Titles by Todd Borg

THE DARK ROAD SUSPENSE SERIES:

WILDERNESS VACATION
WILDERNESS JUSTICE
WILDERNESS PUNISHMENT
WILDERNESS THREAT

THE TAHOE MYSTERY SERIES:

TAHOE DEATHFALL
TAHOE BLOWUP
TAHOE ICE GRAVE
TAHOE KILLSHOT
TAHOE SILENCE
TAHOE AVALANCHE
TAHOE NIGHT
TAHOE HEAT
TAHOE HIJACK
TAHOE TRAP
TAHOE CHASE
TAHOE GHOST BOAT
TAHOE BLUE FIRE
TAHOE DARK
TAHOE PAYBACK
TAHOE SKYDROP
TAHOE DEEP
TAHOE HIT
TAHOE JADE
TAHOE MOON
TAHOE FLIGHT
TAHOE RESCUE

WILDERNESS THREAT

Josie Strong
A Dark Road Suspense
Book 4

by

TODD BORG

THRILLER PRESS

Thriller Press First Edition October 2024

WILDERNESS THREAT
Copyright © 2024 by Todd Borg

All rights reserved under International and Pan-American Copyright Conventions. Published in the United States by Thriller Press, a division of WRST, Inc. www.thrillerpress.com

This novel is a work of fiction. Any references to real people, locales, establishments, organizations or events are intended only to give the fiction a sense of verisimilitude. All other names, places, characters and incidents portrayed in this book are the product of the author's imagination.

No part of this book may be used or reproduced in any manner whatsoever without written permission from Thriller Press, P.O. Box 551110, South Lake Tahoe, CA 96155.

ISBN: 978-1-931296-78-6

Cover design and map by Keith Carlson.

Manufactured in the United States of America

For Kit

ACKNOWLEDGMENTS

Liz Johnston, Eric Berglund, Christel Hall, and my wife Kit are dream editors for reasons too numerous to list.

Graphic maestro Keith Carlson produced a spectacular new look for this new series. So beautiful I want to keep staring at them. I can't thank him enough.

Kit also serves as initial reader, story coach, last reader. She has an unerring ability to find and take out my misjudgments. I can't thank her enough.

On top of their efforts, I dumped five novels on them this year. Not only did no one complain, they dove in with fervor. How lucky is that for me?

Thanks to all, more than I can say.

ONE

After walking their dog named Unknown, Professor Josie Strong and her daughter Samantha rode the bus to Samantha's school. They hugged goodbye, and Josie continued on to a transfer stop. She took another bus to UCLA, where she taught Medieval History. It was the last day of winter quarter classes.

The bus ride suggested a calm day. There were plenty of seats for the passengers, the traffic was mild, and the morning sky was the blue of cornflowers, brilliant yet soft. A hundred springtime floral scents wafted on the breeze.

Josie Strong walked toward the Wabi-Sabi Coffee House on the edge of campus. In keeping with the focus of the Japanese aesthetic that imperfect things are still beautiful, the place was somewhat worn yet alluring in its spare presentation. Josie knew she should focus on the philosophy, which went back centuries. But her guilty secret was her recent addiction to their Shu Kurimu pastries. When combined with the Ueshima coffee that their boarder Amelia Gomez had introduced them to, the result was divine. Josie was no more focused on the wabi-sabi tradition than the medieval history lecture she was about to give in an hour, her last lecture before spring break.

As Josie approached the coffee shop, a man in a gray suit and wearing mirrored sunglasses stopped next to the coffee shop entrance. He stood at attention, feet spread wide, as he faced out toward the street. He reminded Josie of a museum guard, appearing unarmed except for his sentient demeanor. Josie walked past him, entered the coffee shop, and inhaled the delicious aromas. She joined the order line, which was often insanely long earlier in the morning, but reasonable now, and she purchased her favorite pastry and coffee.

Josie took her order to a stool at the counter, hitched one heel over the footrest, took a bite, then a sip, and considered the idea of resigning her professorship in medieval history and becoming a coffee shop dilettante.

As Josie chewed, the side of her face still pulled. It had felt tight ever since the reconstructive surgery to rebuild her cheekbone after the sniper had slammed her to the ground at Fisherman's Wharf. They said she'd be back to normal in three months. That deadline had come. She was better, but far from normal.

She'd barely swallowed when a man sat on the stool next to her. She sensed no coffee in her peripheral vision.

Josie ignored the man and didn't turn to look his way. But as she took a second bite and sip, she sensed that the man hadn't moved, and a dread grew in her psyche. Her day had started off so well.

"Good morning, Professor Strong," the man said in a low voice. "I'm sorry to interrupt your breakfast."

Josie recognized the voice. She turned to look at the man. It was the Governor of California.

Josie didn't know what to say. Just three months before, she'd solved a murder investigation for which the governor had interrupted her life. He'd interfered with Josie's teaching, forced her class to come to a premature end, and he even had his people approach the school that Josie's daughter Samantha attended and requested permission from the headmaster to pull Samantha from school. All this was without consultation with Josie. Not even a phone call or an email warning that the State of California would be disrupting Josie's and Samantha's lives.

Was the governor suddenly appearing at her side so that he could laud Josie's services to the state and thank her for her help in saving his career? Josie didn't think so. She was confident that the man would apply his narcissistic world view to his current situation, whatever it was. He was the kind of person who thought his number one priority should be everyone else's number one priority.

Josie didn't speak. Why should she?

Josie was certain that the governor would have a new problem to deal with. It seemed he had decided that Josie was his new problem solver of choice. Because he knew UCLA board members, he could use them to coerce her. In addition, the man may have thought Professor Strong was more reliable than the other people in his circle, people who were familiar with his self-centered world view and likely resisted his requests.

Josie waited. Let the man speak. Don't even flatter him with the recognition of his identity, never mind his power as the leader of the most powerful state in the union. What was his favorite line? If California were a separate country, it would be the fifth largest economy in the world. The implication was that the governor was due credit for it. Josie thought, Who cares, sir, when you are an insufferable egotist?

Despite her wait, the man didn't say more.

"Good morning," Josie finally said, not even using his name.

"As I communicated to you at the end of December, congratulations again on catching the sniper who killed my best friend's daughter, Mary Jo Telman."

Josie merely nodded. The governor's previous congratulations had come in the form of a short phone call along with the news that Josie would be paid the original fee the governor's office had mentioned plus a substantial bonus. Because UCLA professors are paid a large salary, Josie had decided to donate the bonus to a soup kitchen that catered to old people in one of the less affluent neighborhoods near Santa Monica.

The governor was still talking. "Your report was thorough. We appreciate that."

Josie made another nod. She dreaded what she imagined was coming, another request for "service to the great State of California."

The governor said, "It was especially shocking for us to learn that the sniper was a man who worked in my office and who hadn't been previously known to law enforcement. To think that such a dangerous man can ply his murderous trade without drawing the attention of the California Department of Justice is... It's just shocking." The governor sounded as if he was still trying to come to terms with it. "Of course, my staff failed me in not recognizing the threat that the man posed. But the buck stops with me," the governor said with a puffed-up righteousness. "So I suppose I bear some responsibility."

Josie almost made an audible scoffing sound. Some responsibility? Josie tried to credit the man for not blaming everyone else but him. Yet it was still just part of an act. The man was 99 percent slick-talking politician and only 1 percent earnest human. That he demonstrated no shred of humility was no surprise. That was just another typical trait of a politician.

Josie took another bite of her pastry and sipped some coffee. She knew it was rude not to speak, but she could hardly believe what was happening. The governor had always claimed that his job was to serve the people of California. But his every action suggested the opposite. As if the people of California existed to serve him.

"Clearly," he said, "our systems are not sufficient to identify people who pose a risk to society."

Josie ate another piece of the Shu Kurimu delight. She couldn't ignore the governor, but she tried to make it seem that way.

"Anyway," he said, "I've revisited what we knew and what we didn't know about Mary Jo Telman. After her father—my friend— died, I was proud to walk Mary Jo down the aisle during her wedding. But to learn that she had a kind of hidden life has made me think about the discoveries you made. The business about her house with the secret office and the limited liability company she used to hide her ownership... Well, it made me realize that there is more to learn. For example, in your report after the holidays, you mentioned remaining discrepancies. One of which was the fact that Mary Jo's husband, Ranger Francis Telman, was shot at close range with a handgun, while Mary Jo Telman was shot from a long distance, by the Army-trained sniper you caught."

The sniper who worked for you, Josie thought.

The governor paused. The wait became uncomfortable.

"Did you have a question?" Josie asked.

"Yes," he continued, as if he was unaware of Josie's brusqueness.

Such is a characteristic of megalomaniacs, Josie thought. They can't empathize with anyone else's point of view.

"Because of the different types of shooting," he said, "I'm wondering if, in fact, Francis Telman was also shot by the sniper who killed Mary Jo. Perhaps that sniper simply broke his pattern by shooting at close range? Or, was the situation you alluded to in your report possible… That there may have been a second shooter?"

Josie hadn't just alluded to the idea. She had specifically suggested this very thing. And she had already been over all of this with the governor's aide, Sonja. Josie couldn't remember her last name. At the time, the governor seemed to have no questions or concerns. He was so glad to have Josie identify Mary Jo's killer that he apparently entertained no reservations.

Josie thought that the governor expected her to comment. But she was worn out before she could even think about it. She sipped her coffee.

"So I'd like you to look into this," the governor said.

"You want to reopen the case." Josie's statement was dry and imbued with frustration and tedium.

"The handgun killing that didn't fit with the sniper killing," the governor said. "I think it should be re-examined."

Josie tried not to react. Now he was quoting the very words in Josie's report as if it were his idea. Infuriating.

"If in fact Ranger Francis Telman was killed by someone other than the sniper," he said, "that shooter would still be free. It would be a miscarriage of justice to assume the sniper killed the ranger if it isn't true."

More of Josie's words. Incredible. But Josie knew the governor's motivation. If there really was a second killer, he didn't want to be embarrassed by it on his watch. Another typical quality of a politician.

Josie said, "I said all of these things in my written report and in my discussions with your aides."

"And now I'd like you to act on it," the governor said. "I want you to go back to your findings and see what you can learn about a possible second killer."

"I have a full-time job," Josie said. "A private life. I don't want to disrupt my teaching or my parenting. My daughter is a teenager, an important time for a parent to be around. And my teaching job is the other half of my life."

"I understand. But you have special skills. There is, perhaps, no other person in the state who can do what you do, see things from a unique perspective, bring such education and intelligence to the puzzle, and understand what drives the human psyche to murder. Plus, you are familiar with the case. If there were someone else half as talented and smart as you, I would pursue them. But you are unique, Professor Strong. You are one of the few who have a gift. You found out the truth about my niece living a secret life. You found the hidden room in her Placerville home. The police didn't find that. No one else would have discovered that. I understood from the police report that you enlisted a professional search dog in finding that room. That was very impressive."

Josie paused for a moment on his description of Unknown, their little rescue dog, who, despite her smarts, was no profesional search dog. Josie would have to remember to relay that description to Samantha.

The governor leaned his head back and forth, stretching his neck, then reached up and rubbed the muscles.

"This is a calling," he said, "and you are summoned by that calling. This is your fate."

Josie almost gagged. A colleague of hers who taught creative writing said such words were called purple prose in the writing business, over-the-top verbiage designed to impress those who lacked thoughtful skepticism.

"Please tell me in plain words what you want," Josie said. She'd lost her appetite for the coffee and the pastry. She just wanted out.

"I want you to reinvestigate Francis Telman's murder with an eye to discovering if there might have been a second killer. And if so, I want you to find that man and bring him to justice just like you did with Lucas Herman, the man we knew as Taylor Cooke."

"In other words, you want me to do what I put in my written report."

"Yes, I suppose so. The same conditions apply. But double the fee. The same credential for you to use with law enforcement, the same freedom of decision. No one in my office or at the state Bureau of Investigation will interfere. Any law enforcement organization you mention to us will be told to give you full support. As before, we will all be at your service should you request it." The governor paused and looked at his watch. "Tomorrow marks the beginning of spring break. Today is your last day of teaching, correct? It would be like the last time I asked for your help just before Christmas. You were able to take some time off from your teaching with very little disruption in your life."

As he said the words, Josie was appalled. Appalled! Her class was canceled, her daughter had to leave school and miss important classes, they were shot at, Samantha was nearly killed, and Josie nearly died after being chased by the killer at Fisherman's Wharf in San Francisco. Josie's injuries required multiple surgeries. Now the governor had the gall to depict their sacrifice and near death as causing little disruption to their life.

Josie was speechless at how tone deaf and dense the governor was.

"And while you investigate," he said, "I'd like you to look for the missing woman."

Josie was confused. "You don't mean Elena Soto, the woman who worked for the nursing home and then supposedly went to work at a spiritual retreat owned by the same company?"

"Yes, I think that was her name."

"But your aide, Sonja, assured me the governor's office would find her and make certain she was safe."

"Yes, that was our intention. However, we haven't located her. I was told we never found anyone who knew where the retreat was located. I also understand the woman doesn't answer her cell phone."

Josie was aghast. Finding Elena was one of Josie's most important concerns. And the governor acted as if looking for Elena involved nothing more than dialing her phone number. It was an appalling oversight. Josie felt her stomach clench. She should have checked herself. Ignoring Elena and the concerns of her mother Zoe was a terrible mistake.

The governor continued, "With your skills and a dose of luck, you might be able to find some answers before the start of spring classes. And, if it is necessary, my office is happy to run interference with your dean and other UCLA personnel."

Josie noticed that his figure of speech was very close to reality. The governor's office was very much interfering in Josie's life and every aspect of it that connected to the university.

"And, truth be told," he added, "ever since the sniper you caught died in that horrible explosion, it adds an urgency to the situation."

"What!" Josie said. "Lucas Herman died? The man you employed who used the name was Taylor Cooke?"

TWO

"You didn't know about the sniper suspect's death?" the governor said. He said the words with surprise in his tone, but Josie couldn't tell if the surprise was sincere or feigned.

"No, I didn't," Josie said. "What happened?"

"I don't know much. Because Taylor Cooke worked for my office and knew many top secret details about state government, he was considered a high-value prisoner. So they were transferring him to a more secure jail prior to his trial. The armored transport van blew up on an industrial warehouse road a block or two from the destination jail. The prisoner died."

"This was an ambush?" Josie said.

The governor frowned. "Not that I've been told. I never heard of any specific evidence to suggest such a thing. Investigators said that the van drove over a manhole cover that hadn't been properly seated. The cover flipped up and struck the van's gas tank. It ruptured and ignited. The explosion blew through the floor of the cargo area where the prisoner was held."

"Cooke was killed," Josie muttered, shaking her head, considering the implications.

"Yes."

"What about the guards?" Josie asked.

"The driver and another guard were in the front seat of the van. I was told the prisoner was alone in the back, handcuffed or shackled or however it is that they restrain prisoners."

"There was no guard in back with the prisoner? That seems strange to me."

"Wow, you and I think alike," the governor said. Now his speech had the tone of an immature child delighting in coincidence while ignoring the horror of a deadly explosion.

"I also thought they'd have a guard in back. But I guess they thought prisoner's restraints were sufficient. In the end, no guard was back there. Whoever made that decision saved at least one life."

Or, Josie thought, her mind racing around malicious possibilities, the guards might have been aware of a potential attack. They could have been given instructions to sit in the front. Or, it may have come in the form of a prison rumor.

While death by sudden explosion was shocking, Josie was more surprised that she hadn't heard of it. Wouldn't a prisoner-transport explosion have been in the news media for days? She almost said something, then had second thoughts.

If the governor's office had hushed up the event, it might be better for her if she didn't tell the governor that she was thinking of such a possibility.

"Where was this?" she asked.

"I don't know exactly. But I know the max-security facility is near Stockton."

"When did it happen?"

The governor looked up toward the Wabi-Sabi menu blackboard where items were written in a stylish cursive with colored chalk, but he was probably visualizing a calendar.

"Let me think," he said. "The explosion was right after New Years. And I last talked to you right after Christmas. So it was about a week after I called you to congratulate your success in finding the sniper." He made an exaggerated shake of his head. "I still can't believe that the sniper was a man who worked in the governor's office. He rode in my car!"

Josie remembered clearly that the man had come to her lecture at UCLA and escorted her—nearly corralled her—into the governor's limousine. The same man on whose third-floor balcony Josie had arranged a snare trap.

"Was anyone else hurt?" she asked.

"No."

"I would think," Josie said slowly, "that somebody in your office would have called me after the explosion instead of you telling me now, three months later."

"Yes, I'd have expected that, too! Obviously, no one did. I'll have to look into that. Because you haven't heard about the explosion," the governor said, "maybe you didn't hear about the forensic results on the gun they found in Cooke's apartment near Fisherman's Wharf?"

"No, I never heard anything."

"Oh. Well, you'll be pleased to know that California's Bureau of Investigation ran tests on the rifle. While they couldn't make a definitive conclusion saying that gun was absolutely the one used to shoot Mary Jo Telman, they do think it likely. And they positively connected the rifle to Taylor Cooke, the man also known as Lucas Herman. Fingerprints and such. So the weapon belonged to him, and it was almost certainly used to kill Mary Jo."

Josie knew that the same bullet that killed Mary Jo might have killed Samantha had it not struck Samantha's phone. Because of that, Josie thought of the shooting as a crime against Samantha, intended or not. But she knew better than to say anything that would sound like her judgment was biased because her daughter was also a victim.

Josie remembered what the Army vet Cor Kontos had said. A professional killer would dump the rifle in the ocean or a very deep lake. Which implied that, because Cooke's weapon was found, he wasn't a professional.

Or he was set up and framed.

Josie stood up.

"Will you look into this?" the governor said. His voice sounded plaintive. Almost pleading. "I'd like to know the full extent of what that man was involved in. How he came to shoot Mary Jo. All the things that you intimated in your report to me three months ago. Things I wanted to ignore because I was so glad you'd caught the killer. But now I realize that the rest of the story still has ramifications. You thought there was probably a second killer out there. Now I've come to recognize that you were likely right. This second killer concept feels like some evil thing out in the woods, waiting to take me down."

Josie knew the governor was more worried about blowback

harming his reputation than he was about a killer who might target additional victims.

"I'll think about it," Josie said. "Would my contact be the same woman as before? Sonja..."

"Sonja Gonsalves. Yes." The governor handed Josie a card with Sonja's phone number and email address.

"I'll let you know." Josie nodded at him once, and walked out on the governor of the great state of California. She turned down the street and headed to her office at UCLA's Bunche Hall.

As Josie walked to her office, the governor had her unsettled. Even though he was awkward and self-focused, he was still the most powerful person in the state, which made him one of the most powerful people in the world. And when he made a request of a private citizen, it carried a lot of weight.

For a brief moment, Josie wondered if her resistance to the governor's request was purely about her own life and schedule. Or, was it fueled by her distaste for the man's personality? If he were less self-absorbed, would she be more inclined to help? She realized she would. Which made her reconsider her resistance. Maybe Samantha could help her decide.

THREE

Josie sat in her office for several minutes, grappling with what she'd learned about the sniper dying in the van explosion and the governor's request that she reopen her investigation into who killed Ranger Francis Telman.

Josie found herself worrying most about Samantha. Her daughter very much wanted a normal life, school, volleyball, and walks on the beach with their dog Unknown. It would be hard to break the news that the governor was once again calling on them to help the state. Maybe she could focus on the notion that they might be through with the investigation before classes resumed after the spring break.

But now she had to go deliver her final lecture. Josie walked across campus, trying to focus on what she'd wanted to say about medieval history. But the governor had her mind scattered, and her talk was disorganized as a result.

Her lecture was a summation of the nature of medieval wars and how they fundamentally differed from both ancient and modern wars. She closed by saying that her next class, beginning in spring quarter, would be focused on the development of large siege weapons, the first weapons that were able to blow holes in castle walls sufficient to allow warriors directly into heavy fortifications. She thanked everyone and said she would see them in two weeks, even though she knew it might not happen.

Josie collected her things in preparation for the coming spring break, then caught the bus home. During the ride, she thought about the sniper she had caught in San Francisco, a man whose criminal pseudonym was Lucas Herman but whose real identity was Taylor Cooke, a man who worked for the governor's office.

Josie still had no doubt about her conclusion after the

Christmas holiday case. The sniper she'd caught was likely just one of two shooters. He'd shot Mary Jo Telman, daughter of the governor's friend. However, the initial crime the governor wanted her to investigate was the killing of Ranger Francis Telman, who was Mary Jo's husband. He had been shot at close range. His wife Mary Jo had been shot later from a great distance. Because short-range killings and sniper-distance killings are so different, Josie believed Mary Jo was probably killed by a second shooter.

While Josie wasn't convinced that she would now do as the governor asked, it did fit with the governor's initial request back in December. He'd asked Josie to find the killer of the ranger specifically because she'd found other cop killers. When she identified and found the sniper who shot Mary Jo, the governor thought he was also the killer of the ranger. It was clear to Josie that the governor's position was one of political expediency, not logical thought.

Why had he changed his mind now? Josie didn't know. She certainly didn't think it was because he'd suddenly seen the truth of Josie's original assessment. Something else must have happened, and the governor realized he was vulnerable to political ill winds. He was the kind of man who was always looking out for himself.

What was Josie to do? Although she wanted to tell the governor to go away, she remembered his pressure the last time. He had threatened to intervene at UCLA in a manner that could possibly put her job at risk. Would he do that again? There was no question about it in Josie's mind. He was a man of low standards. Decency didn't matter.

Which meant that Josie was once again trapped. Unless she could find a way to pressure him to back off, she had to acquiesce. Which would be harder? Fighting the governor or finding the other killer?

Time to find another killer.

FOUR

Josie was waiting outside of Samantha's school when she came out.

"Mama! This is fun! Why are you here to pick me up?" Samantha asked.

Josie was enormously glad that Samantha wasn't disappointed to have her mother show up when school let out. Josie imagined that many kids would prefer not to have their mothers come around.

They hugged. Josie gestured toward the bus stop, and they turned and strolled in that direction. Josie noticed that Samantha swung both arms normally. The dislocated shoulder she'd gotten when she fell down the slope after being shot at in the Sierra foothills had fully healed. She was once again playing volleyball. Life was back to normal. At least until the governor had come by.

"I wanted to talk to you. The governor came to see me today."

"No, Mama! Not again."

"Yes. I'm so sorry. He wants us to investigate what I suggested after the last case."

Sam thought a moment. "That there were probably two killers?"

"Yes. The sniper we caught, who shot Mary Jo and you, was one. But the person who shot Mary Jo's husband from short range was probably someone else."

"But I don't want to do more investigation, Mama! We've done enough."

"That's what I think. But after the governor made his pitch and I left, I got to thinking about it."

"You're getting weak?" Samantha said.

"Maybe. I also remembered that we put away a shooter."

"And that's a good thing," Samantha said, her tone softening.

"Yes. A shooter who subsequently died."

Samantha stopped walking. "Lucas Herman died?" She sounded as surprised as Josie had been with the governor.

Josie nodded. "Yes."

"What was his other name?"

"Taylor Cooke," Josie said.

"How did he die?"

"He was being transported to prison when the transport van blew up."

Samantha gasped. "That sounds like spy stuff! A prisoner dying while being hauled off to the clink."

"The clink?" Where did her daughter get these words? Oh, of course. The movies.

"Makes ya wonder, huh, Mama?"

Josie tried to sound like Samantha, "Kinda, yeah."

"Wow, Mama, you can talk without using Professor Speak."

"Workin' on it, girl."

Samantha grinned.

They got to the bus stop and looked vaguely toward the curve down the road where the bus would appear.

"You know, Mama, this whole detective gig, like, really gets in the way of normal life."

"Like totally," Josie said.

"And the guv'nor is way over the line expecting you to find crooks."

"You find the crooks, too."

Samantha nodded. "Right. I SO want that to be over. It's a–what's the word–a default thing that I gotta help just 'cuz I'm your daughter."

Josie said, "What kinda guv 'spects a daughter to find crooks and put 'em in the clink?" Josie barely–just barely–managed to keep a straight face.

Samantha looked very serious. "And sometimes the crooks

get blowed up on th' way to clink life."

Josie started laughing.

Samantha began laughing hard.

"Blowed up," Josie said through her laugh.

Samantha made her face look serious. "He pro'bly got blowed up 'cuz two girls found him. So what's a girl to do? Find a gig chasing crooks? Or a gig being a big-shot prof?"

"I'd stick with volleyball. That is likely more useful to society than being a prof. Gives people something fun to think about."

"Mama! Your pals—oh, sorry—your colleagues would be horrified."

"Some of them already think my class is more about pop entertainment than serious history."

"Why? Because your class is the most popular in the UCLA history department?"

Josie shrugged. "Some people, parents and professors alike, think it can't be serious if it's fun."

"Because if it's fun, it's got no more value than volleyball?"

Josie nodded. "I'm sorry to say that some people might think that. But the governor said this is my calling. Like he thinks that fate chose me to find crooks."

Samantha frowned. "It sounds like you're thinking it might be good for us to do this for the governor."

"Not for the governor. But for the state. Or it might be better to say, for society."

Unknown was waiting when Josie and Samantha climbed up the stairs to their Santa Monica condo. Unknown almost never wagged, but she showed her feelings by rubbing against Samantha's leg, like a cat. In many ways, Josie thought, Unknown was more like a cat than like other dogs. She didn't wag, she didn't bark, she didn't run and play. Was Unknown coping with major PTSD from her past life before Josie and Samantha rescued her? Or, was she simply a world-record-introvert dog?

"There was one interesting thing the governor said." Josie gestured toward Unknown. "He called Unknown a professional search dog."

Samantha's eyes got wide. She picked up Unknown and bounced the dog in her arms. "Hear that, Unknown? You're a professional!" Samantha kissed the top of Unknown's head. "We could probably add your professional fee to the governor's bill!"

Samantha and Josie took Unknown out to the beach walk, a three-mile round trip. When they'd first gone the full distance several months ago, Josie thought it was difficult, and her lungs burned afterward. But now Josie had gotten more used to it. While she still felt out of shape and overweight, she was more confident. She regularly reminded herself that she could walk three miles. They'd started the walk when they adopted Unknown. Josie was grateful to the dog for that, and for many other reasons.

Josie took both her regular phone and her burner phone in case she wanted to make a call that was less easy to trace, a habit she'd developed when Cumberland Durand had explained how vulnerable to eavesdropping phones were, even when they were turned off.

While some probably thought of the beach walk as something for exercise or people watching, for Josie and Samantha it was a time to think and plan. If Josie wasn't thinking, she watched the gulls and the surf, not the people. Josie knew she was unusual in that way, perhaps even weird. She enjoyed watching people in the movies, which occasionally made her think that she preferred people on the other side of the TV screen over dealing with people in real life. She believed her preference developed because people depicted in novels, movies, and shows were scripted and edited. That made them more interesting than people in real life. People on the screen rarely made mindless small talk, at least they didn't in the shows that she and Samantha watched.

Maybe that was why Josie didn't have any really close friends. She had many acquaintances, other professors and school personnel. But no soul mates. There was Ralph Ellison, of course. He'd taken in Cumberland Durand and his siblings, Aiden and Cara. But, kind and helpful as he was, he was a generation older and in a much different part of life than Josie.

Josie had also become quite close to Cor Kontos, the Army vet who was a huge help in Josie's last investigation. But Cor's world of being a soldier was even more distant from Josie's world. Neither Ellison nor Cor seemed like a soul mate.

Did soul mates even exist? Or was that another notion that only existed in books and movies? In fiction, there was a kind of control and balance that the real world lacked. Fictional worlds were, for Josie, more comfortable places to spend time.

Josie glanced at Samantha as they walked. The girl was absorbed in her phone. Josie realized she could do some phone work herself. She got out the card the governor had given her. It had the contact information for Sonja Gonsalves, his aide. Josie used her regular phone to call her.

FIVE

The phone only rang twice before it was answered.

"Sonja Gonsalves."

"Hi, Sonja. This is Josie Strong calling. The governor contacted me today."

"Yes, he had me put that on his schedule. Are you okay?"

"I suppose I am stressed a little. The governor wants me to reopen my investigation into who killed the ranger named Francis Telman."

The woman was quiet for a moment. "For some time he's been fretting about not knowing for certain who killed the ranger. So I reminded him that you believed there was another shooter besides Taylor Cooke. I hope…" the woman hesitated. Josie could hear her breathing over the phone. The woman continued, "I hope that I didn't cause a problem for you in saying that. I imagine you want to be done with this case."

"Yes, I do. But the governor was persuasive. More important, I think, is finding the truth of what happened. The governor said that you could help, so I'm checking in with you."

"I'm happy to help in any way I can."

"The governor told me that Lucas Herman, the man you knew as Taylor Cooke, died in a truck explosion."

"Yes. It was horrible. I saw a picture of the burnt truck."

"The governor told me that the guards were both in the front of the truck, and they survived."

"That's what I heard," Sonja Gonsalves said. "Judging from the photo I saw of the wreckage, they just got out in time."

"I'd like to talk to those guards," Josie said.

"Do you think they… Oh, my, it's a bit shocking to think of what your question implies, that they might know something about the explosion."

"Possibly," Josie said. "Could you find the guards' identities? Their contact information?"

"I have no idea how the prison organization runs their transport system. But let me make some calls. A friend of mine knows a woman who's a commissioner on the CDCR."

"What is the CDCR?"

"Oh, sorry. The California Department of Corrections and Rehabilitation. I'm sure I can find out something. Is this number you're calling from a good way to reach you?"

"Yes. Thanks for your help. I'll wait to hear."

They said goodbye.

Josie and Samantha had just finished their beach walk when Josie's phone rang. She answered.

"I've got contact info for the guards who were driving Taylor Cooke when the prisoner transport van blew up," Sonja Gonsalves said.

"Great," Josie said. "Let me grab a pen." Josie pulled a pen and notebook out of her purse. "Okay, I'm ready."

"Leroy Blomberg was the driver. The other guard was Jimmy John Lasman. They both live near Monterey. In case you don't know the area, Monterey is south of the Bay Area. I've got contact info. Would you like it?"

"Yes, please."

"Okay. They live at the same address. Roommates, apparently." Sonja read off the address. "If you'd like, I can make an advance call for you to prep them for your call. Or maybe you'd prefer they didn't know you were going to call?"

"Correct."

"Okay. Is there anything else I can help you with?"

"No thanks, Sonja. I appreciate it. I'm sure I'll be in touch with you in the near future."

"Don't hesitate. Anything you need. You've got the full cooperation of the governor's office."

"Thank you."

Josie thought about calling the guards but decided she'd be likely to get more information if she simply showed up and knocked on their door.

SIX

After Josie decided to do as the governor requested and try to find the second shooter, she worried.

About Samantha. About all the UCLA students who had already signed up for her spring quarter class, which would begin in just ten days. This project for the governor had the potential to go on for a long time. The fact that the governor's office was willing to intervene and make excuses for her with the UCLA dean or others in the administration was no comfort. Even with the governor's authority, the school would disapprove of her lack of reliability. Beyond that, it was the students Josie cared about. Both of her spring quarter classes were filled. The one about medieval weapons had two dozen students on the waitlist. She hated the possibility that she might disappoint those students. But Josie believed that the governor wouldn't care if his desire completely derailed Josie's career.

The absurdity of trying to find a killer in time to get back to her classes didn't give her pause for long because she didn't have time to wonder about it.

When Josie and Samantha and Unknown returned to their condo, their boarder, Amelia Gomez, had gotten home from work.

Josie discussed her idea for the weekend with them. She asked Amelia if she still felt okay staying in their condo alone.

"I like to be with you and Sam, but I know you have to go do this. Just like the last time you had to leave. I'll be fine alone."

The young woman had been so reliable that Josie felt comfortable. While Josie had been quite strict with their security routine, Amelia had been consistently responsible.

Samantha said she was willing to go along to visit the guards as long as Unknown could join them. Because the governor's aide had said the guards both lived near Monterey, Josie booked a room in one of the area hotels.

On Friday morning, Josie went to her office to finish some work. Then she picked up Samantha and Unknown, and they headed out by noon.

If she hadn't been worried about time, Josie would have chosen to drive up the coast and show Samantha the incredible views of Big Sur, which Samantha had never seen. But it would be faster to take the interstate up the Central Valley.

The route was becoming increasingly familiar with their recent trips hunting fugitives. They went north up the 405, across the San Fernando Valley, then north up the 5.

In the summer and fall, the Central Valley was arid. Often, the dry season stretched nearly to Christmas, as when Josie and Samantha had last been north. Except for the green orchards, every area that wasn't irrigated—ditches and orchard edges and the odd vacant parcel of land—had been golden or brown, depending on what type of grasses and brush predominated.

But now that it was March, the winter rains had turned the entire valley brilliant green, a verdant swath stretching 50 miles west to east and hundreds of miles north to south. The preponderance of green was a reminder that this one single, huge valley produced more food than any comparable area on the planet.

Josie's drive paralleled the twin concrete aqueducts that brought water to the parched southern part of the state. The weather was mostly clear, if windy, and the roads were dry. Samantha mostly looked at her phone. Unknown sat up in the back seat, watching out the window, alert but quiet. Josie had learned to resist her desire to point out the various sights. Samantha responded better to fewer comments. Someday, Samantha might wish she'd listened more to Josie's thoughts.

But as Josie had that thought, she realized it was the futile struggle of all caring parents. You can put your best effort into raising kids, but they rarely turn out exactly as you hope. And Josie had reluctantly come to realize that all aspects of raising a child had been overwhelmed by the addictive nature of social media, wherein the kid is more interested in posting selfies in a misbegotten effort to get likes and friends from nameless, faceless, anonymous others than they are in face-to-face interactions with people they already know. Add to that the reluctance of kids to spend time playing and exploring outdoors the way Josie remembered from her own childhood, and you have a generation of kids who only respond to screen time and don't know how to find a meaningful life disconnected from their phones.

It was because of this that Josie was so glad for Samantha's volleyball. No doubt, parents everywhere were hanging onto sports programs in a last-gasp effort to get kids off their couchs and off their phones.

In spite of her concerns, Josie thought Samantha was great. And she loved spending time with her.

After six hours of driving, they turned off the interstate near Santa Nella and headed west around the San Luis Reservoir.

"Wow, big lake," Samantha said, looking up from her phone. Josie thought she must have lost the cell signal.

Samantha turned her head to take in the size of the water. "They must get a lot of rain, here."

"Yes. It's a reservoir," Josie said. "I read about it."

"Of course, you did," Samantha said.

"Are you making fun of me?"

"A little. Mostly, I'm just observing."

Josie noticed cars backing up behind her. She always drove more slowly than everyone else. On the interstate, the other cars raced by in the left lane. Now, on a two-lane road, she began her standard habit of looking for turnouts so she could let them pass.

"Okay, I'm waiting," Samantha said. "What did you read?"

"The most interesting thing was that much of this water isn't from rain because they don't get that much rain here. You saw the aqueducts as we drove, right? You've seen them on our past trips."

Did Samantha nod? She was checking her phone again.

Josie continued, "The aqueducts carry water from the northern part of the state that gets more rain. But the aqueducts are lower than this reservoir. So they pump a lot of that water up into this reservoir for storage and then release it in the fall. It goes back into the aqueduct and on down to L.A."

"That seems like a waste of energy. Why not just conserve more in L.A.?"

"Good question. Everybody likes that idea. But they argue over who has to make the cuts."

"That's simple. Stop supplying golf courses and swimming pools."

"I think the same way. But it turns out that most of the water goes for agriculture."

Samantha seemed to think about it. "I do like having an orange every morning."

Josie was grateful that the traffic slowed as it backed up on a long climbing section of road. It seemed like there were a lot of vehicles, but that was probably the norm on a Friday afternoon. Like Josie and Samantha, everybody was going places for the weekend. Josie tried not to dwell on the fact that the other travelers were heading for a break from work, while Josie and Samantha were looking for a killer.

They came over a rise, and the traffic sped up as the road descended. Josie tried to keep pace as everyone rushed down the slope, but it frightened her a little.

"Whatsa matter, Mama?" Samantha said. "Your hands are shaking on the steering wheel."

"The cars drive so rapidly, it's scary."

"Mama, you've tracked down something like five killers in the last few months. I don't think you need to be scared of driving."

"Right." Josie felt herself gripping the wheel as if to squeeze moisture out of the plastic.

"I know I won't be scared when I start driving," Samantha said.

"No, I suppose you won't."

"I've got cell coverage again," Samantha announced.

"Good. Maybe you can pull up a map and tell me how to go." Josie gave Samantha the name of their hotel. Samantha directed her, and they were in their room 90 minutes later.

Unknown walked around the hotel room, sniffing. But she didn't lie down, and she didn't seem to find the room inviting. Instead, she stood by the door.

"Mama, I think Unknown is stressed like you."

"She's been in the car all day. Let's go for a walk and get some dinner. We can save some of the restaurant food and mix it in with her dog food."

Samantha clipped on Unknown's leash, and they explored the local neighborhoods. When they went to the hotel restaurant for dinner, the maître d' looked at Unknown as if trying to decide how to reject them.

"She's very well behaved," Samantha said. "She'll just sit quietly by our table."

After a pause, the man nodded. "Quiet. On the leash. No movement?"

"I promise," Samantha said.

They ordered fish and asparagus and sauteed greens, and Josie got a glass of white wine. She immediately took a large swallow.

"Are you okay, Mama?"

"I will be after I drink this wine."

"Wow, that drive really got to you, huh?"

"Yes. I'm a highway wimp."

"Remember a few months ago at Christmas when we got shot at in the Sierra foothills? Cor Kontos came up to the mountains and drove us around. She had a kind of kick-butt attitude when she drove her Jeep."

Josie drank wine. "Right. Cor isn't a highway wimp."

"I didn't mean to imply…"

"No problem. You're just observing how things are."

"Remember, Mama, you're very tough when someone is trying to shoot you."

"No, I'm desperate when someone is trying to shoot me. I'm tough when someone is trying to shoot you."

The waiter brought their food.

"This trip is just information gathering, right?" Samantha said. "No shooting?"

"Correct," Josie said. She took another sip of wine.

"Do you have a plan?" Samantha lifted up a forkful of sauteed greens and looked at it up close.

"Not much of a plan," Josie said. "Knock on the guards' door and ask questions about the prison transport van that blew up and killed Lucas Herman."

"You still think the guards might have something to do with the van blowing up?"

"Maybe. They were there in the van, but not in the back. It seems very lucky that the prisoner was killed and they weren't even hurt."

"Too lucky to be luck?" Samantha said. She started chewing the greens.

"Maybe."

"Kale," Samantha announced. "That's what this is."

Josie nodded. She was eating fish and mashed potatoes. She'd always been guilty of eating the main course first. That was probably why Samantha was thin and she was not.

Samantha asked, "Do you think one of those guards could be the second shooter who killed Mary Jo Telman's husband?"

"That's probably too much to hope for. But anything is possible. It seems too much of a coincidence that Lucas Herman, sniper of Mary Jo Telman, was killed in an unusual van explosion. The obvious approach is to talk to the guards who were driving him to prison. If we get a sense that the transport van explosion was more than just a freak accident, we could pursue that and see where it goes."

"Like pulling on a loose thread and seeing if the fabric unravels."

"There's a nice metaphor."

Samantha took on the serious tone of someone being interviewed. "You see, ma'am, my mother is a professor, so I've learned to think in metaphors."

Josie was sipping wine as she started laughing.

Samantha continued, "She's also First Mate on my ship. I rely on her for first-hand information about the state of our voyage."

"At your service, Cap'n."

"Did you say the two guards live in the same place?" Samantha asked.

"Yes, the governor's aide said they're roommates."

"Have you figured out your questions?" Samantha asked.

"No. I think I'll just play it by feel."

"Is that the way you give your lectures? By feel? Or do you plan them out?"

"I usually have a plan."

"A plan for teaching, but no plan for catching a killer." Samantha was frowning. "Kinda makes me wonder why."

"I think," Josie said, "it's because when I look back in history, hindsight enables me to understand people's dilemmas and choices. Knowing what people did is relatively easy. But knowing why gives me the understanding to teach it. But I'm not good at knowing why someone kills. I have no hindsight that makes it clear how to find them."

"But you succeed," Samantha said.

"That's more from luck than a plan, I think."

They saved some of their fish, got it in a to-go box, and carried it back to their room.

When they went back to their room, Josie noticed that Samantha double-checked the lock on their room door.

Samantha pulled the dry dog food bag out of her pack.

"Please check very carefully for fish bones."

"Always, Mama." Samantha mixed the fish scraps in with some dog food and gave it to Unknown.

The dog ate slowly, carefully, with purpose but no enthusiasm.

"I've seen Christy's Golden Retriever eat," Samantha said. "She practically inhales her food."

Josie nodded. "Unknown isn't like other dogs."

They got ready for bed. Samantha coaxed Unknown up onto

the foot of the king-sized bed. Unknown moved very tentatively as if she still didn't believe that people could be nice to her.

When Samantha lay down, Josie kissed her, and Samantha went right to sleep.

Josie went to bed as well, but it was a long time before she drifted off into a fitful sleep. Her last thought, as she looked down toward the foot of the bed and saw Unknown watching her, was that she and the dog shared the same discomfort and loneliness.

SEVEN

The next morning, Josie went over the route with Samantha. She wanted to memorize the basic roads and turns to get from their motel to the house where the prison transport guards lived. When they got into the Prius, Samantha held Unknown on her lap. Josie was surprised to see that Samantha's phone was not visible. She was about to comment and then thought better of it.

Josie drove toward the address that the governor's aide had given her.

"You're just going to surprise the guards at their house or apartment?" Samantha said. "You don't like it when people surprise us at home. You won't even buzz them into the building if you don't know them."

Josie wasn't sure how to respond. "Professors are sometimes targets for disgruntled students. And a single mom and her daughter need to be extra cautious with security."

"We're still a single mom and daughter and we're going to a strange neighborhood."

Josie nodded. "We'll knock on the door and stay outside. Not too much threat, there. Are you okay with that?"

"Yeah, but there still could be risk," Samantha said.

"Yes, there could. If anything happens..." Josie reached into her purse and pulled out two small pepper spray containers. She handed one to Samantha.

"Mama!" Samantha said. "The warrior I never knew!" Samantha took the canister and held it out in front of her as if to test it.

"You can hold it in your pocket," Josie said. "You rotate the top lever to unlock it and then push down. You can do it all in one motion with your finger tip. But be careful not to spray it at me or Unknown."

Samantha made a single nod. "I've also got Unknown to protect me," Samantha said. She put her pepper spray in her pocket. Unknown was sitting on the floor of the front seat, her jaw resting on Samantha's knee. She lifted her head to look up at Samantha.

Samantha rubbed her head, then turned toward the houses they were driving by. "We're looking for number one eighty-one, and these numbers are getting close."

They were in an old neighborhood of small bungalows. Josie thought they'd been built in the early 20th century. Some were stucco with front porches. Some had clapboard siding and only a tiny gable overhang at the front door. The houses were mostly run down. The vehicles on the street were older pickups and a few old cars.

"Odd numbers are on the right side of the street," Samantha said. "Okay, slow down. One eighty-seven. One eighty-five. One eighty-three. The blue house must be one eighty-one."

There were no parking places in the street. Josie drove past the house and found a place to park on the next block. They walked back to the blue house. Samantha had Unknown on her leash.

"Maybe Unknown and I shouldn't be here," Samantha said.

"You can stay in the car if that would make you more comfortable. But you both make people feel comfortable. Remember that woman in Reno? The mother of the woman who'd gone missing?"

"Zoe Soto," Samantha said. "Her daughter Elena moved away and wouldn't tell her where."

"Right. I hope you never do that. Anyway, I think the whole reason she opened up to us was you. You made her comfortable. You had a kind of magic with her."

Samantha gave Josie a little elbow bump. "It sounds like I'm working above my pay grade. I should put in for a raise."

"Pay grade? An economic lesson from the movies?"

Samantha grinned.

When they came to the house, Samantha stayed back as Josie walked up to the door. Samantha held Unknown's leash in her left hand. Her right hand was in her pocket, no doubt holding the pepper spray.

Next to the door hung a yellow flag with a coiled rattlesnake depicted in black ink. Below the snake it said 'Dont Tread On Me,' with no apostrophe in the contraction don't.

Josie knew it was designed by a general in the Continental Army named Christopher Gadsden, and its message was intended for the British during the Revolutionary War. Two hundred-plus years later, it had been adopted by numerous political groups of many persuasions.

The flag was a potent symbol, and it gave Josie pause before she knocked.

She swallowed, then knocked. After another minute, Josie knocked again.

The blind in the window to the side of the door moved, fingers pulling it just enough for someone to peek out. The door opened. A man in his thirties stood there in jeans with frayed hems and a dirty white T-shirt. He looked at Josie, stepped through the doorway, and, glancing down and behind him at the threshold as if to make sure nothing would block the door, carefully shut the door behind him.

The man was thin, but looked hard and strong. His stringy long hair made Josie think of a nest. Something rodents would make. His mostly-bare feet were embedded with grime, and his sandals appeared to be made from pieces of old car tires. His arms had taut, thin muscles. Up his left arm crawled a tattoo of a snake. The snake disappeared under the short T-shirt sleeve, then emerged out of the neck opening and climbed up the side of the man's neck and face. The snake's mouth was open, revealing large curved fangs that appeared to be ready to strike at the man's eye. The man was holding a phone in front of his chest as if to watch the screen. Or taking a video of Josie.

"Hi, my name's Josie Strong, and I'm wondering if Leroy and Jimmy are in," Josie said.

The man leaned back as if he were farsighted and needed

to get more distance to see her properly. He made a severe frown. He glanced toward Samantha and Unknown, turned as if checking to see down the street, then looked back at Josie. Josie thought his look was calculating. The kind of man who considered the ramifications of anything he might say.

"I'm looking for them, too, ladies. But they, um, are gone fishing, so to speak." He paused. "It figures, considering the rent is due, and the gas and electricity. They headed on out of here like they've got an important appointment, and they left me to handle the bill collectors." As he spoke, his words came faster. "I don't like it. In fact, I'm pretty freaked out about it. I'm gonna get my own place ASAP." He looked Josie over, up and down. "So if you're searching for a pad to rent, be very choosy about your roommates."

Josie thought a moment, trying to think of something that might apply to a roommate. "I can't speak for Jimmy, but Leroy always acts like he's important."

The man made a short chuckle. "No kidding. Driving a truck isn't exactly the most lofty profession. But Leroy's always talking like he's got something big about to go down. Maybe something that would make him need to be armed."

That made Josie wonder. "He's armed?"

"Heck, yeah. I don't know how many guns he has. Self-defense stuff, guns for target shooting and hunting. And guns for sniping."

"He's a sniper?"

"His gig is anything and everything to do with guns. But lately he's been talking like he's gonna develop a sniper cell and go freelance. A buddy of his who had sniper training in the Army came to visit. I'm an Army guy, so we coulda had lots to talk about the five days he stayed here. But it was the longest five days of my life. Every day they went out shooting. No problem there, being I'm, you know, a businessman. I can use the silence during the day to… make my business calls. But every night they talked guns. Sure, I can talk guns, too. But God, the arguments about the reticles in scopes! Normally, I think, go for whatever puts gas in your tank. But now, ever since Leroy's buddy came and warped their brains, Leroy and Jimmy talk about custom stocks and calibrating scopes and hot loads until I can't stand it. And they're addicted to black ops movies."

"What does that mean, black ops?"

The man raised his shoulders and took a deep breath. It looked like the tattooed snake was lifting up as if getting ready to strike.

"Black ops is like secret government military operations."

Josie was feeling very uneasy. She took a deep breath. She could feel her blood pressure rising.

But she still wanted to ask the guards questions. This guy knew something about Leroy and Jimmy's world. If she could keep him talking…

"You said something like reticle. What is that?"

The man made a little snort as if impatient. "It's the little cross hairs in the scope, lady. The cross hairs you line up on your victim. Leroy and Jimmy argued over how much one click would be at a hundred yards. Give me a break."

Josie prodded him. "A click at a hundred yards?"

"If you adjust your scope one click, that'll move your bullet one quarter inch at twenty-five yards. Or a whole inch at a hundred yards. Up or down, left or right. The idea is to make it so your reticle is dead-on accurate. But it's kind of a joke, if you ask me."

Josie raised her eyebrows. "Why?"

"'Cuz if there's any wind or temperature gradients, all your calculations turn to crap." He paused and looked as if he'd revealed something he shouldn't have.

Josie remembered Cor Kontos talking about snipers. Cor was very knowledgeable about guns. But she presented her knowledge as simple facts. Whereas this guy seemed to have an emotional connection to guns.

Josie found the subject of guns depressing. She forced herself to focus on the task the governor had given her.

"Do you know the name of Leroy's sniper buddy?" she asked.

"Nah. They didn't use names when they talked. It was more

like, 'Dude, hand me another beer.'"

"Is there a good time when I could stop back? When Leroy and Jimmy would be here?" she asked.

He shook his head. "Hard to know, lady. Leroy is always acting like he's about to rush off to meet someone important."

"But he probably doesn't say what it's about, right?" Josie was fumbling with her words, trying to keep the man talking.

The man continued, "Tell me about it. Leroy makes like anything he says is letting you in on a big secret. Phone calls where he has to go outside to talk. Him and Jimmy giving each other the special look like some kinda code. And the constant spy-man, cool-man attitude. And then there's times when Jimmy makes a big show counting all the hundreds in his wallet."

Once again, the man looked down the street. Then he looked the other direction.

The man said, "Just this morning, Leroy got a phone call warning about the power shut-off 'cause of the unpaid bill. You know how he likes to act all casual."

"Oh, right. Nothin' gonna rattle that boy." Josie felt so awkward saying it.

The man said, "Leroy told the person from the power company, 'We're hanging at the Bixby cliff, waitin' on our 'pointment. The commissioner wants to talk to us. So maybe this'll be the assignment we're waiting on. So it's not like I can pay a bill when I'm waiting on the commissioner. Out at the Bixby cliff.'"

The man leaned forward toward Josie and lowered his voice. He said, "They always use the word commissioner when they're planning one of their secret missions." Josie could smell multiple foul scents on his breath. Marijuana and cigarette smoke mixed with beer and something else, like cauliflower gone rancid.

"Leroy never told me about these secret missions," Josie said. She was struggling, making up lines to keep the man talking about the guards. She wanted to learn anything that might reveal the guards' involvement in the truck explosion. But she didn't know what to say to turn the conversation that direction.

"The secret missions are just part of acting important," he

said.

"And this was this morning?" Josie asked. "On a Saturday?"

"Heck, yeah. What I put up with... Eight in the morn, my roommates are gone fishin' for some new secret agent job." The man jerked his head toward the neighboring house. "And the guy next door looks down on me for my Budweiser breakfasts. Like he has a clue about what keeps me from sleeping. I could ventilate him just for his superior attitude about me."

"Ventilate?"

"Shoot him full of holes."

Josie was taken aback. She had witnessed so many horrible things in the last few months, she should have been prepared for such talk.

"This Bixby cliff, you mention," she said. "Is that a figure of speech? Or is it a physical place?"

"No figure about it. It doesn't get much more physical than that big dropoff to the ocean."

"Can you tell me how to get there?"

"You've seen it, lady, even if you didn't know it. You just head south to the Bixby Creek Bridge. A little past there is the big meadow that drops off to the ocean. You'll recognize it. Where the tourists go to hike the Brazil Ranch trail."

"I'm sorry, but I don't know that trail."

"But you know the Bixby Creek Bridge, of course. Just look south of the bridge." The man looked off like he was sighting on someplace in his mind. He held out his arm and hand, his fingers outstretched. "Meadow on the ocean side of the highway. Trail up the mountain on the other."

"Is there a sign?"

The man made a wheezing chuckle, as if his lungs were full of liquid. "No sign that I recall. No parking lot, either. People just pull off near the Brazil Ranch road. But from what Leroy and Jimmy said, I think they were going toward the ocean. Probably private land. All I know is, be careful not to fall off. That wind blows like a mother." He looked past Josie toward Samantha. "And don't let go of your dog. He'd be likely to fall off. It's a straight drop to the waves. Scary." He glanced at his phone, which he held with his left hand. He tapped on the screen with his left thumb. "What do you want with them, anyway?" He looked down at the phone again.

Again, he seemed to be scheming. Josie thought the man had more smarts than he presented.

Josie realized that even though she hadn't stated her purpose in stopping by, just asking for Leroy and Jimmy may have been too revealing.

"Leroy and I have a mutual friend, Maryanne. We met her at the Santana Festival. What was it? Three, four years ago? Anyway, Maryanne is getting married and she's having a big outdoor celebration. She lost Leroy's contact info. So she asked me to stop by and invite him."

The man did more thumb taps on his phone.

"Gimme the place and time, I'll pass it on."

"I would, but she also wants me to give him a message in person."

"Why would that be? She doesn't trust me to tell him?"

Josie acted a bit embarrassed, something she was good at. "It's just that she doesn't know you."

"Well, I don't know you, neither. And Leroy doesn't want me givin' out his number. So you better go find that cliff. Leroy and Jimmy are probably there this minute. Plotting their new sniper cell business." His phone beeped. The man stared at his phone. Josie got the feeling he was trying to make a decision. "Gotta go," he said.

Josie asked, "Can you please tell me your name before you go?"

"Snake," he said as he stepped inside and shut the door behind him.

Josie turned, and she and Samnatha walked away. Samantha spoke in a loud whisper. "Did you see that guy's teeth?"

"No. He never smiled."

"But he did this tongue movement, like he had a retainer. It was the same thing a kid in my class does with his retainer. I saw his front teeth. They were pointed!"

It shocked Josie. "He chipped his teeth?"

"I don't think so. I think he purposely filed them into points! I can't imagine anyone hanging with that guy. Male or female. He's disgusting."

"There are all kinds of people," Josie said. "Let's go see where those guards went for their secret agent meeting."

They came to the Prius. Samantha let Unknown into the back.

"Mama, we should eat something before we walk out to the ocean. That little motel muffin doesn't go very far. Unknown needs food, too."

"I agree."

Samantha looked on her phone and directed Josie. They drove over to the highway, turned south to look for a business district that might have a breakfast diner or coffee shop.

A dark gray van came up behind them. They were going up a long curving section of highway when the van swerved into the oncoming lane in a no-passing zone and passed them on the left.

"That guy is going much too fast," Josie said.

"Mama, I think that was the guy we talked to!" Samantha said.

"Snake?"

"Yeah. If so, how does he afford a van? It's not very old, so it probably cost a fair amount. Where would he get that kind of money if he can't even pay his rent and electricity? It's not like anyone would hire him with those teeth."

Josie thought about it. "Maybe he's self-employed."

"Yeah, but self-employed people still have to have customers for whatever they do, right? That Snake guy isn't going to be like Cumberland, working on his computer, getting companies like Google to pay him for hacking information."

"No," Josie said. "He'd more likely be selling drugs or something. Of course, that's just my clichéd view. But his customers would have to be comfortable buying from a guy with pointed teeth."

"That fits a drug dealer," Samantha said. "Like those weirdo druggies who hang out on our beach under the Santa Monica

Pier."

They found a breakfast diner near the town of Carmel By The Sea. Less than an hour later, they were back in their car. Josie turned south on the highway.

Samantha was looking at her phone. "Mama, I Googled Bixby Bridge. Turns out it's the beginning of Big Sur. It's famous." She turned her phone toward Josie.

"I'm driving, hon. I'll look later."

Several miles later, a large bridge with a huge central arch appeared.

"I just remembered where I've seen it!" Samantha sounded surprised. "That's the bridge in Play Misty For Me."

"I've heard that name," Josie said.

"It's a scary thriller with Clint Eastwood and Jessica Walters. Eastwood is a radio DJ and Walters is a psycho listener who stalks him and keeps calling to ask him to play a song called Misty."

"Where did you see this movie?"

"At Cristy's."

"Misty at Christy's."

"I know. It sounds like something in a movie."

"How scary was this movie?"

"Oh, Mama, you wouldn't be able to watch it."

"Why? Did it have monsters and such?"

"No, worse! The psycho woman was a total nightmare!"

Josie kept driving. For a moment, she wondered if this whole sniper murder investigation was going to be a nightmare.

Samantha was staring at her phone. "Get ready to slow down, Mama. We're getting close."

EIGHT

Josie slowed as they drove over the Bixby Bridge, and cars backed up behind them.

Josie said, "Tell me when it's time to pull over."

Samantha looked at her phone. "I already lost cell reception. But I've got the map loaded, and GPS is working. Okay, we're getting close. A half mile to go. Up ahead on the left is the Brazil Ranch road where Snake said tourists go to hike. I'd pull over here. Anyplace you can."

Josie slowed further as she approached a pickup that was parked on the shoulder. She pulled off behind it, moving to the very edge of the gravel. They got out and locked the car. Samantha held Unknown as other cars raced by.

The wind was strong, coming off the ocean from the northwest. Josie wore a coat. She pulled it tightly around her. Samantha wore a short, thin jacket that was closer to a windbreaker than a winter garment. It was unzipped, and she left it open. Josie couldn't understand how a skinny girl like Samantha could stay warm.

The sky above was blue, but a cloudy mist swirled around them. Sunshine was sporadic, one moment brilliant and warm, and the next fading into a fog that was heavy and wet on their faces.

"What do you think?" Josie asked her. "Does anything look like what Snake described?"

Samantha turned a full circle. "He talked about cliffs that drop to the sea. So we should go west. The Pacific is out there somewhere in the fog."

"It doesn't feel like the Pacific back home," Josie said. "It's colder and windier. You can't even see the ocean because of the fog. It feels like the wind could give us frostbite."

"That's the north/south thing," Samantha said, her voice slightly mocking. "That's why we play volleyball down south in Santa Monica and they ski up north in Tahoe." Samantha walked away from the highway, vaguely west. She lifted her knees high as she walked, stepping over uneven lumps of grass. Unknown walked on her leash without pulling like other dogs.

Josie followed.

In addition to heavy, coarse grasses that were hard to walk through, the ground was lumpy as if gophers had turned the soil into endless clumps. Or maybe the meadow used to be for grazing cattle, and their hooves made the ground bumpy. The wind blew harder. It seemed to be a never-ending gale.

Samantha came to a wire fence that sagged between old fence posts made of large logs split in half.

"This is probably a cattle fence," she announced. She picked up Unknown with one arm, put her other hand on the top wire of the fence, pushed the wire down, then stepped over.

"I'll hold the wire, Mama, while you step over."

Josie leaned one hand on the wire and the other on Samantha. She got her leg up and over. The fence wire pushed up too high. Josie couldn't get her other leg over.

"Lean forward, Mama, so you're almost lying on the fence wire. There. Now raise your other leg behind you. Here, I'll help lift it over."

Together, they got Josie over the fence. Josie pushed up, but her purse caught on the fence. She had to jerk to get it free. When Josie was stable, Samantha turned and, holding Unknown's leash, walked into the fog.

The fog was now so thick, the light was dim. It was hard to believe the sun had stabbed through the fog just a few minutes before.

Unknown looked up at Samantha then looked off into the fog, her nostrils flexing in the wind.

Josie called out, "The man called Snake said the cliff drops straight to the water. That could certainly be dangerous."

"Mama, you worry too much. Does it look like I'm about to walk over a cliff?"

"The fog makes it hard to see."

"Nevertheless, I will see a cliff before I walk off it. You're chasing a killer. You don't need to be afraid of fog."

Josie had to call out loud to make her voice carry over the wind. "Don't go too fast. Don't go too far."

"No problem, Mama. I can hear the surf. I grew up with that sound, right? So I'm very tuned to the sound of surf. And now…" Samantha cupped one hand behind her ear and pointed into the fog with the other hand. "Do you hear that?"

Josie stopped and listened. "The barking we heard in San Francisco."

"Yes. Sea lions, Mama. The sea lions are here in Big Sur." Samantha turned and continued walking into the fog.

"That means you're close to the cliffs," Josie called out. "Please be careful!"

Josie tried to speed up her pace. The fog was so thick, she couldn't see anything. She had to lift her knees as if she was marching in order to avoid tripping on the lumpy ground.

"Sam, are you there? Can you hear me?"

"Yes, Mama," came a muffled voice. "I'm here. Everything is okay."

There was a sudden gust of wind, so strong that it caused Josie to stop. The wind seemed to shift direction. The fog got lighter. Then darker. Then it seemed as if the cloud rose up into the sky with such speed that it was like an express elevator. Blue sky appeared, and dazzling sunlight flooded the meadow. The sun was so bright, Josie had to squint her eyes. It shined down and turned the meadow into a brilliant carpet of green.

"Whoa!" Samantha called out.

Josie turned toward her voice.

Samantha was standing on the edge of green, and beyond her was the amazing blue of the Pacific.

"Is this what all of Big Sur looks like? Cliffs and mountains and ocean?"

"From what I remember, yes. Ninety miles of wilderness coastal cliffs."

Samantha seemed to lean out over the cliff.

"Sam, be careful!" Josie hurried toward her, trying not to trip on the uneven ground. Josie slowed as she got close.

Samantha stood near the edge of a dropoff.

"Sam, don't go any closer."

"I'm okay, Mama. I'm just looking down at the incredible view. It's amazing. It…" She stopped.

Josie stopped well back from Samantha.

"Sam…"

"Don't worry, Mama. I'm not moving. But I can see what the sleazeball Snake man meant about the dropoff. If you fell, you'd go straight down into the water, just like he said."

"You're scaring me, Sam."

"What I don't understand is why anyone would meet out here at the cliff edge."

Josie said, "So no one could hear what they said?"

"That makes sense," Samantha said.

"And they'd be far enough from the highway that they probably couldn't be seen. Or, if they could, no one could identify them or the person they were meeting."

"Seems like a long way to walk just to be out of earshot."

Josie said, "I can't imagine what they would be meeting about that they'd be so concerned about being overheard."

"Secret agent talk," Samantha said, laughing. "I can't believe that guy said that stuff."

The fog once again swirled around them so densely that Josie could no longer see Samantha. Josie tried to take deep breaths, tried to calm herself about Samantha being so close to the edge.

Josie spoke into the fog. "The man talked about a commissioner requesting the meeting."

"Yeah. I got the feeling that Leroy and Jimmy would jump at the chance to keep the commissioner happy. And what does a commissioner do, anyway?"

"I remember that the governor's aide referred to the Department of Corrections and Rehabilitation."

Samantha asked, "What's that mean?"

"The people who run the state prisons. I think those people

are called commissioners."

The fog thinned out. Josie could see Samantha as if she were standing on the other side of a sheer drape.

Samantha shook her head. "But it makes no sense that this commissioner would request a meeting out here in the middle of nowhere."

"I agree."

The fog lifted fully and seemed to rise up to the mountains on the east side of the highway. The entire sky was blue as if the clouds had suddenly disappeared. The landscape was almost blindingly bright, especially the ocean.

Josie walked closer to Samantha until she was just a dozen feet from the edge of the dropoff. The sight was dramatic. Huge waves crashed two hundred feet below. The sea lions were barking loudly enough to be heard over the waves. Josie turned around. She could see the mountains that rose up to the east of the highway. Maybe that was where the Brazil Ranch hikers went. The mountains weren't tall like the Sierra, but they would still provide amazing views of the surrounding land and the Pacific in the distance.

That gave Josie a thought.

"Sam, when you say a person falling off the cliff would hit the water, did you mean that in a general way? Like it's a steep dropoff? Or did you mean it literally?"

Samantha looked down toward the water. "Well, it sure seems as though the tattooed guy was telling the truth. That you'd fall into the water. It's not just steep. It's a cliff. Straight down. When the tide goes out, maybe that would change things. But for now, I'd say yes. The dropoff goes straight down to the water." Samantha paused. "But it wouldn't matter, really. It would be extremely unlikely for someone to fall off the cliff, right?"

Josie was looking back at the mountains. "Yes, under normal circumstances."

"But…" Samantha prompted.

"But what if the commissioner called a meeting and wanted to have a picnic lunch out at the cliffs." Josie wondered if her idea was crazy.

"I'm waiting, Mama," Samantha said.

"A sniper could be up on the mountain to the east of the highway."

"Oh, Mama! That is such a wicked idea. Like, the commissioner could ask Leroy and Jimmy to meet him at the cliff edge. They go there and wait. But the commissioner hires a sniper. The sniper takes his shots, and Leroy and Jimmy fall to the ocean below, never to be seen again."

Josie looked up at the mountains. Something caught the sunlight. Or, there was some other source of a bright flash of light. It sounded like a stone plinked on the ground next to Josie's feet.

Josie turned back toward Samantha. "That's not funny, Sam."

"What do you mean?"

"Tossing stones at me when I'm already on edge about you being near the cliff."

Josie heard a faint snapping sound.

"I didn't toss anything at you."

Another stone seemed to jump.

Josie looked back at the mountains. Her purse moved. Josie looked down at it, puzzled. There was a hole in the leather. Then came another snapping sound.

"Run, Sam! Run!"

"What do you mean, Mama?"

"Someone is shooting at us from up on the mountain!"

NINE

Samantha shouted over the wind. "Shooting at us? No! It can't be!" Samantha looked up at the mountains across the highway, her eyes wide and terrified.

Josie shouted back, "Run! Now! We have to run!"

"But where? There's nowhere to go! We're totally exposed."

"Run like a snake! Back and forth! In and out. Back to the car! We have to keep moving so we don't get hit."

"But Mama! You have to run, too!" Samantha ran up to Josie and reached out.

"No, Sam. That makes us an easier target. We have to separate. Hurry! NOW!"

Josie started trying to run. Back and forth. Stepping over the clumps of rough ground. She was instantly out of breath.

Samantha ran past her. Weaving. She carried Unknown.

Josie tried to weave as well. But she didn't have the fitness for it. But if she could just keep moving…

Samantha slowed.

"Don't stop, Sam." Josie was shouting, breathless, paralyzed by fear for Samantha more than herself. "Don't slow down. It's hard to hit a moving target. We have to keep moving. Keep changing directions!"

Samantha ran back and forth, then in a loop around Josie.

Josie tried to mimic her in varying her motions. But she was distracted by other thoughts about the roommate Snake. He'd been tapping on his phone. Then he got a phone call and went inside. Had he called his roommates? Could it be Leroy or Jimmy who was shooting at them?

Then the van had passed them. Samantha had thought the driver might be Snake.

It might be a perfect setup. They could have agreed that if

an unknown person came around asking for Leroy and Jimmy, they'd tell that person about a meeting out at the Bixby Bridge meadow. If any one of them had sniper skills, they could shoot the unknown person as he or she stood near the top of the cliff. With the wind and roar of the waves below, no one would hear the shots. It was unlikely anyone would see them fall to the ground. Maybe they'd even fall off the cliff and into the ocean below. If not, the killer could hike out to the cliff, drag them to the edge, and drop them off. Their bodies would fall to the waves, and the currents would take them away.

Samantha was doing a serpentine maneuver, more back and forth than toward their car. She obviously didn't want to get too far ahead of Josie.

Josie was moving like a slow-motion jogger, barely able to get enough air. But she kept changing directions. Josie thought that the farther they got from the cliff edge, the safer they'd be.

Samantha paused and looked back at Josie.

"Keep moving, Sam! I'm coming!"

Josie remembered that Cor Contos had said that one of the major challenges was adjusting for wind. And the man named Snake had said something like that, too. Josie wondered if the only reason she and Samantha weren't already dead was that they had been saved by the swirling fog and the wind.

They once again came to the fence. Samantha and Unknown almost leaped over it.

"Keep going!" Josie shouted as she pressed down on the top wire of the fence, leaned sideways along the wire, then toppled over the wire onto the ground on the other side. She rolled. Writhed. Felt panic as she pushed up onto her knees, one of which had sharp pains.

"Mama, I can help!"

"No, keep moving! I'll be fine."

Josie stumbled ahead. Another thought intruded.

Why would Leroy or Jimmy or Snake want to shoot her and Samantha? They represented no threat. All Josie wanted was information about the explosion of the prison transport van. That couldn't possibly be enough cause to shoot them. Maybe

Josie had her reasoning turned around.

If Leroy and Jimmy were involved in the explosion that killed Lucas Herman, killing them would eliminate the risk that they might tell someone else. The commissioner could have set up a meeting out on the cliff so he could shoot Leroy and Jimmy.

Was the commissioner involved in the killing of Lucas Herman? And did that same commissioner recently find out that the governor was interested in reconsidering the murder of Forest Service Ranger Francis Telman? If so, maybe the commissioner was trying to cover his tracks.

How would the commissioner know about the governor reopening the case? Probably, the governor worked with the prison commissioners.

As they got closer to their car, the fog swirled around them again, and Josie felt a little safer.

They got to their car, jumped inside as fast as possible. Samantha held Unknown on her lap, pulled her close, and locked her door.

Josie started the car, barely looked for traffic as she pulled a U-turn, and headed north up the highway. She drove much faster than normal, a speed that would normally make her very uneasy.

"Mama, what just happened?"

"I don't know, Sam. Let me drive a moment. I need to breathe."

After several minutes, they came to Carmel.

Josie pulled over and parked in a gas station lot.

"We now have cell reception," Samantha said, "if you want to call the cops."

Josie leaned back in the car seat, closed her eyes, and took a deep breath.

"What would I say? We think someone shot at us but we don't know for sure? We wonder if it was one of the prison guards we were trying to contact, but we don't know why? There's no reason why the guards or anyone else would want to shoot at us. We have no evidence except for a bullet hole in my purse, a hole that looks like it could have happened when I caught my purse on something. And now that I think of it, I think I caught my purse on the fence wire."

"Look inside your purse, Mama. Maybe the bullet got stopped. Or maybe it damaged something else in your purse."

Josie emptied out her purse. There was nothing to see. "Oh, here's another hole you almost can't see. Right in the seam. The stitching is frayed, and it obscures the hole."

"So the bullet went clean through," Samantha said. "Two holes mean you are right, Mama! Someone shot at you. But the bullet will never be found out on that meadow, will it?"

Josie took another breath. "As far as the police or anyone else knows, we just imagined what happened."

"You could call the governor's office. They said they would back you up on this project. They could send out someone to talk to us."

"That's true. But again, what would they do with no evidence of a crime, no motive, no suspect, and no witnesses? They'll think we've just got snipers on the brain."

"This is depressing, Mama." She still gripped Unknown in her lap.

"I agree, Sam. Very."

"What do you think we should do next? I think the sleazy tattooed guy, Snake, drove by us in that van. But I could be wrong. He might still be at his house. Or, back from wherever he went. Should we go back to talk to him? See if he's heard from his roommates, Leroy and Jimmy?"

Josie made a single, slow nod. "Yes, that makes sense."

"Snake could be the sniper, right?" Samantha said. "He was on the highway before us. We went and had breakfast. He would have had time to drive out there, climb up the mountain on the other side of the highway, wait for us to arrive, and then shoot us."

Josie made a slow, thoughtful nod.

Samantha said, "But even if he shot at us out by the ocean, he wouldn't shoot us once he's back home in his own neighborhood, right?"

"Maybe not. Let's find out."

TEN

They drove back to the neighborhood where Leroy Blomberg and Jimmy John Lasman lived with the man called Snake.

As Josie parked a block down, Samantha said, "This is creepy, going back to the world of filed teeth and snake tattoos."

"Yes, it is. Let's just watch for awhile." Josie turned off the car, turned, leaned across Unknown, and hugged Samantha, long and hard.

"We don't have to do this," Josie said.

"Right. But we should do this. I'll be okay. Unknown will protect me. And I've got my pepper spray."

They got out and walked to the house.

Samantha and Unknown stayed on the sidewalk while Josie walked up to the door and knocked. After a minute, she knocked again.

When there was no answer, she moved to the side and stepped over to the front window. She leaned close to the glass to look inside. But it was dark inside, and the light outside made for a bright reflection. She couldn't see anything. She cupped her hands next to her face. She still couldn't see anything.

Josie walked across the front of the house to the other window.

"Mama, are you sure you want to do that? What if someone sees you?"

"I'm not burglarizing the place. I'm just looking."

Josie looked in the other window. Nothing but darkness.

Josie stepped back and looked at the house. It was a small place. One would think that light from a rear window would shine through and illuminate something near the front windows. She tried looking again, cupping her hands like before. Nothing but darkness. Or…

As she let her eyes adjust, she sensed a shape. Dark in tone, like a dark gray. But it was something. And there was a long shape that was slightly different. Darker gray? Brown?

"Sam, can you come and look? I can't tell what I'm seeing. But my eyes are bad. You could probably tell."

Samantha walked up, still holding Unknown's leash. She peered through the window from different angles, cupping her hands next to her face as Josie had done.

"There's something on the floor. I can't tell exactly what. No, wait, it's a person! Mostly out of view. But I can see his leg. I know it's a man because he's got on a big boot. But it's hard to see because the boot is brown and the floor is also dark. But not quite brown. More like dark reddish brown."

Samantha changed her angle. "What's weird is that the red brown seems like a round rug. But the curved edge isn't smooth. It's almost as if…"

Samantha stepped back from the window, recoiling, her eyes looking horrified.

"What's wrong, Sam?"

"Mama! It's blood. The man is lying in a pool of blood!"

ELEVEN

They both ran to the sidewalk.

"Quick, let's get in our car," Josie said, panic in her voice.

Samantha ran, Josie jogged. They got in the Prius. Josie hit the door lock button. Samantha gripped Unknown hard. Josie leaned her head back against the seat and tried to take deep breaths.

"Was the man moving?" she asked.

"Not that I could see. It looked like something in a movie. There was so much blood, he'd almost have to be dead." Samantha seemed very nervous. "I see things like this in the movies, but I always know that movies aren't real. Seeing that much blood for real… That makes me shaky inside."

"Me too," Josie said. "It seems that the right thing to do would be to try to get inside and see if he's alive. Maybe we could help him. But it could be that someone killed him. And the killer could still be inside." Josie looked around, then in her rear view mirrors. "Or outside nearby. I'm going to turn on the car and be ready to drive off, just in case." Josie put her key in the ignition.

"I should call nine, one, one on your phone, so I can use mine to call the governor."

Samantha nodded and handed her phone to Josie.

Josie dialed 911.

"Nine, one, one emergency. Please state your name and address."

The dispatcher was male and sounded young.

"This is Josie Strong. I'm calling from a cell phone near Monterey. The address is…" Josie paused.

Samantha held out a piece of paper with the address written

on it.

Josie read off the number and street. She could barely breathe, she was so out of breath.

"What's your emergency?"

"I knocked on the door of the house. When there was no answer, my daughter and I looked in the window. We saw a man lying in a pool of blood."

"Are you still outside of the house?" the dispatcher asked.

"Yes, but we got back in our car for safety."

"Okay, stay there, and I'll have officers en route shortly. I'm going to put you on hold, but stay on the line."

Josie turned to Samantha. "I'm on hold. You take your phone and listen for when they come back. I'll call the governor's office."

Josie pulled her phone from her purse and dialed. It was answered on the second ring. "Governor's office, Sonja Gonsalves speaking."

"Sonja, this is Josie Strong calling."

"Hi, Ms. Strong. How are you doing?"

"Not so well. We have a situation you and the governor should know about. Remember the prison guards who drove the transport truck that blew up and killed Lucas Herman? AKA Taylor Cooke, who worked for the governor? You gave me their address in Monterey?"

"Right. Leroy Blomberg and Jimmy John Lasman."

"That's it. We're at their house now. We stopped by earlier and they were gone, so we spoke to their roommate. He told us that Leroy and Jimmy had gone out to the Bixby cliff, so we went there to try and find them. That's a long story I should tell you later. But we didn't see them, so we came back to their house. No one answered my knock, so we looked in the window. We saw a man on the floor, lying in a pool of blood."

"Oh, no!" The woman's voice went up in pitch. "I'm so… That is horrible!"

Josie could hear Sonja breathing hard.

"We called nine, one, one," Josie said. "The police haven't yet arrived. I thought you'd want to know."

"Yes, certainly. Let me call the governor about this. I imagine he will want the Bureau of Investigation to look into this as well as the police. Just sit tight, and I will get back to you."

"Okay, thanks. Sorry to sound upset."

"Anyone would be upset. Hold tight, and I'll talk to you soon."

Josie hung up.

"Now what, Mama?"

"We wait and see. Sonja thinks the governor will want the Bureau of Investigation to come out."

Samantha said, "I keep remembering that bad guy who impersonated a Bureau agent." Samantha's voice was dark.

"Yes. He was really evil."

"But," Samantha said, "the Bureau agents were also the ones who were nice to me when Lucas Herman chased us on the wharf in San Francisco."

Josie nodded. "Let's hope they're nice now, as well."

"Mama, do you still think we should be doing this? Trying to find killers?"

"I don't know. It's risky. And stressful. I just want to have a normal life with you at home, walking the beach, watching your volleyball games. teaching. But clearly there are some really bad guys out there. Guys who should be in prison. If we can help catch more of them, that's a compelling purpose to our lives."

Samantha nodded. "Does this new situation with the guards change anything? Like how to find the man who killed the forest ranger?"

"I don't know. I'm too upset to think clearly. I need to calm down."

"Do you think Snake might be the guy lying in the pool of blood?"

"He could be. But this person was wearing boots, and Snake was wearing sandals. Maybe Snake is the person who injured the person lying in the pool of blood."

"You still think we were shot at, right?"

Josie nodded. "No one except Snake knew we were going to be out at the Bixby cliff. Of course, he could have told Leroy and Jimmy, or anyone else that we were going there. It could be anyone who shot at us. But Snake seems the likeliest person."

Samantha nodded. "I see your point. But you know what doesn't fit?"

"No, what?"

"Cor Kontos told us how snipers have to be incredibly trained and focused. But Snake is such a sleazy guy, I don't think he could even make it as a basic soldier in the Army. Never mind being some kind of specially-trained sniper."

"I agree with you. That doesn't rule out Leroy and Jimmy. But I would go further and say that if either of them were trained snipers, they wouldn't live with a sleazy guy like the one we met. They would have discipline, and that discipline would probably translate to picking a more disciplined roommate. Does that make sense?"

"Yeah, it does. Another thing… Cor told us about a sniper who had some kind of major status in the Army."

"Yes, that's right. They called him Typhon after the mythical god of monsters."

Samantha was rubbing Unknown. "Cor also said that snipers usually operate in teams of two. And Snake said something about Leroy and Jimmy and sniper cells. But the Typhon guy that Cor talked about seemed to be a loner."

Josie was staring out the windshield. Down the street were several Monterey Cypress trees, their limbs all leaning to the east, no doubt a result of regular Pacific storms pummeling them from the west as they grew. She felt as if she understood the constant stress that bent a tree. Then she was distracted by another thought.

The governor had called upon her to find the second shooter who'd killed Ranger Francis Telman from short range. Josie had been the first person to propose that the shooter who killed the ranger was a different individual than the sniper who'd killed the ranger's wife Mary Jo and who'd nearly killed Samantha in the process. Josie had caught that sniper, Lucas Herman, AKA Taylor Cooke. But now that Josie and Samantha were looking for the second shooter—the short-range shooter Josie had suggested—

they were possibly being pursued by yet another sniper.

It made no sense. The first sniper, Lucas, was dead. So if there was a second sniper, then that meant one of two things. Either there were a total of three shooters, two snipers and one short-range shooter. Or else Josie's original premise was wrong. One of the snipers was also a short-range shooter who committed the first murder, the killing of Forest Ranger Telman. It could be that Lucas Herman/Taylor Cooke, the man who shot Mary Jo, was both a sniper and a short-range shooter. It could also be that a second shooter, a sniper such as the one Josie believed had just shot at them by the Bixby cliffs, was both a sniper and a short-range shooter.

"You're awfully quiet, Mama. What are you thinking?"

Josie explained her thoughts.

Samantha nodded. "Either way, we still have to find the second shooter."

"But we can't just stumble around," Josie said. "We have to find a way into the problem. A reason to investigate. He could be anywhere. We need a clue about where to look."

"How're we gonna do that?"

"Drive home and talk to people who know the stuff we don't know."

Samantha said, "You mean Cumberland?"

"Right."

"And Cor Kontos." Samantha grinned. "Because she kicks butt."

"She's… well, I wouldn't necessarily put it that way."

"But it's true, right?" Samantha said. "And she knows military stuff. Which basically means she knows the technical side of kicking butt."

A black-and-white police car came down the road toward them, driving fast, its flashing lights on, but its siren off.

Josie rolled down her window and made a small wave.

The police car slowed, then jerked to a stop. The car's window was down.

Josie was alarmed. She kept her hands visible on the steering wheel and spoke slowly and clearly.

"My name is Josie Strong. I'm the person who called nine, one, one."

Both doors of the police car opened. Two uniformed officers got out, both female, one big, one not so big.

The smaller cop gestured toward the house on the next block. "Is that the house where you saw someone injured?" She looked down at a clipboard and read off the address number. "Number one eighty-one?"

"My daughter saw, yes. Inside the window next to the door."

"Have you seen anyone else?"

"No. I knocked, but no one answered. That's why we looked in the window."

"Do you have reason to think anyone else is inside?"

"No. We stopped by about two hours ago. We spoke to a man who answered the door. We were looking for the tenants Leroy Blomberg and Jimmy John Lasman, who are guards who work for the prison system. The man who answered the door said they weren't in. He said his name was Snake. Later, as we were driving, we think the man who called himself Snake drove by us."

"Okay, please stay in your car and wait."

Josie did as requested.

From where Josie and Samantha sat in their car, they could see the officer knock on the front door, then look in the window. The cop turned on a very bright flashlight and shined it through the glass.

The cop spoke into her radio. Went back to the front door. Knocked again. Tried the door knob.

Josie didn't know all the rules about warrants and such, but she knew that police officers can break into a house if they sense someone is in distress.

The smaller cop gestured to the larger one.

The larger one went up to the door. They spoke. Josie and Samantha couldn't hear them.

The smaller cop pulled her gun out of her holster and stepped off to the side so she could see back toward the rear of the house as well as the front.

The larger cop pounded on the door and called out in a voice so loud, Josie and Samantha could hear it from inside their car. "Police! Open the door!" She waited a few moments then unholstered her own gun and gave a hard kick to the door, which broke open.

Both officers, their guns drawn, went inside.

"Can they do that?" Samantha asked. "Break down a door without a search warrant?"

"I think the rule is that it's permissible if they think someone is in imminent danger."

"Like a guy lying in a pool of blood," Samantha said.

The officers were in the house for two or three minutes. The smaller one came back out, stood near the front door, and spoke into her radio.

Another police car came down the street and stopped in the middle of the road, its lights flashing. Two uniformed cops got out. Both men.

A black SUV came from the other direction and stopped nose to nose with the second cop car. Unlike the patrol cars, it didn't have flashing lights on the roof but shining from within the front grill. Two men got out. They weren't wearing uniforms. They both had on dark pants, white long-sleeved shirts, and blue ties.

The officers conferred with each other and spoke on their radios and cell phones. Eventually, two more patrol cars arrived, each angling crosswise, blocking traffic at the intersections at each end of the block. Two more cops got out of each car. A total of ten cops. Josie noticed that all ten officers, seven men and three women, were white. She didn't think it mattered. She hadn't often experienced strong discrimination. But, like all Blacks, she'd learned to pay attention.

Samantha still held Josie's phone. They heard a voice.

Josie reached for the phone. "Hello?"

"This is nine, one, one emergency. Do you have anything else to report?"

"No."

"Okay. Officers are now on the scene, so you can disconnect from this call."

"Thank you." Josie clicked off.

After 20 minutes, one of the men in the white shirts walked over and motioned Josie and Samantha to get out of their car.

They got out but left Unknown in the car.

"You are Josie and Samantha Strong."

"Yes, sir," Josie said. Up close, she could see that his left shirt pocket had a small emblem that said, 'California Department of Justice.'

"I'm Special Agent O'Connor with the Bureau of Investigation." He handed Josie his card. The printing said 'California Department of Justice' at the top and 'Bureau of Investigation' across the bottom.

Josie thought it was a change in the way the Bureau of Investigation was presenting their image.

"May I see your ID?" he asked.

Josie pulled out her driver's license and handed it to him.

O'Connor looked at it carefully, then handed it back. He said, "I understand that you had a bad experience with someone who claimed to be with the Bureau. I'll try not to waste your time."

Josie didn't respond.

The man continued, "I've been told you are working on a special assignment from the governor's office. Can you tell me what you know about this situation and the people involved?" He pulled out his phone and tapped the screen. No doubt, he was recording everything Josie would say.

"Of course." Josie told him what had happened from the time that the governor came into the coffee shop and requested her help reopening the case of Ranger Francis Telman's murder. She explained how they came to this house where the prison guards Leroy Blomberg and Jimmy John Lasman live.

O'Connor said, "Those are the guards who were driving the prison transport truck that blew up and killed the sniper named Lucas Herman, AKA Taylor Cooke?"

Josie nodded. She told him about her conversation with

the guards' roommate Snake and their subsequent drive to the meadow near the Bixby Creek Bridge to possibly meet Leroy and Jimmy.

As Josie spoke, she said only that they hadn't been able to find Leroy and Jimmy. She left out her belief that she and Samantha had been shot at. Partly, she thought she'd lose credibility if she brought up a supposed crime for which she had no evidence. And partly, because if the shooter ever heard or read any report saying that Josie and Samantha believed they'd been shot at, that would tell the shooter that Josie and Samantha were alert to such a possibility. Josie wanted to deny the shooter any advantage that such knowledge might provide. Of course, the shooter may already know that from seeing them run S-turns on the meadow. But it wasn't a given because they were mostly obscured by fog.

When Agent O'Connor was done with his questions, he turned to Samantha and said, "Can you think of anything we've forgotten to address? Any details that you noticed?"

Samantha took her time, frowning. She shook her head. "No, nothing else occurs to me."

The agent turned back to Josie, "Is there anything I can help you with before you leave?"

It seemed a polite dismissal, but Josie sensed an underlying tension.

"Yes. What did you find inside the house?"

"I'm not at liberty to say."

Josie wasn't surprised. "The governor told me that all law enforcement agencies would be instructed to help me. He will notice if my report says that any law enforcement officers weren't forthcoming in my investigation. Of course, I mean to cause no distress. But I also want to solve the governor's case. For that I need all available information."

O'Connor's face went from a pleasant demeanor to a hard scowl. "I'm sure the governor has his reasons for contacting you. But I hardly think a woman like you is going to solve a case like this."

Josie heard a strong pejorative tone in his words 'a woman

like you.'

She spoke with her own steely tone. "What you think about my approach to the case is irrelevant. I work for the governor. And he will decide how to judge what I put in my report." Josie glanced over at the house, where the other officers were working. "Now, you were going to tell me what you found in the house."

The man looked at her for a long moment as if considering the ramifications of his response. Eventually, he said, "I have only the barest of facts," the man's voice was tight. "The rest is speculation."

"One of the reasons the governor chose me for this investigation is his belief that I am judicious and discreet with how I handle information. Including speculation."

The man made a slight shake of his head as if exasperated. "Two men were shot dead at close range," he said. "It looks like a murder and a suicide."

"Could it have been a double murder?" Josie asked.

The man showed no reaction. "Until our crime techs go over the scene and the ME gives us the results of the autopsies, it could be anything."

"But what makes you think of a murder/suicide?"

"There was a note."

"What did it say?"

The man took a deep breath as if he were trying to gather his patience. He pulled a ziplock bag out of his pocket and held it up, out of reach of Josie so that she had to step forward to grasp it.

Inside the bag was a scrap of paper, torn along the top edge as if someone had written something, torn it off, then started again. The writing was in ballpoint pen, with two blobs of ink that suggested the pen leaked.

'I made lotsa mistakes. all gonna catch up with me. my bad. leroy screwed up to. i fixed that. jj'

After Josie read it twice, she angled it toward Samantha. "Can you please take a photo?"

Samantha used her phone to take a photo.

"Were the identities of the dead men clear?" Josie asked.

O'Connor gave her yet another hard look. "The victims each had IDs on them. It certainly looks like they are Leroy Blomberg and Jimmy John Lasman."

"Any sign of the man called Snake?"

"No."

"Do you know anything about Snake?" she asked. "His background? His given name? Criminal record?"

"No. We have no idea who he is."

"There must be signs of him in the house."

"There are two bedrooms. One of them has two beds. A total of three beds. All have been slept in. But there's no indication of a third resident's identity."

"Was a handgun involved?"

"Not that we see. We found a thirty-aught-six rifle that appears to have been recently discharged."

Josie tried to quickly think about what little she'd learned from Cor about rifles in the previous few months. She said, "Many rifles are quite long and would be hard to use for suicide."

The man regarded her and tried to show no reaction.

She gave him a steady look as if they were having a staring contest.

Eventually, he said, "A rifle can be fired with your toe."

TWELVE

The Bureau of Investigation agent told them again that they were free to go. His distaste for them was palpable.

Josie still had questions. But she knew there'd be many more in the coming days. She could contact him later. Or, if she thought he was resistant to her questions, maybe contact his superior.

As they drove away, Samantha said, "That was tense, Mama! But the way you talked to him? You kinda kicked butt yourself! It's like, you kept your voice low and calm, but you made him tell you everything you wanted. You put him up against the wall. I'm impressed."

"The power of words," Josie said. "To tell the truth, he scared me. But I kept reminding myself that I was just doing my job."

"I can't believe the two men we were looking for are dead." Samantha's voice was hushed. "I've only heard about murder and suicide. And now it's happened. Or at least that's what the cops want us to think."

"I agree, Sam. I don't know what to think about it. The murder/suicide explanation the agent gave us is hard to swallow. It could be true. But why? Even if the guards were involved in the explosion that blew up the truck and killed Lucas Herman, why were they suddenly so upset about it that one of them killed them both?"

"Do you think Agent O'Connor was lying about it?"

Josie was slow to answer. "Maybe. But more likely he believes it."

"You mean..." Samantha paused, "it could just look like murder and suicide, yet he thinks that's what really happened?"

"If someone wanted both men dead, they could set it up

so it looks like a murder/suicide. Then the police wouldn't be looking for the real killer."

"A frame job," Samantha said. "The guards could have come home when we were eating breakfast. Maybe Snake killed them both. Maybe he'd just killed them before we knocked on his door!" After a moment, Samantha added, "That would explain why he drove by us so fast on the highway."

"Then what?" Josie asked. "He parked someplace out by the Bixby Bridge, climbed up the mountain, and tried to kill us when we got out there?"

Samantha shrugged. "I didn't see that van parked anywhere. But it could have been hidden behind some bushes."

They drove in silence.

Eventually, Samantha said, "Seeing a dead guy through the window is upsetting."

"I know. I agree," Josie said.

"It's like when Mary Jo was killed. It's too much to take in, Mama. Going after killers is one thing. But if they come after us? That's a whole other thing."

"You're right, Sam. I could easily make the case that a mother's prime responsibility is to keep her daughter safe, away from this side of humanity. Many people would say my number one priority is to protect you."

"But then you'd have to worry about the governor messing with your job. The whole tenure thing. And, frankly, I've told you I want to do this with you. So you have to deal with my desires."

Josie didn't respond.

Samantha continued, "The cops have to deal with this, too, right? Like those cops we just saw at the guards' house. They're all potential targets. Bad guys often want revenge on the cops. So those cops have to live with the same worries. They know that their families might become the target of killers."

Josie knew that Samantha was working through the same things that were on Josie's mind. "But they chose this," Josie said. "They are trained for this."

They were quiet for a minute.

Then Samantha said, “If the governor made you lose your job, Mama, we’d be screwed, right?”

It wasn’t exactly how Josie would put it, but it was accurate. “Maybe I could get a job at USC or one of the other schools.”

Samantha was shaking her head. “That wouldn’t be as good for you. And it would be much harder for you to get to work. USC is a long way from where we live. And if we moved, we wouldn’t be near the beach, I might not be able to play volleyball.” Samantha seemed to settle down lower into her seat. “That settles it, Mama. We’re just like cop families. We have to deal with death. With murder. We have to accept that doing a good thing for society comes with the price of emotional stress.”

“I knew you were a smart kid,” Josie said. In her peripheral vision, she sensed Samantha grinning.

“But you didn’t know just how smart, huh?”

“That’s right, Cap’n.”

Samantha was silent.

THIRTEEN

"What do we do next?" Samantha asked.

"We head home. We'll be there around dark."

Josie drove out to the highway. She headed east toward the San Luis Reservoir.

Josie said, "Maybe we should call Cumberland and see if he can learn anything about the man called Snake."

"How would he do that?"

"I have no idea. Maybe Leroy and Jimmy John used social media. Maybe they posted pictures of themselves and Snake. They might have used his name. You could look for that as well as Cumberland could. Maybe better. But Cumberland will have other ideas. Were Leroy and Jimmy John in the military? Were their names on the utility bills for the house? He might be able to find information that is off limits to us. I'm also wondering what Cor would think about the rifle the police found."

"We could call Cumberland while we drive," Samantha said. "He might be busy with his work. The sooner you contact him, the sooner he could get us on his schedule."

"You could call him. Cor, too."

"What would I say?"

"You're the Cap'n. You're in charge of communication."

"Meaning?"

"You're better at talking to people than I am. You contact the experts. Solicit their help."

"What if… you know, what if they don't want to help?"

"Then you turn on the famous Samantha Strong charm and persuade them."

"You're just saying that to give me confidence. It's a child-raising thing, right? Get your kid to take on challenges by complimenting her."

"What if it is? Is that wrong? Reminding your child of her obvious virtues?"

Samantha grinned. "Okay, where should I start?"

"I would call Cumberland first. Use my phone, because he recognizes the number. I'll talk to him first and then give the phone to you. You explain our situation, what we know and what we suspect but don't know. He already found out about that LLC that owns the house where Mary Jo lived. Remember? Back at Christmas? If he looks for anything related to that, I bet he'll learn some more things that will give us a place to start looking."

Samantha said, "A loose thread that we can pull to see what unravels?"

In Josie's peripheral vision, she could see Samantha smiling.

"Exactly. After you call Cumberland, you can call Cor and tell her what happened. She will have a useful comment."

"Like what?"

"I don't know. That's the beauty of presenting scenarios to experts. They come up with ideas from their own experience. Maybe they're wrong, but they'll still think of things we won't."

Samantha was looking at her phone. "Now I don't have a cell signal. California is supposed to be the technology state, right? But there are so many places where you can't even use a cell phone."

"It's a good reminder of what community provides. Internet. Electric power. Road maintenance. Community water and sewer. Businesses of every kind. And cell service. But rural areas? Not so much."

Josie retraced her drive around the San Luis Reservoir. As soon as they got to the interstate and the openness of the Central Valley, cell reception resumed. Samantha got to work.

Samantha started by using Josie's phone to dial Cumberland. She handed the phone to Josie.

"Hi, professor," Cumberland's voice said.

"Hi, Cumberland. I'm sorry to be brusque, but I want you to know that I'm driving. So I'm going to hand my phone to

Samantha and she can ask you my question. Is that okay?"

"Um, sure, I guess," he said, radiating awkwardness.

"Thanks very much." Josie handed the phone back to Samantha.

As Josie drove, she reminded herself not to interrupt. She didn't want Samantha to feel self-conscious. Josie kept her focus on the road and didn't turn toward Samantha.

At first, Samantha sounded a little hesitant, trying to make a little small talk with Cumberland, then remembering that Cumberland, despite his genius, was well down the autism spectrum and he had little-to-no social skills. So Samantha simply told him what they had experienced, and how they were looking for prison guards named Leroy Blomberg and Jimmy John Lasman. Samantha explained how those guards were just killed.

She was quiet for a few moments during the conversation. Josie could hear that Cumberland was talking, but she couldn't make out any words.

"Yes, it was horrible!" Samantha said. "There was another guy who lived with them, a man with filed teeth named Snake. So now we're looking for him. The cops are, too."

Samantha paused again.

Then she said, "Yes, this is connected to the previous case at Christmas. Ranger Francis Telman, who was shot up by Emerald Bay at Lake Tahoe. And his wife Mary Jo Telman, who was killed by a sniper in the foothills while Mama and I were talking to her. We caught the sniper, thanks to that phone you gave Mama that could track other phones! But there was probably another bad guy that we didn't catch. Now, the governor called Mama about it. So we're back on the case. So if you could learn anything about that, it would be great." Pause. "It's so nice of you to help. I know Mama thinks you're the greatest. I do too."

That statement startled Josie. It was the kind of thing she could never convincingly say. She noticed that Samantha spoke with an ease and friendliness that Josie had never mastered. In preparation for a conversation, Josie often practiced her potential questions and responses in advance. But Samantha was able to converse with ease and in an impromptu manner. She managed to explain their situation without any awkwardness. Josie couldn't easily categorize Samantha's ability. It was as if words flowed organically for her. She exuded comfort and friendliness, and reassurance. Even if Josie said the same words, she knew they would sound forced and stiff.

There was another pause in Samantha's conversation with Cumberland.

"Right," Samantha said. "We want any and all ideas you have. Thanks so much." Pause. "We're driving back from Monterey, so we'll be home tonight. Maybe we could talk again tomorrow? Okay, great." Samantha clicked off.

When Samantha got off the phone, she turned to Josie and said, "Cumberland said he will see what he can find."

"Did he give any indication of when he might find time?"

"He said he'd start right now."

"Wow," Josie said. "How do you do that? Getting a person to want to help you so readily?"

"Just my natural charm, I guess." Samantha suppressed a laugh.

"You say it as if you don't mean it, but it's true, Sam. You have the kind of charisma that makes people so comfortable, they want to be part of whatever you're doing."

"Okay, I'll try my charisma on Cor." Samantha picked up her phone. "You think she'll answer if I call? Or should I use your phone again?"

"Try your phone and see."

Samantha got Cor Kontos's number out of Josie's phone and then dialed it on her own phone. A minute later, Samantha was talking animatedly with Cor.

Samantha explained what they'd been through.

Josie couldn't hear Cor, but she could imagine the words.

"Yeah," Samantha said. "It was so scary. But not as scary as before when the sniper killed Mary Jo Telman and almost killed us. Anyway, we're pretty sure Mama's purse was hit out at Big Sur. A hole right through it. But it could be that something else made the hole. So we… What? No, we didn't get hit."

A longer pause.

Samantha continued, "It seems like it. But no, we aren't positive there was a sniper. Yeah, Mama will really want your thoughts. Me, too."

Samantha went on to say that they thought they were once again dealing with a sniper and they could use advice and comment. After a short silence, Samantha said they'd be home that night, and they could meet Cor anytime. She clicked off and turned to Josie. "Cor's going to come over tomorrow, late morning. Maybe Cumberland will have something by then, too."

"Perfect. You make a good captain."

As they got to the south end of the Central Valley, Samantha's phone beeped.

"I got a text from my volleyball coach. She says there's been a schedule mixup that produced a sudden opportunity for our team to play in a tournament tomorrow on Ocean Park Beach." Samantha was very excited. "Do you think we can fit it in, Mama?"

Josie worried that it would lessen the possibility of her finishing her mission for the governor in time to resume teaching when UCLA's spring quarter started. But she worried more that this project for the governor would have a serious negative impact on Samantha.

"Sure, Sam, let's do it. It'll be fun."

"Thanks, Mama!" Samantha started to lean over to hug Josie, but paused as she realized it wouldn't be smart when Josie was driving.

FOURTEEN

When they got back to Santa Monica, Josie pulled up near their favorite Chinese restaurant, and Samantha ran inside to get takeout.

While Josie waited with Unknown out in the car, her phone rang. The screen showed it was the governor's office. It would be the aide she'd talked to earlier, Sonja Gonsalves.

Josie tapped the answer button. "Hi, Sonja."

"Ms. Strong?" A man's voice. The governor. On a Friday night.

"Speaking." Josie knew she should probably sound deferential. And more conversational. But she was still conflicted about the way he intruded into her life.

"This is the governor," he said. "I'm calling to say that I've heard you work fast and effectively. It's only been hours since we spoke at the coffee shop, and you have already learned of another potential shooter. I'm impressed. I didn't know I had that kind of effect on people."

Josie stifled her instant dislike of the man. She wasn't surprised that he presented her efforts as an example of how important he was.

Nevertheless, she appreciated that he called. He was making an effort, no small thing for a man as self-focused as the governor.

There was a moment of silence. Josie said, "I'm glad you're pleased."

"It was actually Sonja's idea that I call. I think she's worried that you aren't getting enough feedback."

Josie shook her head in disbelief. Just when she was thinking the governor had taken the initiative to call and thank her, he revealed that he did it at Sonja's request.

"So keep up the good work," he added. "And remember that our office is at your service. You need anything, anything at all, just call."

And Sonja, not the governor, will take care of it, Josie thought.

"Will do," Josie said.

They said goodbye and hung up.

FIFTEEN

Each condo in Josie and Sam's building came with a single parking space in the underground garage. Josie pulled in through the security gate, parked, and they skipped the elevator to take the stairs, something Samantha motivated them to do a year before when her volleyball coach explained the fitness benefits of always taking the stairs.

What were Samantha's words? Never sit when you can stand. Never stay still when you can move. And never ride when you can walk.

Samantha and Unknown trotted up three floors. Josie struggled up, breathing hard, thinking once again that fitness wasn't as simple as the so-called experts described. Taking the stairs was, no doubt, good. But even after a year, it didn't make Josie feel any more fit.

When Josie got to their floor and walked in the door, she saw their boarder Amelia Gomez at the kitchen table with her notebooks filled with lists and ideas for her own coffee shop business that she was planning. One side of the open pages had a pencil sketch of a layout for the counters and tables.

Josie noticed that Amelia had no phone or computer on the table.

Amelia gave them her infectious smile.

"I'm so glad to see you!" Amelia picked up Unknown and was smothering the dog with hugs.

They all ate Chow Mein and Kung Pao Chicken.

Josie gestured toward Amelia's notebooks. "Is your business plan still moving forward?"

"Yes. But I'm a little distracted. My boss at the coffee shop offered me the position of assistant manager. She said I was on track to become their youngest manager ever." Amelia gave them a look that was part smile and part embarrassment. "Meanwhile, I'm planning to leave and start my own business!"

"Don't feel bad about it," Josie said. "You have a surfeit of energy and smarts and organization. It's your destiny to do great things and leave behind people who wish they could keep you working for them."

"A surfeit... This means good?" Although Amelia hadn't started to learn English until her parents brought her north to the U.S. when Amelia was ten, she was very fluent in English. Not knowing words like surfeit was more about youth than about being an immigrant.

"Surfeit is an excess. You have an excess of energy and smarts."

Amelia grinned.

Samantha seemed to study Amelia, who, at 19, was older by five years.

Josie thought that Amelia was a good role model for Samantha. Samantha had always had good discipline for volleyball and other school activities. But Amelia's ambition—especially considering her background of poverty—was impressive. And Amelia appeared to be immune to phone distractions, which Josie was beginning to think was an addiction, not unlike other drugs. A moderate amount seemed fine, but phone use quickly grew to take over a person's life. It was one more worry that occupied Josie. It was because Samantha always seemed to be occupied with her phone that Josie noticed when anyone wasn't tethered to their phone.

After they ate, Josie went to bed while Samantha and Amelia stayed up.

In the morning, Amelia served them coffee made from beans she had roasted herself in the oven, a task she was careful to continuously check was still okay with Josie. The heat for roasting was very high, the kitchen exhaust fan ran for hours, and the roasting odor was significant and not completely pleasant. Josie worried that swirling winds might bring those exhausted smells into the other condominiums. But Josie wanted to help

Amelia succeed. And so far, no one had complained.

"What do you think?" Amelia asked after they'd tasted her brew.

"Delicious," Josie said, while simultaneously Samantha said, "Too bitter."

Amelia grinned as if both comments were positive. "I am so glad for your input," she said, exuding a positive attitude. "This will help me perfect my menu."

They had just finished breakfast when the doorbell rang.

"Who is it?" Josie said into the intercom.

The voice in the speaker said, "Cor Kontos, out of her element in this upscale part of town, but available to check on the troops."

"Thanks," Josie said. She pressed the button to unlock the downstairs entrance. Cor knocked at their door seconds later, breathing a bit fast, as if she'd taken the steps three at a time, something Josie had previously witnessed.

Samantha opened the door. Cor stood there wearing camo pants, heavy black military boots, and a sleeveless camo shirt that showed off her muscular, tattooed arms. Her nearly black hair was short and spiky and stood straight up.

"Cor!" Samantha said and threw her thin arms around the much stockier, woman. "Come in."

After Samantha released her, Cor bent down and patted her hands on her knees. Unknown walked toward her and made a tentative wag.

"See, Mama," Samantha said. "Unknown's doing it again, wagging for Cor. She doesn't wag for practically anyone."

Cor said, "Unknown and I connect, one wild animal to another." Cor rubbed Unknown's sides.

"Have you met Amelia?" Josie asked.

Cor turned to Amelia, whose grin made up for Cor's straight face. Cor shook Amelia's hand, giving it a vigorous pump up and down three times. Cor said, "We met on our Christmas trip to San Francisco to rescue the professor from the clutches of the medical industrial complex. Anyway, you know the words. Any friend of the professor and Sam's…"

"Right!" Amelia interrupted. "Same for me."

Josie saw Amelia give Cor's bare tattooed arms a discreet look as if to check for additions to the portfolio. Josie didn't notice any new art. But Cor's Greek skin was a sepia tone that was similar to Amelia's Peruvian complexion. Tattoos didn't stand out well on darker skin.

Cor said to Amelia, "I've heard more about you in the last few months. Your coffee maestro rep is expanding."

Amelia beamed. "They told you I was a maestro?" Amelia glanced at Samantha and Josie.

"Bragged about you, actually."

"Would you like to try my coffee?"

"Sure."

Amelia poured a small mug. "Black?"

"Only way to drink coffee." Cor sipped. "Wow, potent stuff. I love it."

Samantha said, "Amelia even roasted the beans."

Cor turned to Amelia. "You got the coffee chops, girl. I want in when you start your company."

Amelia's eyes opened wide. "They told you I was going to start a coffee company?"

"No. It's just a casual comment based on standout coffee made by someone who roasts her own beans. Only logical explanation is you're starting a coffee company."

"I am! I'm still working out the details and my techniques and the costs."

"You're thorough."

"I believe you have to be thorough to succeed in business."

Cor looked at Josie. "I know I said this about Samantha, but this girl is something, too. Where'd you find her?"

Josie smiled. "We professors develop a kind of good-student radar. I've often gotten coffee at the shop where Amelia works. Multiple times I saw that there was one person who stood out from all the other workers. So Sam and I talked to her. She impressed us in every way."

"And now she comes over and makes you coffee."

Samantha said, "She lives here. For the time being, at

least."

Cor looked at Amelia. "How'd you score a bunk at the Strong BNB?"

Amelia hesitated.

Josie thought understatement was the best response. "Amelia's family is not especially supportive. We are. It was a good solution."

Amelia was still grinning at Cor. "You are a long-time friend of Sam and Josie?"

"Cor was in a class I taught," Josie said. "Another one of those good students. Then she helped us on the little problem we had in Northern California."

"Sniper murders are more than a little problem, girl," Cor said. She put her arm around Josie's shoulders.

Amelia raised her substantial eyebrows and widened her eyes. "Was that when Sam and Josie were almost shot?"

"Like I said," Cor nodded, "it was a big problem. Staying alive was something to celebrate. Y'all are headed to the beach?"

Samantha nodded.

Josie said, "As Samantha mentioned on the phone yesterday, the governor has me re-investigating the sniper case from last Christmas."

"To look for the second shooter," Cor immediately said. "The governor was probably the only one so dense he missed the significance of your recommendation. And now you have new information?"

"Maybe. Can we tell you about it while we take the beach walk? Your input would be greatly appreciated."

"Fortified by Amelia's coffee, this Joe is ready for battle."

Samantha clipped on Unknown's leash, and she grabbed the backpack in which she could carry Unknown in case they went out on the sand where dogs were not allowed.

While they walked down to the street and over to the beach, Cor had an animated conversation about coffee with Samantha and Amelia.

Josie's phone rang. She saw on the readout that it was Cumberland Durand, her former student with the legendary computer hacking skill.

"Hi Cumberland," she said. "Thanks for calling."

"I have some information for you."

"You are so kind to help me. And so fast. But I worry about asking for help. I don't want to interfere with your work."

"You won't. I get my emergency work done first, then most days I have extra time before I pick up Aiden and Cara from school. That's when I do my contract work."

Josie wanted to ask what comprised emergency work for a computer hacker, but decided that satisfying her curiosity probably wasn't Cumberland's desire. She already knew that Cumberland routinely spent time in forbidden places on the internet, rooting out hidden access points to computer systems at big tech companies and governments.

"Is everything okay at Ellison's?" Josie knew that she worried too much. But the Durand kids had been through so much. Their father was recently incarcerated on racketeering charges. In desperation, their mother had a breakdown of sorts and moved to her friend's house in Little Armenia. The family's Beverly Hills house was confiscated by loan-shark associates of Cumberland's father, leaving the three kids homeless. Josie indirectly brought them into contact with Ralph Ellison, and he'd offered to let them stay in his warehouse loft in Montebello. Now it had stretched out over three months, and they were still there. Ellison claimed he enjoyed their company, but Josie imagined he longed for quiet nights alone, sipping wine, listening to jazz. But he was too gracious to suggest it was time for them to find a place of their own.

"Yes," Cumberland said, answering Josie's question. "Mr. Ellison is very nice. But I know he doesn't want us in his house forever. So I keep putting my extra money in one of those investment accounts. Maybe I can learn how to get a house. My siblings could live with me. I've got a bunch of money. But it's not enough for more than a down payment. The houses my computer friends live in cost a lot. So I'd have to get some kind of mortgage. But it's a lot to figure out. I don't know about this house stuff." He paused. "But I didn't call you about that."

"I understand," Josie said. "But I should tell you that I know an economics professor who owns a few houses, one for himself and others he uses as rentals. If you want me to, I can introduce you to him. I know he'd be happy to help. Also, Ellison and I both have homes. We can probably answer some of the basic questions."

"Okay." Cumberland sounded fatigued, as if he found the subject overwhelming.

"Back to your call," Josie said.

Cumberland said, "I have learned something about the dead guards Samantha mentioned. And I found something that connects to Mary Jo Telman."

"The wife of the Forest Service Ranger, both of whom were killed," Josie said. "Do you want to tell me over the phone?"

"I could. But there's an article I should show you."

"Okay, where do you want to meet?"

"Um, well, I'm at this startup company in Venice. Do you still live near Santa Monica? Or maybe you're at UCLA."

"No, we're on the beach walk as I speak. Let's meet on the beach. Look for us south of the Santa Monica pier. Would half an hour work?"

"Okay." He clicked off.

Josie found herself staring at her phone. Unlike most people, Cumberland didn't feel that he needed to put words into blank spaces in conversations. And he had no need for the standard back-and-forth sentences that most people used when saying goodbye. It was fine, and he was efficient, yet his lack of social decorum always made Josie feel as if she had done something wrong.

"You okay, Mama?" Samantha said, turning away from Cor and Amelia.

"Yes. I was just talking to Cumberland."

"And he hung up on you again, didn't he?"

"His style is a little different, that's true," Josie said.

Amelia looked from Josie to Samantha. "Who's Cumberland? Oh, I remember. He came to San Francisco with us at Christmas when we picked up Josie. Anyway, it's none of my business."

Cor looked at Amelia. "You and I both care about the Strong ladies, so maybe it is our business."

Samantha said, "It's okay. Cumberland is a walking dysfunction, who's kind of a homeless, rich, hacker dude. A total beauty, too."

"I remember," Amelia said.

Cor said, "He sat in the back of my Jeep and stretched his legs all the way to the dashboard. Quiet dude. Nice, though. Cor looked at Josie. "How do hackers get to know medieval history professors?"

"He's a former student. When you came and helped us in the Sierra foothills, I knew a little about his skills. So I asked him to help. It was Cumberland who found most of the information we used."

"So he works for you. By hacking?"

Josie nodded. "Yes. And in the previous case we worked on, he found the killer who was hiding in the Yosemite wilderness."

"How does a hacker find someone in the wilderness?"

Samantha said, "By breaking into military satellites that show infrared heat signals visible from…" Samantha stopped herself and turned toward Josie. "Wait, maybe I wasn't supposed to say that."

"Probably not," Josie said.

"I'm sorry, I couldn't make out your words," Cor said, cupping her hand around her ear.

Josie smiled. It was nice of Cor to try to cover for Samantha's revelation.

"Anyway," Josie said, "Cumberland Durand is the one who found out about Mary Jo Telman's nursing homes. He just called now with some more information about Mary Jo. We're meeting him on the beach in thirty minutes."

"Samantha told me on the phone a little about that last case," Cor said. "The case you thought was closed when you caught the sniper at the Wharf in San Francisco."

Josie nodded. "The governor showed up unannounced a couple of days ago."

"He's leaning on you again..." Cor sounded appalled.

"He said he wanted me to reinvestigate the death of the ranger, Mary Jo's husband. Now he thinks that maybe the husband wasn't killed by the sniper who shot Mary Jo."

"Which is what you said all along." Cor shook her head.

"It's frustrating to say the least."

"I remember that you felt that the sniper worked at long distance, and the ranger was killed at short distance, so there was a good chance their killers were different people."

Josie nodded.

"And you agreed to do this again?" Cor asked.

"He's… He knows some people at UCLA who might hold up my tenure track."

"He's using leverage to pressure you? That's disgusting."

Josie didn't comment.

"So this hacker dude has more info about that case?"

Josie said, "He's going to meet us on the beach."

As they walked, Josie told Cor about going to Monterey to talk to the prison guards whose prisoner transport truck exploded and killed the sniper. She explained about meeting the guards' roommate, a man with pointed teeth, who said his name was Snake and who had a large snake tattoo. Snake mentioned that the guards had a friend with sniper experience. And then Snake told Josie and Sam to go to the cliffs near the Bixby Creek Bridge.

"Certainly sounds like a sniper setup," Cor said.

Samantha exclaimed. "How did you know?"

"Isolated setting. Good cover for a sniper nest. Little or no chance of leaving evidence behind. Did you get shot at?"

"We think so, yes. I saw a distant flash up on the mountain and then felt a tug and thought my purse was hit. A second later, I heard a soft snapping sound. It was like you said about how a bullet gets to its target before the sound does."

She showed Cor her purse and the holes.

Cor examined them closely, nodded, then handed the purse back to Josie.

"It could be the holes were made by a sniper round. Or not. What happened after the possible shot?"

"We ran back to our car and drove back to the guards' house. When no one answered our knock, Sam looked through the window and saw a man inside, lying in a pool of blood. We called the police, and they found both of the guards dead. They thought it looked like a murder/suicide."

"And this Snake dude?"

"He wasn't there."

Samantha interjected, "Don't forget, Mama, we saw someone who looked like Snake driving away on the highway, heading toward the Bixby cliff just like us."

They walked some distance before Cor spoke.

"The situation is ambiguous. Snake could be your killer. Or, he could be a potential victim, alive and hiding someplace. He could be dead. Maybe your hacker friend can find out something about Snake."

They came to the beach. Samantha put Unknown in her pack, and they headed out across the sand. A minute later, Josie saw Cumberland coming up the sand from the south. "Here he is, now."

SIXTEEN

They all stopped near the high-water line, the crest of sand where the most robust waves stopped their advance up the slope and ran back to the open water.

As Cumberland Durand approached, Josie could see that he was wearing his usual frumpy clothes, frayed cuffs of his too-long jeans dragging on the sand, shirt untucked and the buttons inserted in the wrong button holes, causing the shirt to hang lopsided. The shoelaces of his dirty sneakers were untied. His dark brown hair was unkempt. Even before he got close, Josie could see his eyes flash intense blue behind long eyelashes, which were so dramatic they suggested mascara, although Josie knew from multiple up-close moments that Cumberland wore no makeup. Josie had learned that Cumberland did not care how he looked. Without trying to, Cumberland succeeded in looking like a bad-boy model. His rakish, disheveled look was unintentional and made for magazine covers.

Josie knew that Amelia had ridden with Cumberland in the back of Cor's Jeep when they came north to pick up Josie and Samantha in San Francisco at Christmas. Yet Josie noticed Amelia stare anew at Cumberland. Her mouth was a little agape. Amelia leaned sideways and murmured something to Samantha. Samantha nodded and whispered back.

"Hi Cumberland," Samantha said as she made a little wave.

If he responded, it was with an imperceptible head movement.

Josie directed everyone to sit on the sand, and they formed a circle.

Cumberland sat down next to Samantha's backpack, which carried Unknown. He touched the top of Unknown's head.

"Hi, dog," he said.

Josie made introductions. "Cumberland, you no doubt remember Amelia from the Christmas trip. And you met Cor then, as well."

As usual, Cumberland didn't look anyone in the eye, not even Unknown. Maybe he couldn't bring himself to that level of intimacy. He looked uncomfortable. Josie realized he was probably only expecting to see Josie and Samantha. A crowd, however small, intensified his shyness.

"You found something interesting," Josie said, hoping to prompt Cumberland.

He nodded and pulled some papers out of his daypack.

"There's a county up near Sacramento called El Dorado County," he said.

"That's where we were three months ago."

"Oh." It was one of Cumberland's words that always sounded awkward. He continued, "Back at Christmas, you asked me to look up a house near Placerville."

"Right," Josie said. "You found out that it was owned by a California Limited Liability Company, and, in turn, that company was owned by a Nevada LLC, which was owned by Mary Jo Telman."

Amelia frowned, but she didn't speak.

"This time," Cumberland said, "I wasn't looking up a specific property. So, I wrote a little program that searched California LLC records for any mention of Mary Jo Telman."

Josie had no idea what that meant, but she understood that she didn't need to know.

"Are these public records?" she asked.

"Yes, but there are some layer issues. At first, I couldn't find anything. Then I got into a Nevada database and found out that Mary Jo Telman is listed as a manager member of several more limited liability companies in Nevada. One of those Nevada LLCs owns a commercial building in Reno, Nevada. The other Nevada LLCs each own a California LLC. Each of the California LLCs owns a commercial building in California."

Josie already knew that the Placerville house was in California's El Dorado County. "This is the same pattern as

Mary Jo's house in Placerville. Properties owned by California LLCs, which in turn are owned by Nevada LLCs?"

"I think so, yeah."

"She bought the properties and then sold them to LLCs?" Josie asked.

"I, um, didn't see anything to suggest that. I think the LLCs were formed first, and the LLCs bought the properties directly."

"So there's no way to trace Mary Jo's ownership of the real estate."

Cumberland shrugged. "It's not easy, anyway. I think that was the point of the process."

Josie noticed that Samantha, Cor, and Amelia glanced from her to Cumberland and back. But they didn't speak. It felt as if they didn't want to interrupt the thoughts of two people who seemed to know what they were talking about. But the reality was that Josie had no idea of what she was talking about. And it seemed that Cumberland was figuring things out as he went.

Josie said, "It seems the entire enterprise was a shell game to hide any connection between Mary Jo and the various properties. I wonder why she went to so much effort and expense."

There was a moment of silence.

Cor spoke up. She had a long piece of reedy grass in her teeth as if she'd been using it for a toothpick, and it bobbed as she spoke. "In the Army, when we went into a community for whatever reason, we always looked for those who were hiding something." The reed grass bobbed. "Where they lived. Where they worked. Who they associated with."

"Because…" Josie said.

"Because if someone was hiding something, it might be connected to some enterprise that ran counter to the community's interest. Or the Army's interest." Cor paused, bit off a piece of the grass, and spit it out. "Of course, it didn't mean they were doing something wrong. These were war-hardened people, and many of them had learned it was best to keep a low profile about everything. Privacy is treasured. Nevertheless, the things that people hide can be revealing."

"Such as..." Josie said.

"Such as they may simply be trying to protect themselves from gold diggers and the crimes they perpetrate."

"Mary Jo's LLCs are hiding ownership of property," Josie said. "So maybe she was worried about gold diggers filing frivolous lawsuits against her."

"Or," Cor said, "the LLCs could be fronts for crime."

Josie turned to Cumberland. "Do you have the addresses for these properties?"

Cumberland held out the papers and leaned toward Josie.

She took them and scanned. "This first one is the house where we visited Mary Jo. Just south of Placerville."

"Yeah."

"This reinforces what I had already thought, that the modern Placerville house wasn't owned by friends of Mary Jo Telman, as she had claimed and as she told the governor, who was her father's friend. In fact, she owned the house and didn't tell people about her ownership because she wanted it to be her hideaway. The privacy aspect even extended to the secret staircase and office, in which she could work without any neighbors knowing where she was or what she was doing. She could invite someone into her house, like she did with Sam and me, without them realizing that she was running any kind of business from there."

Cor nodded. The others just watched.

Josie looked at the papers. "This second property on the list?" She handed the papers back to Cumberland so he could clarify.

Cumberland shuffled the pages. "That's the unusual one. I saw the legal description. Let me find it again. Some numbers, some directional info. And... Oh, here it is. The description refers to the property as an abbey on forty acres."

"Do you mean an abbey in the sense of a religious order led by an abbot?" Josie asked.

Cumberland frowned. "I don't know. It's spelled A B B E Y, if that's any help. I don't know what an abbey or an abbot is."

"An abbey is like a monastery," Josie said. "It's usually run by an abbot."

Cumberland paused. He looked down again at the papers. “Maybe this will help. The seller of the property was the Sisters of Frangelica. Would that explain it?”

“It certainly sounds like an abbey.”

“What does an abbey do?” Cumberland asked.

“It’s a place where nuns or monks live.”

“I always thought those were called a convent or a monastery.”

“That’s what I thought, too,” Amelia said.

Josie was glad that Amelia felt free to speak up. “I think an abbey can be either,” Josie said.

“Oh.” Cumberland shuffled pages. “I also found a newspaper article from fifty years ago. It’s about the abbey.” He pulled out a sheet of paper on which was a photocopy of a newspaper article. He angled it as if to get better lighting. “Sorry, it’s hard to read.” He held it out toward Josie.

“My eyes aren’t very good,” Josie said. “Maybe you could just read it.”

“You want me to...” Cumberland blushed. He took a deep breath.

Josie felt bad. She had forgotten how shy he was. She was about to say something when he cleared his throat as if to begin reading.

SEVENTEEN

Cumberland gave Unknown another pat and then read in a kind of halting, tentative voice, as if he were a young child thinking he would be judged by his reading teacher.

"'In the late nineteenth century, the Sisters of Frangelica were housed in a hotel in San Francisco's Chinatown. They lived there for thirty-nine years. Doris Russo, the San Francisco widow of the man who built the Russo Leather empire, wanted to create a haven for the nuns. Mrs. Russo found out that there was land for sale near the famous Miwok Maze in the Sierra foothills.'" Cumberland paused as if to catch his breath. "'Doris Russo bought forty acres near the maze, and she built a Roman-style villa. She allowed the Sisters of Frangelica to move there at no cost, and, ten years later, she transferred the title of the property to them.'" He paused again.

Josie said, "I read about the Miwok Maze years ago." She frowned, trying to remember. "There was a kind of circular stone maze that dated back many hundred years. It had walls that were as tall as the average person. If I recall correctly, it was laid out on undulating ground so that you couldn't see the whole maze from any one point. You had to walk the paths to try to figure it out. But I've also heard about the Maze of the Sisters of Frangelica. So maybe they were the same thing?"

Cumberland said, "I found another article that says the sisters planted hedges along the stone rows, and they grew up and formed an enclosed maze."

"I see. The sisters lived nearby, so they became associated with the maze."

Cumberland said, "Why would nuns care about mazes?"

"Historically, religious labyrinths were thought to provide meditative benefits," Josie said.

She immediately saw Samantha roll her eyes, turn to Cor, and say, “Professor Speak.”

Josie tried to ignore Samantha’s comment. “It’s similar to the labyrinths in some Christian churches like the Chartres Cathedral. I’ve read that a labyrinth walker is supposed to form an idea that they would think about before they enter the labyrinth. Then, they would concentrate on that thought during the entire walk into the center of the labyrinth and back out. The focus was supposed to force all extraneous thoughts out of your mind. A sort of decluttering of the mind.”

Samantha said, “If it’s hard to figure out how to get through one of these mazes, you couldn’t fill your brain with other clutter.”

“I would think so. But it turns out that calling them a labyrinth or a maze is misleading, at least by our current use of the words,” Josie said. “Religious labyrinths often don’t have a puzzle aspect to them. You just walk a well-defined path until you come to the end, then turn around and come back out.”

“That doesn’t sound fun.”

“No, but the simple act of focusing on walking the path is a large part of what meditation is all about.”

Josie saw Cumberland frown.

“Cumberland, do you think I’m misinterpreting this?” she asked.

Cumberland said, “I wouldn’t know. But I’ve never understood meditation. I’m a computer guy. I think about logic systems all day long. My mind is pretty much always focused and not cluttered.”

“I’m envious,” Josie said.

“But you’d have to have my brain dysfunction to be like that,” Cumberland said.

Cor raised her eyebrows.

Josie had never heard Cumberland refer to himself as having any brain dysfunction. Josie thought she understood something of Cumberland’s brain. “But you aren’t dysfunctional. You’re brilliant,” Josie said.

Cumberland made a single head shake. “All guys like me are

dysfunctional. In lots of ways. Can you imagine me standing around with other guys and talking about, I don't know, basketball or something?"

Josie stifled a little smile. "No, Cumberland, I can't."

"Even if I wanted to, which I don't, I couldn't. The part of the brain that you use for social talk never developed. If they did a brain scan of me, that would be a blank spot on the map."

Josie remembered hearing that phrase. "There was a naturalist named Aldo Leopold who said blank spots on the map are good. If everything is developed and paved over, the overall environment suffers."

"So… That's a good thing about my brain?" Cumberland said.

"I would think so, yes," Josie said. To get back to the topic, she said, "I wonder if Mary Jo Telman was one of the Sisters of Frangelica?"

"I don't know." He looked back at his papers. "The woman who built the abbey, Doris Russo, died. She had funded the Sisters of Frangelica with an endowment to keep the abbey running. But there was some kind of scandal about that money, and it turned out to not be enough. So the sisters had to move out and sell the abbey. Mary Jo Telman's LLC bought the abbey a few years after Doris Russo died."

"Do you have an address for the abbey?"

"Not a regular address, no. As far as I can tell, the abbey's location is recorded like vacant land. It's only identified with a parcel number. So it won't show up on Google maps. I got a satellite picture of it, but the trees obscure the structure, and there's no way to tell how to get there. Obviously, there is a road, but it's like old logging roads, overhung with trees so you can't see it from the satellite."

Cor said, "We could ask a local."

Josie noticed her use of the word 'we.' Josie asked, "Is there a nearby town?"

Cumberland scanned down one of his sheets of paper. "The abbey is in the mountains near a town called Kyburz."

"We drove through that town on the way to Lake Tahoe just

before Christmas."

"I've never heard of Kyburz," he said. "But I've never been to Lake Tahoe, either, so I'm no geographical resource."

Josie heard Samantha mutter, "Geographical resource. Now he's using Professor Speak, too."

"You lead a cloistered life, Cumberland," Josie said and smiled.

"Like the Sisters of Frangelica?" he said. "Maybe they're dysfunctional, too. They could be nerds. Do sisters wear that cape thing?"

"A habit? I don't know. It probably depends on what the abbot requires."

"A habit to please the abbot," Cumberland said. He started laughing.

Josie couldn't remember if she'd ever heard Cumberland make a joke or laugh. His laughter was delightful. Musical even.

"Sisters could be nerds in disguise," he said, laughing more.

"If so, it's a good disguise, pretending to be a God-fearing nun," Josie said.

"Yeah," Cumberland said. "But I don't know any nerds who fear God. Most of the coders I know think they're God." He laughed harder.

Amelia spoke softly. "Makes sense. Nerds have created the world we all use and live in."

"It sounds," Josie said slowly as she glanced at Samantha, "like we need to go back to the Sierra and check out the abbey and the other properties that belonged to Mary Jo's LLCs."

Cor looked at Josie. "You're uprooting your life to please the governor. I'm wondering—and worrying—about why the governor came to your breakfast to dump all this on you."

"I kind of worry, too," Josie said. "He told me that the sniper who we caught, Lucas Herman, AKA Taylor Cooke, was killed in an explosion while he was being transferred from jail to a prison. The guards who were killed in Monterey were driving the prison transport truck when it blew up."

Cor's eyes widened. "I heard about that on the news. But I

didn't know that the guy who died was the sniper you caught."

"Until the governor approached me," Josie said, "I didn't even know about the explosion or that anyone had died."

Cor looked off at the Pacific, thinking, chewing on the remaining piece of her reed grass. "I only heard one story about the truck blowing up. It seemed like a story that would get more attention."

Josie said, "I've wondered if the governor's office covered up the story."

"Because losing a high-value prisoner to a truck explosion was embarrassing?" Cor said.

"Maybe."

"It sounds like you've decided to do what the governor wants," Cor said.

Samantha spoke up. "The gov's got a stranglehold on her school gig."

"You mean he's got influence at UCLA? And they could make life difficult for you?"

Josie said, "He can basically force me to help. But more than that, I feel like I should."

Cor tilted her head the way Unknown did. As if she was trying to figure out exactly what Josie meant. "Kind of like a good samaritan at the state level?"

Josie made a single nod. She didn't expect Cor to think it was a good idea. "If I can find another murderer, that would be a good service to all. But maybe I can't. Maybe I've been lucky with these other cases."

Cor nodded. "You've already been lucky with this case, not getting killed at the Bixby Cliff."

"I missed that part of the conversation," Amelia said. She sounded horrified. "What happened at the Bixby Cliff?"

"We're not sure," Josie said. "But we were frightened."

Cor said, "If you're going to reinvestigate Ranger Telman's death, how would that be affected by this abbey that his wife apparently owned? Nevermind that it's obscured by some kind of corporate shell game."

"I don't know the answer. But it would be a logical place

to start looking because it's new information. The other places involved were assisted living facilities. We followed the sniper from one of them, tracked him on a special phone that Cumberland gave me, and caught him in San Francisco. But now that we know he died in an explosion, that could be another murder. It's something that might not be what it appears to be. Like Mary Jo's secret staircase house. Add an abbey to the mix, and things look even stranger. I should go and check it out."

"I assume you'll take my help," Cor said.

"With great appreciation." Josie glanced down at the martial arts emblem on Cor's sleeveless vest. "Where else would I get a Pencak Silat expert to… you know…"

"To scare the boogeyman?" Cor suggested.

"Exactly. Scare the boogeyman. You're good at that, I presume?"

"None better," Cor said.

EIGHTEEN

Cor spit out the last piece of grass she'd been chewing on. She said, "When would you go to look at the abbey?"

"My spring classes start two weeks from Monday. If I want to have a chance of being around to teach them, I would have to leave as soon as possible. Samantha has a volleyball game in a few hours. So I wouldn't be able to leave until tomorrow."

"Oh, Mama," Samantha sounded very dejected.

"You could stay home with Amelia."

Amelia nodded.

"That wouldn't be right, Mama. I should come. But I don't have to like it. If we leave right away, I won't have any time to savor our volleyball victory!" Samantha smiled.

"No, you won't."

"Cumberland," Cor said.

He turned toward her. He didn't look at her face, but it was an acknowledgment that she'd spoken to him.

Cor said, "I don't know how this hacking world works. So tell me if I'm out of line. I'm wondering, is there any chance you can hack into military stuff, look up this Snake dude, and see if he served?"

"A snake…?"

Cor looked toward Josie.

Josie told Cumberland about the man called Snake.

Cumberland thought for a moment. "You think he was in the military?"

"We don't have a clue," Cor said. "But if he was, it would be helpful to find out. It would give me a sense of his history and maybe even his capability."

"Where would I start?"

"He referred to the Army," Josie said. "Not as though he was actually in the Army. But maybe he was."

Cor said, "I would start with the Army. I don't want to pressure you. Take your time and think about it. I could go on the road with Josie, and you could call me if you find anything interesting."

"Maybe I could look now?"

"You can do that? How? Dial up stuff on your phone?"

Cumberland reached into his pack and pulled out a laptop.

He opened it up, tapped a few times. Then he unzipped a side pocket and pulled out an older phone that was large and had a small keyboard on it. Josie remembered when one of her colleagues used a Blackberry phone that looked similar. Cumberland tapped on the phone, then went back to his computer.

Cor said, "Is it possible to ask you something while you work?"

"Um, sort of."

"I'm just curious about the big picture. How you find stuff without getting in trouble. Or is that a dumb thing to say? Maybe finding is easy, and the only question is how you feel about it?"

Cumberland appeared to ignore Cor.

"He's a white hat hacker," Samantha said. "So it probably doesn't bother him."

Cor turned to Samantha. "What's that mean?"

Josie had been about to ask the same question. Once again, Samantha was talking about something Josie had never heard of. Where did she get this stuff? From the kids in school, no doubt.

"A white hat hacker is one of the good guys," Samantha said. "They do stuff for good reasons, like a company that wants them to find problems in their security. Black hat hackers are trying to do bad stuff. Stealing. Or helping other bad guys. Right, Cumberland?"

Josie saw him shrug in a way that might have been agreement. He was busy on his computer and the old phone.

Cor said, "So looking in private military records is good guy stuff?"

"If it helps catch a bad guy sniper murderer dude," Samantha answered.

Josie was a bit shocked at the way Samantha sounded so confident. Josie resisted her impulse to comment.

Cor said, "I've heard that the military keeps the top secret stuff in something called air-gapped computers. Not even connected to the internet."

Josie noticed that Samantha and Amelia looked at Cor. But Cumberland was focused on his laptop.

Without looking up from his computer, Cumberland said, "Air-gapped computers have pretty good security. But the ladies at Bletchley Park would have figured out how to get into them."

Josie knew that Bletchley Park was where thousands of British women worked in secret during World War II to break the Nazi Enigma code and were only given credit when Britain relaxed their secret status decades after the war. Josie resisted explaining. Being the professor in the room was a hard habit to break.

Cumberland paused, and, still typing on his laptop, said, "Air-gapped computers still have monitor screens. Those monitors give off very faint radio signals. They can be decoded. All it takes is a smart phone with the right software to pick up the signals."

Cor looked from Josie to Samantha to Amelia and then back to Cumberland.

"But you're using an old keyboard phone."

Cumberland tapped on his computer, then on his phone. "Smart phones can be manipulated from both directions. There are lots of advantages to a not-so-smart phone."

They all sat in silence for a minute. The only sound was the crashing waves, which were small enough to indicate that there were no current major storms out in the Eastern Pacific.

Cumberland suddenly said, "Does Snake have a tattoo of a snake going up his arm?"

Samantha exclaimed, "Yes!"

NINETEEN

Cumberland talked as he looked at his computer screen. "Assuming I've got the right guy, Snake's given name is Norman Ploestadter, originally from Idaho. He enlisted in the U.S. Army twelve years ago. After boot camp, he got accepted in a sniper training course at Fort Benning."

"Where is that?" Josie asked.

"Fort Benning, Georgia," Cor said.

Cumblerland continued. "But Ploestadter couldn't finish the course. It doesn't say why."

Cor said, "To be fair, most people who take the course don't finish. It's very grueling."

Cumberland continued, using his fingertip on the screen as if to keep track. "Then Ploestadter got in trouble at the base and was court-martialed for assault and failing to follow orders. He was incarcerated for eight years and received a DD, whatever that is."

"Dishonorable Discharge," Cor said. "You get a DD, you're screwed for life. You pretty much can't get a job. You can't get a loan. You can't get any kind of government assistance for the rest of your life. And you can't own or even possess a gun. It's like being convicted of a felony, maybe worse."

"But," Josie said, "he might still know how to be a sniper."

"Yup," Cor said. "And not being able to get a job could entice him to shop his special skills on the black market."

"Gun prohibition for a DD guy notwithstanding," Josie said.

"Roger that," Cor said.

Cumberland was looking closely at his computer screen. "After his DD, I find one address in Georgia and then nothing."

Cor said, "Few landlords would rent to someone with a DD. And without a decent job, how're you gonna pay rent, anyhow?"

"So he's gotta crash at a friend's pad," Samantha said.

"Friends like the prison guards," Cor said.

Josie noticed that Amelia was looking back and forth from Cor to Cumberland and Samantha. It seemed, Josie thought, that she was somewhat shocked at the conversation, as if she were reappraising the people she was living with.

"Amelia," Josie said, "are you okay with us talking about these subjects?"

"Yes, but I worry that you might not like me hearing these things. Like maybe I don't belong here."

"I'm okay with it. But I'd like to ask that you consider what we're saying to be private and not tell anyone else. That is important to me."

Amelia made an exaggerated nod. "Very private," she said. "I am very good at respecting privacy."

"Good. Thank you for that."

Samantha said, "Mama, I can tell you had a thought, earlier."

Josie nodded. "A sudden thought, yes. Remember when we talked to Zoe Soto in Reno last Christmas?"

"Yeah."

"She was explaining about the letter that her daughter Elena had sent before she took her new job. The top boss had stopped by the Serenity home where Elena worked. I think his name was Bruno Master. He offered Elena a new job as a cook at a spiritual retreat."

"Oh, right. A spiritual…The abbey!" Samantha said.

"It could be. Maybe that's where Elena went."

Samantha's eyes were wide. "She might still be there."

Josie reached for her phone. "I should call Zoe and see if Elena is still out of touch. If not, maybe Elena has been in contact and said something that would be useful."

Josie found the number in her phone and dialed.

"Hello?" A woman. It was Zoe, hopeful anticipation in her

voice.

"Hi, Zoe. This is Josie Strong calling. I'm the professor from UCLA. My daughter Samantha and I spoke to you about Elena back during the holidays."

"Sí." Now she sounded guarded.

"Have you heard from Elena?"

"No." Guarded and worried.

"But something is different," Josie said.

"Sí again. If you are remembering, after Elena went away on her job, my husband Juan is always not trusting Elena's boss. Juan is calling them every day at first. Then every week. Now he gets a call on his phone this morning. Something about Elena. He wouldn't tell me who is calling. He wouldn't give me any details. This means he doesn't want me to be worried."

"Can you tell me about the call?"

"Only that it sounded like something happened yesterday. I heard him say, 'Who died?' And then it was something about how they are all snakes."

As Zoe said it, Josie realized that it could be a reference to the prison transport guards who were killed at the house in Monterey. Josie felt a pang of worry that her actions in Monterey set off stressful events in Reno. When Zoe's husband Juan mentioned snakes, could that be connected to the man named Snake?

"Did Juan say anything else?" Josie asked.

"No. But he listened on the phone for a long time. Then he hung up and told me he had to go meet someone. He left, and I am not hearing from him. Now it's getting late, and I am to make dinner. But I don't know if I'm eating to be by myself or not."

"Would it be okay to stop back in Reno and talk to you?"

"Sí, you can talk to me. When would you come?"

"Tomorrow, if I can get a flight." Josie saw Samantha's eyebrows raise high.

"I am to be home tomorrow, Sunday," Zoe said.

"Thank you," Josie said. "I'll call when I know what time I will come."

Josie said goodbye to Zoe and hung up.

Samantha held her phone up and faced Josie. "It's time, Mama. I have to get ready for my game."

"Oh, of course. Volleyball. You go. I'll be along shortly."

Samantha said, "I'll carry my little honey back to the beach path and walk her home." She picked up the pack with Unknown.

Josie stood, gave Samantha a kiss. She said, "Good luck with your pancakes."

Samantha grinned, gave Josie a fist bump, and walked home with Amelia.

Cor turned to Josie. "What's with the pancake thing? Or is that a private, insider-type comment?"

"It's our mother/daughter equivalent of telling an actor to break their leg."

Cor nodded. "Ah. And pancakes are…"

"A pancake is when a volleyball player dives to the ground to keep the ball from hitting the sand. They try to get their hand under the ball and bounce it back into the air."

"And Samantha's good enough to do the pancake?"

"Yes. She's pretty amazing."

Josie turned to Cumberland. He had pulled a small printer out of his backpack and used it to print some pages.

He gave Josie the printout he'd made. It had information about the abbey and the man called Snake. Josie thanked him profusely.

Cumberland nodded, put his gear back in his pack, made a general wave toward the others, and walked south down the beach.

Cor turned to Josie. "I can help with this new mission."

"You helped us so much back in December."

"It makes me feel good to help. I don't have a lot of friends. You and Samantha are important to me."

Josie had just been thinking the same thing. "That would be so nice of you to help, Cor," she finally said.

"I have to teach my morning self-defense class tomorrow. Then Diane Day takes over the next few classes. Monday morning, I have an appointment just north of Sacramento. A woman wants to start a self-defense school. She wants me to give advice." Cor made a grin. "She says she'll pay me my going rate as a consultant and also cover my travel expenses. Pretty cool, huh? Me, a consultant." Cor gave Josie a little smack on her shoulder.

"That's great, Cor," Josie said.

"So I'll have some free time after Monday. I'll call and see where you're at."

"Thanks so much. I'll be trying to track Elena Soto, who seems to have disappeared into a business that was owned by Mary Jo Telman."

"The woman who was killed by the sniper," Cor said. "And, as you and Samantha mentioned, Elena could be at the abbey Cumberland told us about."

"Yes. After we learn more about that, I might have a better idea of how you could help."

"You lead an interesting life, Professor Josie Strong."

Cor gave Josie a hug, then gave her a fist bump, then turned and left.

Josie watched Cor's athletic gait as she walked away. The woman was strong, and she moved in a way that made Josie think of a jungle cat. A jaguar or something. She telegraphed a kind of power that made Josie envious. And yet Cor had said that she admired Josie's career and her knowledge and the way she could stand up in front of a lecture hall and give talks and field questions. Josie knew it was a different kind of strength, and yet she felt weak. It seemed to take all of her energies to teach, to be a mother to Samantha, and, now, to help the governor of California.

Josie felt unsettled. She had too many questions to answer, too many problems to solve. She had to force herself to move forward. There was work to be done. And before that, she had a daughter who was going to play in a volleyball match. She headed back to the condo to eat lunch and to get a wrap to wear while watching Samantha's match.

Samantha had left a note on the kitchen counter. She had gone to meet her teammate and Amelia had gone to work the evening shift at the coffee shop. Josie ate while Unknown watched her from her bed.

Josie held up her spoon. "You want some lentil soup, girl?"

Unknown didn't move.

Josie found a thick sweater and took Unknown on her leash. Josie wanted to be able to watch from the sand, where dogs were not allowed. So, as Samantha had done earlier, she brought the dog pack for Unknown.

As they walked, Josie thought Unknown seemed more tentative than usual. Ever cautious, of course, but watching everyone as if she sensed potential trouble. Was that the natural sentience of a dog? Or, was Josie simply projecting her own worries onto Unknown? Maybe Unknown was simply unsettled like Josie, uncomfortable because Samantha was gone.

When they got to Ocean Park Beach, where they would head out on the sand, Josie set the pack down, opened it up, and tried to get Unknown into the pack. It was much harder than Samantha had made it look. Josie couldn't get Unknown situated so that her head was coming out the top of the pack. Eventually, Josie got frustrated, let go of the dog, and stood up to reassess the situation. Unknown, still inside the pack, turned the proper direction. All Josie had to do now was lift the pack up. Which, of course, was another challenging task. But she got her arms through the straps, and, with serious effort, managed to lift the pack up on her back. They headed off onto the sand.

Josie recalled that, when Unknown's owner had been murdered, the vet who weighed her said she was only 24 pounds. But it seemed like a lot of weight by the time she'd carried the dog well out toward the ocean.

Josie didn't want to be near the loudest fans, so she found a place that was far enough from the court to be uncrowded. She lowered the pack to the sand and sat down next to it. As long as people didn't stand in front of her, she could see most of the action.

Unknown had her head out of the pack. She looked comfortable. Perhaps, Josie thought, Unknown liked the protective nature of the pack. It was a bit like a miniature dog house. Or maybe more like a marsupial mother's pouch.

Josie didn't pay much attention until the 15-and-under age division began.

As the time for Samantha's match grew near, there seemed to be lots of girls, more than the total number of girls at the charter school, and they made a lot of noise.

Josie was leaning back next to Unknown. Her arms were propped behind her. She sensed movement nearby.

"Mind if I join you?" A familiar voice said.

Josie turned to look.

"Ellison! What a surprise!"

Ralph Ellison looked comfortable as always in faded blue jeans, beige leather sandals, and a white hooded sweatshirt.

Josie reached over with both hands and took one of his. They shook, and then he reached out to pet Unknown, who was watching Ellison closely. Unknown shut her eyes like a cat, seemingly pleased by Ellison's attention. He was one of the few men that Unknown had liked from the time they first met.

"What brings you here?" Josie asked.

Ellison gestured toward the volleyball nets. "There's a website devoted to volleyball. I was glancing through the beach volleyball listings for the various meets and saw Samantha's name. I thought it would be fun."

"You came all the way from Montebello to watch Samantha play volleyball?"

Ellison shrugged. "I had some other business on this end of town, so all I had to do was kill an hour at a coffeeshop."

"Which coffeeshop?"

"There's one near here, just off Santa Monica Boulevard."

"That's the one where our boarder works. Amelia Gomez. You probably saw her."

Ellison frowned, thinking.

"She's a standout of enthusiasm," Josie said.

He nodded. "Infectious smile? Thick curly black hair?"

"That's Amelia."

"Yes, of course! The girl who rode with us when Cor Kontos drove us up to San Francisco at Christmas after you caught the sniper. Amelia brought Peruvian cookies." He looked off, visualizing captivating treats.

Ellison sat down on the sand on the other side of Unknown so that the dog in her pack was between them. "How did Amelia become your boarder?" he asked.

"It's kind of similar to how you ended up taking in Cumberland, Aiden, and Cara Durand. Amelia was in need of a temporary place to live. Her family brought her from Peru when she was ten. They expected her to always live with them as part of an extended family in Bakersfield, close to the farms where they all worked. But when she told them she wanted to start her own coffee business, they balked in a major way."

Ellison made a knowing nod. "So they kicked her out, or at least made her feel unwelcome, and you and Sam stepped in to fill the void." He made a kind of harumph exhalation. "Parents expect song birds to fly the nest. But not their own children. Or, at least, not farther than the next tree." He glanced at the action near the volleyball nets, where there was commotion but nothing that looked organized.

He asked, "Does Amelia make enough money at the coffeeshop to afford rent?"

"Yes. We actually offered to let her stay for free until she found another place. But she insisted on paying us."

"Very businesslike," Ellison said. "That's a good sign."

"Yes. I'm sure it's an indication of her future success in the coffeeshop business."

Ellison had a look in his eyes that Josie couldn't immediately place. She decided that it was a look of appreciation that older people have when they learn of young people who have ambition.

"Are you a fan of volleyball?" Josie asked.

"Somewhat. Beach volleyball, especially," he said. "Just two players on each side. It seems like a perfect mix of individual prowess and team skills. When I was young, I even played a little beach volleyball. I was okay, but not great. I'm intrigued by Samantha's playing."

"I think she's good," Josie said. "But I know nothing about

it."

"She is good," Ellison said. "I saw her once before."

"Really?"

"A similar situation. I was in the area. It fit with my schedule. I looked for you but didn't see you anywhere."

"Oh, I'm embarrassed. Was this about six weeks ago? Because I had a Saturday meeting I had to attend at UCLA."

Ellison thought about it. "Maybe. But no matter. You've got more to your life than Samantha's volleyball."

The current match was over. Losers congratulated winners. New teams came out. Four girls total. Some of the teams had a very tall girl and a short girl. Although as Josie thought about it, she realized that the short girls were probably 5-7 or 5-8, substantially taller than her own 5-3 frame.

Ellison said, "I noticed that Samantha's team is called, 'We'll Bust Your Balls.'"

"I know. I'm somewhat uncomfortable with that."

"It doesn't fit your sense of decorum, does it?" Ellison said.

"No. I prefer a little refinement."

Ellison didn't immediately respond. "Like classical music versus rap or heavy metal rock 'n roll," he finally said.

"Yes. Does that make me a hopeless prude?"

"Maybe," Ellison said, grinning. "Who picks the names for the teams?"

"The players do. When I commented, Samantha made it sound as if their name came from Holly, Samantha's teammate, and her friends."

Ellison reached over and rubbed Unknown's ears. "And Samantha just went along because she's so agreeable."

"You're probably laughing at me for being so naive. For all I know, Samantha helped choose the name and pushed hard for it."

Ellison grinned but didn't speak.

"As long as I'm acting like a prude," Josie said, "I'll also say that I don't like the sexualizing of the sport. These girls are fourteen. Fifteen tops. And they're wearing super short shorts, or even bikinis!"

Ellison nodded. "You'd like people to focus on the girls' athletic prowess and not on the look of their bodies."

"Yes. You are so right. It's one thing for the adult women to play nearly naked. And I recognize that—good or bad—a portion of the audience comes to watch simply because the women wear so little. But when the young girls are also wearing almost nothing, it doesn't seem right."

Another nod from Ellison.

"Do you disagree?"

"No," Ellison said.

Josie thought he seemed uncomfortable with the subject.

"But there's nothing you can do, right?" he said. "A very few people around the world raise their kids to dress and act very conservatively. The Amish. Orthodox Jews. Muslims. Mormons. Some Christians. But the rest of the world embraces revealing clothing. In sports. In advertising. In music and acting and modeling and on the internet. We're on a fast march from the Victorian sensibilities to a racy future. It doesn't seem like many people worry about it. And some of the fundamentalist groups shoot themselves in the foot by claiming modesty as a virtue and then grooming their young boys and girls for body display."

A match ended.

Josie spotted Samantha's teammate Holly Love. Holly was a blonde girl with buzz-cut hair that was shorter than Cor Kontos's hair. At six feet, Holly was even taller than Samantha and heavier by thirty pounds.

Samantha came running out to join Holly. A group of kids started cheering. "Bust Their Balls, Bust Their Balls."

Josie couldn't bring herself to join in and shout the cheer the way everyone else did. It was, to Josie, another example of how different she was from the rest of the world.

It appeared that the match was about to begin. The other team won the coin toss.

One of the girls served. It was so fast that Josie had trouble following the ball. Samantha's partner Holly ran and put out her arms, bouncing the ball up high. Samantha repeated the move. Holly leapt up and slammed the ball down to the ground on the other side of the net. People cheered and yelled. "Bust their balls!"

The next volley was fast. The ball flew back and forth over the net. Samantha blocked it, sending the ball high into the air, and Holly spiked it again. More cheers, more hollering.

As Josie watched, she was aware that she knew very little about volleyball. She was even more aware that she hadn't seen several of Samantha's matches. It was hard to get out of teaching commitments and administration meetings. And Josie was reluctant to cancel any teaching obligations when she knew that her excuse would be judged poorly by other faculty who didn't celebrate kids' volleyball as much as they celebrated their own cultural events like chamber music in one of UCLA's halls or the Jazz-on-the-Grass performances on the campus.

Josie knew that some volleyball players were called defenders and some blockers. But it seemed that they changed positions. The play went rapidly. Often, Josie couldn't tell which team won a point.

Josie heard Ellison making sounds next to her. A roar of appreciation. A grunt of disappointment.

Josie watched him in her peripheral vision. Sometimes his reaction helped her to understand the play. Other times, it was like people cheering football. The players were running and leaping, but only a person well-versed in the sport understood much of what was happening.

Josie could tell when the volleyball match neared the end because the level of cheering increased to a steady roar. But she was embarrassed when it seemed the match was over because she didn't know who had won. She realized that winning points vs winning games and matches were separate things, and she wasn't good at keeping track.

"Well," Ellison said with regret, "I guess the other team busted their balls."

He looked over at the crowd. "Last time I came, I waited around but never got a chance to talk to Samantha."

"It'll probably be the same this time."

He nodded. "Please tell her I liked it."

"She will be so surprised and pleased that you came. She's got the volleyball bug in a major way. Her most recent thing is wanting to go to a volleyball training camp. Something called Origins Beach Volleyball. I told her I was happy to help her apply, and she said you can't apply. It's so exclusive that you have to be invited. Can you imagine that? These are kids, and they treat them like major league sports players. Anyway, that gives you an idea of how important volleyball is to her."

Ellison stood, then bent over to touch Josie on the shoulder and give Unknown a pet.

"Thanks, Ellison. Thanks very much."

TWENTY

As soon as Josie had walked Unknown home, she got on her computer and quickly discovered that every flight from L.A. to Reno was booked solid. If she waited a few days, there were open seats. But she didn't have the luxury of time.

Maybe it wasn't going to be possible to get to Reno and see Zoe Soto.

Her phone rang. It was Ralph Ellison.

"In the post-game commotion, I didn't get a chance to say that Sam has very good skills, movements, judgment, timing. I also wanted to tell her I loved her pancake. It looked painful. But she saved the ball. Very impressive. Could you pass on my thoughts to her?"

"Yes, of course. Thank you for your attention, Ellison."

"You sound distracted. Did I call at a bad time?"

"No. I'm just frustrated. I was hoping to catch a flight to Reno tomorrow morning, and every plane is booked solid."

"You mean the airlines."

Josie was surprised. She wanted to say, 'of course, I mean the airlines.' But she had the good sense to stop herself. She finally said, "Yes."

"You could charter a plane," Ellison said.

That was a new idea for her. "An interesting thought. That would probably be expensive."

"Less than you might think."

Josie was about to say something dismissive and stopped herself. "Do the charter companies post their flight schedules? I should probably take a look at them."

"Most of them are custom schedule. They go when you want to go."

That certainly sounded attractive.

He continued, "For example, there's an outfit that flies out of the San Gabriel Airport near my place in Montebello. They have a couple of those new Diamond Aircraft planes. You could inquire. Of course, if you can wait a few days, you can catch an airline flight. But maybe this is a mission where timing is important."

"Yes, it is. The governor has sent me on another mission."

"Oh," Ellison said with a flavor of disappointment.

"My thought, too." Josie gave him the basics. "We actually met Cumberland on the beach to talk about it a few hours ago. So you might hear his take on it when you next see him."

"Not likely. He was home when I got here, but he's ensconced in his computer work. I can periodically hear his fingers on the keys. But he won't hear me saying this because Aiden and Cara are watching something on the TV."

"I understand. Thanks for the charter plane idea, Ellison. Maybe I'll find one that works."

They said goodbye.

Josie assumed a charter plane would be too expensive. But then she realized that the cost, whatever it was, would be paid by the governor's office. So she got back on her computer.

An hour later, she'd found a company who had a pilot available the next day to fly Josie, Samantha, and Unknown, as well.

Early Sunday morning they parked at the San Gabriel Airport, and were met by the pilot, who walked them out to the plane.

Josie inhaled when she realized that it was a tiny thing, four seats total. At least the plane did look well cared for, maybe even new.

The pilot, a fit young man in his late 30s named James, wore black trousers, shiny black shoes, and a white short-sleeve shirt with black-and-gold epaulets, just like an airline pilot. James pulled on the door latches. The doors turned out to be large window canopies, one for the front seat and one for the back. The canopies opened by swinging up, making it relatively easy to get in and out of the seats.

"Cool plane!" Samantha said.

"This is a Diamond Star aircraft," the pilot said. "The latest small plane in the skies."

Josie thought it sounded like a sales pitch, not a factual statement.

"This plane has no steering wheel," Josie suddenly said, feeling insecure for no particular reason.

"Yes, it's flown by a stick, not a yoke," the pilot said.

Whether stick or steering wheel, Josie didn't think the plane looked substantial enough to fly across the country. The seats were little, and it didn't look like there was any extra space.

"Are these tiny planes safe?"

"This Diamond Aircraft is actually the safest small plane there is. And it also has the advantage of no TSA security screening like with the airlines. We just get in the plane and fly away. I won't even make you sit through the talk on where the plane's exits are." The pilot winked at them.

"Can I sit in front, Mama? Unknown can sit on my lap!"

The pilot said, "I'm sorry, but first I have to ask you to step on our scale, along with your luggage. Your weights are required for our seating position. Where we sit determine's the plane's center of gravity."

Josie hesitated. It felt a little like going to the doctor. She pointed at Samantha, who was carrying Unknown in her backpack. "All we have is our dog and our overnight bag." As she hooked her thumb into the bag's strap over her shoulder, she realized that the question came down to her own weight. How embarrassing. But chunky though she might be, she was still a small person, so her weight probably wouldn't be an issue.

James looked at Samantha and gestured toward a scale.

Still carrying Unknown in the backpack, Samantha stepped onto a steel platform that was so big it could hold a cow.

Josie was next. She held her shoulder bag and looked off as the man inspected the scale's readout. Josie felt very awkward having a stranger weigh her on some kind of cattle scale. She didn't think she was that self-conscious, but obviously was. The pilot was thin. Samantha was thin. Josie was not.

"Thank you," the pilot said. "You can sit wherever you like. I should point out that the flight to Reno is three hours. So, if you need it, you might use the restroom in our office before we take off."

Another discomfort for Josie. Samantha had demonstrated many times that she could hold her bladder forever. Josie could not.

How much coffee had she drunk? Who would have thought that taking a charter flight would involve thinking about such things?

"You better, Mama," Samantha said. "I'll take Unknown over on that grass, then I'll follow you too."

Josie headed toward the restroom, fishing her Dramamine out of her purse as she walked.

Twenty minutes later, the pilot helped Josie over the wing and into the back seat, which was cramped but not as cramped as most airline seats. Especially when she turned a little sideways so her legs could extend into the other rear seat. After Josie was in position, the pilot leaned in and showed her how the seat belt worked. Then he shut the rear canopy window. Once it clicked shut, Josie became aware of the smell of the leather seats. It was quite nice, actually, not unlike a new-car aroma in a luxury vehicle.

Samantha hopped up on the wing and stepped into the right front seat, holding Unknown. Josie noticed again that everything seemed easy for Samantha. Physically and psychologically. Best of all was her attitude. Was that because of how Josie had raised her? Or was it the luck of Samantha's DNA? Whatever the reason, Josie was glad.

The pilot was last in the plane. He went down a list, checking instruments, flipping switches, and such. He said, "You'll find noise-canceling headsets next to your seat. Although this plane is quieter than most dishwashers, you might want to wear the headset to reduce noise. If so, you will also hear pilot radio communications."

He pulled on his headset. Then he talked on the radio.

Samantha and Josie found their headsets and pulled them

on.

The pilot started the engine, taxied to the runway, and spent some time doing checks while the engine was running. He even ran the engine fast for a bit, but the plane didn't move. Josie realized the brakes prevented it. A minute later, he took off the brakes and pushed the throttle. The engine roared, the plane accelerated down the runway, and they took off.

Josie was unnerved by the bouncy quality of the small plane, but she could see that Samantha was excited.

"Mama, this is so cool. I've never been in a little plane. It drives like a sports car!"

Josie resisted wondering how Samantha knew what a sports car was like. It was one of a constant barrage of situations that Josie knew all parents go through. For the first ten or eleven years of a child's life, you have control. Then that control vanishes, and the child's life takes on an arc of its own.

The pilot was saying things in their headsets. At first, Josie thought he was talking to other pilots. Then she realized he was speaking to her and Samantha.

He described their flight path and how they'd first fly around the east side of Mt. Baldy, then head up the Eastern Sierra at an altitude of 11,000 feet and a cruising speed of 170 miles per hour.

Most of the time, the pilot was silent, something Josie appreciated.

Josie quickly became relaxed, a surprise considering this was her first experience in a small plane. After a bit, she stopped comparing it to airliners. They were completely different machines.

It reminded her of her first time on a small boat in the Bay Area. She'd previously ridden the ferry from Richmond into San Francisco. Getting into a small boat that rocked precariously in the slightest of waves, was unsettling at first. But after a short time, the rocking became comforting. Many times as an adult, when Josie had trouble sleeping, she recalled that small-boat feeling and found the memory aided sleep. Maybe this plane ride would do the same.

An hour into the flight, the pilot announced that Mt. Whitney was coming up on the left. Josie and Samantha stared up at the jagged cliffs that rose thousands of feet above the plane. The view of the highest mountain in the lower 48 states was magical. It was nothing at all like looking down at the Earth from 37,000 feet up in the air.

Not long after, the pilot pointed out Mammoth Lakes down to the left, then June Lake.

"If you look to the left you'll get a glimpse of Half Dome mountain at Yosemite Park, just twenty miles away."

"Oh, Mama, that's not a good memory, huh?" Samantha said. "But it does look beautiful from here."

Josie thought that, indeed, their experience near Half Dome almost a half year before had been horrible.

The pilot glanced at Samantha when she made the statement, but he didn't ask.

Next came Mono Lake. An hour after that, Lake Tahoe appeared like a huge blue gemstone nestled in a cradle of snow-covered mountain peaks that looked about the same height as the level their plane was flying.

"Look, Mama! They're still skiing on that mountain. That must be Heavenly Resort. Remember, we saw it when we were in Tahoe last Christmas."

Soon, the pilot began his descent. They dropped far down below the level of the lake and landed at Reno/Tahoe International.

Unlike with the airlines and the long lines through the jetway, the pilot parked the plane in an area reserved for small aircraft, and he brought Josie and Samantha to a small door. He let them into the terminal, and they were at the rental car counter a minute later. Josie realized that, despite small planes being slower in flight than the big jets, the airport protocols went much faster.

"When do you expect to want your return flight?" the pilot asked.

"I'm not sure. A couple of hours at the minimum. Maybe more. Can I call when I have a better idea?"

"Yes. Our fee has two tiers, flying costs and ground costs. I'll know to expect your call in two hours or more."

"Is there a time when we have to head back?"

"No. The weather is supposed to be clear on our route, so we can even head back in the dark, if you want."

Josie said she'd be in touch. Before they left him, she said, "Thank you so much for a very nice flight. Calm and beautiful."

He smiled, and they split up.

They went to the car rental counter and arranged for a vehicle, a tiny little Chevy that felt no bigger than the charter airplane with just the two of them and Unknown.

Samantha used her phone to navigate as Josie drove to Zoe Soto's apartment, where they had visited her at the Christmas holiday.

When Zoe opened the door, wonderful aromas of cooking flowed out. It reminded Josie of their previous visit.

"I'm so glad you brought your dog!" Zoe said. "Last time you came, you left her in the car."

Zoe's eyes were swollen with worry and stress. She bent down and held her hand out for Unknown to sniff. Zoe gave the dog a pet, then gestured toward her threadbare furniture. They all sat.

Zoe's red eyes made Josie afraid to broach the subject of Zoe's husband. But information was why they came.

Josie said, "When I called you yesterday, you said your husband left to meet someone about Elena. Did that go okay?"

Zoe shook her head. "I have not heard. Not the phone, nothing. He went to the meeting and hasn't come back."

"I'm so sorry," Josie said. "Maybe the person he met told him some things about Elena's employer that made him want to look somewhere else, and he went there?"

Zoe nodded. "That's what makes me afraid. It reminds me of words Elena was telling before she went to work at the spiritual retreat."

"What was that?"

"When she was working at the Serenity home. She learned

something. She said it was something she shouldn't be knowing. She wouldn't talk about it. That made me think it was a bad business. Am I wrong?"

"I think you're probably right. Have you heard anything more about where the retreat is?"

"No. I am hoping to know. I showed you that letter she sent before Christmas. But I've heard nothing since then."

"Zoe, we've also learned some things about the woman who owned the Serenity rest home. She bought an abbey in the mountains between Tahoe and the Serenity home in Folsom."

Zoe frowned. "An abbey is the place to worship, sí?"

"Usually, yes. This abbey is of good size, and it might be where the spiritual retreat is located. If there are many people there, they might need a cook with a lot of experience like Elena."

Zoe nodded. "Elena worked four years at the Serenity home. She started as a dishwasher in their cafeteria. In just two years, she grew up to be chief cook and manager. Elena is a wizard in the kitchen. Very smart with the numbers, too. It is smart for them to have her to run the retreat kitchen."

Josie said, "From the aroma of your cooking, I know where she got her cooking skills."

Zoe seemed to think about it. "An abbey sounds like a good location of a spiritual retreat. I am hoping that is where Elena is working. Will you go there and look?"

"If we can find it, yes. Have you had any other communication from Elena?"

"Only the letter I showed to you that said she was going away to work at a spiritual retreat."

"I remember," Josie said. "Zoe, you said your husband Juan got a call yesterday and that something had happened that made Juan go meet someone."

"Sí."

"I'm wondering why someone would call your husband Juan and arrange a meeting. Do you think it was about Elena?"

"I think so." Zoe nodded. "Juan is always pushing about Elena. Calling her boss. Asking the questions. He read the letter many times. He knows she wants to be left alone. But he still wants to talk to Elena. When the workers at the Serenity home tell him Elena is not available, he is just pushing more. Juan is not… How do I say? When you speak with a soft voice."

"Quiet? Accepting?"

"Right. When he got the call yesterday, he went to the meeting. He didn't tell me what they said. That is making me to think Elena is in trouble. But now he hasn't come home. So I am to think he is in trouble."

"Have you tried calling him?"

"Sí. I get his voice message. I will try again." Zoe picked up her phone, dialed, waited. After a minute, Josie could hear a man's voice. Then Zoe spoke rapidly in Spanish. She ended with "Te amo," then hung up.

"It is the same," Zoe said.

"Maybe we could find him," Samantha said.

Josie looked at her with concern.

"If Juan has his phone, we could search it out."

"How is this to work?" Zoe asked.

"There are a couple of ways. If he has a Find My Phone app, we can use that. I can also search phone numbers without the app." She turned to Josie. "It's not accurate like the Hedy Lamar phone Cumberland gave us last Christmas. But it works in a general area. If Juan's phone is turned off, that might make it not work."

"What am I to help?" Zoe said.

"If you and Juan have your phones on a group plan, I can look in your phone and see if you have the Find My Phone app."

Zoe handed Samantha her phone. "But Juan's phone will be finished with the battery power unless he is able to plug it in. So wherever he is…"

"I think phones have some kind of battery reserve so that certain apps still work."

"Like the finding app," Zoe said.

"Right."

Samantha tapped, then looked at Zoe. "All I need is his

phone number."

Zoe recited it. Samantha entered it. Samantha waited, then tapped on Zoe's phone, waited some more.

"Here it is." She handed Zoe's phone back to her. "The map shows he's west of here. That could just be where his phone last made a connection to a cell tower. But it's something. Let me see if I can track it on my phone. What was the number again?"

Zoe wrote on the edge of a utility bill envelope, tore it off, and handed it to Samantha.

Samantha did the same on her phone as she'd done on Zoe's. After a minute, she said, "Same thing on my phone. The last cell tower that his phone pinged off of was up by the town of Truckee."

"I know Truckee. I drove through there for years."

"Does Juan know anyone in Truckee?" Josie asked.

Zoe shook her head. "No one that I am knowing."

Josie said, "We'll drive there and see if we can get a more accurate map of where Juan's phone is. I'll let you know."

"I cannot answer my phone when I'm at work. They are on the very fast schedule. But you leave a message. And then I call you back."

"I understand." Josie wanted to change the subject. "Are you still cleaning?"

Zoe reached behind her, put her palm on her back, and shook her head.

"My back is no more for cleaning. I am a shift manager in the Fiesta Cantina restaurant. Downtown. Right next to the river." Zoe looked at a clock on the wall. "I have to be there at three for set up."

"And Juan?"

"He works at Tires And More on Virginia. But he's off today."

"When does he normally get home on his day off?"

"His favorite show is on at seven o'clock. He's always home for its time. Work day or off day. Then he eats supper and is in bed when I get home from Fiesta Cantina. I would say to call him in the morning."

"Thanks so much." Josie stood up. "What kind of car does Juan drive?"

"He has the Ford pickup. Small size. White." She made an embarrassed smile. "With brown rust. It is not beautiful to see this truck."

"Cars are for driving, not looking at," Josie said. "Thank you, Zoe. I appreciate your help. We'll go now and see if we can find Juan. And Elena, eventually."

"You'll call me if you learn anything?" Zoe's eyes were teary, and she seemed to telegraph hope and heartbreak at the same time.

Josie reached out and took Zoe's hand in both of hers. "Yes, Zoe. I promise. You'll be the first to know."

TWENTY-ONE

Josie and Samantha said goodbye and took Unknown back to the rental car. They drove to a supermarket and got deli sandwiches.

Samantha used her phone to find a wild area where they could get out of the car to eat and walk Unknown. It was on a broad, sagebrush-covered slope above downtown Reno. The tall downtown buildings were below them to the east, and the much taller mountains above them were to the west.

They ate while they walked Unknown over to a small bluff with a view.

"What do you think of Zoe?" Josie asked.

Samantha was slow to respond.

"I think she's a good person. She is very clear about her love for Elena. And her husband Juan is obviously supportive. But..." Samantha stopped.

"What?"

"She described him as pushing with the police. It sounds like he has a temper. It makes me worry. A temper can get a person in trouble."

"Do you think you can find Juan based on that phone map you emailed me?"

"Maybe. We have the screenshot, but that doesn't give me what I need for doing an accurate GPS search. As soon as he goes somewhere else, it would show up on Zoe's phone. But we wouldn't know about it unless she sent us the screenshot. It sounds like she can't spend time on this at work."

Josie stopped walking and looked off across the broad desert depression that was the valley in which Reno was built. Unknown was meandering through clumps of sage, sniffing here and there. The sandy dirt and the aromatic sagebrush of the desert landscape was nothing like coastal Southern California. Or the wilderness of the Minnesota/Canada Boundary Waters where Unknown was from.

"I hope Elena's okay," Josie said. "I get the feeling that all of Zoe and Juan's hopes and dreams are wrapped up in that girl. It's the standard immigrant experience. You start over in a new country, and more than anything else, you want your child to have a good life in that country. For many immigrants, there's nothing more serious."

They walked far from their car as Unknown explored. Josie said, "Remember when we talked to Zoe back before Christmas? Her daughter Elena had a roommate in Folsom," Josie said.

"Lucinda," Samantha said.

"Good memory. I wonder if she's heard from Elena. I might have put Lucinda's number in my phone."

Josie found it and dialed. A woman answered immediately. Her voice was high-pitched and soft, more like that of a teenage girl than a woman.

When Josie had introduced herself, it was as if an emotional log jam broke loose.

"Oh, I've been so worried about Elena" Lucinda said. "It's been months."

"How well do you know her?"

"We were best friends forever. We used to spend all our time together. We're… very close."

"You've had no communication from her?"

"No. Nothing. It's horrible."

"Last December, Elena's mother Zoe showed me a letter that Elena had mailed to her. In it, Elena said she was unhappy and was following a psychologist's advice to take a sabbatical from work. She was going to a retreat in the Sierra. Did Elena tell you about that?"

"Yeah. I knew she was unhappy," Lucinda said. "But that was because of a man at her work named Lucas Herman."

"Do you know anything about him?" Josie asked.

"Only that I heard he was involved in a murder. They caught him in San Francisco. He was selling guns. He's a bad guy. He's one of those animals who eats other animals. Elena talked about him a lot."

"Do you have any idea where Elena may have gone?"

"Nothing specific. But I think Lucas had something to do with it. Another woman I know at the nursing home said she heard Lucas was killed in prison. If we can find out about him, that could help us find Elena."

"Where have you looked for Elena?" Josie asked.

"I've called everyone I can think of. I sometimes think I'm about to crack up over this." The tone of Lucinda's voice matched the tension of her words.

Josie said, "If you hear anything, would you call me, please?"

"Yeah. Absolutely."

They said goodbye.

Josie turned to Samantha and told her what Lucinda said.

"It's like a puzzle, Mama. The next piece is Elena's father Juan."

Josie nodded. "Let's see if we can drive to the place where his phone appeared on the map."

Samantha called Unknown, and they got back in the rental car and followed the freeway from Reno up a twisty canyon toward Truckee. At the bottom of the canyon was the Truckee River. It was a gushing torrent with spring snowmelt. The water was white with turbulence.

"Does the Truckee River water flow to the Pacific?" Samantha said. "It seems like it's going the wrong way."

"The Truckee flows out of Lake Tahoe. And, no, it doesn't go to the Pacific. It flows to the east into what's called the Great Basin of Nevada and Utah. All the nearby rivers do. The Truckee River ends at Pyramid Lake."

"Where does the water go from there?"

"Nowhere. It just evaporates in the hot sun."

"That seems like a waste."

Josie grinned. "From the point of view of the people in Los Angeles who have swimming pools, probably."

"What other point of view is there?"

"The animals. Millions of birds use those lakes."

"Do the lakes ever evaporate so much they dry out?"

"I think so, especially during droughts. When water evaporates, it leaves behind dissolved minerals, such as salt. That's where Utah's Great Salt Lake gets its name. It's really salty. That makes you more buoyant. You float higher in the water."

"Really? Cool. Is that why animals like salty lakes?"

"I don't know. Maybe. And I think there is some kind of shrimp in the lake that birds eat."

Samantha stared down at the Truckee River. "There's a train track just above the river."

"That's where the first transcontinental railroad was built over the Sierra Nevada Mountains. Eighteen sixty-nine. Just after the Civil War. It was mostly built by Chinese immigrants."

"How do you know all that stuff? Oh, that's right. It's your job to know stuff."

After an hour, they climbed up past the town of Truckee, which appeared to be many old buildings nestled in a valley.

Samantha pointed to the south. "What are those stripes on that mountain?"

"They look like ski runs."

"Oh, of course. I knew that."

"Basic life info from the movies?" Josie said.

"Like most stuff," Samantha said. She looked down at her phone, moved her fingers on the screen. "That's called Northstar Ski Resort."

The highway kept climbing up toward snow-covered mountains.

Josie asked, "How will you know when we get close to where Juan's phone was?"

Samantha tapped on her phone. "The GPS app tells me how far it is from our current location and which direction it is from us."

"Does my phone have a GPS app?"

"You have lots of things in your phone you don't know about."

"Did the phone come with those things? Or did you put

them there?"

Samantha didn't immediately answer. "Some of both," she finally said as she was staring at the phone's screen.

"What does it say now?"

Samantha looked. "I don't understand this. Oh, the readout is in meters. Let me see if I can find a conversion."

Josie said, "The sign says Donner Pass is ahead. Are we still going the right way?"

Samantha looked at her phone. "Yeah. We turn off in a few miles." She looked down to the left. "Pretty lake," Samantha said.

"I think that's Donner Lake. Where the Donner Party got stuck in snow."

"My history class talked about that. That's where settlers were traveling to California way back when, and they got trapped in the snow for the winter, and a bunch of them did the big adios. Right?"

"The big adios?"

"Yeah. Gave up the ghost. Met their maker. Croaked. Bit the dust." Samantha flashed a grin.

Josie didn't know if she was surprised or not. "This is popular teenage slang for death?"

"Checked out," Samantha continued. "Gone, baby, gone. Pushing up potatoes."

"Potatoes?" Maybe Josie sounded aghast.

"What? Did I say something wrong?" Samantha looked at her phone. "Oh, we're here. Take the next exit."

"Is this our final exit?"

"Funny, Mama, funny."

"If nothing else, the tragic experience of the Donner Party demonstrated why one should respect deep snowfall."

Samantha looked from her phone to the landscape ahead. "Here it is."

Josie slowed and turned off. She came to a stop at a crossroad that went under the freeway. "Which way, Cap'n?"

Samantha looked at her phone and pointed. "That way."

Josie turned and followed a curving road that wasn't quite

hard pavement but wasn't quite loose gravel, either. It parallelled the freeway.

"According to this map, Juan's phone is very close," Samantha said.

Josie looked left and right. "Unfortunately, there isn't anything nearby except for an overlook. Maybe he left. But I'll turn in just to be sure."

Josie pulled off on the overlook drive. The parking area had good pavement, unlike the road leading up to it. There was an information sign with a map. In the distance down below was Donner Lake looking impossibly blue, and the surrounding mountains were white with snow.

Josie braked to a stop. They got out. Unknown followed Samantha as she walked to the edge and looked down at Donner Lake.

"It's cold here," Samantha said.

"We're somewhere over seven thousand feet, hon. It might be spring in L.A., but it's winter up here."

Josie walked over and looked at the information sign. Samantha followed.

"Mama," Samantha said. "Look over there." She raised her arm and pointed behind Josie.

Josie turned around. At the end of the parking lot was a narrow, paved, one-lane path that went down at a gentle angle, turned, and broadened out to another parking area. It had only enough room for three or four vehicles. The parking area contained only one vehicle. A white pickup. Old. Small. With multiple rust spots.

"Let's go look," Josie said.

They walked down the path. Unknown followed behind.

The white pickup was a Ford. It sat alone, as if looking out over the dropoff. Although the view down toward Donner Lake and the town of Truckee was vast, Josie noticed that the granite mountains of Donner Summit rose up on two sides of the overlook. They were surrounded by walls of granite.

"He's not here," Samantha said after glancing through the truck's windshield. "Maybe he met someone and they went off in the other person's car." Samantha pulled on the truck's door handle to check. The door was locked.

Josie thought the idea made sense.

Josie walked over next to the truck and looked down at the spectacular view. Wind squalls on Donner Lake made the water shimmer.

Unknown moved back from the pickup as if spooked by its smell. Directly in front of the truck was a fence that prevented people from slipping off the edge and tumbling to the rocks below. Maybe she was moving away from the fence. Josie didn't know why, but the dog was definitely uneasy.

Josie backed up to the fence and leaned against it as she gazed up at the mountains above them. A person up on those steep granite slopes would have a clear view of the parking area. And if they weren't moving, they would largely be invisible among the rocks and boulders. If they wore clothing the color of the rocks, gray and mottled, they would be completely invisible.

Without moving, she shifted her gaze to the pickup. Although the truck was painted white, rust was its prominent feature. Large splotchy areas mixed with a myriad of dots. It was strange the way rust attacked an auto body and created such a variety of shapes. As Josie thought about it, the dots of rust appeared almost like they'd been sprayed on instead of being corrosion growing from the inside out.

That gave Josie a macabre thought. She stepped to the pickup and looked at the front door. She reached down and ran her fingertips over the rust. Something didn't seem right. She took a piece of facial tissue, moistened a portion with her tongue, and rubbed the rusty area. Some of the spots wiped off, revealing white paint. She looked closely, but her vision had never been very acute.

"Sam?"

Samantha was looking down at Donner Lake.

"Yeah?"

"Can you come and give me your opinion?"

Samantha walked over. Josie pointed to the rusty spots like the ones she'd rubbed off. "Do these marks look like rust to you?

Or dirt that splashed up on the paint?"

Samantha rubbed at the spots. "I don't know, Mama. Maybe it's…" She paused. "What are you thinking?"

"I'm not sure. Come with me over to the front of the pickup."

"Why, Mama?"

"Just come, please."

Samantha followed her, frowning, a puzzled look on her face.

Josie glanced at the mountains that rose up behind the pickup, then sat down on the pavement in front of the truck. She rocked left, then right, and got herself into a cross-legged position. She patted the pavement next to her. "Sit next to me."

"Mama, you're being weird. It's kind of creeping me out." Samantha sat.

Josie spoke slowly. "I'm wondering if those spots that look like rust might actually be blood."

TWENTY-TWO

"Mama! I can't believe you're saying that!" Samantha leaned forward, then turned and looked up at the mountains behind them.

Josie pulled her back.

"I don't think a sniper would still be here. But why take a chance if we don't have to?"

"You're scaring me," Samantha said, her voice high and shrill and beginning to shake.

"Me too, hon."

"You think Juan came out here to meet someone, but it was really a setup, and Juan was shot just as he got out of his pickup? And his blood sprayed on his pickup?" Samantha's voice rose higher in pitch. "You think a sniper is up on the mountain behind us?"

Josie's voice was a whisper. "I think it's possible."

"Then where would Juan be now? Oh, God, it's like Mary Jo! Juan was near the fence, and a shot pushed him over the fence!" Samantha stared at the fence in front of them. "He could be down below us!"

"It's just speculation." Josie pulled out her phone. "Zoe said she was usually too busy at work to answer her phone. But let me give it a try." She dialed. While it rang, she tried to think of the best kind of message to leave on Zoe's voicemail.

"Hello?"

"Oh, Zoe, it's you. Have you heard from Juan?"

"No. Is everything okay? You didn't find him?"

"Not yet. But I wondered if you could look at the Find My Phone app and see if it shows an updated location for Juan's phone."

"Hold on to the phone while I look."

Josie waited.

Zoe's voice came back. "It still shows the same location. In the mountains near to Tahoe. You didn't find him there?"

"We're still looking. Now that you've checked the map, we know to keep looking. I'll let you know as soon as we learn anything."

"Muchas gracias y bendiciones. I am at work and have to go." Zoe hung up.

"It's the same, isn't it?" Samantha said. She sounded on the verge of tears.

"Yes. According to Zoe's Find My Phone app, Juan Soto's phone hasn't moved."

Samantha looked up at the mountains. "If Juan was shot by a sniper, then it can't be Herman Lucas because he's dead. So who would it be?"

"I don't know."

"What do we do now?"

"We call nine, one, one. But first I want to know if we can gather any more information."

"What kind?"

"I want to look over the fence and see if I can see anything below us."

"But if Juan was shot by a sniper, the sniper could still be up on the mountain behind us."

"He could, yes. But it's highly doubtful. Logic would suggest that as soon as he shot Juan, he would leave the scene of the crime before anyone could summon the police."

"But you would still be at risk if you crawl out into his line of sight."

"Yes. But I think it is a very small risk."

"If the risk is so small, why did you want me to sit down on the pavement next to you?"

Josie thought before she answered.

"Because I was upset, and I wanted your company." Josie squeezed Samantha's arm, then she shifted to the side so she could get on her hands and knees.

"Mama, you're scaring me. You should stay here, and I

should crawl out and look."

"No."

"But what if something happens?"

"Then you call nine, one, one."

"Mama! That is a horrible thing to say."

"I'm just being logical. But I'm convinced the risk is small."

Josie crawled forward. She came to the fence. It was built like a highway guard rail. Heavy wooden posts and a galvanized metal cross beam strong enough to withstand bumping by cars. Josie gripped the fence, stood, lifted one leg over and then the other. She squatted down on the other side and looked down the mountain. There was nothing to see except a steep slope that appeared to drop off toward Donner Lake. Maybe if she scooted forward…

Josie inched away from the fence, toward the dropoff. She craned her neck out, trying to see down. Everything looked the same. She scooted a little farther, looked again. Nothing except a dirty patch of snow in a sheltered spot that wouldn't see the melting heat of the sun until summer. She turned to go back and then had a second thought. The slope was steep. But if she put one leg out like a kind of outrigger, she could get a little farther out and see a little more.

It took some courage, and it reminded her of when Mary Jo's body had hit both Josie and Samantha and knocked them down the slope. Josie got her outrigger foot planted on a rock. She shifted her body farther out and looked down again.

All was the same. Rocks and scrub, and the patch of snow, and…

Wait, the patch of snow looked different. Josie squinted to see better. It looked different because it wasn't a patch of snow. It was an off-white jacket. The jacket contained a man. The man was motionless.

She crawled back over the fence, sat down next to Samantha, and dialed 911.

TWENTY-THREE

It took an hour for the first police officers to arrive. While Josie waited on the phone with 911, Samantha found out that, although they were in California, the county was called Nevada County.

"Talk about confusing," Samantha said. "We just drove from Nevada state."

The first deputies were in an SUV that said Nevada County Sheriff's Office. It took the deputies another hour to get men down to Juan Soto's body, put it on a stretcher, and haul it back up to the overlook parking area. While Josie and Samantha could only see from a distance, it was still obvious that the man had been shot. There was a circular patch of blood in the middle of his white jacket.

The sergeant in charge asked Josie and Samantha many questions about why they were looking for Juan Soto. He seemed doubtful about Josie's motivations. Josie showed him her letter of authorization from the governor's office, and she explained that the governor requested that she investigate the murder of Forest Service Rancher Francis Telman several months before, a murder that took place in El Dorado County to the south. She further explained that Telman's widow, Mary Jo, had been killed by a sniper soon after Telman's murder.

The sergeant was highly suspicious. He took Josie's ID and told her firmly that they were to stay put until he'd made inquiries.

"Where is your car?" he asked.

Josie pointed toward the upper parking area. "That rental Chevy."

He called the governor's office and began asking questions, his voice tense and loud. He walked away as he spoke, but his voice was still audible from a distance. "This woman is connected to three recent murders, and you're saying to let her go?! We should at least take her in for questioning!"

Samantha spoke to Josie, her voice a whisper. "Mama, he thinks we're bad or something!"

"Hush, hon. If I were him, I'd be concerned, too. We just have to wait this out."

The man came back. He was still holding her driver's license. "Spell your name."

He looked at the license as Josie spelled Josephine, a name that not everyone could spell.

"Your address and birthdate?"

Josie recited them.

"Your job?"

"I'm a professor at UCLA."

He made a soft snort and narrowed his eyes as if he thought she was making it up. "My uncle is a teacher there. William W. Johnsrud. Biology. I suppose you claim to know him." His voice was full of derision.

"No, I'm sorry, I don't. There are almost three thousand faculty at UCLA."

"What do you teach?"

"Medieval History."

Another snort. "How do you spell medieval?"

Josie spelled it.

"When was the medieval time?"

Josie wanted to call him on his blatant prejudice, whether it was against her gender, or her race, or something else. But she'd learned to bite her tongue.

"The Early Middle Ages went roughly from the fall of the Western Roman Empire in the fifth century to the tenth century. What we call the High Middle Ages stretched from then until the twelfth century, which led to the Italian Renaissance. Many scholars consider that the Italian Renaissance and the Late Middle Ages came to a close after the Reformation and at the beginning of Modernity at the end of the fifteenth century." Josie paused. "That's what I teach."

"Did you say modernity? That sounds ridiculous."

"It would be if you thought Shakespeare and the Age of Reason and the Enlightenment and all of the other events that occurred then were ridiculous." Josie knew she sounded snarky, but she was barely hanging onto her patience.

The sergeant made a single nod. "It sounds like you know this stuff. Let's say I wanted to check. What is the name of your boss?"

Josie gave him the name and phone number of her dean.

"I just spoke to someone who works as the governor's aide? Do you know his name?"

It was probably a trick question.

Josie answered, "Her name. Sonja Gonsalves."

Behind him, men in uniforms loaded the stretcher with Juan's body into the rescue vehicle. The vehicle drove away.

The sergeant turned back to Josie and Samantha. "This shooting you referred to in El Dorado County. Who investigated?"

"The recent shooting near Placerville was investigated by Sergeant Ham Garner. I don't know who investigated the previous shooting at Emerald Bay. That was before the governor called us."

The sergeant's cell phone shrieked like a hawk's cry. He answered.

"Oh, hello, Sheriff. Yes, I have the suspects right here. They're… What? Oh. You're sure. Okay, will do. Yes... Yes, sir."

The sergeant clicked off.

"The sheriff says you are to be released."

"I didn't know we were being held," Josie said. She felt her blood pressure pulsing in her temples. "We are the people who found the victim. We called you, remember? We're helping you do your job." Josie was mad, and she was tempted to ask for his badge number, and mention the governor again, and maybe make him sweat a little. But she got control of her emotions. She'd learned from the time she was a child that it was best not to irritate people in authoritative positions. But if he ever took a medieval history class from her, she would make him sweat…

TWENTY-FOUR

When they got back in their rental car, Samantha said, "First, we got shot at on the Bixby Creek cliff. Then the guards were killed in Monterey. Then the man called Snake disappeared. A man who went to sniper school in the Army."

Josie nodded. "And now we found Elena's father shot to death. Probably by a sniper."

Samantha was doing a slow shake of her head. "All this killing is scary." She paused. "We have to tell Zoe, right?"

"I suppose that, technically, it's the job of the police to tell her. These Nevada County police will tell the Reno Police, and they will probably send someone out. But we found the body. And that only happened because Zoe was helpful enough to talk to us and give us information. So, we should tell her first. But I don't know how to handle that." Josie felt overwhelmed. "I've never had to tell anyone their loved one died."

"We should probably go to her apartment and tell her in person. But what would we say?" Samantha's voice was plaintive.

"I don't know. The hardest things to face are matters of the heart. And there's no best way to do it. I think we should just tell her that we have very bad news."

Samantha frowned and looked at her phone. "I just remembered that Zoe said she had to go to work at the Fiesta Cantina Restaurant at 3 p.m." Samantha looked at the time. "She's already left for work."

"That's a new conundrum. Do we interrupt her at work to tell her news that will shatter her? Or do we wait until she's done with work?"

"What's that you sometimes say? What would you want if you were the person in question?"

"I'd want to be told as soon as possible. I wouldn't want any delay because someone was trying to adjust for what they think my feelings would be."

"Then we should go to her job and tell her there."

"Right. Can you direct me?"

Samantha looked on her phone as Josie drove down the interstate, through Truckee, and on down the canyon that led to Reno on the desert floor. Samantha looked up the Fiesta Cantina restaurant as they drove and told Josie where to turn.

"I'm nervous, Mama," Samantha said.

"You don't have to come in with me," Josie said when she turned into the restaurant parking lot and parked. "But it would be good if you did."

"Should I bring Unknown in with us?"

"You saw how Zoe was with Unknown, petting her and rubbing her ears. Don't you think that would be best for Zoe? To have Unknown there?"

Samantha nodded.

"We won't have to explain any details," Josie said. "In fact, we don't really know any details."

"Do we even know for a fact that the dead man is Juan Soto?"

"It's true we didn't get an actual ID," Josie said. "But Zoe gave us his number, and we tracked his phone. We found his truck, which Zoe described. Everything matches. And, because we told the deputies that we were looking for Juan, they would have said something if it wasn't Juan. I'm confident it is Juan."

"Should you call Zoe and let her know we're coming?"

Josie thought a moment. "No. Zoe would pick up on the distress over the phone. Better to do it in person."

"Okay, let's do it." Samantha got out of the car and let Unknown out of the back, taking hold of her leash as she jumped out.

Samantha scooped up Unknown, and they walked into the restaurant. Samantha stayed back by the door. Josie walked up to the counter.

The restaurant was a casual design, with a counter and a

menu board above.

There was a short line. Josie waited. When she got to the counter, Josie said, "Hello, we're here to see Zoe Soto. Is she available, please?"

The cashier looked at the clock and said, "Her break isn't for another ten minutes."

"That's fine. We'll wait. Please tell her Josie and Samantha are here."

The woman nodded. Josie walked to the tables in the corner where Samantha was standing.

"What do we do?!" Samantha said in a loud whisper.

"I don't know. We'll just try to treat her the way we would want to be treated. We should both try not to get weepy, as that can make things more difficult."

Josie tried not to let her face tense up because she knew that could come across as stern.

Several minutes went by.

A door to the side of the kitchen opened. Zoe walked out and scanned the restaurant.

"Ready?" Josie whispered.

Samantha nodded. She seemed very tense.

When Zoe saw them, her face seemed to relax for a moment. She started to make a small smile as she walked toward them. Then she immediately transformed. Her face paled. Her lower lip started to quiver.

"Zoe, we came by to…" Josie felt her brain lock up. She didn't know what to say. Just say it!

"Zoe," Josie said. "I'm so sorry to say that we have the worst news. Juan died."

Zoe raised both of her hands to her mouth. Her eyes showed horror and terror.

Josie continued, "He was found at Donner Summit near Truckee. Down below an overlook."

Zoe made a sharp inhalation, a gasp. "What happened?"

Josie couldn't lie. But she didn't want to tell Zoe details that weren't certain.

"We found his empty truck parked nearby. We looked over

the edge where the mountain drops off and saw a man on the rocks down below. So we called nine, one, one. The police hiked down and found Juan's body."

Zoe's face seemed to melt, the beautiful cherry-wood skin sagging and pulling into a contortion of agonizing pain. Her eyes dripped tears.

Josie straightened a bit. She reached out and put her hand on Zoe's forearm. "I'm so sorry, Zoe."

"How did he die?"

"We don't know for certain," Josie said truthfully.

"But you have the guess. You can say if he had the accidental falling. Or, was it the fall when someone pushes."

Josie hesitated. She thought about the euphemisms that people use to avoid speaking plainly. She thought about the value of truth and the pain and stress caused when people won't say what they know or think.

"I don't think he was pushed directly. I think he was shot from a distance, and the shot caused him to fall over the stone wall."

"Shot." Zoe pronounced the word slowly, with a percussive sound to the T. "From a distance," she added.

Josie made a single nod.

"You have the view of the place. An idea of what happened."

"I could be wrong. But I'm guessing that the person Juan was going to see never intended to meet him up close. I think that person told Juan where to go, then hid in the rocks and trees and shot him from some distance away."

"It was a murder that was made with planning. The hunter gunman who touches Elena and shows her his guns."

"We know it wasn't that man," Josie said, "because he was caught months ago in San Francisco." She thought of explaining that Lucas Herman had eventually died in an explosion, but decided that information wouldn't help.

"And then this murderer is escaping and won't be found, and Juan will never be having dinner with me again. And Elena is still gone, too." Zoe made a loud gagging cry. She sagged down onto a nearby chair, her elbows on the table, her face in her hands. She howled. "My family is no more. Gone into pieces."

"Zoe, we're going to try to find out what happened to Juan, and we'll keep looking for Elena. I promise that."

Zoe sobbed, "I am alone forever."

"Zoe, do you have someone who can stay with you?"

Zoe shook her head.

"What about a relative?"

"No. They are in Mexico."

"Do you know someone in your building? Someone who also knew Juan?"

"There is only the carrot lady."

"What does that mean?"

"She grows the carrots in the windows."

"I'm sorry, I don't understand."

"The basement apartments have little window wells at the top of the walls. There is dirt in those windows."

"Oh, of course. I remember. What is the carrot lady's name?"

"Lucille."

"Where does she live?"

"Twenty-one B."

"Do you have her phone number? I could call her and see if she can be helpful."

"She's always staying in her twenty-one B. She never goes anywhere except to get the groceries on Wednesday morning."

"Would it be okay if I asked Lucille to look in on you while we are looking for Elena?" Josie thought that her wording, while awkward, might comfort Zoe a little.

"Sí," Zoe said.

"Will your boss let you leave work now for a family emergency?"

"Sí.

"How do you usually get home?"

"I take the bus."

"We could drive you."

"Okay."

Zoe turned and walked back through the same door into the kitchen. She moved like a robot.

Ten minutes later, they were in the rental car, Samantha and Unknown in back, Zoe in the front passenger seat.

When they got into Zoe's apartment, Josie said, "Samantha? Would you lock the door behind me and stay with Zoe while I see if Lucille is home?"

"Of course."

Samantha sat down with Unknown in her lap. As Josie turned, she saw that Zoe had sat down on an arm chair next to them and reached her arm out to put her hand on Unknown. A dog was always good for comfort, and Unknown seemed to have a special sense that informed her when people needed comfort.

Josie went down to 21B and knocked. The woman who opened the door was a skinny waif in her eighties or nineties. She wore a lavender bathrobe and lavender terry cloth slippers and her frizzy halo of lavender hair seemed to shimmer. The woman's skin was as pale and wrinkly as white crepe paper. In the woman's arms was a long-haired black cat that had white fur on its nose and white tips on its ears. Around its neck was a collar that looked like a lavender ribbon.

"Hello, Lucille," Josie said and then explained who she was and what had happened to Juan Soto.

"I'm hoping you might come with me to Zoe's apartment and spend some time with her while she adjusts to the news."

Lucille frowned, nodded, but didn't speak. She walked to an end table and picked up a floral-patterned cup that contained what looked like tea. Then, cat in one hand and cup in the other, she walked to the door without picking up a housecoat. Lucille shifted the cup into the hand that held the cat, opened the door, then shifted the cup back into her free hand. As she went past, Josie picked up the aroma of the cup's contents. It wasn't tea. More like brandy or some kind of whiskey.

"Do you need anything else?" Josie asked.

The woman shook her head and stepped into the hallway, still carrying the cat.

Josie followed her. "Do you have a key to lock the door?"

The woman shook her head again and walked along the basement hallway toward Zoe's apartment.

Josie checked the door latch to see that it wouldn't automatically lock the woman out of her apartment and pulled the woman's door shut.

Samantha let them into Zoe's apartment.

"Lucille, this is my daughter Samantha. And this is our dog Unknown."

Samantha made a little wave.

Lucille set the cat down on the hassock, took a sip from her cup, then set the cup on Zoe's table. The cat and Unknown sniffed each other's noses, slowly, but not cautiously. It was as if both cat and dog knew that the other was safe.

Lucille sat on the arm of Zoe's chair and rubbed the back of Zoe's neck. Zoe put her hand on Lucille's other hand. Lucille had still not spoken a word.

Josie realized that either Zoe and Lucille had a non-verbal relationship or they simply felt that this was a time for touch, not talk.

After a couple of minutes, Josie spoke.

"Zoe, I gave the police your phone number. They will contact you when they have more information. I will also contact you when I learn more."

Zoe looked at Josie. Zoe's eyes revealed enormous psychic pain. "Gracias," she said in a tiny voice.

Samantha reached over and touched Zoe's arm. "I think we'll find Elena," she said.

Zoe didn't respond.

Samantha gave a small tug on Unknown's leash, and they turned to leave. As they went out the door, Josie got another glimpse of Zoe and Lucille and her cat. Three lives that were intertwined from circumstance, not necessarily desire, yet they all served each other well.

TWENTY-FIVE

When they got back in their rental car, both Josie and Samantha took deep breaths. Samantha gripped Unknown in her lap.

"I hope I never have to do that again," Samantha said.

"Unfortunately, the older you get, the more death comes into your life and the lives of the people you know." Josie immediately realized her comment was inappropriate, considering Samantha's recent experiences.

"But I'm young," Samantha said, "and I've faced death a few times now in just the last few months."

"You're right. I'm sorry, my comment was obtuse. I should be providing you a childhood filled with nothing but happy times." Josie felt a sudden clutch of anxiety over what she was doing as a mother.

"You try, Mama. But the governor pushes his concerns into our lives."

Josie reached over and squeezed Samantha's leg. "You put up with so much…"

Samantha sensed the discomfort. "So where do we go next, Mama?"

"The abbey. We have many questions about the abbey. We need to go there to find answers."

"We don't even know where it is." Samantha's frustration was obvious. "We can't just drive around the forest. Especially in a little rental car. We'd need something like Cor's Jeep."

"We can search for it from above."

"But Cumberland said that the satellite photos mostly just show forest."

"Those are photos from hundreds of miles above. I'm thinking of James the pilot and his little plane."

Samantha's eyes widened. Immediately, Josie sensed that her daughter's dark mood lightened with a new focus for their investigation.

Josie dialed the number James had given her.

"Josie Strong calling."

"Hello, Ms. Strong. Are you ready for your return trip to L.A.?"

"I'm sorry, but not quite. I'm wondering if you can first fly us over the Sierra. There's an abbey in the forest I need to inspect from above. But not very far above, if that makes any sense."

"A low altitude recon mission," James said. "Where is this abbey?"

"I'm not sure, and it doesn't have an official address. It's more like vacant land. Somewhere near the town of Kyburz on Highway Fifty. So I guess we'll have to fly around and look for it."

"Does this abbey have a name?"

"I don't know. But, at one time, it housed a group of nuns called The Sisters of Frangelica."

"Got it. I'll see if I can find anything on my pilot charts. In the meantime, our plane is gassed up and ready to go. After you return your rental car, call me, and I'll find you near the rental counter."

"Thanks, James."

Josie clicked off.

Fifteen minutes later, they pulled into the airport and drove to the rental car drop-off lane. Shortly after that, Josie called James from inside the airport.

"I'll be right there," he said.

James showed up with a professional, pleasant smile on his face. "I trust your meeting went well," he said. When he saw Josie's and Samantha's faces, his face lost its smile.

Josie hesitated. "We got the job done," she said. "Thank you. Will this search mission for an abbey work with your schedule?"

"Yes. In fact, I was able to post a question about the abbey on a pilots' discussion website. I got a response from someone saying that he's flown over what looks like an Italian villa shrouded in tree cover—his words not mine —about fifteen miles southwest of Lake Tahoe. It's near the Ice House Reservoir, which is north of Kyburz. The pilot wrote that the reservoir was frozen when he flew by, but that the Abbey is in a valley that lies lower by a thousand feet, and it faces south. So, it is accessible most all of the year."

"Do you know where the Ice House Reservoir is?" Josie asked.

"I looked it up. It should be easy to find."

"That sounds like what we're looking for. Is there something we need to do? Get permission for a… what are the words. A flight plan?"

"No. We're flying VFR. Visual Flight Rules. We can just take off and go. We still have lots of daylight. If it doesn't take too long to see what you want, we'll still have time to head back to SoCal. If we spend lots of time looking for this abbey, fuel might be an issue. But we won't know until the time comes."

"This is great, James. Thank you for being so flexible."

They went back out to the plane. Josie once again got in back, with Samantha and Unknown in front. The pilot did his checks, spoke on his radio, and they were in the air twenty minutes later.

James took off to the south from Reno Tahoe airport. After climbing for several minutes, he banked to the west as he climbed up above the mountains that encircled Lake Tahoe.

The lake spread out before them, huge and blue. The pilot headed straight across the water at an altitude that wasn't much above the mountains. Initially, Josie was uncomfortable looking down. Something about flying near the mountain peaks and not far above the vast blue of the lake made her uneasy. Eventually, she relaxed. But then the pilot flew over a ridge of mountains just beyond the West Shore. The mountains were covered with a thick white blanket of snow with only sporadic outcroppings of rock.

Josie once again felt short of breath.

"This ridge to the west of Tahoe is what's called the Sierra Crest," the pilot said. "From here, the West Slope of the Sierra Nevada goes gently downhill to descend almost ten thousand feet to the floor of the Central Valley sixty miles to the west."

Josie knew that Samantha would be resisting such a didactic explanation, but Josie found it interesting.

"This pointy mountain just to our left is Pyramid Peak at ten thousand feet. The lake you see in the far distance ahead is Ice House Reservoir. The other pilot wrote that the Italian villa sits in a valley to the south of the reservoir."

"The information you read calling it an Italian villa, did it also refer to it as an abbey?"

"No."

That wasn't good news. But Josie had no choice but to wait and see what came into view.

"What's the big canyon over to the left?" Samantha asked.

"That's the canyon of the South Fork of the American River. Next to the river is Highway Fifty. Down in that canyon is the town of Kyburz."

"Mama, that's the road we drove last Christmas when we went up to Tahoe so you could meet the entomologist, and Unknown met that giant Great Dane."

"I remember."

A few minutes later, they approached the reservoir.

The pilot pointed. "There it is. Down in that valley just south of the reservoir. Like an Italian villa made of light-colored stone. Maybe even marble. It even has columns and cloisters. Very formal, those Sisters of Frangelica."

The pilot looked left and right. "No other planes appear to be out in this airspace. How would you like me to fly? I can stay high so we don't draw too much attention from those on the ground. Or I can go in low, bank around in a tight circle, and give you a bird's-eye view. Because we're in a rural area, we're allowed to fly just five hundred feet above private property."

"Let's go down part way," Josie said. "Sam, can you get photos? I'm not looking for anything in particular. So lots of photos gives us more opportunity to identify things later."

"Sure, Mama." Samantha already had her phone out.

The building was clearest from a distance, because the low angle enabled them to look under the trees. As they got closer, the tree cover obscured their view.

Samantha was taking photos.

"Oh, look, Mama! Over to the side is the Sierra Maze Cumberland talked about. It's all grown up with bushes the nuns planted, but you can stll see that it's a maze."

Near the maze, up the slope several hundred feet, were patches of snow. Something about the snow seemed significant to Josie, but she didn't know what.

"Okay, going down a little," the pilot said. He pushed the stick forward. The nose of the plane angled down. James brought the plane in at a gentle angle.

"We're now about six hundred feet above ground level. This will give you a good view of the grounds. Oh, look, there's our welcoming party." He joked and gestured over to the right of their plane.

Josie looked where he pointed. There were two men out in a clearing.

"One seems to be wearing a strange shirt," Samantha said. "But it's hard to see from this high up. It has a dark sleeve and a light sleeve."

"Those boys have rifles," the pilot exclaimed. "Whoa! They're raising them! They're pointing them at us!"

Just as Josie thought the pilot would climb high up into the sky to get away from any potential rifle fire, James pushed the control stick to the left and forward.

The plane banked to the left and dived, and the plane's engine roared. James wavered the control stick left and right, and the plane went into wild gyrations, banking left and then right. Josie gasped and put one hand to her chest.

The pilot aimed the plane toward a bunch of trees that were grouped at a point on the upper edge of the canyon. The plane raced. Josie stifled a scream as the pilot went within yards of the trees and then pushed the control stick even farther forward.

The plane plunged down just as the canyon dropped away.

The plane seemed to fall into the canyon. Not far below them was a steady line of vehicles coming and going from Tahoe.

Now Josie understood. James knew that the safest way to escape potential rifle fire wasn't to slowly climb high into the sky, but to make a sudden plunge into a nearby canyon, out of view from the men with the rifles.

"Sorry, ladies," the pilot said as he leveled out, flying through the canyon. "Didn't mean to cause excitement. But I didn't know if those men were serious or not when they raised their weapons and pointed them at us."

Josie was gasping for air. Samantha seemed to squeeze Unknown.

"Now we're out of range, so I'm going to climb back up."

Josie took a deep breath. She could still feel her heart thumping.

He pulled back on the stick, and the plane climbed its way out of the canyon.

"Do you think those men fired at us?" Josie asked. Her voice wavered.

"I have no idea. I saw no muzzle flash. And I didn't feel any impact on the plane. So maybe they were trying to scare us away without firing. It's even possible they thought it was a joke. If so, that is a very stupid, very dangerous joke." After a pause, he added, "I'm assuming you didn't expect there to be men with guns at the abbey."

"Oh, my God, no," Josie said. "I thought the abbey might be unoccupied. But either way, it's legal to fly over someone's private property as long as you don't go too low, right?"

"That's correct."

"So there's no cause for someone to shoot weapons at a plane. Or even act like they're going to shoot?"

"Correct," the pilot said.

As Josie focused on taking deep breaths, she began to wonder if every aspect of her mission for the governor was going to involve men with guns. Because Lucas Herman had been in the business of selling illegal guns, she expected it to some degree, but this seemed severe.

"We'll stay far away from the abbey as we head east back over the Sierra Crest," the pilot said.

He made a banking climb, keeping up a steady chatter to try to ease the tension that his passengers were clearly feeling.

Not long later, he pointed out Kirkwood Ski Resort, Caples Lake, and then Hope Valley, as he flew back to the Highway 395 corridor and turned south toward Southern California.

After Josie had calmed, she thought back to when the governor contacted her a few days ago. Initially, Josie had thought that catching the sniper last Christmas in San Francisco meant the current task would be looking for a man who shot the ranger at close range, presumably with a handgun that is suited to close-range shooting. But it seemed that a sniper fired at them from long range in Big Sur. Then they found Juan Soto, who had likely been shot from long range at Donner Summit. Now, they'd had yet another experience with rifles. It was as if she and Samantha had wandered into the old west. People shooting guns everywhere. But the reality was probably just that Mary Jo Telman and her ranger husband had gotten involved with a group of very violent men. With nothing but suggestions and circumstantial evidence, Josie suspected that Mary Jo's secretive life, with properties hidden behind limited liability companies, involved a criminal enterprise, and that in turn suggested the kind of men who carried guns.

James cleared some mountains and put the plane into a banking turn to the right. Josie could see they were flying along a long line of mountains that stretched as far as she could see.

"Did our detour make it so we need to get more gas?" Josie asked.

"Not unless we encounter substantial head winds. The forecast for winds aloft shows north winds for the next several hours. So we'll have a tail wind for much of our trip down the Eastern Sierra. That will ease any fuel concerns."

Josie thought about the long drive from the airport to their condo. "Will we get to the San Gabriel airport before dark?" Josie didn't feel safe driving at night, even on a well-lit freeway. But as she asked the question, she was aware of the irony worrying about safety considering they'd just been in a very unsafe situation where they could have been shot down over the Sierra wilderness.

The pilot tapped on the touch-screen cockpit panel.

"With our current tail wind, our ground speed is about one hundred seventy-five miles per hour. That will put us on the tarmac about forty minutes before sunset. So, even after doing our paperwork, you'll have an hour of light for driving home."

"Thank you very much."

Josie noticed that James had discerned her concerns even without asking about it. She made a mental note to remember his name in case she ever needed another charter flight.

Less than three hours later, they touched down at the San Gabriel airport, and Josie, Samantha, and Unknown were home in Santa Monica a little over an hour after that.

TWENTY-SIX

Amelia was out working her evening shift when Josie and Samantha got home.

They made some dinner and ate it sitting side-by-side at the dining table so they could look at Samantha's photos of the abbey while they ate. Samantha slowly swiped at the photos. The abbey and the surrounding territory were quite clear.

Josie's phone rang. The screen said it was Cor Kontos.

"Hi, Cor. I'm glad you called."

"Did you get to Reno?"

"That and more. Sam and I are still trying to digest the day." Josie told Cor about the charter flight to Reno, talking to Zoe Soto about her daughter who was still absent, finding Zoe's missing husband dead, going back to give Zoe the terrible news, then flying over the abbey and seeing men point rifles at their plane.

"Whoa, that's terrible. Any chance you got a photo of the men at the abbey?"

"No. We've got some photos of the abbey, but, unfortunately, no photos of the men with rifles."

"Any trouble finding the abbey?" Cor asked.

"The pilot found it for us. He saw a location description on a pilot website. Some other pilot had posted a message about seeing what looked like an Italian villa west of Lake Tahoe. Our pilot used that information to find the abbey. Now that we've seen it and the men with rifles, I need to drive back there and figure out how to see the abbey up close."

Cor said, "I think I mentioned I'm heading up to Sacramento tomorrow to talk to someone about setting up a self-defense school?"

"Yes, you did, but I don't remember the details."

"It's an actual consultant-type job." She paused. "I'm a bit giddy about it. I've never had someone pay me for information, sit down-style at a coffee shop in some neighborhood called Midtown Sac. Anyway, the abbey isn't far from Sacramento. Maybe seventy or eighty miles up in the mountains? So I can go take a look at this abbey after my meeting. Can you email me whatever you've got on the location? Photos that show the layout? GPS coordinates? Whatever you've got."

"Sure. Samantha could do that. But what would you do? Knock on their door? Or would it be more of a surreptitious visit?"

"I should see what I can observe without them knowing I'm there."

"What if the men at the abbey stay inside all day?"

"An individual might stay inside for a long time. But if there are two or three people, someone is going to stick their head outside, if only to get fresh air. I keep my binoculars in the Jeep, so I can scope out any security camera placements. Once I know that, I can figure out the camera shadows. From that, I can go in closer if I want."

"Does that mean you put tape over the camera lenses?" Josie asked.

"No, that's TV stuff. If you take out a camera, the moment they notice it's off-line, it just advertises your presence, and they go on hyper alert. You don't want to alert them. So you work around their defenses. Once I know the camera shadows, the places the camera misses, I can get in closer. Maybe even up to the windows."

"I'm foolish to give you my ideas. You're the expert."

"Actually, I'm not. I worked a bang-and-burn sabotage once. But I've never worked dark missions. However, I've seen all this stuff from a distance. So I know how it works. Have Samantha shoot me the abbey info, and I'll see if I can find out anything. I'll let you know later tomorrow after I head for home. I'll be back in L.A. by the middle of tomorrow night. I can call Tuesday morning."

"I really appreciate your help."

"What are friends for, anyway? You gonna be at work or home tomorrow?" Cor asked.

"I have some office work to do in the morning, but we're on spring break, so I won't be there long. Then I'll return home. I'll have my cell with me, either way."

"Talk to you soon, give or take. Cross your fingers they have no dog."

"We didn't see one, if that helps."

"Okay, thanks."

Cor clicked off.

Josie had Samantha email Cor the photos they took from the plane along with the location coordinates of the abbey.

The next morning, Samantha headed off to meet friends for volleyball practice. Josie called the El Dorado County Sheriff's Office. She had to navigate two computer-voice phone menus in order to leave a voicemail for Ham Garner, the sergeant who'd investigated the sniper killing of Mary Jo Telman back before Christmas.

He returned her call shortly.

Josie thanked him for calling back, briefly reminded him about the previous case, and then explained that the governor was once again asking her to look into the murder of Ranger Telman.

The sergeant wasn't as friendly as she'd remembered. Maybe he didn't like the idea of pursuing something because the governor wanted it. "What do you want me to do?"

"Something happened that bears looking into."

Josie told Garner about Mary Jo Telman's LLC, which owned an abbey in El Dorado County, in the mountains above the town of Kyburz. She explained how, the day before, she and Samantha had come to fly over the abbey, and they saw two men with rifles who pointed them at their airplane.

"You get a picture of that?" the sergeant asked.

"No. I should have, but it was very stressful, and we didn't think to get photos."

"Do you have evidence of a crime at this abbey?"

"No. But we have reason to think that a woman who worked for one of Mary Jo Telman's rest homes is working at the abbey under duress. Possibly against her will. She hasn't been seen for months."

"You think she was kidnapped?"

"Not technically. She did send a letter to her mother saying she was going to live at a spiritual retreat. But the mother thinks the letter was coerced."

Josie heard the sergeant on the other end of the line taking a deep breath.

"I'm sorry, professor, but a mother's worries about her daughter's lifestyle choices do not constitute kidnapping."

"There's more," Josie said. "Two days ago, the daughter's father went up to Donner Summit to meet with someone who called him and apparently had information about his daughter. He was shot and killed."

"What does that mean, 'apparently?'"

"The mother heard her husband talking on the phone, and she said it sounded like the call was about the missing daughter."

"Did she hear anything specific?"

"No, not to my knowledge."

"Do you have evidence that links that shooting to Mary Jo Telman's shooting? Or the abbey? Or any actual evidence that suggests the daughter is not at the abbey under her own free will?"

Josie had to swallow before she answered.

"No," she said. "I should probably tell you that the two guards who were transporting Lucas Herman, the sniper who killed Mary Jo Telman, were found murdered in Monterey." Josie didn't think it would help to explain that she and Samantha were the people who found them.

"Herman is the prisoner who died in the truck explosion," Garner said.

"Correct. It may not directly impact this current case and the abbey, but it does indicate that the criminal aspects of Mary Jo Telman's circle run very wide."

Sergeant Garner paused before he spoke. "I'm sorry, professor, but with no direct evidence of any crime, regardless of whether it's connected to Ms. Telman or not, there is little I can do. Even though the governor has his desire, we still can't contravene the law. We don't even have circumstantial evidence of a crime other than you seeing two men point rifles. Certainly, brandishing a weapon is a crime. But without photos, it's their word against yours. The District Attorney takes property rights very seriously. If I were to bring him your story, he would wonder how low you were flying. He would wonder if you trespassed with the airplane. If you went below five hundred feet, then you were trespassing."

Josie heard the man slurping something. Morning coffee, perhaps.

Garner continued, "It sounds to me like the mother really misses her daughter. And it sounds like the father got involved in some criminal enterprise that ended up getting him killed. No one involved has heard of a crime. It's just supposition. In that situation, I can't do any more than make a friendly visit to talk about the weather. But if the property is fenced and posted, I can't even go on the property without breaking trespassing laws." He paused. "Any chance you saw a fence from the airplane?"

"Yes. It looked like a wrought iron fence quite far out from the abbey building."

"Then my hands are tied. I'm sorry, professor, but you need a credible report of a crime for me to do anything. Physical evidence or witness testimony."

"Wouldn't the District Attorney want the chance to uncover an unreported crime in the county?"

"Sure. But only if there is hard evidence. District attorneys are elected officials. You know how politicians are. They are often driven by political spin. If they get a rep for investigating law-abiding citizens, they will be eviscerated by public opinion."

"But this abbey is owned by a business."

"That's worse. Businesses usually have significant financial resources. A business can often hire a team of expensive lawyers that can completely out-maneuver the county. And their followup will be to humiliate the DA in the next election."

Josie didn't want to hear it. But she understood.

"Thanks for your time, Sergeant. I'll contact you if I learn anything that changes the situation."

That night, Cor called at 10:30 p.m. Samantha and Amelia were in Samantha's bedroom, maybe already asleep, or maybe watching YouTube videos. But Josie was up with insomnia, stressing about the case.

"Hey, Josie, am I calling too late?"

"No, Cor, I'm up. But please talk a little louder. Your background is somewhat loud, so it's hard to hear your voice."

"Sorry, road noise. I'll talk louder. I've got a dash-mounted phone holder, so it's not very close to my mouth. And the Jeep is buttoned up tight. But the sidewalls still buffet in the wind and leak noise. I can slow down, too." She paused. The buffeting lessened. "There, down to fifty-five. Hear me better, now?"

"Yes. Thanks. Did your consultation go well?"

"Yeah, that was one sweet gig. I spent an hour and a half telling this woman the critical aspects of starting a self-defense school. She paid me five hundred! I've never made that much in such a short time. Then I headed up into the foothills. Past that place where we found the sniper's nest back in December."

"Did you have any luck finding the abbey?" Josie asked.

"Yeah. Sam's GPS info and the photos made it easy to superimpose over a topographical map, so I could figure out where to hike with the least chance of being snowbound. I figured out to go east on Fifty, then turn off on Ice House Road and climb up to the closest reservoir. I parked in the woods about a mile from the abbey and hiked up a ravine. There was still some snow on the north-facing slopes. But nothing dramatic. My approach was good for not drawing attention. No way they'd guess anyone would approach from that way."

"You found the abbey?"

"Yeah, nice joint. All fancy architecture like what a religious group would want for their… For whatever nuns do."

"Did you see anyone?"

"No foot soldiers, but I saw the young woman."

"Elena?! That's fantastic."

"Let me back up and say that the place is fenced with wrought iron with spiky pointed verticals. Not exactly inviting. But great for privacy. They obviously don't want people trespassing. There's a heavy gate with security cameras. There are other cameras scattered about. And there's no doorbell. Whatever they're doing there, they can do it in privacy."

"Anyway, I wasn't able to talk to Elena, as she was a long way off. What I did was hike around back to where I thought the kitchen entrance might be. You know, like a service entrance? Because you said she was supposed to be a cook, right?"

"Yes."

"Anyway, when I went around the back side, I stayed in the forest, maybe a hundred yards out. A door opened and the woman came out with one of those roller buckets with a mop. She brought the bucket over to a slope and tipped it over to dump out the wash water. There was no one else. I could tell she was going to go back inside, so I made my bird whistle. It doesn't attract a lot of attention, but she lifted up her head and looked out into the forest. I stood tall and waved both arms back and forth."

"Did she see you?" Josie asked.

"Yeah! And you won't believe what she did."

"What's that?"

"She pulled a flashlight out of her pocket, aimed it toward me, and blinked out SOS in Morse Code."

"Really? That's amazing."

"She had one of those new LED lights that are super bright, so it's obvious even in daylight. The message was clear. Three short flashes followed by three long, then three more short. She did it twice. Then the door opened behind her. She slid the flashlight into her pocket and turned away from me."

"Do you think the person who opened the door saw that she had a flashlight?"

"I don't know. I hope not."

"Is there any chance you got a video of that SOS?"

"No. It happened too fast. And I wasn't prepared."

"What happened next?" Josie asked.

"She put the mop back in the empty mop bucket and stepped down on the squeeze lever. She dumped out the remaining water, then rolled the bucket back through the door and disappeared inside."

"This is fantastic, Cor."

"I thought it might be the indication of trouble that you were looking for. I'll email some pics and then show you the rest when we meet."

"Thanks again. This is great! Will you please call me tomorrow?"

"Will do."

They clicked off.

TWENTY-SEVEN

The next morning, Josie downloaded the photos that Cor had emailed. She pondered what Cor had said on the phone the night before. She thought of calling the sheriff's sergeant and telling him about Cor seeing Elena signal an SOS. But compelling as Cor's report was, Josie could easily imagine what the sergeant would say. Once again, there's no evidence of a crime. Not even video. The woman wasn't being abused. She didn't run out and scream to Cor that she was being held captive. Josie could easily imagine a different officer of the law thinking it would be appropriate to drive up to the abbey and make some inquiries. But Sergeant Garner had already made it clear that he wasn't willing to go through a locked fence or gate. He wouldn't pursue it without hard evidence of a crime.

Amelia had a morning shift at the coffee shop and had left very early.

When Samantha came out of her bedroom, wiping sleep from her eyes, Josie told her what Cor had said about seeing Elena Soto at the abbey and how Elena had flashed an SOS help message with her flashlight. They looked at the photos Cor had emailed.

"So poor Elena really is trapped there," Samantha said. "That probably means she's in trouble big time, huh?"

"I'm afraid it does. I'm going to think about it, and I don't want it to be a problem for you. But sometime soon, I'll want to get your ideas on how you think we should proceed."

Samantha was nodding. "We need to go in and bust their balls."

Josie grinned for a moment. "Yes, I suppose that's what we need to do. So maybe you can leave tomorrow open?"

"Gol, Mama, I have so many important things to do.

Volleyball practice. Keeping up with my network of friends. Maintaining my social media pages. Spending quality time with Unknown."

Samantha said it with sarcasm, and yet Josie realized that it would benefit herself if only she did some of the same social things and focused on more than just being a mother and teaching medieval history. Josie further realized that it would be most beneficial if she did so face-to-face.

Samantha got a text from a friend who lived just three blocks over. Samantha told Josie she was going to meet the friend for a couple of hours. Then Samantha left.

After Josie had another cup of coffee, she left a note saying she was walking Unknown in case Samantha came home before she returned. Instead of texting, she wrote on a Post-it, something she did much more often since Cumberland had instructed them on how easily hackers can learn every detail of people's lives from their electronic communications.

For a change from the beach walk, Josie walked Unknown east. She chose the street that passed the old auto garage that had been reconfigured as an art studio by the painter Shuluwish Ojai, a woman who seemed wise beyond her 80 years. Josie didn't know what created the perception of wisdom. Maybe it was Shulu's way of stating things in an understated way, or maybe it was enhanced by the fact that the woman simply didn't talk much. Josie had noticed in the past that people who use fewer words often have more impact when they speak. Shulu Ojai was as self-contained as anyone Josie had ever known. Josie wondered if it was a characteristic of Shulu's Chumash Native American roots.

Although the woman's studio was usually closed to the public by a fence and roll-down metal door, today it was open.

Josie stopped on the sidewalk without stepping forward onto the broken asphalt parking lot that stretched from the street to the studio building. Josie had gotten the sense over the years that it was impolite to simply walk in even when the gate was open. But she had spoken to Shulu enough to think it would be equally impolite to walk on by without saying hello.

So she waited with Unknown to see if Shulu might appear from the back of the garage studio. The woman would either wave, as if waving at someone she expected to pass by, or make a beckoning motion, inviting Josie to come in.

A few minutes later, there was movement. The woman appeared from behind a huge artist's easel, noticed Josie, and beckoned. Josie made a little return wave and walked with Unknown across the broken parking lot, past Shulu's rusted old Dodge van. The glass garage doors were open, so Josie and Unknown stepped freely into the studio space.

As befitting an auto-repair garage that was built before the availability of modern, bright light fixtures, Shulu Ojai's studio had large windows on the side walls and two glass roll-up garage doors on the front. Shulu had added two skylights, so the place was flooded with natural light, appropriate for a painter of birds on sunny SoCal beaches.

"Hi Shulu. It's good to see you."

Shulu nodded. She reached down, gave Unknown a pat, and then glanced down at her painting apron, which was daubed with paint of many colors, but especially blues and turquoise, beiges and whites. The colors of ocean and beaches and birds, her most frequent subjects. She untied the apron and lifted it over her head.

"Time for a tea break for me. Join me on the roof?"

Josie said, "That would be very nice, thank you."

Shulu nodded, pointed up the stairs, and walked through the door to the back.

Josie understood that she was to go up to the roof and wait while Shulu prepared tea.

She and Unknown walked up the long stairs and went through the door out onto the roof deck, which had a view of not just the parking area and street, but all the way to the Santa Monica mountains and the Pacific.

Shulu had two umbrellas in floor stands, one colored sky blue and the other a deeper marine blue. There was a small turquoise table made of metal mesh, and two metal chairs that matched in style but were a deeper shade of blue with a hint of green in it. It was another color Josie had seen in the ocean.

A bit winded from the climb up the stairs, Josie was grateful to sit down. She unclipped Unknown's leash, who then looked at her as if wondering if unclipping the leash was a mistake or a genuine indication that she was free to roam.

"It's okay." Josie waved her hand. "You can poke around."

Unknown turned and explored the small roof deck, moving slowly and gently as was her tentative, cat-like style.

Josie heard footsteps on the stairs. She stood up and held the door open as Shulu came through with a ceramic teapot in one hand and a plate in the other. On the plate were two ceramic mugs, two cloth napkins, and four small biscuit cookies. Like the various blue colors of umbrellas and furniture, the pot and mugs and plate were individual in details but coordinated in style.

Shulu poured tea and then sat down.

She didn't immediately speak and instead gestured toward the cookies.

In some ways, Shulu reminded Josie of Cumberland. Shulu felt no need to fill silent space with words that had no substance. She only spoke when she had something thoughtful to say.

"Thank you," Josie said as she sat down. "This is very nice."

Shulu picked up one of the cookies and a napkin and took a bite. Josie followed. The cookie reminded Josie of something their boarder Amelia might make as she developed her choices for a future coffee shop.

"I love these," Josie said. "Not very sweet, yet addictive."

Shulu nodded. She lifted her mug and held it out.

Josie understood that it was for toasting.

They brought their mugs near each other but didn't clink. And neither said anything.

Josie admired the woman's reserve as much as she enjoyed the artistic expression that imbued all aspects of Shulu's space. She lived and worked on a busy street in what used to be an auto garage, yet her roof deck was as inviting as a deck at a cozy Malibu beach house.

"Sometimes I see you and your daughter walk by," Shulu

said. "Samantha has a presence. And I no longer see her in black clothes. What are those called? Gothic?"

Josie nodded. "Fourteen-year-old kids seem to move through phases every few months. I'm glad the Goth period is over. Some time back I gave her a raspberry-colored T-shirt."

"Enticing her with color," Shulu said.

"Yes. Just yesterday she wore it for the first time."

"She is going to grow up to be an elegant woman."

"Thank you."

They both sipped tea. The movement made Shulu's amazingly-thick gray ponytail shimmer. Her hair was straight like that of many Native Americans, and her ponytail was as long as her arm.

Unknown was sniffing a pot of geraniums in a sunny corner of the deck. She walked over into the shade of one of the umbrellas and lay down on the boards.

Shulu held the handle of her mug with one hand and cupped it with the other as if trying to absorb the heat.

"But even when your child embraces color and light, something else comes along and threatens darkness, right?" Shulu said. "There is always tension in making difficult decisions."

"Is it that obvious?"

Shulu paused. "The world looks to artists with the hope of seeing beauty. I won't say my job is easy. But it doesn't come with moral dilemmas..." Shulu let the thought stand unaccompanied. Eventually, she added, "I imagine the demands the world makes of professors are complicated."

For a moment Josie wondered if Shulu was simply speaking in broad terms, or if she could tell that Josie was facing stressful decisions. She decided it was an opening nevertheless.

"I'm pursuing an assignment for the governor. Six people have been killed. He wants me to find the killer."

Shulu widened her eyes as she frowned in near disbelief.

Josie explained, "A Forest Service Ranger and his wife. A man who worked for the wife and sold illegal guns. Two prison guards who transported that gun seller after he was caught. And the father of a young woman named Elena Soto. Elena also worked for the ranger's wife."

Josie worried that it was too much to be telling Shuluwish, too much burden to be sharing. She waited for a reaction. Shulu didn't talk.

Josie continued, "Now Elena is in trouble. Her mother lives in Reno. I believe they are from Mexico. Elena's trouble might not be severe. But I fear the worst. I think her father was killed because of her troubles."

"Why is the governor interested?"

"He was friends of two of the people who were killed."

Shulu nodded. An invitation to continue?

Josie explained that Mary Jo Telman, who'd been killed in the Sierra foothills, owned some nursing homes. "I suspect that those nursing homes are acquiring drugs ostensibly for the use of the nursing home residents. But I think the nursing homes are skimming some of the drugs and selling them through some type of distribution network. Mary Jo also purchased an abbey in the mountains east of Sacramento."

"A religious abbey?" Shuluwish asked.

"Yes. It is beautiful but very remote. We've seen it from an airplane. There are armed men there. I think the abbey might be headquarters for the drug distribution. I have a friend who sneaked up through the forest to get a look at the abbey. My friend saw a young woman that could be Elena Soto. The woman used a flashlight to flash an SOS Morse code signal to my friend."

"Meaning," Shuluwish said, "that the woman is probably being held captive."

Josie nodded. "That's my assumption, yes."

Shulu's frown intensified. "The police will go and get her, right?"

"Probably not. I talked to a sheriff's sergeant, and he told me that he needs video or some other direct evidence of a crime. He called my report of the men pointing rifles at our plane a 'he said, she said' situation and that the District Attorney might think we were flying too low, which is trespassing. He also said that, because the abbey is fenced and gated, he can't trespass through a locked gate without evidence of a crime. So law enforcement won't help."

"You considered other options?"

"To the best of my ability, yes. I can think of no legal way to investigate what is happening to that young woman inside the abbey. Her circumstances are alarming. But we have a clear call for help in the form of her flashlight SOS." Josie paused. "There are some actions I might take. But I'm wondering what you think about it?"

Shulu sipped tea.

Josie waited.

Shulu ate a biscuit cookie.

Josie noticed that Unknown lifted her head off her paws and looked at Shulu.

Shulu said, "Like most women, I know something of how men can take control over women. My people have a history that is passed on by oral tradition. The stories are still told about what the Spanish missionaries did to our people hundreds of years ago. They took by force what was ours. They captured our people and made them slaves. The women, especially, were victimized in the worst ways. My guess is that this woman, Elena Soto, cannot afford to wait while her potential rescuers consider how to take action that passes the inspection of men in law enforcement."

Josie thought about it. "You are saying we shouldn't be too concerned about getting legal permission. That makes sense because we may not be successful in getting permission."

Shulu nodded and looked off toward the nearby mountains. Her face showed great concern. "I worry for this woman you talk about. I think it's time to assemble an army of sorts and make a plan."

"To rescue the woman," Josie said.

"Yes. You know how they did it in medieval times. Breach the ramparts and storm the castle."

TWENTY-EIGHT

Josie thanked Shulu for her thoughts, said goodbye, and walked back home with Unknown.

During the walk, her cell phone rang. The readout said it was Cor Kontos.

"Hello, Cor."

"Hey, prof. Sorry I'm calling later than I'd expected. But we had a bit of a schedule problem. Diane can't teach her classes today. So I'm filling in. If it's okay with you, I'd like to meet you later and go over what I saw up at the abbey."

"I'd like that. And a delay is okay, Cor," Josie said. "You're helping me. I'm grateful for whatever help you can give, whenever you can give it."

"Glad to hear it," Cor said. "Can I call you later today? Or maybe tomorrow morning?"

"That's fine. I'll be here. Thank you for your effort. And I hope Diane is okay."

"She is. It's a family thing. She'll be back teaching as soon as tomorrow or the next."

"Good," Josie said. "I'll wait for your call. Thanks again."

When Josie got back home, Samantha was still gone. So Josie texted her that she was taking Unknown and heading to her office at UCLA. As they walked to her office in Bunche Hall, something made her recall what Ralph Ellison said about history dogging us all. In a quirk of thought progressions, she thought about how helpful he'd been to her and Samantha over the previous months when he made them a branding iron and then helped them out after he bumped into them in Yosemite National Park. Josie was especially pleased that Ellison got along so well with Samantha. Not many older, bachelor men would find any common ground with a young, female teenager.

The thought of Ellison accidentally meeting them in Yosemite brought a faint memory. At first, it seemed to be one of those extraneous, free-association thoughts that had no bearing on anything. She remembered that several months ago, before the trip to Yosemite and even before the wilderness trip to the Quetico in Canada, she'd been in her office in Bunche Hall. She was going through the mail and came to an advertisement on an over-sized postcard. She couldn't remember the details of the advertisement, but it caught her attention because it featured heraldic symbols. Medieval symbols. She couldn't remember the name of the business that sent it.

Josie pondered the odd memory as she climbed the steps to her office. Once inside her office, she shuffled through the papers on her desk. Unknown sat on her cushion to the side and watched her. Josie looked in some drawers. Opened her file cabinet. Glanced in her waste basket, even though she knew it had been emptied by the office cleaning crew several times since. There was no particular reason for Josie to think that she had saved the postcard. But she couldn't remember throwing it in the recycling bin. Josie knew she was strange that way. An oddity of her mental organization was that she could often remember items she threw away better than items she kept.

She stood up from her desk and walked over to her bookcases. The shelves were full with textbooks and journals and notebooks filled with papers written by graduate students.

On the top shelf of one bookcase was her handmade crossbow, the replica of a medieval crossbow. Josie had built it for her Ph.D. dissertation fifteen years ago. It was the same crossbow she'd used to kill a murderer in the recent past, the criminal case that had drawn the attention of the governor. The crossbow fired iron bolts instead of arrows, bolts that Josie had made herself in the same manner used by medieval blacksmiths. She had worked under the tutelage of a blacksmith, who had died two or three years later. She still had six of the original bolts left. They were stacked in a shallow pyramid made of three rows. It was, she thought with macabre humor, a pyramid of death.

Leaning against the crossbow was the postcard.

Josie realized that she must have associated the medieval symbols on the card with the medieval weapon and she had unconsciously set the postcard nearby. She picked it up.

The images were as she remembered, a coat of arms, a halberd, and a shield.

The advertisement was about wrought iron fabrication. At the time she received the advertisement, she'd never had any interest in metal fabrication. Because the advertisement came to Josie, it had probably been sent to a mailing list that was not properly focused on the kind of businesses or people who would need iron work.

Josie turned the card over. The other side had the business information. It said, 'Ellison Blacksmithing, specializing in Medieval designs.'

The shop address confirmed that the card came from Ralph Ellison, and it had arrived long before she looked him up online and went to meet him.

Josie remembered when she had looked for a metal shop to create the branding iron that she and Samantha used in Yosemite. At the time, she hadn't thought of the postcard. But was there a subliminal connection? When she saw Ralph Ellison's name during her online research, maybe it was reinforced by the postcard that had sat in her office for a few weeks. After all, she'd kept the card and put it next to her crossbow.

As Josie thought more about it, it produced a cascade of other thoughts, one of which made her inhale with shock. She sat down at her desk, leaned back in her chair, and took deep breaths to calm her racing mind.

Because it didn't seem likely that she would be on any mailing list for blacksmithing, was it possible that Ellison knew of her before he mailed it? Did he specifically look for her address before he sent it? She looked at the card again. Her address was written by hand. Nearly all advertising mailers were printed by computer. Even older ones had computer-printed labels.

Josie thought about multiple scenarios. A few minutes later, she came to a decision. She picked up her phone and dialed

Ellison's number.

"Ellison here," he said.

"Hi Ellison. It's Josie. It sounds like you're driving."

"Hold on, let me stop."

Josie waited, pleased that a man who had little respect for what he called mindless laws nevertheless obeyed the ones that made sense.

A minute later, he was back. "I've pulled off the road. What's up?"

"I have a question. I'm wondering if we can meet."

"Happy to," he said. "I'm near downtown. Where are you?"

"At my office at UCLA."

"I'll come to campus. With parking and such, better give me half an hour. But that's faster than you coming to me."

"I hate to ruin your day," Josie said. "We could plan a future day when it would fit with your errands."

"Errands are already done. I was just about to head home. Shall I come up to your office?"

"It's such a nice day, let's meet in the sculpture garden."

"Got it. The one just north of your building. See you soon."

Josie put Ellison's advertising mailer in her purse, took Unknown, and walked across the UCLA mall. She dropped off some materials she had promised another professor, and walked back to the sculpture garden. She was barely aware of her movements, so distracted was she by her question for Ellison.

She sat on a bench near a Deborah Butterfield horse. The sculpture was constructed of a few disparate pieces of bronze shaped such that they appeared to be weathered driftwood. Yet the full-size horse it represented seemed amazingly real, graceful and beautiful. Josie thought it was a kind of magic similar to when painters create a good portrait. No matter how a viewer tries, they don't see paint strokes on canvas. They only see the subject of the portrait. Josie was looking at relatively few sticks. Despite looking like sticks and being cast in bronze, Josie could only see a beautiful horse.

Ellison showed up five minutes later. "Just me," he said as he approached, apparently not wanting to startle her. He tapped on the bench as he sat next to her, an enduring type of formality from a man who knew it was good to err toward less touching with women.

"What's up?" he said.

Unknown had been sitting next to Josie. The dog stood, walked over next to Ellison, and sat down so close that her jaw was touching his leg. He gently rubbed Unknown's head.

Josie wasn't sure of the best way to broach her question. "Some months ago, I received a postcard advertisement about your blacksmithing. It was sent to my office here at UCLA. At the time, I didn't know you, and I didn't pay attention other than to notice that the postcard mentioned medieval design."

Josie watched Ellison as he nodded.

She continued, "As you know, I came to you to have you make a branding iron, which I used in Yosemite Park. I'm wondering why you sent that card to me."

Ellison shrugged. "Businesses try to find customers in a variety of ways. As most businesses go online, snail mail is becoming more noticeable than it ever was before. Post Office mail stands out."

"But that doesn't actually answer my question. That's not really why you sent it, is it?"

Ellison turned to look at her, then looked off at the Butterfield horse sculpture. "I sent it because I'd found out about you, and I wanted you as a customer."

"And…" Josie prodded.

It was a long moment before he replied. "And I thought that, if, against all odds, you ever wanted me to do some blacksmith work for you, I could get a sense of you."

"Of me and Samantha?"

"Yes, Samantha, too."

"And you wanted a sense of us because…"

He paused again. "I'm getting the idea that you know where this is going. So I'll just say it. I wanted to get to know you and Samantha because I think I'm Samantha's grandfather."

TWENTY-NINE

Because of her previous revelation about Ellison sending her the postcard, Josie was prepared for the admission that Ellison was Samantha's grandfather. But the words still hit her like a blow that could knock her to the ground.

It seemed to suck the air from her lungs. She couldn't breathe. She sat up straight on the sculpture garden bench and tried to expand her lungs. Gradually, a little air seeped into her lungs. Josie started to cry. Her tears weren't for joy, but neither were they for sadness. Her tears were for the thoughts of what could have been, pro or con, calm or stressful, certainty or uncertainty. They were tears for a life of potential experience that hadn't been realized. It was a feeling that she increasingly experienced as she considered the narrow scope of her job and even her very existence.

Finally, Josie said, "Why didn't you just approach me directly?" She felt indignant.

"Because, sorry to say, I wasn't sure that I wanted a relationship with either of you. I've lived the majority of my life alone, and I've been happy with that. I didn't want to upset that world unless I felt a strong pull toward something else. But I also wasn't sure you'd want to have me in your life, no matter how small an involvement it was. If I'd originally approached you with this info, that could have been a huge upset that you might not have wanted. I wanted to respect the cohesive bonds of your world and not barge in with information that would stress that."

"So you came to Yosemite because you thought we'd be there?"

"Yes. As I told you at the time, I've often camped there. So when you were in my shop, picking up the branding iron, you mentioned Yosemite. I got the idea that you were going to go there. So I thought, why not go and observe a bit."

"The advertisement you sent me was like a fisherman putting out a line and bait, trolling. See if I take the hook. Reel me in and check me out." Josie felt a growing anger.

"I confess, it's true."

"You didn't think that was manipulative?"

"It was definitely manipulative. And I'm sorry for the discomfort that gives you. But trolling seemed necessary if I wanted to avoid crashing into your world. If I had seen things in Yosemite that suggested my presence would be a big upset to you, I would have stayed away and left you in peace."

The statement sounded suspicious to Josie.

Ellison said, "Imagine if I'd simply called you up and said, 'I'm a semi-retired blacksmith who might be Samantha's grandfather. But I don't have a clue if we three could develop a comfortable relationship. I have no family experience. I fathered a son who was a failure by every measure, and part of his failure is directly connected to my failure to require his mother to allow me a role in his life. But now I want to dip my toe in the waters of a familial relationship. If it suits me, I'll maybe hang around. If not, I'll disappear back into the woods.'"

Ellison paused. "Would that have been a good approach? Would you have thought, this guy seems nice? Or would you have run in the opposite direction?"

Josie nodded. "You're right. I would have thought of Jabari and figured you were probably looking to scam me out of money or worse. I'd have thought you would likely be a terrible influence on Sam."

"Also," Ellison said, "if I'm honest with myself, I have to admit that I didn't know if I would like either of you. I wasn't just concerned whether you'd tolerate me joining your life in some way. I was worried that I might not be able to tolerate either of you."

He looked at Josie as if gauging her reaction.

"What?" Josie said, making a wan smile. "You thought there was a possibility that we wouldn't be adorable?"

Ellison kept a straight face and nodded. "The thought occurred to me, yes."

"So now that you've come to know us, do you want an ongoing relationship with us?"

"Yes." No hesitation this time. "I've never cared about anyone else like I care about you two."

"How do I know you're not just a grandpa wannabe? How do I know your real goal isn't just to be able to tell grandpa stories so you can keep up with the rest of the grandpa geezers?"

Ellison suddenly seemed blocked. His mood, his demeanor, his personality all locked down, the shutters closed.

Josie waited, wondering if her words had been terrible or if she'd merely asked a reasonable question.

It was a long moment before Ellison spoke. "I don't go to bars. I don't even have friends with grandkids. In fact, I have very few friends."

"God, not another person like that," Josie said. "I don't have friends, either. Fortunately, Sam has friends. She's good at connecting with people."

They sat for a moment in silence.

"I'm sorry," Josie said. She lightly touched Ellison's wrist. "That was very rude of me to say such a snarky thing about being…" She trailed off.

"A geezer gramp wannabe?" Ellison said.

"I'm so sorry. That sounds horrible when you repeat it back to me. Please forgive me. I'm just shocked. And unsettled. You sort of dropped me into a whirlpool just now, and I'm spinning around."

"Apology accepted. And I understand your upset. I should have been straight from the beginning."

"No, you shouldn't have. Because I would have recoiled and pushed you away. Jabari was no ambassador for anyone. He was a slick, charming, handsome, sexy con artist, who belongs where he is, in prison."

Ellison made a single nod.

Josie said, "If you had approached me using Jabari as your point of connection, not only would I have assumed you were untrustworthy, I might have called the police."

Another nod.

Josie took a minute to do some deep breathing. The doctor had told her that practicing relaxation techniques was good for reducing blood pressure.

Eventually, Josie said, "Tell me about you and Jabari."

Ellison took his time. "I quit the Army when I was twenty-seven. I tried some different things, looking to get an idea of what I might do with my life. I was a lifeguard in Newport Beach. I parked cars at a restaurant in Palm Springs. I apprenticed with a blacksmith. Years later, a musician I knew from way back got me the best job I ever had, working as a roadie for a company that managed concert tours. One of their acts was Diana Ross. It was just grunt work hauling equipment, but I felt like I was part of something big, something that produced value by every measure. You're young. But you probably know that Diana Ross was the greatest ever. On one of her tours, I met a singer, Tara Moreau, who did backup harmonies for Ross.

"Tara and I had a short, passionate, tempestuous relationship. Emphasis on tempestuous. By the time Tara knew she was pregnant, she had quit me weeks before. She didn't even tell me she was pregnant, never mind telling me I was the baby's father. I found out from a friend of hers. I tried to insert myself into her life. I repeatedly asked her for access. I even tried to pressure her. But she would have nothing to do with me. In retrospect, I should have simply insisted. But I didn't.

"She named the child Jabari. Jabari Moreau. Apparently, he was trouble from the beginning. I knew because, even though she refused to let me into her life, she started calling me to vent. Three or four times she called to say that the little boy made her life hell, and it was my fault. She said she had brothers and nephews and all were good. So, simple deduction proved that I had given Jabari my bad genes. She called him a little monster. And, from what I heard from another friend, it sounded true. Before the kid could walk, he was climbing out of the baby crib, pulling down the drapes, knocking over and breaking every little thing. He ate the dirt out of the plants. He managed to climb up and turn on the faucet and close the sink drain and flood the apartment and two apartments below it. He screamed for fun, grinning the whole time, yelling so loud in the middle of the night that the neighbors called the cops. When they came, he grinned at them and yelled even louder. One time, when Jabari was about two years old or maybe less, the neighbors called again. Three in the morning. They'd heard pots and pans falling on the floor, and they thought gangbangers were having a fight. The cops came and found Tara trying to cradle Jabari in her arms while she sang to him. But every which way she turned, Jabari managed to grab another item off the counter or the wall and throw it to the floor. When Tara was exasperated, she handed Jabari to a cop and told him to try to rock him to sleep. Jabari got the cop's holster unsnapped and tugged the gun out. It fell to the floor and went off. No one was hurt, but everyone was scared to death. The cop was suspended for having a round in the chamber and the gun cocked. He later said that the noise and the wailing coming from the apartment as the cops approached made them think that the neighbor was right, that gangbangers were fighting inside the apartment. So he came in with his gun out and cocked. He holstered it without thinking.

"Despite all that, I still asked Tara if I could get involved with her life. She said no way. She said one bad male in the family was enough."

Ellison was leaning forward, elbows on his knees. He rubbed his palms together as if to rid them of dirt.

"Tara died in a car accident when Jabari was sixteen. I tried to entice the boy to come live with me, but he went to live with friends instead. I called several times. He wouldn't take my call. I knew some people who were the parents of one of his friends. That's how I learned more bits and pieces of his world. Six months after Tara died, I tried again to contact him, but he would have nothing to do with me.

"As you probably know, Jabari eventually took up with a hairdresser named Persimmon Jones, a Dutch, Cherokee, French Canadian mix who was tall and thin and charismatic. Just like Jabari. It seemed that they were made for each other.

But when she got pregnant, he didn't use any common sense and got in more trouble than before. You probably know the rest of the story. After Persimmon gave birth, she ran off with a truck driver from Colorado, leaving Jabari to take care of Samantha. The very concept of Jabari caring for a baby contravenes all known laws of the universe. Not long after that, you met him. I surmised from my distance that you were more taken with his child than you were with him. And you understood that Jabari was singularly ill-equipped to be a loving dad. So when Jabari saw the opportunity to pass the little girl off to you, everyone who was connected to Jabari and Samantha knew it would be an improvement."

Ellison straightened up and took a deep breath. "I tried to keep my distance. But from what little I could tell, based on things people I know told me, it seemed you were a dream mother, whether you thought of yourself as a temporary baby sitter or a foster mother or stepmother or whatever. You had a heart of gold, an intense focus on doing what was right, and more than anything, you loved that little girl. And I loved you from a distance for loving that young girl. You saved that child, Josie. You saved her from a life of struggle, emotional and intellectual and financial, a life of what probably would have been misery. You gave her love and stability and hope and ambition. Everyone owes you. Jabari, me, society. Most of all Samantha."

Josie stood up and walked over toward the horse sculpture. She found a tissue and wiped her eyes. She looked to the horse's face as if looking for wisdom.

Eventually, she turned and came back to where Ellison still sat on the bench.

"It was right of you to wait before telling me. But I'm glad you finally did, even though it's a shock and very upsetting."

"I always feared the subject because I worried it would upset you."

"Will you keep this between you and me?" Josie asked. "For now, at least?"

"Yes. But you should know that just as you came to figure out who I am before I said anything overtly, Samantha will, too."

Josie nodded, frowning.

"That kid is not just excessively smart, Josie, she's excessively perceptive. What do they call it? Emotional intelligence. She can read you. And, frankly, you're not a natural poker player. You have a lot of tells."

Josie thought about what he said. It produced a growing dread in her.

Ellison said, "Can I ask you a question?"

Josie nodded.

"Sam knows you're not her biological mother, right?"

Josie felt her tears flow as if a valve had been opened. "I haven't said anything!" she gasped, choking on her cries. "Jabari made me promise not to tell Sam about him. It was part of our agreement before he would sign the adoption papers. He was embarrassed at being sent to prison, and he couldn't bear the idea that his daughter would grow up thinking she came from scum. Those are his words not mine. So I've never known what to do or how to handle it. I've wanted to break that promise many times. But had I not made the promise, I would never have been able to adopt Sam!"

Josie sat down on the bench, leaned her elbows on her knees like Ellison, and lowered her forehead to her palms. She spoke into her hands, her voice muffled, her words garbled with tears. "Even when I've been sorely tempted to tell her, I've never known how to do it. So I kept putting it off. I kept thinking I should wait until the time was just right."

Ellison touched her leg, three fingers just above her knee.

Josie found it enormously reassuring to have someone understand something about her biggest secret, even if it was the person who was instrumental in spilling the story.

"When I first started metal sculpting," Ellison said, "I took a class at the community college. Over the course of eight weeks, the instructor explained all about design and technique and materials and art history. Nothing in depth because the class was designed to be as broad as possible, although it had a bit of focus on the craft of sculpture. Near the end of the class, the instructor announced that she was going to tell us the single most important thing about making art. She said that if you want to be successful at it, you can't wait for the right time or the right place or the right mood or the right idea. You can't wait for inspiration or acquiring a certain amount of study or finishing a series of classes.You just have to do it."

Josie said, "The stars will never all line up, will they?"

"No. I think the principle applies to lots of things in life. I believe it will be better for Samantha to hear it from you than to hear it from someone else."

Josie nodded. "She probably won't be too angry with me."

"No. She's still your daughter, regardless of not having shared DNA. She looks up to you. She loves you. I've watched you two. It's obvious."

"When do you think I should tell her?"

"Now. Tonight when you are both home."

"How do you think I should bring up the subject?"

"Don't even think about. Just sit down with her and tell her you have something you need to say."

"What if she hates me?"

"She'll get over it."

Josie sat up and looked at Ellison. "How do you know all these things?"

"I don't know any of these things. I'm just guessing."

"I'm about to turn my life and my daughter's life upside down based on the guess of a bachelor who's never been married."

Ellison nodded. "A wannabe geezer grandpa bachelor."

Josie inhaled in a kind of short gasping cry, choked with emotion.

"Your call," Ellison said.

THIRTY

Before dinner that evening, Samantha made popcorn and poured two iced teas. She said, "Hey, Mama, I've found two Netflix choices we might like after dinner. Wanna give me an opinion? Amelia's gone for the night again, so we can choose a romantic comedy without wondering if she thinks we're lame for watching them."

Josie was thinking about Ellison. "Actually, I was hoping we could sit and look at the view and talk."

"Oh, no, not another one of those mother/daughter talks we hear about in our family education class."

"No, not one of those. But somewhat similar. A second cousin to that kind of talk."

Samantha made a big sigh, grabbed her bowl of popcorn and plopped down on the sofa. "Okay, lay the mother/daughter talk on me."

Josie sat next to her. "I don't know where to begin. So I'll just say it. Forgive me if it sounds harsh or shocking. Please don't hate me."

"Just say it, Mama!"

Josie took a deep breath. Held it. Blew it out slowly.

"I'm not your biological mother."

Samantha was chewing popcorn.

"That's your big deal?" Samantha didn't appear to have any reaction.

"Maybe you don't understand," Josie said. "I'm not, you know…"

"Mama! I wasn't born yesterday. It's no surprise," she said. "We don't share DNA." Josie noticed that her words were almost the same as Ellison's.

"How did you know?"

"Well, I didn't really know for a fact. But it's pretty obvious. I'm tall and skinny. You're not. You're dark chocolate. I'm chocolate mixed with butterscotch. My hair isn't dense black like yours, and it's more wavy than curly. Whereas you could grow an afro two feet in diameter." Samantha paused. "But it would be a saggy 'fro."

"Saggy?! If I wanted, my hair could be tough as a black volleyball."

"Face it, Mama. You're getting older. Your hair isn't as springy as it used to be. Never mind the gray."

"Gray?! Girl, you start slamming one of my better features, you're gonna have to cook dinner for the next month."

"Fine. Unknown loves to come with me to pick up Chinese takeout, 'cuz they always give her treats."

Josie couldn't believe she'd gone from being afraid to talk to Samantha to getting defensive about her hair.

"Another obvious difference is I'm an early technology adopter, totally drawn to the techie world. You're stuck in the Middle Ages. What did you call it? You're a Luddite. I like rap, you like classical and jazz. I love volleyball. You hate all sports."

"I don't hate all sports!" Josie was appalled that her feelings were so transparent.

"You can't fool me, Mama. There could be the greatest sports matchup in history, and you wouldn't take the time to even watch it on TV, never mind actually going to see a game in person. I bet you never even watched Venus and Serena take over the world with their tennis rackets, right?"

"But I like some sports. I like watching figure skating," Josie said. "And ballet." Josie felt silly trying to defend herself. Samantha was right. Or maybe Josie's brain was secretly seizing on ways to avoid talking about the actual subject she brought up.

"Figure skating and ballet are dance," Samantha said. "That's more like—I don't know—more like art than sports."

"So we have some different interests," Josie said. "That made you think I'm not your biological mother?"

"You want the truth? All my life, you've studiously avoided

talking about my origins. And my dad, especially. It's always been obvious that he was a troublemaker or some kind of major problem. Maybe he died, maybe he went to prison. Either way, you're embarrassed about him. So you've kept that part of my background secret. But you're no good at secrets, Mama. I'm guessing that he broke up with my biological mother. Maybe she was a druggie or something and imploded. Maybe she died. So he was stuck with me and then he took up with you. Then his life imploded, too, and you raised me by yourself."

Josie shook her head. Ellison was right. Samantha was so perceptive, it was impossible to keep much from her.

"Frankly, I'm pretty amazed, Cap'n," Josie said. "You nailed it. You described your background perfectly."

"Aye, Matey. My bigger question is why haven't you told me everything before?"

Josie sighed. "Because your father made me promise not to tell you, or he wouldn't sign the adoption papers. You were only two years old when he went to prison. But you were really smart, and he was so impressed by you. He felt terrible about the idea that you would ever know about him and his failures. Of course, that didn't motivate him to be a better person. But he cared a great deal about what you thought. So he made me promise not to reveal to you his name or his crimes or his background."

"Are you ready to break that promise?"

"I'm thinking about it," Josie said, "now that you've already figured out the basics."

"Then do your professor thing. Analyze the reasons for and against keeping your promise."

"It sounds like you've thought about this."

"My ethics teacher did a section on promises."

"I still can't get over you having an ethics class in middle school. Where I grew up in Richmond, we only had the basics. Reading, writing, arithmetic, and science."

"It's one of the benefits of being economically privileged." Samantha said it in a casual way as if she accepted her privilege as a fact of life and there was no point in being distressed by it. "Anyway, my teacher explained that people often justify breaking promises by saying they want to produce the greatest good for the greatest number. Which may happen. But my teacher says there's no justice in that. She said countries break their promises of truce or alliance and go to war, do terrible things, and kill people using the greater good justification."

"It sounds like there is another way to think about breaking a promise," Josie said.

"Yeah. She said the more ethical way is to consider whether breaking a promise between two parties will leave no one worse off while it makes one or both better off." Samantha was mumbling because she was stuffing popcorn into her mouth. "So the question is, if you break your promise to my dad, will it make him no worse off while it makes us better off because we're able to talk freely about something important?"

Josie thought about what Samantha said. She tried not to get distracted by the power of the kid's mind.

"If I break my promise to your father, I will have to confront the fact that my promise is not rock solid. I'll lose some self respect. You'll probably respect me less, as well. Because you'll know that, in certain situations, you can't trust me to keep a promise."

"Here's an idea," Samantha said. "I'll tell you what I think. If I'm right, you nod. If I'm wrong, you shake your head."

"That's somewhat like a sin of omission versus a sin of commission. It's still a sin because it's designed to mislead, but in a way that makes the sinner feel less bad."

"If we play this game, and you agree to what I already know or what I guess, will it make you feel less bad?" Samantha asked.

"Yes, probably."

"Okay. If I say something you disagree with, then you can refuse to respond. And the only downside will be my supreme disappointment."

"Ouch!" Josie said. "That's mean!"

"Okay. First question. Is my dad's name Jabari Moreau?"

"What?! Where in the world did you hear that?!"

"I've heard it multiple times from you. Years ago, you

would say the name in your sleep. You always sounded angry. It happened quite a few times. Sometimes it would be Jabari. Sometimes Moreau. Sometimes his full name."

"You never said anything," Josie said.

"Why would I say something? It was obviously something that made you upset. I didn't wanted to dredge up things that were uncomfortable for you."

"I never knew…" Josie didn't finish the sentence.

"And I've seen some mail with the name on it."

"What kind of mail?" Josie felt a shock.

"Years ago. There was a notice from a court. I think it said something about an adoption judgment."

"You never said anything about that, either!" Josie had thought the subject would turn Samantha's world upside down. Instead, things were turning upside down for Josie.

"When I saw the letter in the box, I left all the mail there so you wouldn't think I saw it. I didn't want you to be upset."

Josie reached over and took Samantha's hand. "You are so sweet. How'd I get so lucky?"

"That's one of the questions I'm trying to get you to answer. Please tell me how you got so lucky."

Josie took several breaths and then explained that Jabari Moreau's mother was Tara Moreau, a backup singer to Diana Ross. She also explained how Jabari was a difficult child and how he continuously got into trouble.

When she was done, Samantha said, "So Tara Moreau was my biological grandmother on my father's side."

"Correct."

"Who was my paternal grandfather?"

Josie took another deep breath. "Maybe it's like your father's name. Maybe you already know it."

"I guess we won't know until you say it, Mama."

Josie said, "Ralph Ellison is your grandfather."

Samantha did a kind of leap straight up so that she ended up standing on the couch, her head near the ceiling. "Ellison is… is… Grandpa Ellison?! Oh, my God! That is the best thing I've ever heard!"

THIRTY-ONE

After learning that Ralph Ellison was her grandfather, Samantha stepped down off the couch. She sat next to Josie. But she bounced. She couldn't sit still.

"Were you planning to tell me about Ellison today?" Samantha asked. "Or is that another thing you thought you'd keep secret for the next who-knows-how-long?"

It seemed to Josie that Samantha was both glad and mad at the same time, if that were possible.

"I couldn't keep it secret because I didn't know it!"

"What? How could you not know Ellison is my grandfather?"

So Josie explained everything. How Ellison talked to friends and neighbors of his son Jabari and his girlfriend Persimmon Jones, who gave birth to Samantha. And how Ellison came to suspect that Josie might be the woman who adopted the girl. And how he sent the blacksmithing postcard advertisement to Josie thinking that, while it was a long shot possibility that she might one day need some iron work, it was worth trying. And how after they went to his blacksmith shop to have a branding iron made, he figured out they were going to try something in Yosemite. So he went camping in Yosemite on the chance that he might meet them both.

And from that point, Samantha knew everything else.

"Should I call Ellison now? Or should we go to his loft? And speaking of that, what should I call him? Ellison? Or Grandpa Ellison?"

"I think Ellison, unless he says otherwise."

"Will he be okay with having me in his life now that I know who he really is?"

"He'll be more than okay."

"Really? Are you sure? Will he still like me? I won't just be a kid anymore, sometimes fun, sometimes exasperating. I'll be… I'll be his grandkid."

"Sam, Ellison thinks you are the best thing in the world. He adores you. So, yes, he will still adore you. And he has never thought you were exasperating."

Samantha went quiet. She sat still for a time, drinking her tea. She stared at the gas fireplace. She no longer ate popcorn by the fistful but instead put one kernel at a time into her mouth.

Josie stayed silent so Samantha could think about this new world. Unknown sat on the floor near them, her jaw lifted up at a steep angle to rest on Samantha's knee. It was just like she had done with Ellison.

"I can't believe that the man who helped us in the San Bernardino mountains and nearly got clubbed to death is my grandfather."

"Yes. It's a joy to discover that a relative is a good guy instead of, well…"

"A bad guy," Samantha said.

Again, Samantha went silent. Josie understood how much mental processing was involved when your life is suddenly reordered as if by decree.

"Mama?" Samantha eventually said.

"What?"

"Because I have Ellison's DNA and I don't have yours, you don't feel bad, do you? You're still my mother in my eyes. I really want you to know that. And I want you to know that I love you even more for telling me these secrets."

Josie leaned over so that her head landed on Samantha's shoulder. "And you're still my daughter, and I love you even more." Josie hugged her daughter hard.

After dinner, Josie dug around in the cabinet under the kitchen sink and found a bottle of Riesling she'd been saving for some time. She had to search to find a corkscrew.

"Are you having wine to celebrate our new truthfulness?" Samantha said. "Or is it more of a relaxation medicine?"

"Both," Josie said. She poured a couple of inches in a small, stemmed glass.

Samantha picked up the glass, sipped it, and then nearly spit it out. "Yuck, that's awful! Don't they make, like, a sweet wine or something so it's easier to drink?"

"This is a sweet wine. That's why I bought it. Wine connoisseurs seem to mostly like dry wines, but I can't drink that stuff."

"What's dry wine like?"

"Not sweet."

"Why would someone call a liquid dry? Why not just call it unsweetened, like chocolate?"

"I don't know. It might be because dry wine makes your mouth feel dry. But ask the French or Italians."

Samantha nodded and sat back on the couch next to Josie.

"I still don't know anything about my biological father or mother. Let's start by telling me about my father."

Josie paused. "He's very smart, but he mostly uses his smarts in a bad way."

"Like?"

"Like figuring out how to commit crimes."

Samantha nodded. "What else?"

"He's charming and charismatic to a fault."

"What kind of fault?"

"The fault is that he uses his charisma to captivate others and get them to do what isn't in their best interests. People are immediately taken with him. He has a kind of star power. Like you. But with your father, the result is that people trust him when they shouldn't."

"You mean, like lend him money when he won't pay it back?"

"Exactly. Although he spins stuff in a grander way. He won't ask someone to lend him money. He'll ask them to invest in his business. He won't ask for a charity meal. He'll ask to come over and talk about his new invention over dinner."

"Their dinner," Samantha said.

"Exactly. He always has a line or a story, and people fall for it. They think he is so convincing. And he makes everything fun. So they want to get onboard with whatever scheme he's cooking up. They get excited."

"And then they get burned," Samantha said.

Josie nodded.

"What's he look like?"

"He's beautiful. Imagine a Maasai warrior, very tall, six-four, muscular, shiny skin the color of black walnut, broad forehead, bottomless dark eyes, braided hair that naturally shines as if it's got a gloss coating, cheekbones so wide and sharp they could cut you, a perfect smile with broad teeth, whiter than teeth have any right to be."

"The kind of looks that give you big advantages in life," Samantha said.

"Yes, but only if you have your act together. Jabari's looks and charisma could have made him a movie actor. Instead, his beauty got him into trouble. He grew up knowing the power of his looks. From the very beginning, he used that power in a bad way."

"To take advantage of people who were distracted by his looks?"

"Yes. People immediately fell for him. Women, of course. But men, too."

Samantha stared again at the mantel above the fireplace. "Where is he now?"

"He's in the Mojave Valley Prison, where he's serving a twenty-five-year sentence for armed robbery."

"When is he eligible for parole?"

Josie immediately felt a gut punch of worry that Samantha would want to meet Jabari. Maybe even spend time with him after he got out of prison.

"You were two years old when he went to prision. So he's served twelve years so far. I think his first parole hearing comes up in four years."

Samantha seemed to think about it. "Good," she finally said. "I've got a few years before I have to worry about deciding whether to engage with him."

Josie exhaled a long, slow breath. Music to her ears.

"What about my birth mother?"

Josie gritted her teeth. This was the kind of Q & A that she'd always dreaded.

"Your birth mother was Persimmon Jones, a hairdresser. I learned from Ellison that she was part Native American—Cherokee—part Dutch and part French Canadian. She moved away with a truck driver from Colorado and left Jabari to take care of you."

"She abandoned me to a guy who couldn't take care of me."

"Yes."

"Did you ever meet Persimmon?" Samantha asked.

"Just once briefly. I saw someone I knew at the grocery store in the San Fernando Valley. She was with Persimmon. We got introduced. We chatted just long enough that I could see that she was tall and thin and pretty. Smart too, but also something of a scatterbrain. The butterscotch in your skin is from her. I later learned that she had already planned to leave you and Jabari and head to Colorado."

Samantha was quiet. "What happened that made it so my father decided he should let you adopt me?"

"Partly, he realized it was too much work taking care of a baby. And, even though he was naturally irresponsible, he also realized that he took too many drugs to ever be sensible. He did some crazy things when he was on drugs."

"Like what?"

"One time he used you to try to rob a bank. He held you up and said they had to give him all their money or else. He didn't specify any threat. He was just on drugs and desperate, and he thought it seemed like a good idea at the time. Witnesses said you started screaming louder than a fire truck siren. You ended up okay, but your very loud voice made it so Jabari couldn't focus. He ended up leaving you at the teller window and running out of the bank. The police were waiting outside."

"My dad couldn't properly rob a bank because he brought me, a baby, along." Samantha sounded appalled.

"Yes."

"So how did you actually take over raising me?"

"I offered Jabari money."

"Wait." Samantha shook her head. "Are you saying my father sold me to you?"

"Yes."

"My own father sold me to you! I can't believe it!"

"It is hard to believe. To be fair, I don't think he thought of it as a commercial transaction. I believe he just realized that it would be best for you if I had full custody of you and you lived with me. Coincidentally, he understood that I had a good job and a steady income. So it made sense to him to request a fee for his favor."

Samantha was shaking her head. "I was a commodity. Like a car or something."

Josie didn't respond.

"Was I expensive?"

"More than a car," Josie said. "But cheap considering I got the best little girl in the world." Josie leaned sideways on the couch and hugged Samantha again.

Samantha was quiet for a minute. "When you first got involved with my father, were you so attracted to him that you could look past all of his problems?"

"The truth is that I was so attracted to you that I could look past his problems. But regardless of how attractive he was and could be, I knew I could never be drawn to him in a deep, permanent way. But I fell in love with you at first sight. The very first moment I met you, I was hooked. Completely hooked. Because you belonged to him, I was willing to do almost anything to have you in my life. When he continued to screw up and get in trouble as if he had no regard for your welfare, that made me even more determined to figure out how to make a good life for you."

"I was the puppy you got so smitten with that you wanted to take me home even though you hadn't planned on acquiring one."

Josie nodded. "And to extend the metaphor, he was the

dog who was show-dog-beautiful but was so untrained and impulsively wild that I knew it would be best to get you far away from him."

"How did you first meet me?"

"I was visiting a friend when a friend of hers stopped by. That friend brought Jabari. We all chatted, then he asked me out to coffee. I liked him, so I went. We met for coffee a few times. The second time he brought you. From that moment, I barely saw him anymore. You had a kind of power. You were just learning to talk, yet already you said clever things."

"Like what?"

"Like, 'I can sing, I can dance, I can hit a home run!'"

"Really?" Another big smile.

Josie grinned back at her. "Really. I don't think you even knew what a home run was. But that just made it more charming."

"You never got married to Jabari," Samantha said.

"No. We barely had any relationship at all. There was only you. I wanted you so badly that Jabari realized I would do anything for you. Furthermore, Jabari was facing prosecution for taking you to rob the bank. Then, when one of his druggie friends posted his bail, he robbed another bank. Meanwhile, the state had already taken you after he used you to rob the first bank. Jabari realized that you were facing a life as an orphan in the foster care system. He wanted to prevent that. But he had no family who could take you in." Josie sipped her wine.

"I also knew the stakes. So, I got a message to him in jail saying I would love to adopt you. As he thought about you ending up in the care of strangers, he was very inclined to have me adopt you. Then he would at least know the woman who raised you. And—I'm sorry to say—he realized I would pay for the privilege."

"How did that work? You paying to adopt me?"

"I wrote up a simple contract and had it reviewed by a friend who is a lawyer. I can show it to you sometime if you like. It basically says, 'With the goal of providing the best possible upbringing for Samantha Moreau, Jabari Moreau and Josephine Strong recognize that Josephine has a more stable life.

Jabari Moreau agrees to transfer full custody of Samantha to Josephine. And Samantha will become her legal daughter and take the name Strong as her last name.'"

"Wow, that's… I don't know. Smart, I guess," Samantha said.

"We had to jump through a bunch of bureaucratic hoops to get the California authorities to go along. But once they investigated Jabari and me, they were eager to have me adopt you."

Josie sipped wine. "Then we made another contract between us that we never showed to the state authorities. It said, 'In return for Jabari's consideration and favor, Josephine Strong agrees to put money in a time-release financial instrument that becomes Jabari Moreau's the day that Samantha turns eighteen, with the qualifier that Samantha has lived her life with Josephine Strong as her legal guardian."

"So there's a big chunk of money waiting for him when I turn eighteen? This is like a soap opera."

"That was the lawyer's idea. I gave Jabari some cash when we signed the deal. The lawyer said I should also put cash in an investment bank in such a way that Jabari would be motivated to leave us alone until you are eighteen."

"Oh, I get it," Samantha said. "That way, if he waits to get the money, he won't try to disrupt the adoption agreement. And after I turn eighteen, I'll be a legal adult and can say where I want to live."

"Exactly."

"Wow, Mama. You're even smarter than I thought."

"Mostly, I was pretty motivated to get you and keep you."

"I'll be envious when I turn eighteen and my loser dad gets money."

"You'll get money, too."

Samantha turned sideways on the couch. "What?"

"When I opened the time-release account for him, I also opened one for you. I put twice as much money in the account for you."

"And I'll get that money? And I can do with it what I want?

Mama!" Samantha stood up and did a little dance. Unknown stood, as well, watching Samantha. Unknown tipped her head sideways, trying to figure out what was going on.

"Is all this—I don't know the right word—official? Like, let's just say the governor of California is unhappy with your work for him. You already said he could screw up your teaching job at UCLA. But he can't screw up us, right?"

"Correct. Our mother/daughter relationship is fixed by state law and official with the authorities. My lawyer has copies of everything. And all of my copies are in the filing cabinet with the elephant charms sitting on top."

"I don't remember seeing anything there," Samantha said. Then she added, "Not that I was spying on you. But when I was looking for where you put my school report, I looked in the cabinet."

"The adoption papers are in a folder marked, 'Class Notes - The Papacy and the Western Schism.'"

Samantha grinned and nodded. "You are good, Mama. Devious, but good. What kid would ever look for candy in a Western Schism?"

"Candy?"

"When my school report grades are all As, you let me buy whatever I want. Remember? Two years ago, you let me get a giant bag of M&Ms. Last year, chocolate elephants. So I just..."

Josie filled in, "You think of good grades as a bargaining chip?"

"Of course. Any kid would." Samantha turned and looked toward the filing cabinet. "But mostly I stay away from that file cabinet because if I ever bump it, the elephant charms tip over. I can never put them back exactly where they were, and then you would notice, and you would wonder."

Josie made a slow nod. "And you think I'm devious."

Samantha shrugged her shoulders and looked embarrassed.

Josie said, "The elephant charms started with Jabari."

Samantha turned and gave Josie a questioning look.

Josie stood up and walked over to the file cabinet. She

picked up one of the charms, brought it over, and handed it to Samantha.

"When Jabari first said I should be your mother, he gave me this elephant made of green glass. He said it was a symbol of the strengths of motherhood."

"Why an elephant?" Samantha asked as she turned the little sculpture over in her hands.

"He said that elephants are the most powerful and committed and devoted mothers in the animal kingdom. He saw me as having the same characteristics as an elephant mother."

"Is it true?" Samantha asked.

"I don't know about me. But I've read about elephants. They are amazing. Many predators look at baby elephant calves as a potential prize meal. Lions, tigers, hyenas. Even crocodiles. I hate to be graphic, but a baby elephant would feed an entire pride of lions. But if the mother elephant is healthy, predators mostly don't have a chance. An elephant mother will fight off any and all creatures that want to attack her calf."

"What if a bunch of lions come?"

"The other female elephants will join with the mother and surround the baby."

"How can an elephant fight lions? Lions have fangs and claws, and they can run super fast."

"True. But an elephant is so much bigger and stronger, they can easily kill a lion by stomping it. Elephants are also the smartest animal after humans, chimps, and dolphins. If lions pick a fight, they had better be prepared for a brilliant competitor. Intelligence usually wins over strength, and an elephant has both of those characteristics in greater quantity than a lion."

"Is that like you, Mama? Are you able to catch killers because you simply have more intelligence than they do?"

Josie made a little laugh. "Well, I don't have any brawn, so I better keep finding some way to track them down and subdue them."

Samantha looked out the window. It had gotten dark, which was a relative concept in Santa Monica. From their partial ocean view, they could see some of the sparkling lights on the ferris wheel on the Santa Monica Pier.

Josie could still imagine the complete darkness of Yosemite Park or Mary Jo's modern house in the foothills heading up to Tahoe. There was dark, and then there was real dark.

"You know what, Mama? Your smarts are pretty obvious. But I think the most important thing you've got going is your persistence. You just won't give up."

Josie realized that Samantha was right. Even Einstein had referred to the same thing in his famous, if apocryphal, quote that what often appears to be genius is mostly just persistence. The people who succeed the most are the people who try the hardest and never give up.

Josie sipped some wine.

The phone rang. It was Ellison.

"Hi Ellison," Josie answered.

"I'm sorry for calling late. But I wanted to give you some time to, you know… I'm just checking to see if everything is okay."

"Yes, everything is okay." Josie watched Samantha who had stood up and was bouncing on her toes. "Your timing is perfect. Sam and I were just talking about you."

"Did you tell her about me?"

"Yes."

"Does she hate me?"

"I'll let her tell you what she thinks." Josie handed the phone to Samantha.

Samantha took the phone and shrieked. "Oh my God, Ellison! I can't believe you're my grandpa! I'm so excited. This is the best news of my life!"

Josie could tell that Ellison was responding, but she couldn't hear the words.

Samantha said, "Tomorrow? Yes, of course! I'm on spring break. So I can go do any kind of stuff you want! But I don't know about how to do granddaughter stuff. Or even what that is." Samantha paused, thinking. "But Mama and I have some stuff we have to do for the governor." Samantha looked at Josie.

"Right, Mama?" She turned back to the phone. "I think we have to do some planning, and that will take time. What? Oh, let me give Mama the phone."

Samantha handed Josie the phone. "He wants to talk to you."

Josie spoke into the phone. "I meant to say thanks."

"For…?"

"Everything. You were right on all fronts." Josie looked at Samantha. "My darling daughter already knew Jabari's name and other aspects of her past."

"Glad it worked out," Ellison said. "Now I have another thought. Samantha mentioned your current governor's project."

"Yes. It appears that we can't count on law enforcement to save Elena Soto, the young woman who we think is trapped in an old abbey in the Sierra foothills. So we may have to break into the abbey and rescue her ourselves."

"I may be hopelessly deluded about any help I could provide. But I'd like the opportunity. And I have a good meeting space. Some of your potential helpers, such as Cumberland, already live here. And, not to engage in too much hyperbole, Samantha may want to look at this place anew now that she has a clearer picture of the world around her. So why not meet here? Morning works for me."

"I'm expecting an update from Cor in the morning. After that would be good."

"I'll look for you any time."

THIRTY-TWO

Amelia got home late, shortly before Josie and Samantha were going to bed. Before Josie fell asleep, she could hear Samantha and Amelia making loud, excited comments about the news of Ellison's relationship to Samantha.

The next morning, Amelia was up before them. She had made coffee. A new blend, she said. She poured both Josie and Samantha a cup.

Before Josie had taken her first sip, Cor called.

"I covered for Diane yesterday. She's back on the job this morning. So I can meet."

"That would be great. I want to figure out how to rescue Elena Soto."

"The woman trapped at the abbey. We'll make an extraction plan for her."

"Meaning how to go into the abbey and take her out."

"Yeah."

"Do you know the best way?" Josie asked.

"There is no best way. We examine the territory, consider our priorities, discuss our options."

"Okay. That would be great. I'm wondering if you'd be willing to meet at Ellison's. He wants to help. You met him at the hospital in San Francisco."

"We didn't just meet. While you were recovering in the hospital, Samanatha arranged for Ellison and me to caravan together up to San Fran from L.A. at Christmas. Remember? Ellison and Cumberland and his young siblings and Amelia, too?"

"Oh, right. Sorry. My brain was not functioning very well while I was at the hospital. Anyway, Ellison's place is in Montebello, east of downtown. You can meet us there, if you like."

"Where are you now?"

"Home," Josie said.

"I'm nearby, so I'll pick you up. Twenty minutes? Maybe less."

"Perfect. In case you're hauling things in your Jeep, I should let you know that Amelia may want to come, too. With Unknown, that might be crowded in your Jeep."

"Not at all. And less crowded than your car."

"Okay," Josie said.

They clicked off.

Josie turned to Samantha and Amelia. "Cor is driving us to Ellison's." Josie looked at Amelia. "I told Cor you might come, as well. But only if you want to, of course."

"I want to help. Whatever you plan to do, I'll help."

"You have your job…"

"You're trying to save a woman who is in danger, right? Helping with that is more important than my job. And anyway, I have six vacation days saved up. They can usually adjust the work schedule. I'll call and ask them."

Josie reached over and squeezed Amelia's hand. "Thank you."

Amelia nodded and took her phone out on the balcony. She came back inside in a couple of minutes. "They're fine with it. The assistant manager will rearrange the schedule." Amelia walked into the kitchen and filled a thermos with her coffee. She put it and some food items into a small backpack.

Samantha was looking out the deck slider door. "Cor just pulled up," she announced.

They quickly gathered their things and went down the stairs and out to Cor's Jeep.

Samantha picked up Unknown and squeezed into the back seat. Amelia joined her. Josie got in front. She was still buckling her belt when Cor accelerated away.

When they were on the 10 freeway, Cor put an earpiece in one ear, then touched her phone, which sat in the dashboard holder. The phone came to life. Cor tapped some buttons and hit the call button. After a moment, she began talking.

Josie knew that Cor wouldn't mind Josie overhearing what she said. Otherwise, she wouldn't have placed the call. But there was too much road noise to hear much.

The conversation went on for a few minutes. Then Cor clicked off.

"Diane Day's morning class was her only one today, so she's going to join us at Ellison's."

Josie was surprised and a bit concerned that Cor invited Diane without talking to Josie first. No doubt, Cor knew Diane could be helpful. But Josie was uneasy about having too many people involved in planning something that might require them to operate covertly.

Josie said, "Do you think Diane won't mind helping?"

"No. This is her field. She has a phrase for it. The emancipation of women. When she hears about a woman under threat, she goes into superhero mode. Look out bad boys. Diane Day gonna kick your ass."

"She uses self-defense skills?"

Cor was nodding her head rhythmically as if to a song no one else could hear.

"She uses whatever seems appropriate."

"When you first mentioned her some time ago, I think you said she was really small."

"Like a little wildflower. Emphasis on wild. Even if people didn't underestimate her, which, natch, is a bonus for her in any situation, she still would surprise. If Diane comes after you and you want to stop her, you pretty much have to shoot first."

THIRTY-THREE

Josie directed Cor through Montebello to Ralph Ellison's warehouse loft. Samantha and Unknown ran ahead, taking the stairs two at a time. Amelia stayed back with Josie and Cor. Josie knew the young woman could probably trot up the steps at a fast rate, even if nothing like Samantha. But Amelia knew how to be winning, even ingratiating. She and Cor matched Josie's pace going up the long flights.

They heard laughter and shrieking from up above.

Cor looked at Josie and frowned.

"Sam and Ellison's first hug since the grandpa revelation," Josie said.

"Say that again?" Cor said.

"Ralph Ellison learned years ago that he might possibly be Samantha's grandfather."

"Oh, I can see a fractured family coming from a long way out."

Josie nodded. She gave Cor the basics of the situation. "Samantha just found out last evening."

"Ah. A big deal, that." Cor looked at Amelia's backpack. "You're bringing food?"

"Alphajores," Amelia answered. "Cinnamon flavored Peruvian cookies. I went to my friend Alejandra's place, and we made these cookies for Dia de los Muertos, and they were very popular at work."

"Day of the Dead?" Cor said.

"Yes, a treat for our past ancestors and relatives and friends."

Josie was huffing as they turned up the last flight of stairs. More shrieking came from above.

"And the thermos?" Josie said. "I noticed you making more

coffee this morning after we'd already had the first pot."

"It was that last Arabica roasting I did in your oven. I'm trying a new technique. It's not as bitter as you might be used to in the big coffee houses."

"Sounds good," Josie said.

They came to the top of the last flight. The big sliding warehouse door was open.

Inside, Samantha and Ellison were doing some kind of dance.

When Josie and Amelia finally walked through the big door, Samantha was next to the statue of Athena. She held Ellison's hands and danced him around in a circle, pulling him with her.

She turned to Josie. "Mama, Ellison says I should still call him Ellison. He said the only other choice is Geezer Gramps Wannabe. What do you think?"

"The Geezer Wannabe concept is compelling. But I'd probably stick with plain old Ellison."

"Then Ellison it is!" She spun him the opposite direction. "Turns out my grandfather can…" She looked at Ellison. "What did you call dancing?"

"Cut a rug."

Samantha spun, then jumped toward him. Ellison caught her with a bit of a grunt, held her up in a hug, and turned in a circle.

Josie grinned with delight at their enjoyment. "Sam, you might want to…" Josie stopped herself. Any comment about whether Ellison could be so physical without injury would sound bad to both him and Samantha.

Ellison set her down. He was breathing hard.

Samantha picked up Unknown. "C'mon, Unknown, let's go upstairs and see Cumberland and look at the view."

Unknown didn't like the metal-grate stairway because it was hard on her paws. Samantha carried her up the stairs to the loft.

Without stepping forward, Cor leaned into the door opening and looked in and up at the big space. Amelia stood a step back and watched. Josie saw Cor scan the high ceiling of glass, the metal staircase that led to the loft, and the rolling metal cabinets and counters that comprised the kitchen. Cor's eyes came to the Athena sculpture. Her look traveled from the base of the sculpture up to Athena's crown, which was bathed in light from the glass ceiling above.

"Meet Athena," Josie said. "Goddess of Wisdom."

Cor had a look in her eyes that Josie hadn't seen before. Maybe it was awe.

"This is where you live, Ellison?" Cor asked.

"Yes, come on in."

The three women walked in. Cor lagged behind, doing a full rotation as she looked around the loft.

"Ellison, you remember Cor Kontos."

"Yes, of course. She came with us to San Francisco last Christmas."

Ellison stepped forward and shook Cor's hand.

Cor said, "I'm trying to remember. I don't think I call you Mr. Ellison, correct?"

Ellison nodded. "If you just call me Ellison, I'll feel significantly more comfortable than that Mr. Ralph Ellison fellow ever feels."

Cor smiled. "I get it. When I'm called Ms. Kontos or, God forbid, ma'am, I'm likely to put someone in an arm lock or face down on the floor."

Ellison pointed at the Combat Action Badge on her sleeveless shirt. "Army," he said.

Cor nodded. "Twenty years. You?"

"Six."

She paused. "Vietnam?"

"Tail end of it, yeah."

"Don't let his reticence fool you," Josie said. "He was serious about it."

Amelia stood nearby.

"Ellison, you remember our friend Amelia Gomez. She also came with you to San Francisco at Christmas."

"Yes, she of the mouth-watering cookies."

Amelia's eyes crinkled with delight. "Does the last-name-only thing apply to kids like me?"

"Yes, please," Ellison said.

Amelia gave him the huge smile that Josie had learned was an amazing social lubricant. Amelia wasn't beautiful, but people melted when she smiled. She took her cookie container out of her backpack and handed it to him. "Alphajores for you."

Ellison beamed and carried the container over to the big stainless-steel rolling counter. Amelia followed and put her coffee thermos next to them.

Amelia said, "The name Ralph Ellison seems familiar. Aren't you famous or something?"

"Or something," Ellison said.

Josie said, "The famous Ralph Ellison from long ago was an author. And this Ralph, named for the earlier Ralph, is a remarkable man in more ways than I can count."

"I remember now," Amelia said. "English class. Bakersfield high school. It's coming back to me. The book was Invisible Man! Am I right?"

"Indeed," Ellison said.

Amelia put on her biggest smile.

"Feel free to check out the loft and the view of downtown," Ellison said. "I'll take your backpack."

"Thank you." Amelia trotted up the long flight to the loft.

Josie turned to Cor, who was once again standing back, her head cranked up to look at the Athena sculpture.

Ellison walked toward the big sliding door, which was still open.

"Another woman is coming," Cor said. "Diane Day, my fellow self-defense teacher. I called her as we got to your building. She told me she'd be fifteen or sixteen minutes late."

"Not just late, but 'fifteen or sixteen minutes late?'" Ellison said. He showed no surprise at the addition of another person.

Cor nodded. "Correct."

Ellison looked at his watch. "Such precise timing reminds me of my days in the military."

"Diane Day is ex-military like me."

Ellison nodded. "I'll leave the gate open." As Ellison turned, he glanced up toward the loft. Josie followed his gaze.

Samantha and Amelia were talking, possibly even to Cumberland, whose corner chair was out of sight from down below. Although Josie suspected that Cumberland was lost in his computer. Samantha's and Amelia's voices were audible, exclaiming the delights of the view toward downtown Los Angeles in the distance.

Ellison spoke to Josie and Cor in a soft voice. "This young woman, Amelia Gomez... When we spoke at the volleyball game, you said she's living with you?"

Josie nodded. "She and her roommates lost their apartment. So we let her move in with us and sleep in Samantha's room. It's not long term. Months, I think. She insists on paying the same rent that she paid for her room in her previous apartment."

"You know her well?"

Josie couldn't tell if his tone was disapproving or just worried.

Josie shook her head. "No. But she's kind and generous and steady and very hard-working. A positive influence on Sam, I think. It's good for Sam to get to know others who haven't had so many advantages, especially someone as ambitious as Amelia."

"I'm a good character read," Cor said. "I say Amelia's personality has legs. Reliable. Long term."

It was a moment before Ellison responded. He looked at Cor as he spoke. "I know Cor is ex-military. So she's all about discretion. But regarding the things you told me that the governor is requesting, plans you have that are—how shall I say—somewhat surreptitious, you trust Amelia not to talk about them?"

"Completely," Josie answered. "Amelia is a Dreamer child from Peru, undocumented. She grew up here since ten years of age. So she really only knows this country. We have the benefit of growing up here and being successful. But she lives much further outside of the mainstream than we do. As you heard, she speaks English like you and me. She has no formal education beyond high school. Her family has nearly disowned her because she dared to leave the migrant farm community in Bakersfield and come to Los Angeles. Being brown and female and without citizenship is a huge obstacle to getting ahead. Amelia's very survival requires discretion."

"Does Amelia fit the requirements of the Dream Act?" Ellison asked. He added, "I don't trust the politicians who are mostly demagogues and would throw kids under the bus to keep their voters happy. And, hence, keep their jobs."

"I think so, but I haven't talked to her very much about it. She's very forthright about her parents bringing her to the U.S. illegally when she was ten. They paid most of their savings to a coyote smuggler who packed them into a truck and drove them north, where he dumped them at the Texas border in the middle of the night. They waded and swam across the Rio Grande in the dark and connected with another coyote who trucked them to a town where ranchers come every day to find laborers. Eventually, they came to California's Central Valley where they had some relatives working in the orchards. I think the Dream Act makes it so that she can gain permanent resident status after she fulfills the various requirements. Down the road, citizenship is a definite possibility."

Josie leaned her back against the wall, her hands clasped behind her, a thinking position she'd developed at UCLA. "What I've seen so far is that she works harder than anyone I know. She has a barista job that is more than full time, and she's planning to start a coffee shop and roasting company. She spends all of her free time working on her plan. She never hangs out, she never spends time on social media. Sam and I have to beg her to watch a Netflix movie with us. She would rather be reading her library books on business. You should see her notes. Multiple pads of paper filled with business analysis. She saves all her money and doesn't even have a phone because she says they're too expensive."

"Kind of like you in her focus," Ellison said.

"More so." Josie looked up at the Athena sculpture, feeling that it represented a role model for ambitious women.

"Do you think she can help you with this task the governor

has given you? When you go into battle, the details of your plans have to be kept top-secret."

Josie understood Ellison's skepticism as a holdover from his military days.

"In the short time Amelia has lived with us, she's been a help in everything we do. She will, no doubt, help with this project, too. And she keeps Sam centered and focused. So yes. Whatever role she takes on, she will do well. Perhaps more than anything else, she is a good role model for Sam."

Ellison smiled.

Cor said, "If mom says something, it's sometimes dismissed. But if someone not much older than Samantha says the same thing, it gets through."

"Exactly."

"How old is Amelia?" Ellison asked.

"Nineteen. Five years older than Sam."

The sound of footsteps echoed up the stairs outside the door. They all turned and saw a small-but-sturdy blonde woman with hair cut short like Cor's but curly instead of spiky. Unlike Cor, she had no visible tattoos. Like Cor, she wore Army green jeans but without the camo pattern.

"Hey, Diane," Cor said. "C'mon in."

Ellison looked at his watch.

"Exactly fifteen minutes," he said.

THIRTY-FOUR

Cor made introductions. Diane was polite but not warm as she shook hands with Ellison and then Josie.

After minimal chat, Ellison said, "We should get to the task at hand."

He walked over to the long, rolling, metal table that he used as a dining table, conference table, and very large desk. He rolled the table over near the Athena sculpture, reached out with the toe of his shoe, and pressed the brake levers on two of the wheels.

Josie called up toward the loft. "Sam? Amelia? Time to come down."

Samantha called back, "You want Cumberland to join us?"

"Yes, of course. I wasn't sure he was up there."

Diane walked over to a stack of conference chairs. Although Josie knew from experience that the chairs were heavy, Diane lifted them three at a time and positioned them at the table. Josie thought to help but realized that Diane probably preferred to have a task to herself. Diane spread six chairs around the table.

Amelia and Samantha came down the stairs. Samantha carried Unknown.

Josie said, "I want you both to meet Cor's friend Diane Day."

The two young women shook Day's hand. They were all a study in contrast. Colors, builds, heights, ages, hair styles.

Josie turned to Ellison. "Are Aiden and Cara in school?" she asked, even though she assumed they were.

Ellison answered. "Yeah. Big bro Cumberland will walk them home after school. That is, if he can tear himself away from his computer." Ellison glanced up toward the loft. "That guy can spend more time looking at a computer screen in a day or two than I have in my entire life." Ellison paused. "But for the money he makes, I guess that's to be expected. Now if only he would get organized about his finances. His payments get deposited in some kind of brokerage account. When I asked him about it, he didn't know any of the details. So he printed out some pages and showed me. They revealed big dollar amounts. I said he should pay attention and at least keep track of his balances. He shrugged and put the sheets in a cardboard box under his bed. I'm fine with him living here, but I was, frankly, wondering if he had an idea of how to find a house where he and his siblings could eventually live. So I asked what his plan was for dealing with his money. He said he didn't know what to do with money."

Ellison held his hands out, palms up, fingers outstretched, the question still on his face. Then he walked over to his kitchen area and opened his fridge. He pulled out a pack of pre-washed carrots, a glass that held six-inch celery sticks standing up in a quarter inch of water, and a bowl of raw broccoli florets that had been sliced in half. Ellison cut open the plastic carrot bag and dumped the carrots into a bowl. He set all the veggies on the big table. As Josie watched, she realized how he stayed so fit and trim. Veggies and stairways. She should use him as her role model.

Over at the wall was a metal cabinet the height of an armoire. He pulled out a box of Saltines, a bag of corn chips, a jar of peanuts, and set them on the table. He looked at the assembled foods, went back to the fridge, and removed a jar of salsa. He picked up a stack of paper napkins and another bowl and set them next to the veggies and salsa.

"Is it okay if I help with glasses?" Josie said.

"Please do."

Josie got glasses and filled a pitcher with water. Then she found coffee mugs and brought them to the table.

Cor was talking to Ellison.

Josie couldn't hear all the words. Ellison said something about how multiple tours meant a serious commitment. And

Cor said something like six years was serious as well.

"How serious was he?" Samantha said as if announcing to an audience in a theater. "I'll tell you." She started singing in a dramatic and unnaturally-low voice, the beats of music matching her feet on the stairs. "'Fighting Soldiers from the sky. Fearless men who jump and die.'"

"Green Beret?" Cor said to Ellison. "Let me shake your hand again. We had some Special Forces guys working with us in Afghanistan. I was impressed with their focus."

Diane Day stepped toward Ellison and high-fived him.

"I'm just a regular guy," Ellison said in an awkward voice.

"A regular Green Beret guy who sculpts," Samantha said, grinning.

"Now I'm an embarrassed regular guy," Ellison said. He looked at Samantha and then at Cor and Diane. "I'm surprised you both know the Green Beret song, considering that you're about forty or fifty years too young."

"Sadler's song has deep roots," Cor said. "I've even read some of his books. Gladiator stuff, but really fun. But how do you know the song, Sam?"

"I didn't learn it until I met Ellison," Samantha said. She added, "And I didn't even know what a Green Beret was until Mama told me about Ellison."

Diane Day had been standing quietly nearby. Ellison glanced at her. She gestured toward the Athena sculpture. "You made that?"

"I'm a blacksmith, and I have a metal fabrication shop. So I fiddle a bit in my spare time."

Diane Day made a slow nod. "More than fiddling, I'd say. It's kind of got a certain look. What's that called?"

Ellison shrugged. "I was looking at a lot of classical Greek sculpture when I made it," Ellison said.

"Cor Kontos is Greek," Day said, gesturing toward Cor.

Ellison said, "I thought Kontos might be Greek. What about the name Cor?"

"Short for Corinthia," Cor said. "It's a place in Greece."

Ellison frowned. "If I remember correctly, that's kind of near the epicenter of western sculpture."

"Those ancient Greeks figured out a lot of stuff," Cor said. "Too bad I was such a screwup as a kid. Maybe I've got sculpting in my genes. Maybe I coulda been a contender."

Ellison seemed to think for a moment. "The director of On The Waterfront, Elia Kazan, was Greek, right?" Ellison said.

"Oh, God," Cor said. "You not only know the movie with the quote, you know the director. So you're a film-literate, embarrassed, regular, Green Beret, sculpting guy."

"But I didn't try making art until my mid-fifties, so I've got a lot to learn."

"You give me hope," Cor said.

Ellison turned to Diane Day. "Josie told me you and Cor teach self-defense to women. Do you show them street-fighting techniques, or weapons, or..."

"Mostly we focus on recognizing and avoiding dangerous situations," Day said. "When we get physical, I show them some moves based on Pencak Silat."

"Is that the Indonesian stuff?" Ellison asked.

"Yeah."

For a moment, no one spoke.

Josie gestured at the chairs. "Let's all sit at the table," she said.

Ellison called up toward the loft. "Yo, Cumberland Durand. Got your lunch, here." Ellison set the box of Saltines and a Diet Coke in front of one of the chairs. They took chairs at the table. Ellison ended up between Diane Day and Josie.

"Some guys," Ellison said to Day as he pointed to the Saltines and Coke, "are rigorous about getting a healthy diet."

Cumberland ambled down the stairs.

Ellison turned the other way and whispered to Josie. "At least, he's fully dressed today."

Cumberland walked over and sat in front of the Saltines. He was frumpy, his wrinkled jeans sagging with no belt to hold them up, navy shirttails hanging out from beneath a gray sweatshirt, shoes untied, his hair disheveled and hanging down over his pale skin like the rock-star model he could have been.

He didn't look at any of the others.

"Cumberland," Josie said, "you know everyone here except for Diane Day, who's a friend and business partner of Cor."

Maybe Cumberland made a little nod of acknowledgment, but Josie couldn't tell.

Unknown walked over to Cumberland. She looked up at him, looked around at the other people, then sat down next to Cumberland and watched him. It was as if she'd realized that the greatest likelihood of dropped crumbs would come from him. Or maybe, Josie thought, Unknown sensed a camaraderie with Cumberland, an outsider among people the way she was an outsider among dogs.

Amelia passed her container of cookies around, then lifted up the thermos and walked around the table. She offered coffee, and everyone took a cup except Cumberland. Everyone ate.

"What are these amazing cookies?" Cor said.

"Alfajores," Josie said. "A Peruvian specialty. Last winter, Amelia baked them for Navidad. And for the Day of the Dead."

"And the coffee?" Ellison asked.

Amelia answered. "My personal blend. I roast the Arabica beans and grind them with a tiny bit of pepper and cinnamon."

"You make this yourself?" Cor asked.

"Sí."

"Wow," Cor said. "I understand why you're going to open a coffee house."

Amelia turned to Samantha and Josie and gave them a high-wattage smile.

"That's her eventual plan," Josie said.

"I don't have much," Cor said, "but I'll be an investor if you need that."

Ellison set his cup down and licked his lips. "Me too."

Amelia's grin grew, and her eyes moistened.

They ate cookies and sipped coffee. The celery sticks and carrots and broccoli sat lonely on the table, only Ellison eating them.

Ellison spoke. "Before we get into the intricacies of what we're here to do, I'm thinking Josie should give us all an outline of the problem and her proposed solution."

"The problem, I can outline," Josie said. "The solution is something I'm hoping you all can help me figure out." She turned to Cumberland. "Cumberland, you said you could project my pictures on your computer screen."

He nodded. "I'll use Ellison's TV screen. It has a better picture." Cumberland was chewing Saltines as he answered. He reached out his hand.

Josie unlocked her phone with its password, and handed it to him.

Cumberland tapped further, then handed it back. "The photos will transfer when you touch them."

"Great. Thanks." Josie turned to the others. "You all mostly know how this problem started. Back before Christmas, the governor asked me to find the killer of his friend's son-in-law, Ranger Francis Telman. To the best of my knowledge, we didn't succeed. However, during our investigation, the ranger's wife, Mary Jo Telman, was killed by a sniper. Sam and I came under fire as well. After investigating Mary Jo Telman's companies, which are rest homes owned by limited liability companies, we learned of a young woman who worked as a chef for one of the rest homes. Her name is Elena Soto. She agreed to cook at a spiritual retreat. Elena's mother felt that part of her motivation was to get away from the constant attentions of one of Elena's bosses, a man named Lucas Herman. Lucas told Elena he'd been a sniper. The man talked about his guns, and he wanted to show them to Elena. It was, to say the least, peculiar, trying to impress a girl by showing her his guns.

"When we spoke to Elena's mother, she gave us a phone number she'd gotten from Elena's phone, a number connected to many of the calls Elena received. Cumberland was able to identify that number as belonging to Lucas Herman."

Josie noticed that when she mentioned Cumberland's name, he showed no reaction and continued to focus on his Saltines and Coke.

"Because of what we heard about Lucas and his guns, we tracked Lucas. We were able to do that with a high degree of accuracy by using a special phone that Cumberland provided us. We followed Lucas to San Francisco and observed him at an apartment near Fisherman's Wharf. He was showing multiple rifles to another man he met at the Wharf. So we set up a snare trap, which ultimately led to catching the man with Lucas. Lucas saw me and chased me to the Wharf. The police came, and he was taken into custody.

"He was denied bail. While in a prisoner transport van, the van exploded in a freak accident. His death looked suspicious. So the governor asked me to reinvestigate and see if anyone else is involved. What we've found so far is that the two guards who were transporting Lucas Herman were recently shot and killed. Their roommate, a man named Snake, disappeared. Cumberland found out that Snake was dishonorably discharged from the Army. Prior to that, he had also been in the Army's sniper program."

Josie paused and drank coffee.

"A convoluted plot," Ellison said, shaking his head.

Josie nodded. She brought up an aerial photo of mountains and forest.

It showed up very clear and bright on Ellison's TV.

Josie continued her explanation. "Cumberland found an abbey in the mountains that Mary Jo Telman, the sniper victim, owned by way of another limited liability company. The abbey was built decades ago by a San Francisco woman named Doris Russo who built it for a religious order called the Sisters Of Frangelica. You can see the abbey near the center of this photo. It looks like an ancient Roman villa. Columns and promenades and cloisters. Very dramatic. Let me zoom in more. You'll see that the abbey has a roofed portico similar to what one would find at a hotel so that you can have cover during rain. And over here is a parking area with room for four or five cars." Josie pulled a laser pointer out of her purse and pointed with it.

"A big place," Ellison said.

"Yes, it is," Josie said.

Amelia's eyes were wide. "We learned something about Doris Russo in school. I think she built her abbey near something called the Sierra Maze?"

"Yes. Hundreds of years ago, the Miwok Indians created an ancient stone maze with various paths. Not unlike a Christian labyrinth in churches like Chartres Cathedral in France. However, the Christian versions were not mazes but meditative walking paths all set in a circle. In contrast, this was a maze made of stone walls that were four or five feet tall. And the Sisters grew hedges and vines that added height to the stone walls."

"Wow. It still exists," Amelia said.

"Yes," Josie said. "Good memory. Unfortunately, Doris Russo's endowment ran out, and the sisters were unable to keep the abbey. They disbanded. The abbey was put up for sale, and it was bought by an LLC owned by Mary Jo Telman."

Ellison asked, "What did Telman do with the abbey?"

"I don't know for certain what goes on at this abbey, but I suspect it is used in connection with a drug sales network, where Telman's nursing homes over-prescribe drugs for their residents. Those excess drugs are probably sold on the street, and I'm guessing the money is collected at the abbey. From there, the money is laundered through a casino and laundromats that Telman LLCs own.

"Sam and I chartered a plane and flew over the abbey. Two men pointed rifles at our plane. We don't know for certain, but we believe the abbey is also the so-called spiritual retreat where we think Elena Soto is being held against her will."

Ellison asked, "Do you have reason to think that the people at this abbey are violent?"

"After those men pointed their rifles at our plane, yes. And it fits with the violence of the man named Lucas."

"Mama!" Samantha suddenly said. "I just realized that one of those men with rifles was wearing what looked like a multi-colored, long-sleeved shirt. I thought one sleeve was light and the other was dark. But maybe the dark arm wasn't a sleeve! Maybe it was the sniper guy from Monterey, the guy named Snake who had a dark tattoo of a snake going up his arm!"

Josie felt a sudden revulsion. "I think you're right, Sam. Connecting Snake directly to the abbey pulls these components into a tighter circle."

"Yes. And there was another murder that I haven't yet mentioned. The missing woman, Elena Soto, has a father named Juan. He was recently killed by a sniper near Donner Summit." Josie sipped coffee.

She continued, "Two days ago, Cor hiked to the abbey, which is in a wilderness area and is fenced and gated. Cor approached the back side and saw a woman wearing a white cook's apron and hat come out of a service door. It would appear that the woman in the cook's apron is Elena Soto. Cor whistled and waved from a good distance away. The woman's response was to pull out her flashlight and flash a Morse Code SOS at Cor. Then the cook was interrupted by a man, and she had to go back inside the abbey."

Josie tapped on her phone and brought up another photo.

"So this Elena Soto woman," Ellison said, "appears to be held captive. Do you have an idea of why that might be?"

"I think she was simply kidnapped to do forced labor." Josie felt her eyes tear. "I desperately hope she is not forced to do anything else."

"Mary Jo Telman was killed by a sniper," Ellison said. "Any idea why she would be targeted?"

Josie nodded. "I can only surmise. My best guess would be that someone wanted that cash flow. In the big picture of drug sales, this is likely a small operation. But it still might generate many millions each year. By killing Mary Jo, a person could try to take over the business. One thing Sam and I heard was that the rest home employees get most of their instructions and guidance through a morning email. It made me think that Mary Jo could run her business remotely. It's even possible that most of her employees had never met her. Maybe her only face-to-face contact was with a few lieutenants, so to speak.

"It seems possible that if someone had access to Mary Jo's passwords, they could kill her and move into her role, continuing to issue morning emails and trying to run the business the way

Mary Jo had. With little or no in-person contact, employees would continue to do their jobs, and they might never know that the person in charge had been killed and replaced. Of course, in order for the killer to benefit, he would have to know how to get into Mary Jo's bank account. But that could also be done online. It's possible that someone found where Mary Jo kept her password book. That might list Mary Jo's passwords for her email as well as her bank accounts."

Cor said, "So the killer had to take out the husband, Francis Telman, first, because, as a cop, he would know what was going on the moment Mary Jo was killed. He might even realize who the killer was."

"I think so, yes," Josie said. "Later, the killer might kill Elena Soto's father, Juan Soto, simply because he kept pestering them for information about Elena. Maybe he learned incriminating information in the process."

Josie looked up at the screen. "This shot shows the abbey from higher up. Notice that the area to the east is covered by snowpack, whereas the abbey and the area to the west are lower, so the snow has melted. The snow gave me an idea of how the killings could be connected." Josie brought up a new photo, this one from a Google satellite photo.

"In the center of this photo, I've drawn a circle showing the abbey's location, just north of the town of Kyburz. It's hard to tell by looking at the photo, but Kyburz is down in the American River Canyon, and the abbey is in the mountains above the town."

Josie shifted the picture on the screen.

"The right side of this picture shows Emerald Bay at Lake Tahoe. That is where Ranger Francis Telman was shot and killed. I've also drawn a circle on the lower left part of the photo, an area near Placerville, which is a foothill town down below Kyburz. The area where Mary Jo Telman was killed by a sniper was near that town.

"Cor found the sniper's nest in the foothills, where the sniper lay when he fired the shots that killed Mary Jo and nearly killed Sam and me. In a boot print at that nest, I found a bug that possibly connects the sites of where Francis and Mary Jo Telman were killed and the site of the abbey. An entomologist in Tahoe identified the bug as a snow scorpionfly, an insect that is found at high elevations such as in Tahoe, thus providing a possible connection between Mary Jo's killing and Francis's killing miles away and at a much higher elevation." Josie paused to think through her timeline.

"One of the puzzles about the ranger's death at Emerald Bay was that the killer got to Emerald Bay in a stolen car, which he left there. Then he stole back-country skis from near Telman's cabin. But those ski tracks led up into the mountains. I wondered why a killer would head up into the mountains in the middle of winter. By studying topographical maps, I realized that if the killer was able to ski up to the crest of the Sierra, it would be a continuous downhill run of about fifteen miles to get to where the snow cover ended."

"Which was near the abbey," Ellison said.

"Yes."

Diane Day had been quiet up to this point. "You're suggesting the bug could connect Emerald Bay at Tahoe to the town of Placerville, and the snow could connect Emerald Bay to the abbey."

"Yes. It only suggests a connection. I could be wrong."

"But the idea suggests an action."

"Yes," Josie said, pleased that Diane Day was engaged.

"And that action is…" Ellison said.

"I called the sergeant on the El Dorado County Sheriff's department. He's the man who investigated the shooting of Mary Jo Telman. I explained all of these connections and told him about the men at the abbey who pointed rifles at the plane we charted. He said there was nothing they could do. They can't even go over the abbey's fence without specific evidence of a crime. He thought that no matter how much sense my speculation made, there was no way he could get a search warrant. And with the abbey fenced off, they can't even get to the front door and knock."

Cor spoke up, "But the professor has an idea of how to do

what the cops can't, right?"

Josie made a single nod. "I was recently talking to a very wise painter I know and respect. She is peaceful, like her Chumash Indian ancestors. But when I told her about my situation and asked her opinion about what to do, she said that the likelihood that Elena is being held captive means it's time to breach the ramparts and storm the castle."

THIRTY-FIVE

Ellison looked thoughtful, but worried as well. "You want to break into the abbey?"

Josie nodded. "I think the answers will be found at the abbey. But breaking in would be asking to get killed, in addition to being a flagrant crime in itself. Instead, I want to drive the workers out of the abbey and do it quickly enough that they don't have time to think clearly."

Ellison said, "So this wouldn't be a home invasion. But anything that would drive them all out fast sounds like a war. Not that I mind."

"I mind. But it helps me that in medieval history, there are antecedents for this. The philosopher Saint Thomas Aquinas, who was possibly the first medieval superstar, wrote about the concept of a Just War. He justified the very thing I'm proposing."

Samantha rolled her eyes. "Professor speak, Mama. Can you cut to the essence?"

"If we can drive the men out of the abbey and do it with enough surprise that they don't have time to plan how they flee, that will expose what they're doing."

Samantha said, "What do you think would happen to Elena if we drive everyone out?"

"The men would want to take her. But if our actions force them to hurry, they might not have enough time to consider how to keep her under their control."

"Meaning she might escape," Samantha said.

There was a moment of silence.

"Do you have a medieval approach on this?" Ellison asked.

"I think so," Josie said. "Warriors in the middle ages didn't always fight with swords and bows and arrows. There were other ways to make people abandon the castle. One obvious way is fire. But that has substantial downsides, including potentially fatal risk to the occupants, including Elena."

Ellison raised a single eyebrow. "You have an idea that isn't obvious?"

"I think so. But I'm going to need help figuring it out and more help implementing it."

THIRTY-SIX

"I'm thinking of something that is slower and less deadly than fire, but nearly as compelling."

Josie felt an intense gaze from all but Cumberland.

Josie put a new photo up on the screen. "Here is the abbey, and this black line is the wrought-iron fence and gate around it. As you can see, it isn't easy to get to the abbey's exterior without climbing the fence." She used the cursor to point at the photo.

"Here is the gravel drive that comes down from this old logging road. This area is for parking. There was only one vehicle there as this photo was taken, but the tracks suggest as many as five vehicles commonly park there."

Josie put up another photo.

"Some distance to the north is the maze. It's obscured by the hedges that the sisters planted. But the important thing I want to show you is this wide, light gray line on the east side of the photo." Josie pointed with her cursor. "It's several feet wide, and it makes a series of gentle turns."

"I love it," Ellison said. "You want to dam up a concrete water canal."

"Yes. There are several of these throughout this part of the foothills, all bringing water to the various reservoirs." Josie zoomed out another notch. "I don't think it would be easy to dam. But a flood could be a very effective way to get the abbey's occupants to flee."

Josie moved her cursor. "If you look closely at these topographical lines, you'll see that the water in the concrete canal flows toward the south at about forty-eight hundred feet of elevation. The abbey sits at about forty-six hundred feet. Now look at these A-shaped topo lines where the top of the A is at higher elevation than the lines farther down. That shows a ravine, in this case a gentle ravine." Josie moved her cursor back and forth as she talked. "If we could dam up the canal in this area, the water would flow down toward the abbey."

Cor stood up and walked over to the TV screen. "If that's the case, doesn't that suggest that even a heavy rain would send water into the abbey?"

"Yes, however rain that falls on a gentle ravine probably seeps into the ground rather than running to the abbey. Also, most buildings have some drain channels to direct water. Even most small houses have gutters and downspouts and channels to direct water away from the house."

Josie moved the cursor.

"My thought is that damming the canal here, or here, would direct a large amount of water down toward the abbey, hopefully overwhelming whatever water mitigation the abbey designers put into the building. I'm thinking the water collected and directed into concrete canals is probably much more than heavy rain."

Josie pointed to another area on the photo.

"I can't be sure, but the drive is probably designed to drain water away. Maybe we could interfere with that."

THIRTY-SEVEN

Ellison stood up, walked over to the TV screen, and looked at the photo up close. Unknown turned away from Cumberland to look at Ellison.

Cumberland said, "The main drainage mitigation at the abbey is a culvert next to the driveway, just above the gate."

The group turned to look at Cumberland.

"What makes you say that?" Josie asked.

"I got the building plans from the county." Cumberland clicked and tapped on his laptop. The plans replaced Josie's photo on Ellison's TV screen. Cumberland reached over and pointed. "If you get much of the canal water to flow toward the abbey, it might be diverted by this culvert. But if the culvert could be plugged with a log or something, it would make the flood much more effective."

"How did you know to get those plans?" Cor asked.

"I didn't until the question just came up. So I looked in the county's building records."

"You hacked into the county."

"Yeah." Cumberland tapped on his computer's touch pad. The building plan went away and the previous picture came back on the screen.

"And you're in their system right now," Cor said. "Like a second-story burglar or something."

"Yeah."

Cor made a long, slow shake of her head.

"I like this idea," Ellison said. "It would take a big flood to make a big impression. If they just find a wet floor, they'll assume there's a plumbing leak, put down some towels, and go back to bed. But if we could make them think a river was flowing through their abbey… That would be something! But the abbey is big. The concrete ditch may be shallow. Do you think there's enough water to do the job?"

Josie nodded. "I looked up concrete water canals. Their carrying capacity varies considerably. Based on the photo, this canal is about five feet wide. I did some calculations and got many figures. But my best guess is that, considering it is now spring and we have a lot of snowmelt, this canal carries tens of thousands of gallons an hour. One of my calculations suggested seventy-thousand gallons an hour. That's probably the upper limit. And how much of that water would flow across the ground and not seep into the soil, I have no idea. How thoroughly could we seal up the flow in the canal? Would a good part of the water continue down the canal? I'm looking for all ideas. Especially regarding how to dam the canal and how to do it without anyone from the abbey knowing what we have done. At least, not until it is too late."

Everyone seemed focused except Cumberland. But Josie knew he had provided much of her information, including the very existence of the abbey, so there was not much new for him.

"Damming the canal should be relatively easy in principle," Ellison said. "We imitate beavers. Logs, branches and sticks. Stones and mud. I don't have any of a beaver's skills, but I bet I can still dam up water as well as most beavers. For a couple of hours, anyway. Of course, beavers probably work twenty-four-seven." He walked over and looked closely at the photo on the screen. He pointed. "It's hard to tell what this foliage is, bushes or trees or something in between. But it's probably got what we would need to build a dam. We should show up with hand saws and axes, so we can cut wood without making much noise." Then he looked off toward his big warehouse windows and frowned. "Actually, we might want anyone who later investigates to think our dam was actually made by beavers. In that case, we couldn't use saws. The saw cuts would give us away. But if we used an ax and hatchet, those marks look more like how beaver teeth cut wood. And in this era of saws, most people looking at branches and sticks cut by an ax would assume the cuts were made by beavers. I could look at beaver cutting images online and get a sense of how to imitate the look."

Cor said, "Let's say we cut a tree so that it falls across the canal. It will bridge from one side of the ditch to the other. That might not help, right?"

"I see the problem," Josie said. "The sides of the concrete ditch will hold up the tree, and the water will still flow beneath the tree."

"So we do the beaver architect thing," Ellison said. "They build up their dam bit by bit. We scope out a range of good spots that might have some trees that can be felled beaver style. Once we drop a good-sized tree over the ditch, we look for other large chunks of downed wood. We add branches and rocks. Eventually, we move toward progressively smaller stuff to fill in the gaps. Maybe we even pack in mud. All the components can be wedged and interlocked so that the big tree over the ditch holds them all in place."

Amelia spoke up. "My family and I once picked oranges near the big concrete aqueducts that bring water from Northern California to Southern California. We often saw stuff floating down. So this little concrete river might have floating stuff, too. It will help dam up the water."

Ellison grinned. "Eventually, the water rises behind our dam and spills over onto the ground. It could even end up looking somewhat natural, so that no one immediately assumes it was a criminal project. A cop coming along might even think the tree was cut by a beaver, and then flotsam came down the ditch, caught on the log, created a jam-up, and then more stuff accumulated to clog the ditch."

"Cops could tell that our wood cuts were fresh," Cor said. "And the green pine needles would show the tree was fresh."

"Like when beavers have been recently working," Ellison said. "I've read that beavers continuously work on their dams. They're always adding new trees and branches. Even so, we muddy-up the fresh wood cuts with dirt to give them a natural-looking stain."

Samantha said, "Wouldn't damming the canal make a lot of

noise and alert the guys at the abbey?"

"I worried about that," Josie said. She pointed at the photo. "But where I want to dam the canal is half a mile away from the abbey. And there is this rise in the land between the canal and the abbey. It's like a low hill. I'm pretty sure it will block the line of sight between our dam and the abbey. If we work in the middle of the night, they won't hear us unless they are out prowling."

Cor spoke up. "If I'm reading the topographical lines correctly, the ravine will direct the water around that rise and on down to the abbey."

"Correct. Unfortunately, there is a potential problem a hundred yards or so to the side." Josie pointed with her curser. "The topo lines show a small flatter area here. It still slopes gently toward the abbey, but it will slow down the water on its path to the abbey. It could make it so the water spreads out and seeps into the ground. If we bring shovels, we could make a better channel of sorts to keep the water going in the correct direction down the ravine."

Ellison frowned. "It might be very difficult to dig. And shovels make noise when they hit rocks. If we need pickaxes, those make even more noise. Every time you hit a rock with a pickaxe, it makes a clink. Doing it in the middle of the night when people are asleep would be good. But we still risk waking anyone within hearing distance."

Cor said, "They could have someone on guard duty. They might sleep with windows open."

No one said anything for several moments. It made Josie think of her classes, when she would ask a question and the students would clam up.

Amelia spoke first. "I saw something in the vineyards that might help. The men who ran the irrigation tubes always struggled with coyotes. The coyotes would bite through the irrigation tubes to get water to drink. Sometimes a large amount of water would collect in small ponds. The men had trouble digging the dirt to help the water drain. The water made it hard for them to use their pickaxes because they couldn't see the dirt beneath the water, and their pickaxes would splash when they tried to dig. So they had tools made of those thin metal rods they use to reinforce concrete."

"Rebar," Cor said.

"Yeah. The metal bars were eight or ten feet long, and they had wooden handles. The men would hold the rebar tools at a shallow angle and insert the rebar into the water-covered ground. If they hit a rock in the ground, they'd pull it out and try another place. Once they got the rods into the dirt, they'd lever the bar up to loosen the dirt. Once they loosened the ground, it was easier to push a shovel into the dirt. Then they could get the water to flow toward the trees. Sometimes they had to pull off the wooden handle and pound on the rebar with a sledge hammer. That made noise. But mostly it was pretty silent."

Ellison smiled. "Brilliant," he said. "I can make a couple of those rebar tools."

"The result would mean that we make a channel for the water to flow to the abbey." Josie pointed with her curser. "I'm guessing the distance across this area is about a hundred feet. The more dirt we could remove, the better. But I'm thinking that, initially, maybe we shouldn't make the channel go all the way through."

"I see where you're going with this," Ellison said. He stood next to the screen and moved his finger in a circle. "These topo lines make it look like water from the dam will pool in this area, making a pond of sorts. We could create a channel through this area but wait until the last minute to cut the last section. When it comes time to do that, the water will rush through and on down to the abbey."

Josie was nodding. "You said it better than I could."

Cor said, "This flat area where we'll dig is potentially in view of the abbey. We couldn't use lights."

Ellison said, "Right. So when we're in view of the abbey, we mostly work in the dark. If we absolutely must turn on a light, we use the old-fashioned flashlights that are relatively dim compared to modern lights. And we wrap the rims with black tape so there is little light wash to the side."

"Did medieval warriors plan for operations at night?" Cor asked.

Josie answered, "Yes. And they were sneaky. Each army had sentries and advance scouts. They climbed trees and nearby hills, or mountains, or castle walls. I think our sentries should be Sam and Amelia. They can be at good lookout points." She pointed at the topo map. "Here, and over here. They can alert us if anyone comes out of the abbey while we're working."

Cumberland spoke up. "I can get everybody a mic headset so we can all communicate while we're at the abbey."

"Those are real?" Josie said. "I thought those were just a TV show fantasy."

"They're real."

Josie backed up from the TV screen as if to get a broader sense of the area. "Our goal is to drive everyone out of the abbey in a hurry. So we need a plan for when that happens."

"There's always the ruse de guerre," Diane Day said.

"Great idea!" Josie said. She saw confusion on Samantha and Amelia's faces. She clarified. "Deception. Like a Trojan Horse." She looked at Diane. "Any thoughts on what type?"

Diane shrugged. "Cor has a lot of military experience. Add in Ellison and me, we could come up with a believable-but-fake military operation. For example, imagine the bad guys pile into their vehicles and drive away. We set up a fake traffic stop. We tell them an evacuation has been ordered."

Cor said, "I know where to get a magnetic light bar for the top of my Jeep."

Josie nodded. "That could work in concert with a flood."

"Yeah," Cor said. "Anyone fleeing the abbey comes to our traffic stop. We explain how a truck crashed into a concrete ditch, which has now been compromised, and the Army is working with the sheriff's office to coordinate an evacuation. In the process, we can see if there is a woman in one of the bad guy's vehicle."

There was a pause.

Samantha made a little wave with her hand. "If we dam the canal half a mile away, the water might take a very long time to get to the abbey. There'd be no way to know in advance."

"Good point," Diane Day said, "Even if it did successfully flow to the abbey, we couldn't predict how long that would take, right? How long do you think it would take for the water to reach the house?" Because we'd have to add that flow time to the time it takes us to build our dam."

"I don't know," Josie said.

"Too many variables to even guess," Ellison said. "It would depend on the volume of water, the porosity of the soil, current dryness of the land. We could never guess the answer."

Cumberland spoke up. "Group intelligence excels at this kind of problem."

Josie turned to him. "What do you mean?" she asked.

At the same time, Cor said, "What's group intelligence?"

"Oh." Cumberland paused. "Well, there was a British dude named Sir Francis Galton. He was the polymath who formulated the concept of the wisdom of crowds. Of course, many times crowds get things terribly wrong. But there are narrow situations where crowds are really smart."

"Is this an urban myth?" Cor asked. "Or is this a real thing?"

Cumberland looked afronted. Josie knew that Cumberland's mind never entertained sarcasm or hyperbole. Not even small talk. Every aspect of Cumberland was earnest and sincere. It was part of his semi-autistic world.

"It's a real thing," he finally said.

"I've heard of it," Diane Day said.

"I think I remember," Ellison said. "Is this the story about the ox at the county fair?"

Josie turned and looked at Ellison. Another in the ongoing surprises of the man's knowledge.

"Yeah." Cumberland munched another saltine. "In ninenteen oh six in Britain, a fair held a contest. The emcee brought a big ox out from the barn and tied it to post. He got the ox to step its front hooves onto a big scale and then do the same with its back hooves. Only the emcee and two judges could see the readout on the scale. They added up the weights from the front and rear of the ox, and the emcee wrote the total down on a piece of paper. He put it in an envelope and tacked it up on a board. Everyone could see that the envelope remained untouched. The challenge was to guess the weight of the ox. If someone could come even close to the correct answer, they would win a big prize. Everyone wrote their guess on a piece of paper and put it in a jar. The emcee then pulled out each entry, and read off the guesses. It turned out that no one was close. He opened the envelope and showed the crowd that the correct weight was one thousand, one hundred, and ninety-eight pounds."

Cumberland slurped some Diet Coke. "Francis Dalton happened to be there observing, and he got an idea. After the contest was over, Francis Dalton took all the entry slips of paper, totaled up the guesses and divided by the number of entries, which gave him the average of the guesses."

"And that was correct?!" Samantha blurted out. "No way!"

"Nearly correct," Cumberland said. "The average of the guesses was just one pound off the actual weight. None of the individual guesses was even close. But the average was accurate."

"Does group intelligence have any application in the real world?" Cor asked.

"Yeah, it's huge," Cumberland said. "When you Google something, the top response on the search page is often exactly what you're looking for, right? That is, the top response that isn't a sponsored ad." The words could have been enthusiastic, but Cumberland's voice, as always, was kind of monotone. Josie had always noticed that Cumberland spoke like the shy, reserved kid he was, soft voice, low pitch, tone very dry.

Everyone nodded.

"This happens in spite of the fact that there might be millions of websites that have stuff that is similar to what you're looking for. The reason Google often gets you the perfect site at the top of the list isn't because Google is inherently smart. It's because Google uses group intelligence. They count how many links on the world wide web point people to any given website that has information about your search subject. That's like counting how many people are guessing the ox's weight. Google knows that the more guesses there are, the more accurate the weight average will be."

Samantha was shaking her head. "But most people aren't wondering about number stuff. They want things like the best chocolate cake recipe."

Cumberland made a single nod. "Okay, take a search for the best recipe for chocolate cake. Google looks for all sites that have chocolate cake recipes, and then it ranks those sites according to how many other sites link to the chocolate cake sites. The chocolate cake site that has the most links pointing to it is likely to be the most useful site for most cake bakers."

"Wow, that's how Google works?" Cor said. "Group intelligence? Very cool."

Josie noticed that everyone seemed both interested and also surprised at this sudden burst of information from Cumberland.

Cor said, "You brought up group intelligence when Josie was talking about breaching the canal. What are you thinking?"

Cumberland made a small nod. "If any of us guesses how long it will take for water from the dam on the canal to flow down to the house, we'll probably be way off. But if we all guess without knowing what anyone else thinks, our average will probably be much closer to reality."

Samantha said, "Even though there's only…" she counted, "seven of us."

"Yeah. Not a large sample. But seven is better than one."

Samantha said, "Okay, everyone, write down how long you think it will take the flow of water to go the distance to the house." Samantha sounded excited.

Josie handed out scraps of paper. Ellison found some pens and handed them out. "One for you, Amelia," he said.

"I shouldn't participate, Ellison," Amelia said. "I'm kind of an outsider. I'm not really part of your group."

"Yes, you should," Cumberland said. He sounded firm.

"Oh," Amelia said. "Okay."

They all wrote.

Josie collected the pieces of paper and handed them to Cumberland. He glanced at them briefly and said, "The average of our guesses is twenty-one hours and forty-seven minutes."

Cor said. "Shouldn't we get a calculator so we get an accurate average?"

"Cumberland's a human calculator," Ellison said. "Get an electronic calculator and you'll get the same result."

Cor's eyes widened a little.

"Okay," Josie said. "That gives us an estimate to work with. Twenty-two hours. That means we have a two-night project. The first night, we make our preparations, damning the canal and digging a better channel throught the semi-flat area."

Ellison added, "And plugging up the culvert Cumberland found on the building plans."

Josie nodded. "To go back to Diane's question about the total time involved, if it actually were to take twenty-two hours for the water to be diverted, then we'd hope to finish damming the canal in the early morning hours the day before. Say, four a.m. Then we'd be back twenty-two hours later. Two a.m. No, scratch that. We need to allow for the water getting to the abbey sooner. If it takes three hours less than our group intelligence estimate, then we'd want to come back at eleven p.m. If it takes three hours longer, then we'd expect to wait until five a.m."

"What happens the second night?" Samantha asked.

"We all get into place," Josie said. "You and Amelia at your lookouts, while Cor and Diane and Ellison prepare their ruse de guerre."

Samantha said, "So the dam works, and the flowing water builds up in a pond. Once we cut the last channel of our temporary pond, the water will rush down toward the abbey."

Ellison said, "If we're successful at plugging the culvert, our flood vandalism will probably drive the inhabitants out fast."

Amelia frowned. "But what if the abbey is, you know, kind of water tight and the water doesn't go inside?"

"Maybe we could make a hole," Ellison said.

Cor raised her eyebrow. "Are you thinking of an explosive charge?"

"No. We'd need to use medieval assaults as our model."

"We hit the front door with a battering ram?"

Ellison frowned and shook his head.

Josie looked at Ellison. "You have a pickup truck. Could it haul a boulder?"

"Great idea. The truck's old, but it's a three-quarter ton truck. You're thinking of rolling a boulder down to the abbey?"

Josie nodded. She pointed to the map. "The abbey's driveway is here. Above it is this old logging road. The topo lines show a slope from the logging road down to the house. What if you could get a big boulder in your truck and then drive to this point? Would it be possible to park your truck so that the rear end points down the abbey's driveway and door? Then you roll a boulder out of the back of the truck. We plan it so the boulder goes down, blasts through the fence, and hits the abbey right where the water is flowing. Could a boulder punch a hole in an abbey?"

THIRTY-EIGHT

Ellison thought about it. "A big enough boulder could. The key would be if the slope is steep and firm enough to let a boulder roll freely. If a boulder could build up a good speed, eight hundred or a thousand pounds could probably punch a hole in a building wall."

"But where would you get a big round boulder," Samantha said. "And how would you get it in your truck?"

"Right, Sam. I know a landscape company that sells rock. But their boulders are chosen for artful landscaping, which means unusual shapes. Whereas we need something round so it would roll. Something like a giant cannonball. But I can check with them. If they had a round boulder, they could put it in my truck with their backhoe. That leaves the problem of how to get the boulder out of the truck when the time comes."

Now Sam was pacing as the others sat. She bent over, picked up Unknown, and carried her back and forth.

Cumberland spoke, a low voice, directed down at the table. "Archimedes said he could move the Earth if he had a lever that was long enough."

Cor stared at Cumberland.

"Who was Archimedes?" Amelia asked.

"A Greek mathematician. Worked with geometry, mechanics. Stuff like that." Cumberland looked at Josie. "Is that right, professor?"

"I believe that is correct. But that was before my time."

Amelia looked puzzled.

Ellison said, "Josie means the time of her expertise. Her focus is medieval history." He looked at Josie. "Sort of the fifth century to the fourteenth century, right?"

Josie nodded.

Ellison said, "The ancient Greeks were, well, ancient. A thousand or more years earlier than the medieval dudes."

Josie smiled.

"I'm the one who's Greek, and I don't know any of this," Cor said.

"Glad to know I'm not the only one who doesn't know stuff," Amelia said.

Cor was shaking her head. "You know barista stuff. Coffee roasting and baking and running a business. You're probably gonna get rich off what you know."

"So we do as Archimedes did," Josie said, "and use levers to get the boulder out of the pickup." She added, "Although, it would still be hard work. It's not something I could help with."

Ellison glanced at Cumberland, who hadn't yet given any indication if he was going to come along and help assault the abbey. Ellison turned and looked at Cor.

"I'll help Ellison," Cor said.

"Perfect," Ellison said.

"We should have backup, as well," Ellison said. "A second boulder. Miss with the first, fire off the second. I'll park the truck just so, at an angle so the bed of the truck points down and back. We'll sneak down and plug the culvert. Speaking of which, there's a construction site I drive by. They used those rolls made of hay for erosion control. They've got a big pile of extra rolls. I could borrow one of those and cram that stuff into the culvert."

Cor said, "So we have an abbey with bad guys and maybe a kidnapped woman. We're going to drive them out with a flood. And that water is going to do its thing about twenty-two hours after we dam it up. Sounds like a decent plan."

"This flood would totally damage the abbey, right?" Samantha said, breaking the silence.

"Yes, that bothers me," Josie said. "But it's made of stone. It would survive."

"And it's worth it to rescue the kidnapped woman and maybe catch the sniper," Cor said.

THIRTY-NINE

"So we force the men to leave the abbey," Ellison said. "Where do you imagine they would go?"

Cor said, "I'm guessing they'd intend to drive out toward Ice House Road, which leads down to Highway Fifty at the bottom of the canyon. But we'll stop them from going anywhere."

"And see if they have Elena with them and rescue her," Josie said.

"That's our first goal."

"It would also allow you to judge the men, as you perform your military traffic stop," Josie said.

Ellison said, "Yeah. How many. Their level of competence. Attitude. Readiness."

Cor looked doubtful. "I don't know. They will probably have guns. If we try to prevent their escape, they might try to kill us."

Diane Day was nodding. "We need to deceive them in some way."

Josie said, "There's a bird called a Nighthawk. The female feigns injury in an effort to draw potential predators away from the nest. Deception is present in most animals."

Cor looked at Ellison. "I think a basic military approach is best. You and Diane and I present ourselves as official Army personnel. My Jeep will pass as Army. I'll wear my threads. What about you? Do you still have your old uniform?"

"Yeah, I'm embarrassed to say that I've kept it all these years. Why, I don't know."

"Now you do know. We'll create what looks like an official Army traffic stop. Someone escaping the flood at the abbey is going to come by vehicle, right? Driving late at night. We stop them to warn them of the flood. They will think it makes perfect sense because they've just seen the flood up close.

"When they stop, we get a look at their vehicle, the people inside. They won't have a problem with official Army personnel as long as we look the part. Maybe we should check out your threads."

Ellison shrugged, walked over to an amoire and pulled out a hanger with a jacket. He pulled the jacket on and turned to face everyone. It still fit well.

Josie was impressed that Ellison had put on no extra pounds over the decades. But it made her feel a little inadequate. She was substantially heavier than she'd been in her early twenties. It wasn't much consolation that she'd earned a Ph.D. while she was munching all those chips and sweets.

"Oh, my God," Cor said. "Check out the chest candy!" She turned to Diane as she pointed at Ellison.

"You mean my badges and ribbons?"

"Yeah! Pins, too. If non-Army people saw you, you could pass for a Captain or Major! Especially at night. I'll be your driver. Diane will be your Sergeant. We'll be Army outreach, going out of our way to help citizens during a natural disaster." Cor turned to Josie. "What say you, professor?"

"I'm sold," she said.

Everyone was quiet, as if Diane and Cor's idea made their plan more real and, as a result, more frightening.

FORTY

Josie said, "As we do this, let's remember that our main goal is to free the kidnapped woman, if in fact she is in there. Catching the men is secondary. We need a good approach."

Cor looked at Diane Day.

"The woman can be my assignment," Diane said. "When I see her, I stick by her, hustle her off into the wilderness if necessary. If someone gets in our way, I stop him."

Josie said, "This sounds dangerous."

"My specialty," Diane said.

Amelia Gomez looked worried. "This is scary. Years ago I heard about a cousin of mine who was kidnapped in Colombia. Something to do with pressuring her partner who was involved in the drug trade. She lived, but he was killed. I never met her, but this reminds me of what I heard about. A real-life nightmare."

"I agree," Josie said. "I should stress that you are all free to not participate in our plan," Josie said. The words were strong, but her voice was gentle. "In fact, you shouldn't even consider participating unless you have a burning desire to be part of this."

"That's the thing," Amelia said. "Because my cousin's experience was so traumatic, it makes me want to help. But once we make this flood, then what?"

"Didn't you say that the governor's instructions were to subdue and hold the shooter?" Cor said.

Josie nodded. "Yes."

"I'm confident these men are holding Elena," Cor said, "because I saw her. I saw the SOS, so I know she's under major stress. We can take the men at gunpoint," Cor said, glancing at Ellison. "We can disarm them, make citizen's arrests if that's appropriate, zip-tie their wrists and ankles, and sit on them until the cops come. Maybe the cops charge us like we're vigilantes or whatever. Or maybe they appreciate us handing them some bad guys."

"I've known some cops over the years," Ellison said. "If we tied these crooks up, it might be more practical to disappear before the cops come. That way the cops can focus on the gift of the bad guys. Maybe they'd think what we did was inappropriate and even criminal. But I bet they would be relieved to not have to devote so many resources to processing us."

Josie turned to the others. "Let's see how it would play," Josie said. "Our advantage is having the governor back us up. It could be that he gives us total cover. I don't want to hurt anyone with our offensive. But in case they attack us, what do we do?"

"Diane and I have weapons," Cor said.

Josie stared at her.

Cor said, "I've got an AR-Fifteen, a Colt Forty-five, and a pocket Glock."

"I don't know what that means," Josie said.

"Big rifle, big pistol, small pistol. All serious and legal, and I have a California concealed-carry permit for the handguns."

"That sounds special. Is it?"

"It just means that, because I teach self-defense, which sometimes attracts dangerous men who take personal exception to the idea that a woman might want to defend herself against dirtballs, the sheriff's office gave me a permit."

"Can anyone get such a permit? Like me, for instance, if I bought a gun?"

"The short answer is no. You have to show need, and you have to demonstrate proper training."

"Do police officers have concealed-carry permits?"

"Not generally," Cor said. "They carry guns. A peace officer's badge is her permit."

Josie looked at Diane.

"I also have a concealed carry permit for several sidearms," Diane said. "But the ones I always carry are my Beretta Nano and a Hellcat."

"You say that as though you are carrying them now."

Diane nodded.

Josie felt a sudden thickness in her throat, as if she didn't realize the extent that many people go to in preparation for violence. But then, she'd been close to multiple gun deaths these last few months.

"If these men get violent," Josie said, "would you shoot them?"

Cor continued, "The best use of guns is to intimidate, not kill. A gun can be a very effective threat. But if it gets to the point where people are actually shooting, it shows that things have gone very wrong." Cor paused.

Diane said, "My desire in a serious situation is only that someone understands or suspects I have a gun and they perceive that I know how to use it. A gun that remains unused can even be of use when a situation escalates to violence. I've had times where my opponent is so focused on whether or not I'm about to pull my weapon that he doesn't notice that I'm shifting my stance to strike with my feet."

Josie said, "Sam and I each have pepper spray. Do you think that's a good idea?"

"Diane, you have experience with spray, right?" Cor said.

"It's good to have," Diane said. "But you need to know that it has to be a surprise. If you make a show of pulling it out, your opponent is likely to shoot you."

Samantha set Unknown down on the floor. She said, "I've heard of bear spray and mace. What's the difference between them and pepper spray?"

"As far as I know, they're pretty similar," Cor said.

"They all have a significant level of capsaicin," Diane said.

Ellison added, "That's the active ingredient in hot chili peppers, right? Okay to eat. But put it in your eyes… Look out. As I understand it, the main difference between the various sprays is that sprays made to use on humans come in small containers that are easy to hold in your hand without being obvious. They're designed to be used up close. Good for surprise, like Diane said. Bear sprays come in big containers that can shoot thirty or fifty feet or more. You need that distance to deter a charging bear. Those containers are big and obvious. A bad guy could tell you're carrying one from far away."

"And blow you away before you get close," Samantha said.

Josie had heard the term 'blow you away' before, but it made her uncomfortable to hear it coming from her 14-year-old daughter. Josie wondered, was she was making a big mistake to even let Samantha join her in such meetings? Maybe, but Samantha was her best and most helpful companion.

"I know where to get bear spray," Ellison said, "if you decide it's a good idea."

"We'll think on it," Josie said. She frowned as she thought of a question. "At this point, I'm not inclined to tell the authorities what we're planning. But if I do tell them, I should probably anticipate how they would respond. Cor, does your Army background give you credibility with the police? If they show up, would you have any sway over their response?"

"Depends on the cop. Right Diane? Ellison? The secure ones respect that you've put in time as a soldier. And some of them have been in the military as well. They know you understand threat assessment, weapons, discipline, etc. But the insecure ones might dismiss you as a grunt who doesn't understand the nuances of police work. There are soldiers who reinforce both points of view. On the whole, if a cop shows up and sees a situation under control with no loss of life and no one waving weapons, they're likely to think a soldier makes a credible witness, and they will appreciate her help in the situation." Cor looked over at Ellison as if to see what he thought.

Ellison nodded. "I agree."

"It seems like having a military presence is a definite advantage," Josie said, "even if it isn't official military."

"I think so," Cor said.

Josie nodded. "I remember that you have a gun, too," she said to Ellison.

"A Colt Government," he said, "and I also have a concealed carry permit because I often deal in cash and my shop is in a rough part of town."

"You three are like having a private Army," Josie said.

"As long as I don't get sucker-clobbered over the head," Ellison said.

It was Cor's turn to frown.

"Josie didn't tell you?" he said. "A few months back, Josie got dragged into a different case, which was probably what precipitated the governor's request for help with this current case. Long story is I went along on her plan to trap a killer up in the San Bernardino mountains. It was impressive as hell. She got two killers instead of one. But before that happened, I got stalked and clobbered. Pretty embarrassing. Special Forces my ass. I was a special idiot. Might as well have been asleep on the job."

"Don't believe what he says," Josie said. "Before that, he helped Sam and me find a killer in Yosemite. And then helped us figure out how to lure another killer to the San Bernardino Mountains. He even provided the venue."

"Don't forget Cumberland," Samantha said. She had moved over to sit next to Cumberland at the table and was sharing his crackers. Unknown sat on the floor between them, watching their hands move from the box to their mouths and back.

Cor turned toward Samantha.

Samantha said, "Cumberland hacked into satellites that the Mil…" she stopped suddenly and turned to look at Cumberland, as if realizing that she was about to reveal classified information. She started again. "Cumberland provided major computer support. He was our secret weapon."

Cor seemed to scan all the people, looking from Josie to Diane to Samantha to Amelia to Cumberland to Ellison, and back to Josie. After a pause, she spoke to Ellison in a low voice. "Precipitated is a cool word."

It took Josie a second to remember that Ellison had used the word earlier.

Ellison smiled. "I took chemistry in college. But I'm more interested in how human activity precipitates a response than I am in how chemicals precipitate out of solution like water vapor turning to rain and falling out of the sky."

Cor said to Josie, "Can I ask… In this previous situation that

Ellison mentioned, how did you catch these killers?"

Josie answered, "As Ellison said, we set a trap in an abandoned garage."

"Did you have a weapon?"

"Yes. A medieval-style crossbow I built as part of my Ph.D."

"It works?" Cor said, surprise in her voice.

"Very well, yes."

"Did you fire it?"

"I had to. I killed one man and injured the other."

Cor's eyes widened. "Do you… Does a person need a permit to have a crossbow?"

"Not the last time I checked. But there are rules that apply to all weapons, including crossbows. You can't hunt with a crossbow except during the specific hunting season. And killing someone with a crossbow is no different than killing someone with a hammer or in any other manner. The police and court system put you through an intense examination. Your justification better be convincing and your explanation very good. Otherwise, the District Attorney will charge you with murder. In my case, the weapon saved my life. Of course, there are many kinds of medieval weapons. They don't have to be as sophisticated as crossbows."

"I can bring my sling bullets," Samantha said.

"Sling bullets?" Cor looked at Samantha.

"Like David and Goliath," Samantha said. "I'm pretty good with it. You get a two-inch rock flying at your head at, what speed, Mama?"

Josie shrugged. "Sixty miles an hour? Eighty?"

"Okay," Cor said. "Like you said in class. Medieval weapons are serious stuff. Would you bring your crossbow on this mission?"

"I… I haven't thought about it. I suppose I should."

After a moment, Cumberland said. "I can give computer support. But I can't come with you. I have to stay with Aiden and Cara. Is that okay?" He looked over at Ellison. "Us staying here when you're gone?"

"Of course."

"What about the abbey's electric power?" Josie asked. "Could that be turned off? Can a person—how should I put it—infiltrate the electrical grid and turn off the power?"

Cumberland shook his head. "In this case, the grid probably isn't involved." He pointed at the photo on the screen. "On the south side of the abbey is a bank of solar panels." He held up his index finger, sighted across it to the screen, and counted. "It looks like the rectangle of panels is four panels high by twenty panels wide. Eighty panels. That would probably be twenty-four thousand watts or more, depending on the type of panel. That's a lot of power, which suggests it's a complete off-grid system and the abbey's residents are self-sufficient."

"So you couldn't turn that off," Josie said.

"The typical way to turn off their power would be to find their main breaker box, which is probably inside. And the battery storage will be inside, too. Either we'd have to physically break in, or I'd have to get into their computer system. I don't know where…" Cumberland stopped and started typing on his laptop. He frowned, typed some more. "If I could find solar installation contractors who work in this area, maybe I could luck onto the company that put in the solar system."

Ellison said, "The contractor who installed a system that size would have pulled a permit. So the county would have a record of the contractor."

"Yes, of course," Cumberland said as he typed.

Josie turned to the others. "To recap, the first night, we dam the canal in the early hours of the morning," Josie said. "I expect that will be a long job. Then we make sure to leave the area before dawn."

Josie had made some notes on a pad of paper. She flipped a page. "The next night, we return. We check to see if the dam overflow is draining toward the abbey and making a temporary pond. When the time comes, we use our picks and shovels to cut the last bit of channel and release the water from the pond. From there it will rush down the last part of the ravine toward the abbey. Cor and Diane will plug the driveway culvert and while Ellison drops the boulders."

Samantha said, "What if the canal water has moved so fast toward the abbey that it's already overflowed the pond and driven the occupants out?"

"That's a good point. If that happens, we will have failed. Their crew would leave and take Elena with them along with any evidence of whatever criminal activity they are involved with. Better we hope our overflowing dam works as planned and our temporary pond is storing the water until we're ready to set it free." Josie scribbled a note, then continued. "If everything is copacetic, we proceed with…"

"Mama..."

"What? Oh. If everything looks good, we go to the next step in our plan."

Cumberland spoke. "I won't say that taking out their power is totally doable." He was staring at his computer screen, and typing, and dragging his finger on the trackpad. "But it's possible. They have one of the most common home security programs. If I…"

"Wait," Cor interrupted. "Do you think you can hack into their computer even when they're off the grid?"

"I'm in their system now."

"What?!"

"They're off grid with regard to their power. But they still have internet through this satellite dish." Cumberland pointed at the TV screen, then, picking up the laser pointer that Josie had previously used, directed the laser dot around a small gray oval on the screen.

"Wait," Cor said. "You can hack into the abbey's computer through a satellite?"

Cumberland shrugged. "The only difference is it connects to the internet through a satellite dish instead of through a cell tower or a cable connection."

Cor looked shocked.

Cumberland said, "So plan to call me with advance notice. If I can cause a power disruption, I should do it at whatever you think is the most effective time."

"What do you think of this sequence?" Josie said to the others. "After our dam is redirecting water toward the abbey and the culvert is plugged, Cumberland turns off the power when Ellison is ready to roll the boulder. Then, hit or miss, Ellison drives his truck away from the abbey and hides it in the brush. Meanwhile, Sam and Amelia can be posted in their hiding places. They watch through their binoculars, and give us all a running report on what they see."

Cor said, "Then Ellison joins Diane and me in my Jeep. We put on our Army jackets, and we set up our fake traffic stop, which we use to warn them about the flood that they are already fleeing. That is our opportunity to look for the woman."

"Right," Josie said. "My question is, what do we think these guys will do?"

Ellison shifted his posture and took a deep breath. He seemed reluctant to speak. "In Vietnam, we learned that you don't plan for what you think the enemy will do. You plan for what the enemy is capable of doing."

"Mama, when we were in the Quetico wilderness, that's exactly what you said about medieval war planners."

"You're right." She turned to the others. "What are those capabilities?" Josie asked, looking from Ellison to Cor to Diane and back.

Cor said, "The men in the abbey are capable of finding the dammed-up canal before we come back on our second nighttime visit. They are capable of sensing a trap and putting out their own sentries who would lie in wait for us to return. If they caught us, they could kill us, or torture us for information and then kill us. They are capable of meeting us with major gunfire, shooting to kill. They are capable of driving at speed through our checkpoint and crashing into our vehicle. They are capable of killing Elena to keep her from talking."

Josie felt her face change, and she knew her skin had gone ashen. "That's very frightening. Considering those possibilities, do you think we should change our course of action?"

"How, Mama?"

Josie thought for a moment. "Let's say our flood succeeds

in bringing the men out of the abbey. What if we see Elena and we're able to verify that she's being held against her will? Is that the evidence we need to call the local sheriff's office?"

Josie's question was met with silence.

She continued, "The governor wants me to pursue this independently from local law enforcement. But that doesn't mean he wants me risking a gunfight with killers."

Cor looked at Diane and Ellison.

Ellison said, "You might tell the governor what you know and let him decide that question."

"Okay. I'd like any opinions on whether to talk to the governor. Sam?"

Samantha said, "The governor called you because he didn't think the cops would find the cop killer."

Cor was shaking her head. "If you tell the governor where and what," Cor said, "he'll botch it, I'm sure. He'll tell someone, guaranteed. Also guaranteed is that the person he tells is not a person you would tell. The result will mean major fallout. Elena could get killed. The shooter could get away."

Cor seemed to look hard at Josie. "Then again," she added, "you could decide not to tell him anything revealing and just get a read on his level of commitment to the situation. You could ask the simple question. Call the local cops or go it alone?"

"That's a good compromise."

"When would you call him?" Ellison asked.

"No better time than now." Josie pulled her regular phone out of her purse. She found the governor's number and dialed.

"Good afternoon, this is the California State Governor's office, Sonja Gonsalves speaking." The woman's voice was pleasant and calming.

"Hi Sonja, this is Josie Strong calling."

"Oh, hello, professor. How is everything? Are you okay?"

"Yes, I'm okay. Things are going about as I expected, and I've learned some things. I want to ask the governor's advice."

"Yes, of course. But he's flying back from the P-REF. Oh, sorry, the Pacific Rim Economic Forum in Honolulu. He texted me twenty minutes ago that he was going to try to grab a couple of hours of sleep before the plane lands."

"Then perhaps I could get your advice."

"Well, I can't say that I know what he thinks about any given thing, so I prefer to get his response. I can only guess at his thoughts. What can I help you with?"

"Maybe nothing. I think I know who killed Ranger Francis Telman, and I think I know where he's hiding. But I have no physical evidence or witness testimony, so I wanted to see what the governor thought."

"I better call and get the governor's input," Sonja Gonsalves said. "Maybe he's still awake. Can you hold?"

"Yes." Josie was suddenly visualizing the men who pointed rifles at their plane. She thought Samantha was likely right, that one of them was the man called Snake. Josie wanted to mention that a man who'd been through sniper training in the Army was connected to Lucas Herman, the sniper who killed Mary Jo. She wanted to explain how Snake lived with the two guards who were transporting Lucas when the truck blew up and Lucas was killed. Josie also wanted to explain that they were the same two guards that Josie and Samantha found dead in the Monterey house. But as Josie had the thought, she realized she shouldn't say it. She didn't want to clutter the governor's aide with the idea, and it wouldn't help answer the question of how far the governor wanted Josie to take her investigation.

Josie turned to the others who were looking at her. "I'm on hold. She's trying to reach the governor, who's on a plane coming back from Hawaii."

Gonsalves came back on the phone in a minute. "I spoke to one of his staff on the plane. She said the governor's asleep and he told her not to wake him unless it was an emergency."

"Okay." Josie took a deep breath, breathed out, tried to calm herself. "Let me ask you my main question. Do you think I should be involving law enforcement on this?"

"That's not my place to decide such issues."

"But you could advise me."

"I don't know about that. And, frankly, I probably wouldn't want to know about anything you've learned. I have enough trouble sleeping as it is. It sounds like you're making good progress, so maybe you should continue your investigation as you've been doing up to now. If you think it's inappropriate to work with local law enforcement, then don't involve them. After all, that is why the governor brought you into this case, right? Because he thinks traditional law enforcement hasn't been effective."

"I don't know that I'm being effective, either."

"Not to hear the governor tell it. He keeps mentioning how you caught Lucas Herman. He likes to say, 'Don't ever think you've got the upper hand when you're dealing with the professor lady.'"

"The governor said that?"

"Those very words. It's because of his high regard for you that he wants you to have our full support."

"Thank you," Josie said. "If I should still want to talk to the governor, when do you expect him home?"

"His plane lands at LAX this evening at nine p.m."

"Oh."

"Is something wrong?" Sonja asked.

"No. I just keep making the same mistake, thinking that, because the state capital is in Sacramento, he would come and go from there."

"I see. Well, we do, of course, have the Sacramento office, but the governor does most of his work out of Los Angeles. Warmer in the winter and cooler in the summer than Sacramento."

After a moment, Sonja Gonsalves spoke again. "Don't get me wrong. We consider Sacramento very important, and the governor uses his office there for important functions."

"I understand. I'll consider what you have said as I move forward. Thank you for talking to me." Josie took a deep breath and let it out slowly.

"Roger that. Good luck, professor. We're rooting for you. After the governor lands and is awake, I'll tell him what you said. If he has a different point of view, I'll call you immediately. He might even call you himself."

Josie hung up and looked at the others.

FORTY-ONE

"Did you learn anything to help you make a decision?" Cor asked. "Are we telling the cops our plans?"

Josie shook her head. "Not unless the governor calls me and says otherwise. The fewer people who know about our plan, the less chance it gets back to the men at the abbey, some of whom may know members of local law enforcement. I think the governor's liaison understands that point of view even though she made it clear that she has no authority to advise me."

"What's the next step, Mama?" Samantha asked. She had bent down to pet Unknown, then picked her up and held her, rocking a little, back and forth.

Josie suddenly felt hungry and she looked long and hard at the chips and dip. Then Amelia's cookie container. She could eat them all. Instead, she took a sip of water, then picked up a single piece of celery and used it to scoop up some dip. Meanwhile, Ellison pulled a carrot stick out of the jar. It was hard to feel good about people with food discipline, Josie thought. Then it occurred to her that she was doing what Ellison did. Using food discipline. Was it as hard for Ellison as her? She doubted it.

"Mama?"

"Oh, sorry. You asked what next. I'm thinking."

"Any chance these guys have a dog?" Ellison asked as he reached toward Samantha, who was still holding Unknown. He ran his hand over the dog. "If these men have a dog, it would hear us or smell us and bark, and that could ruin our plan."

"I saw no indication of one when I was there," Cor said.

"Would we bring this hound?" Ellison asked, gesturing toward Samantha.

Samantha said, "Of course. We have to bring Unknown, right baby?" she said as she lowered her head next to Unknown.

"Unknown is good at alerting me to anything out of the ordinary, but she doesn't bark."

"Then how can she alert you?"

"She whines. Real soft."

Ellison nodded, but it didn't look like he was convinced.

He turned to Cor. "You were at this place. How many guys do you think we're dealing with?"

"No way to know after a short observation. I saw the woman I think is Elena at the back of the building. Later, I saw two guys get into a Suburban. But I didn't have a clear sight line. There might have been more. When the vehicle left, I couldn't see into it through its smoked windows. After the Suburban left, I saw a third man outside the abbey, walking along, talking on his phone. That makes three guys, one woman. But I had the thought that the guy talking on the phone was outside because he wanted privacy from any others inside. If so, there might be four guys, maybe more. You can fit eight people in a Suburban. Did they all come in the Suburban? I doubt it. And they would want a second vehicle for backup."

"So it's possible there's a bunch of guys there," Ellison said. "Maybe they've got a kidnapped woman. Maybe one of the guys is a sniper."

Josie said, "Cumberland, you said you'll be here with your siblings. Are you okay with computer support in the middle of the night, even when your brother and sister are sleeping nearby?"

He nodded. "Aiden and Cara will sleep through Sierra assault mission ground control. Maybe I can shut down the abbey's power. But I guess I won't get another chance to see you nail some dude in the eye with your homemade crossbow."

In Josie's peripheral vision, she sensed Cor turning to look at her.

"Is that true?" Cor asked.

Josie felt a little embarrassment. "He had already killed someone else, and he had shot me and was going to kill me next. The law of the wilderness. Kill or be killed."

"Whoa. I didn't realize you were, um… So kick butt. Yes,

let's go get these scumbags."

"Oh, I'm late," Cumberland said in a sudden raised voice. "I forgot to pick up Aiden and Cara." He shut his laptop and rushed out the big gate. They heard his steps going down the stairs.

"In case it matters, I still want to help," Amelia said, changing the subject back to what Josie had been talking about.

"We want you." Josie turned toward her daughter. "Sam, I shouldn't just assume you want to join in this stressful stuff. It could be dangerous."

"Of course I want to help, Mama."

Josie thanked everyone, and they made a plan to head to the Sierra two days later, giving everyone some time to prepare. Ellison planned to acquire a boulder or two, bring shovels and pickaxes, and he said he'd remind Cumberland to see about getting two-way radios and headsets with mics.

When they left Ellison's warehouse loft, Cor and Diane trotted down the stairs with Samantha and Unknown. Amelia and Josie lagged behind and walked down the long flights together.

Josie wanted to change the subject and say something that would be less stressful than talking about Elena's kidnapping and the men at the abbey. But nothing came to mind.

Amelia did it instead.

"When your friends said they would invest in my coffeehouse company, was that just, you know, casual talking?"

"I don't think so. I think they were serious."

"Do you know how that works? Getting investors?"

"Only in the vaguest sense. But I can help you figure it out. There are people who can give you advice."

"That would be so great. I'm so lucky that you know these people. You've helped me so much with my confidence."

"I can help in other ways, too."

"How?"

"I'm also interested in investing."

FORTY-TWO

Two mornings later, Josie, Samantha, Amelia, and Unknown got in their Prius and headed back north to the Tahoe foothills. Not far back, Diane Day and Cor Kontos were in Cor's Jeep. Ellison was an hour behind, driving his old pickup, which was laden with two boulders he'd gotten at a landscape company. He also had some wooden boards for levers, several shovels and pickaxes, two axes, and two rebar pieces that he had outfitted with wooden handles to make it easier to dig hard, rocky soil.

Josie had reserved three rooms at a motel 25 miles from the abbey. So their plan was to meet at the motel in the late afternoon.

Ellison was in one motel room. Cor and Diane in another. Josie, Samantha, Amelia, and Unknown in a third.

They assembled in Ellison's motel room late in the afternoon to discuss their plan. Josie got out her maps and the satellite photos, and they went over the details of the plan they'd created in L.A.

When things seemed settled, Cor said, "I have another idea. The last time I was there, I saw an abandoned mid-seventies Chevy Vega on the side of the road. It's got two flat tires, a smashed windshield, and it's been stripped of license plates. Eventually, someone - Caltrans or something - is going to tow it to the junkyard. My idea is, why not tow it under cover of darkness to a spot on the logging road above the abbey? The Vega is dark brown, and the paint is degraded so it looks blotchy. Quite camo, actually. I could position it in the trees next to the logging road near where Ellison is planning to drop the boulder. Right after we drop the boulder out of Ellison's truck and pull out onto the nearby logging road, we could release the brake on the Vega, shift it into neutral, and let it roll into the road. That would block the logging road in the other direction and would force the men out toward the highway. They would probably plan to go that direction anyway. But this would block the alternative. The junk car wouldn't appear to be clear sabotage. It would just look like some scavengers tried to haul it off into the forest, but gave up and left it in the road."

Everyone looked to Josie for her reaction.

"I think it's a great idea. How would you tow it?" Josie asked. "Especially with flat tires?"

"I'd spray flat-tire sealant in the tires. It's not guaranteed to do the job, but I've used it before. It works pretty well for temporarily inflating tires."

"How would you tow it?"

"My Jeep has a tow bar, and I've got a snatch strap. The car is less than a mile away from the abbey, and I've done some towing in the past. I'm pretty sure Diane and I can get the Vega into position."

Josie nodded. "I don't mean to sound negative, but I'm just checking. Cars need keys to turn the steering wheel and shift the gears, right?"

"Modern cars, yes," Cor said. "But this car is before all that. I'm not sure, but I think the front wheels will track when it's towed."

Josie nodded. "I like it. Let's do it. Do you and Diane want help towing the abandoned car?"

Diane quickly shook her head. Josie thought she was probably one of those people who prefer to work alone because it means no discussion.

Cor put the thoughts into words. "No help necessary. It's straightforward. The most likely problem we'll have is if someone comes by while we're hooking it up. If so, we can say that the car belongs to a friend and she asked us to tow it."

They discussed some more details. When they were done, Josie said, "Let's order in some pizza, and then try to get a nap. I'll wake everyone at nine p.m, which will give us time to head into the mountains at ten. That should get us to the concrete canal by about midnight, so we can work on our dam without anyone watching us."

"Oh, one more question," Josie said. She turned to Cor. "Do you think you'll be able to lead us to our destination in the dark?"

"Yeah. Diane and I are both good on GPS navigation. Also, I've got a cutout switch on my Jeep, so I can drive without lights."

Ellison said, "Don't need a cutout switch on a pickup as old as mine. Push in the headlight switch, no lights. Simple as that. But brakelights are a different story. Same for Josie's wheels."

"I didn't think of that," Josie said. "My car has lights that are constantly on when it's running."

"We brought duct tape for that," Cor said.

FORTY-THREE

They left at 10 p.m.

Because the first night of their mission was to dam the canal, they left Ellison's truck with the boulders at the motel. However, they transferred the tools from his truck to the back of Cor's Jeep. Ellison also pulled out three large garbage bags stuffed with erosion-control hay tubes. Ellison rode with Diane and Cor, who took the lead in her Jeep. Josie, Samantha, Amelia, and Unknown followed. They drove up into the foothills, turned off on Ice House Road, and climbed up into the forest. With Cor navigating, they arrived at their predetermined spot about a mile away from the water canal.

Josie had gotten everyone LED lights on elastic head bands and explained that they should only use them when they were in the forest a long way from people. "The lights swivel from straight ahead to down. Let's keep them pointed down as much as possible."

Under Cor's direction, they left their vehicles under trees and brush. They found some branches to put over the vehicles for disguise. Cor pulled out a roll of blue painter's tape and used it to cover the few remaining exposed headlights and parking lights.

"This way, there'll be no reflection should anyone come along and their lights shine this way."

Samantha pointed at the ground. "The snow has mostly melted, but there's still some snow in places. It shows our tire tracks here." She turned. "Over here, too."

"The weather forecast showed a substantial warming trend," Josie said. "Let's hope they're right, so the snow will melt and erase our tracks." She reached into the Prius and pulled out five pairs of work gloves in various sizes.

They hiked to the concrete canal. Samantha and Amelia sped through the dark to the concrete waterway. They dipped their hands in the fast-flowing water.

"Wow, it's freezing!" Amelia said.

"Probably came from snow that just melted a few hours ago," Cor said.

She looked at the nearby trees and hefted her hatchet as if its weight would help her judge what she might cut.

"What do you think of this tree," Ellison said. He had turned so his headlamp shined on the trunk of a fir about eight inches in diameter. He touched the trunk with the point of his ax. "It leans a little toward the canal. I think it's tall enough to reach the canal if I can drop it in the right direction. Once the tree falls over the water, it could be our main anchor point. It will be heavy enough to stay put as we wedge other branches under it." He turned to Cor. "What do you think?"

She looked up at the tree, then looked back at Ellison. "I'd say it's about ten times your height. Sixty feet or so. I think that will reach the ditch. Let me pace it off."

Ellison nodded.

Cor paced toward the canal, taking large, exaggerated steps. "Thirteen paces at about three feet per step."

"Thirty-nine," Ellison said. "So it will work if it falls the right direction."

Ellison raised his ax.

He spread his feet wide, touched the trunk with the ax blade for a sense of measurement, swung the blade back, and brought it down at a slight angle in a gentle chopping motion. The blade hit the wood, then skipped off in an arc toward his foot.

"Kind of scary," Ellison said. He spread his feet farther apart.

He made another chop. The blade made the tiniest bit of wood fly as it skipped away again. On his third chop, the blade made a decent cut into the wood, and a larger chunk of wood flew. "Does that look like what a beaver might cut with his teeth?"

"Works for me," Cor said.

Josie had never seen tree cutting up close. But Ellison seemed to know what he was doing.

He began a steady chopping.

Cor walked over to a tree that was quite small, only seven or eight feet tall. "If I cut this, no way would it fall anywhere near the concrete waterway. But beaver drag small trees, right?" She looked at Josie.

"I don't know," Josie said. "Let's assume they do."

"Yes, they do," Ellison said.

Cor began chopping.

"Timber," Ellison said. "Stay back."

Everyone turned to look. The tree he'd been chopping was leaning just a degree or so. Gradually the lean increased, not precisely toward the ditch but in the general direction. There was the snap and crackle of wood fibers breaking. The tree leaned more and began to fall at a faster rate.

There was a deep, thudding crack.

Josie immediately worried that the men at the abbey could hear it.

The tree, though not large, accelerated down toward the concrete canal. It struck the concrete with a thunderous impact. It flexed in a big bend over the concrete, then snapped back the other way, then settled. The air was filled with floating needles and little broken branches and dust that shone blue in their headlamp light beams. A strong conifer aroma filled the air.

Samantha said. "Ellison, you're like Paul Bunyan."

"Yeah, me 'n Paul," Ellison said, holding up crossed fingers. "I hope it didn't break the concrete."

They walked over and shined their headlamps on the canal.

The water flowed as before. Only now it was bridged with a tree across the top of the waterway.

"Just as we hoped," Josie said. "Now we drop rocks and branches and other debris and try to dam this river up."

"Timber, number two," Cor said, as her hatchet brought down the smaller tree.

Cor slipped her hatchet into her belt holster. She picked up the trunk of the small tree and dragged it over to the concrete ditch. "This little baby must weigh two hundred pounds. I can barely drag it."

"Perfect," Ellison said. "Its weight will help it stay put. I'll help you jam it down beneath the other tree."

"Already here," Diane Day said from behind Cor.

Cor and Diane wrestled the tree into position. The bigger tree held it in place. The smaller tree poked into the water and created a significant obstruction to the flow.

The others started dropping rocks into the ditch. Cor and Ellison each chopped down another small tree. They angled them under the first two trees, gradually creating a log jamb.

Ellison paused to catch his breath. Diane took his ax and chopped down a medium-small tree. It took all three of them to drag it over to the ditch.

While Ellison, Cor, and Diane each cut more small trees, Samantha and Amelia worked on finding and hauling rocks and heaving them into the ditch. Josie suspected that beaver wouldn't move rocks, but she didn't think it was enough of a concern to worry about.

Gradually, the dam took shape, an awkward, irregular, growing obstruction.

The water rose as it tried to flow past the growing dam. When the first water spilled over the edge of the concrete waterway, the group made a small quiet cheer. Urged on by their success, they increased their effort at poking in more branches and old logs.

Josie angled her light to shine on the concrete trough just below the new dam. "There's still water flowing down the ditch, but it's a fraction of what it was before. Most of the water is flowing over and out onto the ground."

"Now the question is whether Cumberland's group intelligence prediction is correct," Ellison said.

"Twenty-two hours before it gets to the abbey, right?" Amelia said. "Give or take a few." She walked over to where the water was pouring onto the ground. "The ground is pretty flat. It looks like the water is just soaking in."

"We'll know tomorrow night," Josie said. No beaver specialist would be fooled. The individual cut branches couldn't be matched up to a larger tree from which they'd been cut. No doubt many aspects of their dam didn't fit classic beaver design. But it was good obfuscation. Someone who didn't really know beavers might be fooled. Josie imagined they would be telling the story for years to come. 'Beavers near Lake Tahoe had rebelled against human intrusion into their world, so they dammed up an above-ground water canal.'

As the water flowed down the ravine, they all hiked ahead of the flowing water and down toward the flatter area where they hoped a pond would form near the abbey.

Not far away, the abbey seemed to glow in the starlight. It looked beautiful even though Josie thought of it as evil.

Josie whispered. "We're close enough to the abbey that we have to be as quiet as possible. And we can't use lights. We'll have to go by starlight."

They had two shovels, two pickaxes, and the rebar levers between the six of them. Although it was hard to see in the dark, Cor, Diane, and Ellison discussed the lay of the land in whispers and hand signals. They decided on the best location for excavating a channel that would help cut through the area where they expected the pond water would pool.

Diane was the first to go to work with the shovel. She stepped the shovel into the ground, hit something solid, moved to the side, stepped again. The shovel went in just a couple of inches. She levered out some dirt, moved her shovel a little more, repeated the process.

"That's a hard job," Josie said to Diane. "I really appreciate your help."

Diane was grunting as she dug. "A sister's held captive. I'll do whatever I can to bust her out."

"Thank you," Josie whispered.

Cor started with a shovel and then switched to swinging the pickax. It made a clinking sound nearly every time she plunged it into the ground. Some of the sounds were loud and made Josie wince with worry.

When Diane and Cor hit solid rock, Ellison probed with his rebar tool. He went in at a very shallow angle, then levered it up.

Cor set the pickaxe aside and went back to using a shovel.

"That helps," Cor whispered.

Samantha picked up one of the pickaxes. "This is far too heavy for me." She set it down and picked up the other rebar lever. She moved toward the abbey and tried to insert the rebar the way Ellison had.

It was slow work. No matter how hard they tried to be silent, the tools hit rocks and made more loud, metallic clinking sounds.

Samantha switched off with Amelia. Josie also took a turn with the lever. She anticipated that it would be hard work, trying to push the rebar into the soil. But it was much more difficult than she expected. It wasn't long before she handed the rebar back to Samantha.

Josie whispered to Ellison. "I feel worthless, watching you guys do all the work," Josie said.

"We don't mind," Ellison said. "A general needs mental space to ponder strategy."

After a couple of hours, they'd succeeded in making a decent channel that came to an end right where the ravine got steep above the abbey's driveway. It wasn't as deep as Josie wanted. But she was convinced that if the soil wasn't too porous, a pond would form.

"I think this is far enough," Josie whispered.

"I'll tiptoe down with the anti-erosion tubes and see if I can plug the culvert near the driveway," Ellison said. He opened two of the plastic bags and pulled out the contents. They were constructed like tubular hay bales, the hay rolled up and held tight by loops of twine. Each tube was about 18 inches in diameter and three feet long. Ellison grabbed two of them and hugged them to his chest.

"How are you going to see in the dark?" Josie asked.

"I won't. I'll go by feel. Very slowly. You all can carry our tools back to the vehicles. I'll meet you back there."

The five women headed back, took the camo branches off their vehicles, put their tools in the cars, then removed the tape from the lights. They waited for Ellison.

After an hour, Josie was getting very worried. How long could it take to stuff a bale into a culvert?

She heard a noise from the logging road. She almost gasped.

"Just me," Ellison whispered. He appeared in the darkness.

"Did you have trouble with the culvert?" Josie asked.

"No. I had trouble trying not to get lost. Thus, walking back on the logging road."

They drove back to the motel in the foothills just as it was getting light.

They slept late the next day. Amelia and Samantha were occupied with their phones. Cor and Diane left to do some errands. Ellison took a nap.

Late that afternoon, they met in Josie's motel room and revisited their plan one last time.

"Try to get some rest," Josie said. "I'll set the alarm for eleven p.m., and we'll plan to leave at midnight."

FORTY-FOUR

They left at midnight and turned onto Ice House Road at 12:30. They drove as a caravan with Cor and Diane in the Jeep, then Ellison in his truck, and Josie, Samantha, Amelia, and Unknown taking up the rear.

After several miles, they pulled over. Cor put tape over the running lights on Josie's car. She taped white paper over their brake lights.

"This will make it so no one can see you unless you are braking. White paper will allow us to see each other brake. Let's go light on the pedal and not ride the brakes."

"I can't see anything," Josie said. "How can I even follow you?"

Cor said, "Your night vision will get much better after ten minutes or so. I'll turn on a flashlight and put it on the floor in front of the rear seat in my Jeep. That will give you something to follow. I also got us flashlights that don't spill light to the side." She handed everyone lights. "If you slide the focus sleeve, the light becomes a narrow beam. I've put tape over all but the tiniest opening. You can drive by holding the light out the car windows. But when we get very close, the lights stay off. Once our eyes adjust, we go by starlight only. The higher slopes have snow that reflects the starlight and make it easier to see."

Thirty minutes later, they came down the logging road and drove toward the abbey. Josie felt like the territory was vaguely familiar even though she'd only seen it from the airplane. Soon, Cor pulled over again, the others followed, and they turned off all their lights.

When Josie stepped out of her car, she gasped. Ice water flowed into her shoes! She whispered, "The ground is waterlogged! The dam is working!"

Ellison bent down and put his fingers on the ground. "This is flowing at a good rate. Let's hope it hasn't yet driven the abbey's occupants out of the building."

They proceeded to the area where they hoped water would collect in a pond.

Even in the black of night, they could see that it was more like a small lake than a little pond. They all marched through water-logged soil around the perimeter and saw that their little dam had held, preventing water from gushing down toward the abbey. But it was obvious that when they cut the last bit of earth that blocked the pond, the water would flow vigorously.

"We were successful," Josie whispered. "The abbey looks quiet. It is still dry."

"But not for long," Ellison said.

"Now we should put on the radio headsets Cumberland got us," Josie said. "When you touch the button, we can all hear you. If you push it farther, the button clicks in and the mic stays live."

They tested the headsets and found the reception was adequate, if scratchy, with static.

Josie said, "Cor, you and Diane go to work on towing the junk car you found. Ellison, you get your pickup positioned for rolling the boulders. I'll help Samantha and Amelia get to their sentry lookouts. When each of you is in place, let us know over our headsets. When all is ready, I'll give the okay. Cor and Diane and I will cut the final passage to release the water. Ellison will roll the boulders. Then he and Cor and Diane will all meet to set up their ruse de guerre traffic stop."

They split into groups.

By two in the morning, Josie saw Cor positioning the towed Chevy Vega in the forest above the abbey, blocking one of the access roads that the men at the abbey might use. Off to the side, she saw Ellison parking his truck with its boulder cargo in the trees nearby.

By three in the morning, Josie, Samantha, and Amelia hiked through the water-logged forest. They found a good place for Amelia to hunker down at the edge of a broad dome of land covered with small trees and brush. They got her ensconced under the heavy boughs of a fir tree, from which she had a view toward the abbey.

Josie squatted next to Amelia. "Are you comfortable?" Josie whispered.

"Yes. I'm fine," Amelia whispered back.

"You have your headset turned on."

"Yeah."

"And you have my cell number. If anything happens, you can call out. You are not alone."

"Yes, Professor Strong. I'll be fine."

But Josie heard the waver in Amelia's voice. She was clearly scared at the prospect of being left alone in the dark forest.

"Please call me Josie." Josie felt that the familiarity of first names would make Amelia more comfortable.

"Josie," Amelia said. "I'll let you know when I see anything move. I'll be fine. Don't worry about me."

"My job is to worry."

Even in the black darkness, Josie could see Amelia's brief attempt at a grin.

Samantha spoke. "And I'll be just over there," she gestured at the dark forest.

Amelia nodded. "Okay."

"See you soon," Samantha said. She grabbed Josie's arm and pulled her away.

"You're too much," Samantha whispered as they walked away over water-logged soil. "You're so busy trying to reassure that you make people worry even more."

"Yes, I'm too much."

"But you mean well."

"Yes, I mean well," Josie agreed.

When they came to a good place with what seemed like dry soil that was elevated by tree roots, Samantha got down under the boughs of another fir tree, hidden from easy view even though she too had a good window to look through. Samantha pulled Unknown down next to her.

Josie sat down on Samantha's other side. She immediately

felt ice water soaking into her pants. Uncomfortable, but worth it for a moment with her daughter. Josie put her arm around Samantha's shoulder.

"Is it dry where you're sitting?" Josie asked in a whispered voice.

"Pretty much. But it's just my butt getting wet. It's not like ice water is going down my back. You?"

"Mostly, yes. Your phone is on vibrate?"

"Check," Samantha said. "Your phone, too?"

"Yes." Despite the headsets over their ears, they could hear each other well.

Josie rubbed Samantha's back. "Does your shoulder feel okay?" Josie was referring to Samantha's shoulder, which was dislocated back when Mary Jo Telman was shot and killed.

"Yeah, Mama. My shoulder is all healed."

"Will you feel comfortable being left here alone?"

"I've got my protector at my side." Samantha reached over and stroked Unknown.

"Kind of handy that she doesn't bark," Josie said.

"Yeah."

"But her whine can be loud."

"When I put my hand on her, she quiets down," Samantha said. "You can stop worrying. You can go now." Samantha gestured. "Amelia is nearby. You need to get to your First Mate's command position."

"If I call, and you sense someone within hearing range when your phone vibrates, don't answer. I'll assume you're okay but just being cautious." As Josie said it, she realized it wasn't true. If Samantha didn't answer her call, Josie would fear the worst. But it was important to give Samantha as much psychological comfort as possible. She might be very smart and confident. But she was still just a 14-year-old girl.

"No problem, Mama. You worry too much. Like I already said, I'll be fine."

As Samantha said it, Josie sensed Samantha reach up and touch her Four Virtues necklace.

"You know what, Mama?"

"What?"

"I know I sound frustrated when you keep checking to make sure I'm okay. But the truth is you do a good job of making me feel safe. I mean, I know this isn't safe. We're dealing with a killer, right? But you plan for everything, so we're as safe as can be, considering the circumstances."

"I'm just doing what anyone would do."

"That's not true, Mama. I bet Jabari wouldn't do it, would he? He couldn't and he wouldn't."

"No, I suppose not. But your father never had the mental stability to handle situations like this."

"That's my point, Mama. You have what it takes. You can make a complex plan and then you… You have follow-through."

"Like you, Cap'n. Persistence is all." Josie kissed her fingertip and pressed it against Samantha's forehead.

Samantha looked in the direction of the logging road they'd driven on as they came to the abbey. "I'll report any movement on the road or anywhere else."

"Okay, hon," Josie whispered. "Be good, Cap'n."

"Aye, Matey."

Josie gave Samantha a hug and stood up. She felt ice water running down her legs as she hurried away through the dark trees.

It was a moonless night, now nearly four in the morning, an hour or more later than what Josie had wanted. But it was still two hours before the first hint of dawn, so they should be okay. Josie moved by the light of the Milky Way. She carefully walked down the slope, through the forest, moving her feet with deliberation, step-by-step, staying in the brush and trees. She held her arms out in front of her to keep from walking into unseen branches and tree trunks. Josie moved slowly, trying to will herself to see in the dark. Bad vision was one thing. Bad vision in the dark was another.

There was enough breeze to create a rustling in the brush and a swishing in the needles on the trees above. It was perfect for cover. As long as none of them made a noise that was obviously manmade—a clank of metal or something similar—their sounds might be assumed to be natural.

As she got farther away from Samantha, she knew she was drawing closer to where Ellison and Cor and Diane were working. Yet she suddenly felt a great loneliness as if she were heading off into the forest of an alien planet, a mysterious place where the enemies threatened to destroy all.

Josie worked her way up a slope and found her command position, as Ellison had referred to it. It was a place they'd identified from the topo maps and satellite photos. A tangle of manzanita grew where the gradual slope came to a steep embankment that went down to the abbey. Despite the darkness, Josie had a view of the abbey and driveway and the surrounding grounds, even though they were all just vague dark shapes. She climbed over heavy twisted limbs of manzanita. There was a curved branch shaped vaguely like a U. She wiggled down to sit in the curve. The U was a bit too narrow for her hips and hence quite uncomfortable as it put a vise grip on her hip bones. But it allowed for some rest. She leaned back a bit, thinking she'd possibly contact another branch, which would give her back a rest. She hit a large branch, like the trunk of another manzanita. This one was vertical and rock solid, positioned even worse for comfort. But it was better than nothing.

The trunk pressed through her backpack with its angular contents, the medieval crossbow she'd hand-built as part of her Ph.D. dissertation.

Josie had disassembled her crossbow into its two main pieces, the stock-and-trigger assembly and the bow. Josie had built it using a medieval version of a mortise and tenon joint. It was a classic wood-joining approach that had been used for centuries. To reassemble the pieces, Josie would snap the joint together and push in the locking piece. Disassembled, the two main components just fit in the backpack. But it was uncomfortable to lean against. So Josie turned sideways a little, getting her shoulder propped against the manzanita trunk. It helped take some strain off her back.

Josie hoped that bringing the crossbow was excessive

preparation. But she wanted to have something with which to defend herself, just in case. It had worked before with devastatingly effective results.

She touched the mic button on her headset and spoke to the darkness, hoping her troops could hear her.

"Amelia and Sam are in position with a good view. How is your progress, Ellison?"

"Getting my levers in position. Almost ready to roll the boulders," Ellison said.

"Cor? Diane? Need any help?"

"No. We got this."

Josie recalled Ellison saying she was the general. The person who made the decisions and gave the directions.

But Josie didn't feel like a general. She was just a teacher, in far over her head. She could talk at length about historical battles. But now that she was about to launch her own battle, she felt unprepared and unsuited for the job.

She got out her phone and texted Cumberland. "Ready for power cut-off if you can manage it."

Half a minute later, Ellison's voice came over the two-way radio. "Ready to roll on your command."

Cor said, "Logging road blocked by junker. Diane and I are ready to dig out the final bit of dirt."

"Okay, let's do it," Josie said.

"Tailgate's down," Ellison said over the radio. His voice was soft but intense. "I levered out the main wedge. I don't understand…"

After a moment, "The boulder ain't moving. The boulder looks free," Ellison said. "It is free, damn it. But it's not moving. Let me get up in the truck bed. I'll change the position of this lever."

Cor's voice came loud. "Water's beginning to flow."

"I'll get my back behind this lever and push with my feet," Ellison said. There was a loud crack. "Damn!" Ellison said. "The lever broke. That was loud enough to wake people. Not to worry, I'll get this other one in position."

"Water's coming faster," Cor said.

Ellison's voice sounded frustrated. "Maybe I left a small chunk of wood under the edge of that bastard."

"Look out, Poseidon," Cor said. "Prepare to be swallowed by the sea."

Ellison said, "Lemme turn so I can work the lever while I use my feet against the boulder. Roll, you sucker!"

"Oh, mother," Diane said. "This is a gusher. Look out, Cor. You could lose your footing. You'd ride whitewater."

"It's moving," Ellison said. "It's rocking. It's happening. Oh, baby, here it goes. SWEET."

Josie heard a very loud clanking noise. The creak of metal, clang of cymbals, thud of rock banging on metal, then a duller thud of boulder on pavement.

"Liftoff," Ellison said.

Josie tensed, listening for any hint of sound that might come through the air instead of her headset.

But the loudest sound was her phone vibrating. On an incoming call.

FORTY-FIVE

"The ball of doom is rolling free," Ellison said in Josie's ears.

Josie's phone vibrated again.

"The boulder is already going down the drive," Ellison said. "It's moving faster. Straight toward the front door of the abbey. This is gonna be so good… Oh, wait. It's veering to the side. Crap. It's off the drive. Rolling toward the parking area."

Another buzz on Josie's phone. Josie struggled to focus. She released the mic switch on her headset so she wouldn't broadcast to the others.

She glanced at the screen. It was blinding in its brightness. She'd forgotten to turn down the brightness. She squinted her eyes. Saw that the caller was Cumberland!

"Hello, Cumberland," she answered, holding the phone near her headset so she could hear both it and what came over the headset.

"Professor. I got into the computer at the abbey and was able to trip a thermal cut-off relay that… But you don't need to know that, do you? Anyway, it looks like I shut down their off-grid electrical system until someone who knows the system can do a manual reset. So they'll probably be without power for a little while at the minimum. And without power, their satellite internet is down in addition to their regular lights and stuff."

"Great, Cumberland!" Josie whispered loudly. "You are amazing!"

"But I'm calling because I learned something you might want to know about the abbey."

"Okay."

Ellison was back in her ears. "The cargo almost stopped rolling, then sped up a little. It's heading toward… There are two

Suburbans parked near the abbey." He sounded very stressed. "Oh, whoa, baby. The cargo is… Right into the Suburban. Front and center."

Josie heard the thud of rock and crunch of metal in her headset and through the air at the same time.

Ellison said, "That SUV isn't going anywhere soon."

"The second baby is on track. Not so big, not so round. But… What the heck, number two is rolling straighter. Oh, now it's veering the other way. Toward the fence. What am I seeing? A rooster tail of water. Perfect. Number two is rolling through water. Wow, Bam! Through the wrought iron gate!"

Josie heard the crash.

"The fence slowed the boulder to a stop. Now it's starting to roll again. Yes, yes, yes. Another rooster tail. Right toward the front door. Not fast enough, though. Here we go. Bulls eye! Front door held, but it looks like it might be a little broken. There's so much water here, it can't help but be gushing into the front door."

Cor said, "Ellison, they could be running out soon! You should get your truck out of there and find us at our meeting place."

Cumberland was still talking in Josie's phone. "Remember when you told me about the secret door and stairway in that lady's house?" Cumberland said. "It made me curious. So I looked at more Building Department records."

"Okay," Josie said.

Ellison's voice came over the headset: "Okay, I'm in my truck and out of here. One Suburban down. Front door of the abbey dented."

Josie heard Ellison's truck engine.

Then she heard shouts. Muffled. From the direction of the abbey.

"Did I call at a bad time?" Cumberland asked. He could probably hear noises over Josie's headset.

Josie hesitated. "No, you're fine. What's up?"

"Remember you told me about the house near Placerville and that it had the secret staircase?"

Josie had a hard time concentrating on who was speaking.

Amelia's voice whispered in the headset: "The front door of the abbey is opening!"

Josie stared down toward the abbey. Did someone move over by the abbey's door? She squinted. Dark shapes on a dark background. Maybe she was seeing things. Or maybe someone was out in the dark. She realized that Cumberland had been talking. "Sorry, I didn't hear the last thing you said."

"I said that the county issued another building permit to her."

"Mary Jo Telman? For which house?"

"It was for the abbey. A few months after her LLC bought it."

"What was the other building permit for?" Josie asked Cumberland.

"It was for a tunnel and an underground garage at the abbey."

Josie stared through the darkness, willing herself to see what Amelia was seeing, as she continued to speak to Cumberland on the phone. "There's a tunnel and an underground garage here? I don't see any signs of that."

"Um, well, I'm looking at the building plans. The tunnel goes from the basement level of the abbey, through the ground to the underground garage. What's strange is the entrance to the tunnel is at the back of a utility closet. That seems unusual. Let's say you drive to the abbey and park in your underground garage. If you want to carry something from your car, like groceries or whatever, you wouldn't normally want to go through a utility closet, would you? Also, this closet looks kind of small. That made me think the tunnel might be secret. And because the lady had another secret passage, it sort of makes sense, right?"

"Absolutely," Josie said.

Amelia's voice in the headset: "The person who came out of the abbey is acting weird. Stomping across to the drive. Like he's trying to make his feet splash."

Josie heard a man's voice coming through the darkness. "What the hell is this?! The power is out here, too. And we've got some kind of major flood! The driveway is a river. There's water everywhere! And some giant rock rolled down and smashed the door. The water is coming in!"

Josie had heard the voice. It had a nasal quality. Something about the voice made her visualize a tattoo.

Snake!

The distant man's voice called out through the night. "Sanford! Bo! Wake up and get out here! We've got something freaky happening! I came out for a smoke and found a flood. It's like a lake out here! It's coming in the abbey!"

Josie was thinking about what Cumberland said about an underground garage with a tunnel connecting it to the abbey's basement. She reconsidered the area near the drive, looking for a location that could hold an underground garage. It was probably someplace without trees. Nothing seemed obvious. And the vehicles were parked out in the open. If they had an underground garage, why wouldn't they park in it?

Cumberland said, "There is writing on the architectural plans near the drawing of the garage. An arrow points to the garage door. The writing says, 'garage door mechanics are reinforced to accommodate the weight of the camouflaged door.'"

"That's interesting." Josie said. "As you look at the plans, can you describe where the garage is compared to the front door?"

"Let me rotate the plan so I can explain better. Okay. Pretend you are standing at the front door of the abbey. You are looking straight out at the driveway."

Josie looked at the doorway, where the unseen man was still shouting in the dark. She tried to visualize what it would look like if she were standing in the doorway. "Okay. I'm looking where you say."

Cumberland continued. "If straight out is at noon and nine o'clock is to your left, the garage is at eleven or eleven thirty. It's about a hundred feet from the abbey's entrance door. Maybe more."

"It's dark out," Josie said, "so I can't see much. I'm no good at judging distance. But it looks like there's nothing there but a slight rise and some bushes that lead up to where I am hiding.

But of course, the garage is underground, so I wouldn't be able to see anything."

Cumberland said, "The plans show two vent pipes at the garage. One's labeled, 'air intake.' The other's labeled 'air exhaust.'"

"Which could be hidden among the bushes," Josie said. "Thanks, Cumberland. This is very helpful."

"Okay, bye," he said and clicked off.

Josie stopped and reconsidered. She had a sudden realization. She reached one hand behind her and tapped her knuckles against the manzanita trunk she was leaning against. The knocking sound of her knuckles was a metallic thud. It wasn't manzanita. It was a pipe.

Josie realized the underground garage was directly below her.

Amelia's voice came in the headset. "Oh, no. Someone is coming toward me. No! Stop! What are you doing?!" Then a scream.

"Help!"

"Amelia?!" Josie shouted. "What happened? Are you okay?"

But there was no answer.

FORTY-SIX

When Amelia went silent, Josie's throat seemed to lock up with an intense pain. She couldn't breathe. Couldn't swallow.

"Mama!" Samantha's voice said in Josie's headset. "What should I do?"

Josie felt frozen. "Stay where you are," she finally said. "Stay hidden! Stay quiet! Everyone else... If you can hear me, Amelia was taken. I don't know where. And Cumberland says there's a tunnel from the abbey that leads to a hidden underground garage. I'm not sure if that changes what we're doing. But be aware. There might be men who will come out of that garage. Or maybe men will hide in it. Maybe that's where they took Amelia."

Josie had to get back to where Amelia had been hiding. Maybe the entrance to the hidden garage was close to where she'd left Amelia.

But it was so dark, she wasn't sure of her position.

She ran into some branches, twigs poking her in the cheek and sharp points gouging her shoulder. She backed up, tried to go around, felt her outstretched fingertips brush something. Something rough and hard. A tree trunk. Josie fumbled her way around it and continued through the darkness.

She had no idea what happened to Amelia. She and Samantha had left her a good distance from the abbey. Had someone seen them? Someone like Snake, with night-vision goggles? Had that person run all that way from the abbey's front door to grab Amelia?

Josie spoke to her headset mic. "Amelia? Can you hear me? Say something. Amelia!"

Again, there was nothing.

Josie came down the slope that she now thought was the roof of the underground garage. She hit a hard level surface. The drive. Where was Amelia from here?

She could barely make out the dark shape of the Abbey's front door. There was more movement by the door. Josie couldn't see a person. There was no light coming out of the abbey. Then a flashlight turned on. It was blindingly bright.

The movement of the flashlight was awkward. Like the person holding it was doing something unusual. Running through water.

The flashlight moved in a jerky fashion, over to the vehicles.

The interior light came on inside one of the SUVs. Was it the one that Ellison damaged with his rolling boulder?

Josie sensed one of the vehicle doors opening. Then another door on the opposite side. It looked like they put something into the back of the SUV. Their movement made Josie think of luggage.

A voice carried through the darkness. "God, there's a giant boulder that smashed into the front of the Suburban! The flood must have dislodged it from up by the road. We have to move our gear into the other Suburban."

"Why? We could just dig in, here. So what if some stuff gets wet?"

"No way. I heard about natural disasters. The fire department comes through. Maybe cops, too. Help me get those file boxes and duffles out of here! You know what the boss will do if some outsider sees those duffles?!"

None of the voices sounded like Snake. Where had he gone? Was he the one who found Amelia? Grabbed her?

The voices got muffled as if the men went back inside. In a minute, people came back out.

Doors opened on another one of the vehicles.

Josie could see moving flashlights. It looked like they were moving luggage.

More movement by the abbey's door. More flashlights. The men weren't running. But they were moving fast. As they got closer to the light from the SUV, Josie could see two people. Then a third, smaller person. The three people got into the SUV, its interior lights illuminating their shapes.

Two more men ran out of the abbey, both with flashlights wavering. Their movements were less smooth, like they were big and clumsy. Or maybe they were just carrying something. They appeared to put bags in the back of the vehicle that wasn't damaged. Then they ran back to the abbey for another trip.

On their return to the Suburban, there was a third flashlight. They got in the SUV. That made a total of six people, Josie thought. Five men, and a smaller person. Yet it was a large vehicle. Someone else could have been there in the dark. If anyone didn't have a flashlight, it would be nearly impossible to see them.

Josie pushed in the button on the headset mic.

"I don't know where Amelia is," she said, her voice choking. "I think everyone is getting into one of the Suburbans. I counted six people. Five looked like men. One was smaller. Maybe a woman. It could be Elena. Maybe Amelia. But I didn't see any movement near where Amelia was hiding."

"The flood has them panicked," Ellison said. He was breathing hard as if he was moving fast. "It could be everyone who was at the abbey is now in the Suburban."

Josie heard the faint sound of doors closing, and the interior lights of the vehicle turned off. An engine started. Headlights came on, shining across the dark landscape. The SUV started driving.

"The SUV is pulling out," Josie said, "and headed your way. Cor, Diane, Ellison? Are you all okay?"

"That's affirmative," Cor said. "When Samantha tells us which way they turn onto the logging road, we'll intercept them. Ellison is just now getting into my Jeep." There was a pause and then the sound of a car door shutting.

"Any word from Amelia?" Cor asked.

"No," Josie said. Then, "Samantha? Watch for the Suburban coming your way."

"I haven't seen them yet," Samantha said. "I'll let you know as soon as I do."

"Okay." Josie was about to click off her mic. Something stopped her. "Cor, can you talk while you drive?"

"Of course."

Josie had a sense of a fleeting thought that was hard to grasp, but nevertheless seemed important.

After a moment, Cor said, "Are you still there? Josie? I'm driving up the shortcut trail. We'll be nearing the logging road in a bit. That will put us in front of the men leaving the abbey."

Josie said, "You just said the word 'affirmative.' What's the difference between 'affirmative' and 'yes'?"

Josie could hear Cor breathing.

"I don't get it." Cor sounded confused. "What does that have to do with our plan?"

"I think it will tell me who the killer is."

Cor paused. "You're serious?"

"Yes."

"I don't know about affirmative." Cor sounded frustrated. "It's an Army thing. It's more precise. Some people use 'yes' for a range of things. You can even answer the phone with 'yes.' And 'yes' rhymes with other words. If the communication channel isn't very clear, you might think someone said 'mess' or bless' or 'guess.' But almost nothing rhymes with affirmative. It can only mean one thing."

"Thanks. What about the phrase 'roger that?' I've heard the phrase, but what does it really mean?" Josie asked.

Cor said, "It simply means, 'Message received.' Some use it for 'Message received, and I agree.'"

"So if someone says 'affirmative' or 'roger that,' would you assume they were in the military?"

Cor answered, "I've heard the phrase many times with no connection to the military. So connecting 'roger that' to the military is a weak connection. I give it a 'maybe.' How 'bout you, Ellison? Diane?"

"Roger that on a possible connection," Ellison said, his voice grim. "But I have no doubt Josie has a reason for asking."

Samantha said, "I see a glow of approaching headlights.

They're slowing and approaching the logging road. I can't tell yet which way they're going. They're almost coming to a stop. It's like they're trying to decide… Left! They're going left. Away from the junker."

"We're ready to intercept these guys," Cor said, "Josie, will you be along soon?"

"I'm still looking for Amelia. I assume they grabbed her as a bargaining chip. But I never saw any sign of her. I'll head to my car, pick up Sam, and we'll be along. If we're not there when you meet the men, you'll still do the same performance. Only now you should look for both Elena and Amelia. Sam and I will hear the broadcast version in our headsets."

Cor, Diane, and Ellison had planned to stop any vehicles, look for Elena and see what they could learn about the occupants. Josie had planned to run to her car, take the tape off the lights, and drive with Samantha. If possible, Josie would catch up with the vehicle.

Josie had to slow as she rushed to her car. She was breathing so hard, her lungs burned. She got to a part of the drive that she recognized. It was near the point where Cor and Diane had dumped the junk Chevy Vega. Josie's car would be up the logging road near Ellison's truck. Josie tried to remember the layout. She thought it was about 50 yards away. She tried to walk fast up the slope, but the effort had her gasping for air.

Cor's voice spoke in the headset.

"We're in position. I've got the flashers on and the magnetic red cop light stuck on the roll bar. Ellison's out of the Jeep next to the big lantern. He's got on his chest-candy jacket, so we're ready. The SUV is approaching. I'll leave the headset mic on so you can monitor."

Josie could only hear her own breathing as she tried to listen to her headset. There was silence and background noise and the soft, resigned baritone voice of Ellison saying, "Let's do it." It might not be a frightening situation compared to the war in Vietnam, but he was probably thinking about when he got clobbered up in the San Bernardino mountains.

There was the sound of the Jeep door opening, then

shutting. Then the sound of a vehicle engine, increasing, then decreasing.

Cor's voice: "U.S. Army Colonel Ellison would like a word, gentlemen."

Ellison's voice, "This traffic stop is so we can alert area residents and travelers to a flood in the Army's Five Thirty-One fiber-optic corridor. Have you seen any flood waters?"

"Are you kidding?" said a man. "The whole mountain is wet. What could cause that? Some damn thing the Army did?"

"We speculate a damaged water canal, sir."

Josie imagined that Cor and Diane were peering into the Suburban as Ellison spoke.

Another man's voice: "Sorry, dude. This does not compute. My buddy is Army. He woulda told me of any Army crap around here. I think you are full of it."

Cor's voice: "Sir, you are speaking to an Army colonel. I understand you've been drinking and are surprised by our presence. But please show some respect. We're only looking out for your safety."

Josie heard the sound of a vehicle door opening and closing.

Man's voice: "And what is this Jeep? This ain't no regulation Army vehicle. Show me your ID and I'll call my buddy."

Cor's voice: "Sir, stand back."

Man's voice: "What are you gonna do about it? And who's this little blonde hottie? Two Army ladies for one colonel?"

Cor's voice: "I won't ask you again. Please step away."

Man's voice: "I'll get in your face if I want. You look like a pretender to me. And this little blonde is hardly big enough to shoot a… Ugh!"

Josie heard an exhalation and then a thumping sound as if someone slammed into the side of a vehicle.

Man's voice: "What the…! You're gonna be sorry, angel. Aargh!"

Josie heard a car door open. A feminine whimper. Running steps.

Another man's voice: "Stop, girl, or I'll take you down!"

Diane's voice: "Run Elena! Go a mile, then hide. We'll find you come daylight."

The other man's voice: "I'll show you why not to mess with…" There was a sudden cracking sound and then a loud oomph sound as the man's breath seemed to explode out of his mouth.

Josie heard a big thud and then another. Some sounds that Josie couldn't identify.

Cor's voice was loud and close as if she were bending her head down to speak to Josie. She said, "Three men down. Their wrists and ankles are zip-tied. Woman victim freed. Ellison has the other men at gunpoint."

"Oh, God," Josie muttered to herself, trying to stifle the words even as she uttered them. She'd hoped that things wouldn't explode to this level. Ellison's using his gun?!

Ellison's voice: "On the ground!" he shouted. "All of you. Do it! NOW!" There was a pause. "You mess with the Army, we'll put you in the Sierra Army Depot lockup for obstructing an official Army operation! Nighttime desert temps push below freezing this time of year, and they're gonna strip you. Have you heard about the Army Depot lockup? No defense lawyer has ever gotten in to see an inmate in eighteen years. You will be removed from the human race. It's like being put on Mars, men. And you are one twitch of my trigger finger from mortal injury. Give me an excuse, you miserable miscreants! Go on! Try me!"

A man's voice: "Oh, honey, ignore this old geezer. I'm gonna show you how a real man handles a woman like you…" There was another big thud. A man hollered and then screamed long and loud.

Ellison's voice. "Easy, Sergeant, you don't have to show them just how tough a small woman can be."

Another man laughed and mumbled something in a taunting way.

Diane's voice: "You bastard." Her voice was a hiss. "I can make it so you never again grab another woman like that."

"Try me, cutie pie."

Josie heard a sound like branches snapping. Then another

howl followed by a man whimpering. "Oh, God, you broke my hand. You're never…Oh mother of God, that hurts. No, don't do that. No, don't…" There came more snapping sounds, and his words turned to a prolonged scream.

A minute later, Cor's voice: "Five men down, wrists and ankles zipped and tied to each other. Patted down, weapons, phones, and car keys confiscated. I'm gonna double zip them, then hog tie them, then pants them."

Ellison's voice: "They're not going anywhere until the cops get here."

Josie heard other sounds. Some that were clearly pain. Some that may have only been psychological misery.

Diane's voice, almost too faint to understand: "After all that with your friend, you try to trip me, you piece of crap? Here's a lesson you will never forget about underestimating women. We can be just as tough as your worst nightmares."

Josie heard another howl of agony.

Diane's voice calling out over a man's sobbing: "Here's a souvenir to take home so you always remember."

A man screamed louder than before.

Cor's voice: "Six men down."

Josie didn't even want to know what had happened.

Josie knew she should be driving toward them.

Josie stared out at the darkness. She worried about Samantha out alone in the dark. "I'm still here, Sam," she said as if talking to the faceless night. "I've got something else to check out. Are you and Unknown still okay?"

"Yeah, Mama."

"Ellison? Cor? Do any of the men have a large tattoo of a snake on their left arm and up their neck?"

"Let me check," Cor said. After a minute, "No. All they have is girlie tattoos and super hero tattoos. Adolescent stuff. Nothing of substance. No art, no emotion."

"Thanks. Can you give me a little longer?" Josie said.

"We've got the rest of the night to sit on these dirtballs," Ellison said. "We could count their money for fun."

"Are you serious?"

"Yes, ma'am. Four duffle bags of it. Used bills, banded by denomination. Can't imagine how much it is. A good portion of the bundles are hundreds. A serious piece of change. Millions, probably."

"Won't the authorities be eager to see that." Josie thought she should give up her wait and join the others when she sensed something. This time it wasn't sound or light. It was a vibration. Coming from the slope that Cumberland said was an underground garage.

FORTY-SEVEN

A deep rumbling sound seemed to come from the ground. A vague glow appeared over on the far side of the domed hill, an area out of Josie's line of vision. Cumberland had mentioned a camouflaged door on the building plans. Apparently, what looked like a slope was, in fact, an opening to the underground garage.

The glow got brighter. Bright light shined on some bushes. A car appeared, coming up at an angle as if on a ramp from underground.

The last people to leave the abbey?

The car's headlights reflected off the surrounding trees. The glow made it easier for Josie to see. She stepped up her pace. The place where she'd hid her Prius was close.

She pressed her mic button as she went.

"Watch the logging road for one more vehicle," she said, panting. "I can't see what kind. Smaller than the Suburban. A car. It came from an underground garage. Its occupant will probably be armed. I'm worried. If he's the sniper and he realizes that we've set him up, he can stop well back from you and shoot you from a distance."

"I see headlights coming," Samantha said.

Josie was winded, trying to both talk and run. She stopped talking so she could get more air.

Although she was moving away from the car that had left the garage, she was aware that its headlights changed their angle. She turned to look back through the forest. It was no longer near the abbey driveway. It was heading in a new direction through the forest. A hidden path from the hidden garage?

"Stay down, Samantha. Everybody, stay down and turn off your lights. The car is heading your way, but it's on a trail we haven't seen before."

Josie got to her car, took off her pack with the crossbow parts and set it inside. She peeled the blue painter's tape off the headlights. Seeing where she was driving was more important than hiding. Especially now that the abbey's occupants were mostly detained by Cor and Ellison.

Samantha's voice whispered in the headset. "The car is heading over toward that big hill. Where we saw the maze."

As Josie started her car, she had the shocking realization that whoever had Amelia could hear everything they said on Amelia's headset. Josie was breathing fast, hyperventilating. She drove as fast as she dared.

"Hey everybody," Josie said, "they took Amelia. That means they can hear everything we say. So don't reveal locations. And Sam, you stay hidden. They can't find you."

The beam from the other vehicle's headlights disappeared.

Josie slowed.

The other headlights reappeared as a sudden flash through the forest, then went out again. Josie drove through the dark. She was choked with emotion, worrying about Amelia and wondering if this rescue mission was a terrible mistake.

If the woman Diane and Cor saw was Elena, then maybe Amelia was in the car that had driven into the forest. Since Cor said there was no man with a snake tattoo among the men she stopped, maybe it was Snake who was driving the car with Amelia.

"Remember, Sam, please don't move. I suspect the other car is Snake's. He probably has Amelia. He's probably listening to us right now. We should all keep our mics on. I'll report as soon as I know where he's going."

"Okay," Cor said.

Josie could barely breathe as she chastised herself over her mistakes. What have I done? Amelia was helping us! Helping me! And now I've… Josie wiped her eyes, trying to see through her tears and the trees and the terror.

How could she not have seen this coming? She had believed that they kidnapped Elena Soto. Yet she brought Samantha and

Amelia here! What was she thinking?!

Josie's Prius bounced as it went over the bumps and dips of the forest floor. Her headlights shined on a trail that split off from the more traveled road. There were fresh tire marks in the mud. Josie turned to follow it. The trail was primitive. Dirt tracks through the trees.

Josie raced along the trail. Turned hard around trees. She jerked on the steering wheel as if to rip it from the dash.

Ahead of her came a flash of red. Tail lights were visible for a moment, then disappeared as the road curved. Josie tried to drive faster. She came to a hard right-angle turn. She went around it, skidding in the dirt, the Prius rocking violently to the side. For a moment she could again see tail lights through the forest.

There was another turn.

Josie realized the dirt trail was not going anywhere near the logging road. They wouldn't come near the others at the road block. Josie was being led farther off into the mountains. Away from the abbey and the highway. Away from anything.

The distant car's headlights flashed through the forest. The light beams washed over something that didn't look like trees. It was a wall. Vines over stone.

FORTY-EIGHT

Josie saw no more taillights on the vehicle she was following. Around a curve? Or had the other vehicle stopped? Engine and lights off?

Josie had been trying to drive even faster through the darkness. There was a sudden sharp turn.

She hit the brakes. Too hard. The car skidded. She slid to the edge of the road. Josie tried to steer to counteract the skid. She overcompensated. The car skidded the other way. It went across the road. Just before she came to a stop, the front wheel dropped off the edge. The undercarriage of the car grounded out on a high section in the trail. Long ago she'd heard someone talk about such a predicament. They called it being high-centered.

Josie felt herself begin to panic. She shifted into Reverse. Gave the car power. A wheel spun, but the car didn't move.

Josie's breathing was short and fast. In a moment she was hyperventilating.

Maybe if she rocked the car. She shifted into Drive and hit the accelerator. She was worried she'd shoot down the slope.

Again there was the sound of rubber spinning on gravel. The Prius didn't move.

One more try in Reverse.

Nothing.

Josie could barely breathe. She looked in her rearview mirror and then looked ahead, scanning for any sign of light or movement. Nothing.

Josie turned off her car. She reached behind her for her pack. She couldn't feel it.

Where had she put it?!

She turned halfway around, leaned into the back seat. Felt the seats.

There. Heavy nylon fabric. Hard pieces of crossbow wood inside.

She lifted the pack forward to her lap, opened her door, and nearly fell out.

The ground dropped away. Either there was a deep depression in that part of the trail, or she was on the edge of a precipice. She had to slide off the edge of the driver's seat before her shoes hit the dirt. She slipped, her shoes sliding on the dirt and gravel, and she went down on her butt. Her pack slammed down on the tops of her thighs.

Josie scooted forward in the dark without even trying to stand up. The night was cave-black. Where was her flashlight? Her phone?

In the car.

She scrambled on hands and knees up to the car. The door was still open. She felt around in the dark. Eventually she found her phone on the passenger seat. The flashlight had fallen onto the floor. She put the phone in her pocket and held the flashlight.

There was a flash of light on a mountainside a long distance away. The light on the mountain moved, growing brighter, then dimmer. Josie had no idea where the source of the light was. Nearby and shining away? Or far away and shining near?

Josie took her pack and tried to crawl away from her Prius. She felt herself losing control and sensed little whimpering noises in her throat. She gritted her teeth and swallowed. She was not going to be taken without a fight!

Besides, she was the hunter, not the other way around. She was following the last person to jump ship at the abbey.

She stood up, slipped the pack straps over her shoulders, and started walking slowly through the dark, taking tentative steps, hoping she wouldn't step into a hole or trip over a root.

She was on a section of road that went up at a steep angle. After just a few steps, she hit grass. Had she stepped off the trail? There was no way to know unless she turned on her flashlight. But she was loathe to use it as it would make her a target and destroy whatever night vision she had.

The darkness was complete. But she could see some stars. After a short time, she could see a great many stars. With no artificial lights, her night vision was slowly becoming more effective, something she never experienced in Los Angeles.

Despite the slow appearance of stars, she still couldn't see anything other than those pinpoints of light. She moved by feel, her arms out in front of her in the hope that she wouldn't walk into anything. She sensed that she was on a trail for the simple reason that she hadn't hit brush or trees.

As Josie moved, she tried to remember what she'd last seen in her headlights. But nothing came to mind. There'd been a flash of light from the car she was following and then the view of the curving trail lit by her own headlights. Now there was nothing.

Josie was moving forward in baby steps, shuffling her shoes along the dirt, when she sensed that the trail was going up.

After a minute of shuffling, she was breathing hard. Why, when she was moving so slowly? She realized she was going up a substantial rise. After a long minute of going uphill, she sensed a widening and lightening of the sky. Maybe it was an opening in the trees. Or maybe there was light from somewhere. Was it the approaching dawn? No, there was no light in the sky. She kept moving, trying to see through the tree canopy.

There. A flash of light shining through the tree branches in the sky to the east.

A sliver of moon, just above the horizon. Rising before dawn.

Josie was careful not to look at the moon, as whatever advantage its light might give her would be lost as it dulled her night vision.

When the trees closed in again, the darkness increased, demonstrating how much light came from that moon sliver.

The trail crested a small hill, went down just a few yards, and then began climbing a new slope, steeper than before. Josie felt she must be getting close to the maze. But she saw nothing in the darkness. Then she sensed a new light.

Josie walked toward the light. After some distance, the light elongated, split into two, then went back to one. Josie realized what it was.

The sliver of moon was reflecting off something shiny. A car, probably new and recently washed, so that its paint glistened.

The car was parked in front of a wall of rock. The edge of the maze.

She assumed that no one was in the car, but there was no way to tell. If she shined her flashlight, that would destroy her night vision, and, if the car had darkened windows, she still might not be able to tell if anyone was inside. She thought of trying the door handle, but that might set off an alarm. Better not take the risk.

Josie realized she might be very close to people. Someone like Snake might have taken Amelia from the car and gone into the maze or at least to the other side.

Josie had her weapon, but it would do her no good in her pack. She walked away toward a group of trees that were slightly lit up by the moon. She could find a place to sit down and assemble her crossbow.

A car door closed someplace close. Not in front of her. Maybe behind her. How did someone get behind her? Did the person she was following sense where she was and call for help?

Josie started running to the side, away from the car and the sound of the closing door.

She sensed more moonlight. Not enough to clearly perceive trees and bushes. She sped up, pushing herself until she was nearly running. Her jacket caught on some branches. Fabric tore. The ripping noise seemed like a roar in Josie's ears. She tried to run faster.

A light flashed through the forest, then went off.

Josie kept trying to run.

Now a flashlight turned on, its obvious beam bouncing and jerking through the trees where Josie was running. Despite her heavy panting, Josie heard sounds. Footfalls. Branches breaking. Twigs snapping. Heavy breathing.

A man was coming for her. Josie realized she'd never be able to outrun him. Snake didn't look fit, but he was certainly in much better shape. It was hopeless. Her only chance was to hide.

She looked for places as she ran through the woods. Maybe she could find a log on the ground and lie next to it. Maybe she could pull branches over her.

But there wasn't time. It was too dark to see anything in the forest. He was coming. He was close. She didn't even have time to put her crossbow together. Josie plunged through the dark forest. Her uncontrolled whimpers seemed to grow against her will. It was part of her panting breaths. Air going in and out, with a little cry on each exhalation.

The forest seemed to get darker. More dense. The moonlight couldn't come through the tree canopy. But then the forest floor seemed to glow. Josie realized she'd run to an area where there was still snow. The forest was dense enough that sun couldn't come through to melt it. Two or three inches. Crunching underfoot. Spilling into the tops of her water-soaked shoes.

Which meant that she was leaving footprints. If the man saw them with his flashlight, it would be easy for him to follow.

She couldn't even hide.

Then the white went away. The trees became less dense. The forest seemed to come to a stop. Josie paused for a moment, trying to breathe, trying to understand what she was seeing. There was an open meadow. The snow was gone because it had been melted by the sun. The meadow was dark even though the sliver of moon was shining down. Darker than Josie would have expected. Much darker. Then she realized why.

Not far away was a dark fence. A wall of dark rock. She'd somehow circled back around to The Sierra Maze.

Josie realized this was her chance to hide. If she could get to the maze and find the entrance, she could get lost in its passages. She could find a corner far back in its recesses, a place where she could get down next to a wall. If she didn't move, it might take hours for the man chasing her to find her location in the maze.

Josie ran across the meadow, nearly sprinting. The ground was uneven. Each placement of her feet felt risky. The slightest hole could twist her ankle and bring her down in the dark. But she didn't have a choice. All she could do was run through the dark and focus on speed. She needed to get into the maze before her pursuer could get to the meadow and shine his flashlight at her as she ran across the meadow.

Josie came to the rock wall. Despite the little bit of moonlight, the dark wall was featureless. Josie put her hands out, touching the rock. She let her fingertips drag across the ice-cold rock as she moved sideways, looking for the entrance, feeling for an opening. She tried to remember when she and Samantha saw the maze from the airplane. Could she recall any helpful details? Not much.

The outer wall of the maze was a circle just like medieval labyrinths.

Josie kept her hands on the stones, feeling as she ran to the left. The rock was cold and rough and slippery with frost.

Then the rock wasn't there at all.

The entrance.

FORTY-NINE

Josie stepped into the opening. She went from dark night to an even darker space inside the maze.

Yet, even though the maze felt similar to a cave, it had no roof. But there were some vines that bridged from one wall to the next. Moonlight came through the vines and provided a small bit of illumination. But the rock walls were so dark, it was nearly impossible for Josie to see how the passage went. Her touch on the rock made it seem that the passage went to the left and then gradually curved to the right. Josie went by feel, going clockwise around a circular path like in a traditional labyrinth. She followed the curving path and ran into a wall.

Fortunately, she had her arm out, and she hit the rock with her hand and not her face. She reached out with her hands. Felt another wall. Was she at a dead end?

Josie's recollection from reading about the Sierra Maze was that it wasn't like a labyrinth with one long path designed for contemplation. The Sierra Maze was designed like a puzzle, with multiple choices of passages and openings.

She turned and walked forward with her arms out. There was another passage going back the way she'd come. It was one of the curving loops, typical of a labyrinth. Now she was curving again, this time counter-clockwise. Labyrinths had concentric circles. She was now on the next ring.

Josie continued on. Came to a corner. This would be an opportunity to put together her crossbow.

She sat down in the dark and, working by feel, pulled the components out of her pack. She'd assembled and disassembled the bow many times over the years. It should have been easy. But she'd never done it in the dark. The pieces didn't feel familiar even though she'd spent hours making them a dozen years ago.

Josie stopped and took a deep breath. She closed her eyes, which immediately felt ridiculous. It was too dark to see, anyway. But consciously closing them calmed her.

She lifted up the parts of the crossbow. Ran her hands and fingers over the wood. Established which piece was which. Figured out the orientation. Found where the pieces joined.

One piece of Josie's homemade weapon was the curved bow made from pieces of wood she'd steamed, bent into shape, and then laminated with glue. The curved bow had a heavy cord that held the wood in its curved shape.

The other piece was the long stock with the trigger assembly and the groove for the bolt. The two pieces fit together with a mortise and tenon joint that used no glue. It was a joining approach that Josie took from medieval designs. Because building the crossbow was part of her Medieval History Ph.D. dissertation, she was meticulous in conforming to the construction approach that went back a millennium.

She pushed the wooden pieces into position, wiggling them into a tight fit. Then she pushed in the wood dowel that locked the joint.

In a clip on the foregrip of the stock were four bolts. They were held in place with a leather strap the size of a man's bracelet. Josie loosened the strap, pulled out a bolt, and inserted it onto the track of the stock. Like the rest of the crossbow, the bolts were handmade using medieval techniques. The bolts were hand-forged of iron, heated to a malleable temperature, then pounded into shape, about five inches long and half an inch in diameter, and honed to a sharp point. The bolts were heavy. They didn't fly with the speed or accuracy of a modern bullet or even an arrow shot from a longbow. But they were relatively heavy. In many situations, they were deadlier than nearly any projectile that wasn't explosive.

Josie slid the bolt forward until it hit the stop. She pulled back on the cord and hooked it over the rear of the bolt. The winch crank had a ratchet catch. Tensioning the cord would make noise, a clicking that seemed very loud. But the weapon was useless until it was tensioned.

Josie began to turn the winch crank very slowly. Each click made a loud metallic snick.

As the cord was pulled all the way back, it put enormous tension on the bow, tension that would propel the bolt when the release trigger was pulled.

All Josie needed to fire the bolt was to disengage the trigger lock.

Josie stood and put her backpack on. She held the crossbow in her right hand and felt the rock wall with her left. She moved forward once again. The wall turned. She had gone several steps when she came to an opening on the inside wall of the curve.

Josie turned through the opening. She ran her hand along the wall. The passage turned right. Several steps more, it turned left. Then came another opening. Once through it, she could go either way. It was an arbitrary choice. She chose right. She went several steps and came to a wall. She felt left and right, turned around, re-checked. She tried to get a visual sense of the layout by the scant light of the sliver of moon shining through the overhanging vines to the rock walls below. Her vision had never been good, and that was a serious hindrance. Nevertheless, she concluded that she'd come to a dead end.

That was frightening. She felt hopelessly lost in the dark. In the wilderness. All alone except for someone who was probably a killer.

If the man pursuing her found her, she'd have no escape. But that also had an advantage. He couldn't sneak up on her from behind. If she were ready with her crossbow, a dead end might be useful.

But where was Amelia?

Did he have Amelia? Had Snake tied her up and stashed her at some dead-end part of the maze? Did he leave her in the trunk of the car? Shouldn't Josie continue to search in hopes of finding her?

Maybe she could get a look over the top of the stone walls. The faint moonlight might illuminate the maze.

Moving very slowly, Josie set the crossbow on the ground, point down and leaning against the rock wall to her right. The walls of the dead end had rounded corners. She stood in one of those corners, within arm's reach of the crossbow, and raised her arms up, hoping to feel where the top of the wall formed the corner. But this section of wall had a top edge made of smooth, rounded stones. She couldn't get a grip. She shifted her hands sideways over the stones, moving to the left. She found an area where the stones had edges. She was able to wrap her fingers over the top. One stone was too sharp. It would cut. Another stone was irregular but not so sharp. She grabbed it with her fingertips. She held onto the stones, then lifted one of her feet a foot off the ground and slid the toe of her shoe over the surface of the wall, feeling for more roughness where she could get a grip with the sole of her shoe. There was a small gap between two of the rocks that made up the wall. She tried to cram the edge of her sole into that gap. She pulled with her hands and managed to rise up a foot.

Josie scrabbled her other shoe against the wall. She tried to find a grip, frantically moving her shoe left and right, up and down. She was about to lose her hand grip when her shoe lodged in some type of gap. With her two shoes barely gripping the wall, Josie was able to pull herself a bit higher. She peeked over the walls. The moonlit expanse of maze and meadow was dramatically lighter than the cave-like blackness within the maze The relative lightness was a relief.

Until she saw the bobbing beam of a flashlight off to her left.

The light came from within the maze! The man was not far away, and he was coming in her direction. Maybe there were walls between him and her. Josie hoped so, but she couldn't tell. She knew she couldn't stumble blindly ahead. She might walk right to him, and she would have no chance without a weapon.

Josie stepped down, squatted down, and sat on the ground. She reached out, found her crossbow, and leaned back against the end of the passage. She remembered her flashlight and got it out of the pocket in her pants. She would be facing her attacker if he found her.

She sensed a light and looked up toward the top of the

wall.

Light spilled across the top of the walls. The light seemed to bob. The light got brighter. And much closer!

Josie gripped her crossbow, her finger accidentally hitting the trigger.

Josie inhaled. Fortunately, the crossbow didn't fire.

Moving in slow motion, she set the crossbow down, took off her jacket, and picked up the crossbow. She carefully draped her jacket over the crossbow, keeping the fabric away from the tension cord and the bolt. By adjusting the fabric, she thought it would partially obscure the weapon.

Her next effort was to shift over to the side wall. She knew that if the man came down the passage and shined his light on her, he would see her cowering against the wall, in a corner of the dead end. She would hopefully look so fragile and debilitated that he would perceive no threat. Josie thought that most killers would hesitate to shoot a woman cowering on the ground.

Now that Josie was in position, all she could do was wait.

The ground was hard and covered with what felt like sharp stones. But she focused on her weapon. She knew a weapon was only useful if the person holding it had the will and focus to use it.

FIFTY

Josie wondered about her decision. She could still stand up and go on a hunt for the killer. That would require her feeling her way through unfamiliar passages. If she didn't move by feel, she would have to use her flashlight, which would alert anyone to her presence.

A better choice was to sit tight and focus. She'd be like bait in a trap, waiting for the predator to find her. That had the advantage of maximum stealth. No one would know where she was until they stepped into her sight, exposing themselves to her deadly weapon. That seemed more effective.

The driver of the car she'd followed would have seen her headlights in his rearview mirror. He knew that she was out here somewhere. He probably knew that Josie had heard Amelia's cry for help in her headset. He had every reason to believe Josie would come after him in an effort to save Amelia. As long as Josie was patient, he might eventually walk into her trap.

Then she remembered that her headset was on. If any of the others spoke, it would be easy to hear. She carefully ran her fingertips along the headset, feeling for the on/off switch. There was a curved wheel. Volume. Next to it, a raised bit of plastic. She gave it a gentle push. Nothing. Pushed it the other way. It moved with a click. Hopefully, that turned the headset off.

Josie took a deep breath and tried to calm herself. But then the words 'affirmative' and 'roger that' bothered her. Cor had used them. But she'd heard them before. Where? When? It had been recently, she thought. Somebody she didn't know well. Somebody she'd met. Then it came to her.

When she'd first gotten into the governor's limousine at UCLA three months ago, he'd said something, turned to his aide Sonja Gonsalves, and asked if his information was correct.

Gonsalves answered the question the same way that Cor had. 'Affirmative.' Josie thought Sonja had also used it more recently, as well.

Now Josie wondered if Sonja had also been in the military. Lucas Herman, operating under the alias Taylor Cooke, was one of the governor's assistants. He learned his sniper skills in the Army, and he turned out to be the sniper assassin who killed Mary Jo. Was it possible that the governor's other employee, Sonja Gonsalves, had also been in the Army?

Sonja had been so supportive, so helpful. She couldn't be involved with the people running the abbey, could she?

But when Josie had recently spoken to Sonja on the phone, the woman used the phrase 'roger that.' Before that, she used the word 'affirmative.'

Cor and Ellison made it seem that the words weren't strong indicators of military experience. But they also agreed that military people use both phrases.

Josie went over what she knew about Sonja, which was basically nothing. But what could she surmise? The woman was efficient and focused, clearly a good resource for the governor. It seemed unlikely for a typical employee in Sonja's position to use the word affirmative. Certainly, Josie didn't know any professors or secretaries who used those words.

Josie didn't know anything about the military. But she'd met people who'd been in the military. Many of them had characteristics similar to Sonja and Cor. They had good posture, whether standing or sitting. They didn't engage in much social conversation. They were efficient. They didn't wear trendy clothes or much, if any, makeup. They had short hair and polished shoes. Their clothes were neat and clean, their shirts tucked in. They called people by titles, Mr., Ms. or ma'am. Or Professor. They showed respect for those around them.

Josie remembered that the governor had said that his good friend was the father of Mary Jo Telman. But Josie also remembered that, when she and Samantha met Mary Jo Telman at her hideaway home near Placerville, the woman mentioned her father in disparaging tones.

Josie's thoughts were interrupted by a thumping sound. Maybe even a distant voice? She listened to her surroundings. Everything was silent.

After a few moments, Josie returned to her thoughts about Mary Jo.

When Mary Jo had spoken of her father, Mary Jo referred to him as King Lear. At the time, it seemed such an unusual description of one's father that it stuck in Josie's memory.

What did it mean to describe a man as King Lear?

To Josie, King Lear was only a character in a play by Shakespeare. Had she seen it? Years ago? Josie couldn't recall for certain. But what was King Lear about? Josie had a vague memory that King Lear wanted to give his empire to whichever of his three daughters loved him the most. Two of the daughters competed for his favors, telling him lies about their love for him. Those two daughters were also in love with the same man. As Josie thought about it, she remembered that one of King Lear's daughters murdered the other!

Despite the darkness in the maze, Josie shut her eyes for a moment as if that would help her retrieve her memories.

Was it possible that Sonja Gonsalves and Mary Jo Telman were sisters? Did they both love Francis Telman? Did Sonja join the military and get training to become a sniper? Did she kill Mary Jo? Why? Because she loved Francis? If so, why would she kill Francis? To punish him and Mary Jo for falling in love? Or could it all have been a scheme to take Mary Jo's businesses and property?

The ideas all seemed ridiculous.

But why did Mary Jo mention King Lear? She must have suffered major family stress to compare her father to King Lear. And behind that direct comparison might be an implied comparison of King Lear's daughters to Mary Jo and a sister, if she had one.

It probably wouldn't take much research to find out if Mary Jo had sisters and if one of them was Sonja Gonsalves. Cumberland could figure it out. The governor was connected to both Mary Jo's father and to Sonja. As a favor to his friend, who had recently died, the governor walked Mary Jo down the aisle at her wedding. Maybe the governor also hired Sonja as another favor to his friend.

Josie heard a thump. She paused her thoughts to concentrate on the night sounds. She had thought the man pursuing her was close. But the curves of the maze might have forced him around to the other side. Her surroundings were silent once again.

Josie thought that if Sonja had killed Mary Jo and taken over her business, she might still be at the abbey. Sonja might have had the men leave first so she could escape under cover of darkness. Maybe the men didn't even know she was there. Sonja could wait and then escape out through the tunnel and the underground garage. If she had somehow discovered Amelia, she could take her as a bargaining chip. Then, when she realized she was followed, she could hide out in the maze.

The concept seemed wildly implausible. But so was murdering someone with a sniper's rifle from a long distance, and someone had done just that, multiple times.

Implausible or not, taking over Mary Jo's business might not be difficult, especially if Mary Jo had been largely running the business through email from her hideaway house in the foothills. Sonja might figure out Mary Jo's email password and simply step into Mary Jo's role without the employees even realizing it. Or, Sonja could impersonate Mary Jo and tell the employees that she was retiring and a new manager named Sonja was joining the business. She could even use a pseudonym.

Josie thought about the man named Snake. If Sonja was now running Mary Jo's empire, Snake might be her right hand man.

But why would she send Snake after Josie? It could simply be that she thought Professor Josie Strong was likely to unravel the scheme and the true nature of the rest home business.

Sonja might have had Snake kill the two prison guards so that they couldn't reveal what they knew of the scheme. She might have directed Snake to kill Josie and Samantha out at the Bixby Cliff. Snake or Sonja could have been watching for Josie all along. When the flood appeared, Snake might have been ready and waiting.

Cumberland discovered that Snake had sniper training before he was kicked out of the Army. If Sonja had been in the Army, she might have also learned sniper skills.

Josie remembered how Cor had talked about a legendary Army sniper they called Typhon, after the Greek god of monsters. Cor had explained that long-distance killing required exceptional training to develop complex, precision technique. It was a skill of delicacy, not a skill of strength. A sniper was like a surgeon, not a fighter. Something a woman might excel at.

That didn't fit what Josie had learned of Snake. He seemed more brash and bold than what was required of a sniper. Snake was closer in personality to Lucas Herman, who had bragged and boasted to Elena about his hunting skills. Josie thought that both Lucas and Snake were showboaters. Cor had said that typical snipers were quiet and reserved. Like Josie's perception of Sonja.

Cor had said the legendary Army sniper was referred to as Typhon because his identity was secret. There were rumors regarding Typhon's superiour accomplishments and skills, but he/she was nevertheless unknown to everyone. As Cor had explained, even the person giving the orders might not know the sniper's true identity.

As Josie went over what Cor had said, she remembered Cor saying that Typhon was good at both long distance kills and hand-to-hand combat. That fit with Mary Jo being killed from a distance, while her husband Francis was killed up close.

Josie recalled Cor saying that Typhon had a technique he used in close-quarters fighting. He held his flashlight straight out from his right side to create the illusion that he was a couple of feet to the side of his actual position. Then he would fire his pistol with his left hand. If his victim was able to return fire, he would probably shoot toward Typhon's flashlight, which would mean he'd miss Typhon's body.

Josie heard a sound. A thud. A scuffling. Was it Snake in the maze? Hitting the walls in the dark? But he had a flashlight. He could see.

A flash of light bounced off rock. Her stalker was close.

There was a noise. Then a shout. "Don't try it!" A garbled woman's voice. An explosive gunshot, loud as a bomb, shook the air.

An almost-instantaneous second shot, almost as loud, had a different sound.

A muffled voice said, "Got him. Stay back. Let me check." Then a pause. "He's dead."

After a moment, the woman's voice spoke more clearly, calling through the darkness. "Josie? Hello? Are you in here?"

Josie was shocked. It sounded like Cor Kontos. Could it be?

Josie nearly called back, but realized that if there was a second stalker, Josie's voice would tell the shooter where she was.

Cor called out again, "When you didn't come, we started to worry. Sam and I came together. We got the man with the snake tattoo. He fired. I fired back."

There was no other sound. After a long moment, Josie decided it was safe.

"I'm here," Josie called out. "I'm at the end of one of the passages."

"Mama!" Samantha called out. "Oh, my God, I'm so glad you are okay!"

Josie heard Unknown start whining.

A vague shape appeared in front of Josie. Was it Cor? Josie stayed hunkered down. As the person moved, moonlight touched the person's head. It was Cor. Another shape suddenly appeared from behind Cor. Josie couldn't tell for certain, but the person did not seem tall and skinny like Samantha.

"Cor!" Josie called out. "Look out behind you!"

A flashlight beam turned on, illuminating Cor's head from behind. A shooter fired. The gunshot was even louder than the others. Josie saw blood spray as Cor spun away and fell to the ground.

FIFTY-ONE

Josie gasped in terror. Where was Sam?!

Josie shouted. "Sam, run!"

The shooter seemed to leap sideways into the dark. There was a grunt, then a cry.

Samantha called out. "Let me go!" Samantha screamed. The shooter turned. Josie was nearly blinded by the shooter's flashlight. But Josie could tell the shooter held Samantha's arm.

Josie tried to flatten herself to the wall just as there was another gunshot.

The brilliant muzzle flash was blinding, and the sound numbed Josie's ears. Josie felt fire on her upper arm as if someone had stabbed her with a red-hot branding iron.

Josie realized the shooter was going to kill her and Samantha too. If Josie were to prevent that, she'd have to shoot toward Samantha and potentially cause great harm. But it might be worth the risk compared to certain death for Samantha.

Josie reminded herself what Cor had said, that Typhon was a left-handed shooter who misdirected adversaries by holding a flashlight out to the shooter's right side.

Josie aimed her crossbow two feet the other direction. If it were possible that Typhon was Sonja, that would mean she was shorter. Josie lowered her aim a bit.

But Sam was in the way. There was no way to reliably get Samantha out of the way so Josie could attempt to shoot the killer. But if they were all going to die...

Josie had a sudden idea. "Pancake!" she shouted.

Josie sensed a movement, saw a dark shape drop to the ground. The other shape seemed to bend forward a little, as if hanging onto Samantha but staying upright.

Josie pulled the crossbow trigger.

There was a thudding grunt. The shooter's flashlight dropped to the ground.

For a long moment, there was nothing but silence. The flashlight lay on the ground, its beam making an intense white circle on one of the rock walls.

"Sam! Sam, are you okay?" Josie's voice was choked.

"I'm okay, Mama." Sam's voice. Tiny and scared.

Then came a choking catch in the shooter's throat. The reflected beam of the flashlight showed a dark shape sliding down the stone wall and hitting the ground with a soft thud.

Josie couldn't breathe. Couldn't think. But she gathered her strength.

"Cor?" she called out. "Cor! Answer me, Cor!"

Josie got to her hands and knees. She held her flashlight in one hand, turned it on, and scrambled forward. Electric pain shot through her shoulder. It jolted her with every move. It was a staccato pain, like machine gun fire, as bad as any pain Josie had ever felt.

"Are you okay, Mama?"

"I'm okay. Mostly."

Josie did her best to ignore her pain. She crawled over and, using her good arm, picked up the flashlight and shined it and her own flashlight at the shooter.

Sonja Gonsalves's eyes were partially open as she squinted in pain. Her right eyelid twitched uncontrollably. Her jaw quivered. Her pistol was on the ground next to her.

Josie swatted it away into the dark and then crawled toward Cor. Josie could barely move, so intense was her pain. But she continued to crawl.

"Sam, are you still okay?" Josie asked as she crawled. Her voice was choked with worry. "You're not shot."

"I'm okay. My knee hurts, but I'm okay." Samantha rolled on her side, reached out, and grabbed Josie as she crawled past. Josie fought back the pain and lowered her face to Samantha.

Samantha said, "Where's Cor? Is Cor okay? I'm so afraid!"

"We need to be strong. Come shine the flashlight on Cor."

Josie handed the killer's flashlight to Samantha. Then she

crawled, and Sam trotted, toward the limp form of Cor on the ground. Sam shined the killer's flashlight.

Cor was lying on her back. There was a gaping hole in her upper chest, near the left collar bone, just above where Josie thought her heart would be. Blood was spilling out. Not a spurt, but a steady, dramatic flow. Josie felt an involuntary gasp coming. She managed to stop it.

Cor's mouth was open. She was trying to breath. She gurgled as she tried to speak.

"I'm not...," Cor said.

Josie gasped again, her own breath catching. "Please focus on staying with us." Josie tried not to cry. Then she said, "You'll be fine, Cor." Josie said, believing it was a lie. "You're going to be fine," she repeated.

She stared at the bloody bullet hole, trying to remember what to do. Stop the bleeding, right?

"Shine the light on the wound, hon," she said to Samantha.

She put her right thumb over the bullet hole. It wanted to slip off because of all the blood.

"Sam, I need you to plug this wound."

"How?!"

"Put your thumb in the hole. If that doesn't work, push down on it with the heel of your hand."

Samantha kneeled next to Cor and pushed with her thumb. Josie saw Samantha's thumb slip into Cor's body. Cor groaned. Samantha switched to her palm.

"I'll see if I can get a cell signal."

Josie pulled out her phone. It said 'no service.' Samantha's phone used the same carrier, so she wouldn't have service, either. Josie would have to drive up a hill or something. She remembered her headset. If Ellison was in walkie-talkie range, he could call 911.

Then she had a better thought. Try Sonja's phone.

She held her own flashlight as she crawled back to Sonja. Josie shined the light on her.

The bolt from Josie's crossbow was embedded in Sonja's

right abdomen.

Josie put her finger tips on Sonja's neck to feel the carotid artery. The woman had a fast, weak pulse. Josie didn't think she would be able to put up any resistance.

Sonja's eyes no longer twitched. Josie believed Sonja was close to death.

Josie felt Sonja's pockets. She had a phone. Josie got it out and pressed the button.

The screen lit up. But there was no phone-dialing keypad. Josie pressed the home button again. Nothing else appeared. Josie started to feel panic closing in. She knew Cor was close to death as well.

"I can't make it work," Josie said. "And there's no passcode screen, so I don't know why."

Samantha said, "Is there a symbol with curving lines like a fingerprint?"

"Yes."

"Okay. That means it has fingerprint recognition. You have a few chances to use Sonja's fingers before the phone locks down. Start with her index finger, then her thumb."

"She's left handed. Does that make a difference?"

"Then try her left hand first. If her thumb or index finger don't unlock it, I'd try her right hand."

Josie did as told.

The phone unlocked. It showed one bar of reception. Josie found the phone symbol. She went through Sonja"s contacts. There was one under the Gs that said Guv. Josie hit the button.

The phone rang five times. Then the governor answered.

"Hi Sonja. How are you?" he said.

"Governor, this is Professor Josie Strong calling on Sonja's phone. Sonja was your second shooter."

"What?! No, that can't be true."

"Believe it. She shot at least one of my group. That person is dying. Sonja is dying as well. I need medics and police fast! Please listen carefully. I'm at the Sisters of Frangelica Abbey in the Sierra foothills up near Lake Tahoe. It's off Ice House Road and up above a town called Kyburz. I believe there is room to land an ambulance helicopter. Please put that in motion now. I'll wait on hold."

The line went silent.

"How is Cor?" Josie called out.

"Still breathing," Samantha said.

"Have you been able to slow the blood?"

"Not much, if at all. It's like she's bleeding, but the blood is going inside her chest. Cor's in bad shape, Mama. Real bad."

"I know."

The governer came back on the line.

"How is it that Sonja is dying?" he asked.

"We need an ambulance helicopter on the way! Is it coming?"

"Yes. It is on the way." The governor sounded shocked and subdued.

Josie paused to wonder if there was anything else that was a higher priority than talking to the governor.

She said, "After Sonja shot Cor Kontos, she shot me as well. I was able to shoot back. But Cor is seriously wounded. A bullet through the chest."

"Oh, no. Oh, God. I can't… I'm so sorry. I don't know exactly what to do. Sonja always handles my crises."

"I'll tell you, sir. First call nine-one-one on our behalf. Your contact in this area would be the El Dorado County Sheriff's Office. There is a sergeant named Ham Garner who is somewhat familiar with our situation. The first priority is a medivac helicopter. We're down to seconds, governor, or more people will die."

"Yes, I did that. The ambulance helicopter should be there in minutes." It sounded like the governor was crying.

"Good," Josie said. "Now you need to work your magic with the California Bureau of Investigation. They need to get up here immediately. We have several dangerous men we've detained. Another man is dead in the Sisters' Maze near the abbey. The woman the men kidnapped has run off into the wilderness. and we have another woman who was taken and is missing. The men have several duffle bags full of what is almost certainly illegal cash. Sonja works for you, sir. So this has the potential to blow up into the biggest political scandal in California history. Send the bureau by helicopter, too, but don't let them get in the way of the ambulance chopper. I have to go now."

Josie hung up before the governor could say anything more.

The light beam showed Cor's blood flowing in larger volume. Blood was everywhere. It looked like someone had poured a quart of blood on Cor's chest, and more was on the ground. Samantha's hands and clothes were coated with blood.

Josie leaned down next to Cor's prostrate, motionless form. She felt for her pulse. It was still beating, but Josie could detect no breath.

"Stay with us, Cor. A medivac chopper is on the way. You are one tough woman. You can do this. Please, Cor, please." Josie's pleading voice was soft and wet and full of tears. "Please," she said again. "Stay with us," she repeated.

Cor's lips were moving. She was trying to say something.

Josie leaned forward, her ear next to Cor's lips.

"I'm not ready for Flanders Fields," Cor said.

FIFTY-TWO

Josie sensed herself fading out as her own injury and blood loss and fatigue took their toll.

The events became blurry.

After a minute, Sam was talking to someone.

Another voice responded. A man's voice. Ellison.

Then a woman's voice. Diane Day. "I've got Amelia. She was tied and taped back in the maze." Diane saw Cor on the ground beneath Samantha.

"Oh, mother of God..." Diane dropped down next to Cor. Samantha was still holding her hand over Cor's chest.

Samantha mumbled something Josie couldn't understand.

Amelia appeared. "Oh, Cor! She's covered with blood."

"Mama's bleeding, too," Samantha said. "Badly."

"I'm on it," Ellison said.

Josie sensed movement and pain in her upper arm.

There were more words, but Josie couldn't tell what was said or who was speaking, because there was a thumping sound in the distance that obscured the words. The sound grew into a distinct, rapid thwacking as a helicopter approached.

FIFTY-THREE

When Josie opened her eyes, she had to squint against the bright light.

Her vision was blurry. Gradually, she came to realize that she was in a hospital room.

"Mama! You're awake! Ellison, she's awake!"

Josie felt Samantha lean over her, her head next to Josie.

"Oh, Mama, I was so worried! You scared me to death."

Josie felt reassured by Samantha's hair in her face, Samantha's voice in her ear, Samantha's weight against her.

"Scared me too." Ellison's voice. Deep but soft. Josie couldn't see him. He must have been off to the side.

Josie blinked hard, trying to clear her vision. Maybe it would clear her brain fog as well.

"Can you hear me, Mama? You're not talking!"

Josie wanted to talk, but her voice wasn't working. Or maybe it was her brain that wasn't working. What was that called? Aphasia. Josie could think. Sort of. She felt like she'd been in a deep sleep and was struggling to wake up. Anesthesia?

"Cor?" she tried to whisper.

Samantha lifted off of Josie. "She can talk!" Samantha said. "What are you trying to say? The doctor said that traumatic experiences can cause PTSD. So don't worry, Mama. You lost a lot of blood, and they had to do surgery on your upper arm where the bullet went through. The doctor said it nicked your brachial artery, and that's, like, a totally major thing. So they gave you a bunch of blood and stitched you up using some synthetic material, and they think it's likely you'll recover the use of your arm."

It was obvious to Josie that Samantha was taut with worry and stress. But Josie wasn't in any condition to comment.

"Cor?" she tried again.

"Oh, now I understand. You said Cor! Cor is all messed up like you, only worse. But they think she's going to have a full recovery. A bullet went through her lung and all the way through her body—like the bullet that went through your upper arm—but it missed her heart and aorta. So it was, like, the perfect place to shoot someone if you want them to…" Samantha turned to someone out of Josie's sightline, probably Ellison. "What did the doctor say, Ellison?"

"She said that the bullet hole will leave a nasty scar that Cor will be alive to brag about. Just like your scar, Josie. The surgeon saw the scar on your leg and said it also looked like a bullet wound."

"So Mama, get this," Samantha said. "The doctor and nurse, who are both women, asked me what line of work you're in where you regularly suffer bullet wounds. I said you were a medieval history professor at UCLA. And the two women looked at each other. One said to the other, 'Did you know that history professors are bullet-hardened?'"

Josie made a weak grin.

"So remember that, Mama," Samantha continued.

"That I'm a bullet-hardened super hero," Josie said, forming her words slowly and carefully.

"That's true," Ellison said.

Samantha reached out and caressed Josie's face. "You're gonna be okay, Mama. I'm so glad. I can't tell you how glad."

Josie focused on forming words carefully. "Wha… What day is it?"

"It's Saturday. You were shot late last night after we made our escape. The doctors did something last night—I can't remember what—something that stabilized you. Giving you blood, I think. Then you were in surgery early this morning. Same as Cor, actually."

"Where are we?"

"UC Davis Medical Center."

"Is Cor here, too?"

"Yes. You're both on the same floor. I think it's where they put trauma patients."

"What about Sonja and Snake and the others?"

Ellison answered. "First, they didn't want to tell us. So this granddaughter of mine called the Bureau of Investigation! She told them you would get the governor on their case if they weren't forthcoming about the ongoing risk to you. After all, you'd been shot and could have been killed. You have a right to know if your would-be assassin was still out there gunning for you. So they 'fessed up and said that Sonja Gonsalves was deceased as was her associate, a man whose name they don't know. But they said the man had a huge tattoo of a snake going up his arm."

"So it's all good."

"Well, not everything is good," Ellison said.

"How's that."

"They said you won't get your crossbow back for some time because it was used in a homicide."

"What's not good about that?"

"What Ellison means, Mama," Samantha said, "is that, without your weapon of choice, you will be defenseless if anyone attacks you soon."

Josie thought about it. "I've still got you with your sling bullets."

"True."

"One more thing," Ellison said. "When you were coming out of anesthesia, you were kind of talking about King Lear and was Sonja the sister of Mary Jo Telman."

"So I called Cumberland," Samantha said. "It took him only fifteen minutes to find out that Sonja Gonsalves was, in fact, Mary Jo Telman's sister. I don't know what all that means, but it sort of fits with your idea that someone wanted to take over Mary Jo's business empire. Cumberland even got into Sonja's..." Samantha stopped speaking and looked around to see if anyone was listening.

Josie realized that Cumberland must have hacked into something that shouldn't be talked about.

Samantha started again. "Let's just say that Cumberland was

able to uncover some communication between family members showing that Sonja and Mary Jo had ongoing family squabbles and a long-running feud. And you figured it out."

"It was a lucky guess," Josie said.

"No. The governor made it clear. You professor types are able to see things from a different perspective."

"But I'm never working for the governor again," Josie said.

"Good call, Matey," Samantha said. "Because, as Cap'n, that's my new rule on this ship. No more work for the governor."

EPILOGUE

They were out on the beach in Santa Monica.

Josie sat on a small, folding beach chair. Next to her, Cor Kontos sat on a matching chair.

The day was in the mid-70s, and the sun, hazy in a misty sky, provided a gentle heat. Good for healing, Josie thought.

Josie wore a light short-sleeved blouse that was loose enough to accommodate the bandage, which wrapped all the way around her upper arm. The most recent bandage no longer showed red from leaking blood.

Cor wore a sleeveless T-shirt. Her bandages covered much of her chest and back, obscuring many of her tattoos. Cor also wore a type of elastic truss with multiple straps that stretched from her waist to her neck, holding her bandages in place.

Unknown was in the backpack that Samantha had carried and then set in the sand before she headed over toward the volleyball courts. Unknown stood up, turned around within the confines of the pack, and lay back down.

Ellison walked over. He sat down, reached into his sweatshirt pockets, and pulled out two cans of beer.

"These might be verboten on the beach. But if any beer police show up, we'll just tell them they are prescription medicine for you battle veterans."

He handed one to Cor. She popped the top and drank half of it down.

"They don't have white wine," Ellison said to Josie as he held out a beer. "But a beer might help mitigate your pain."

"No thanks," she said.

"I'll take it." Diane Day said as she and Amelia walked up. Diane was wearing a magenta T-shirt, black cargo shorts, thick magenta socks and black hiking boots. Her shirt said, 'Warning:

This Joe is armed with Pencak Silat.'

Diane popped open her beer and sipped it. She sat in the sand on the other side of Cor.

Amelia sat down next to Josie and Unknown. "I brought some alfajores and coffee." She took off her backpack, opened it up, and pulled out a thermos, mugs, and cookie container. "Would you like some? They are guaranteed to help healing."

"Please," Josie said.

"Well," Ellison said, "in that case, I'll have cookies and coffee, too."

They all watched the volleyball. Samantha and her teammate Holly appeared to be in an intense match against another team who looked and moved like professionals.

Periodically, Samantha flexed and rotated her knee that had been injured while wrestling with the killer in the Maze.

"Prognosis?" Ellison asked, facing Josie and Cor.

"Good, but will take some time," Cor said.

"Good, but will take some time," Josie echoed. More than the pain of being shot, she felt weary. Worn out.

"And you, Amelia? After being kidnapped by Snake?" Ellison asked as he popped one of her cookies in his mouth.

"Good, but will take some time." Amelia made a hint of a grin.

Ellison took another cookie. He sipped coffee as he looked at Amelia. "This stuff is heaven."

Josie noticed Cumberland Durand and his siblings Aiden and Cara approach. Cara smiled. Aiden didn't smile, but he had a pleasant look on his face. Cumberland frowned, looked down at the sand, and looked awkward. Josie gestured at the sand near her and Cor.

The three siblings sat.

Amelia passed them the cookie container. "We have to save a couple for Sam, so..." She flashed them the electric smile.

Aiden and Cara each took one. Cumberland took a handful, then paused, looked in the container, and put two back.

"Your information saved us once again," Josie said to

Cumberland.

"More accurate than the info we were usually given on military missions," Cor said.

Diane Day made a single nod.

Cumberland nodded but didn't look up and didn't say anything.

Ellison looked at Cor and Diane. "What I don't get is how you two took down all those men. I was right there watching, but it was dark, and I couldn't understand your moves. That was quite a demonstration. You took their weapons, too."

Diane pointed to the words on her T-shirt. "A typical guy, confronted with women, is completely overconfident. In this case, you can't even imagine the stupidity of six guys who think they're going to take down two women."

Cor nodded. "With our training, it was like dealing with toddlers at a pre-school."

"It must have been an eye-opener for the police when they came upon those guys."

"Sergeant Ham Garner called me," Josie said. "He said the El Dorado County District Attorney is still adding charges to the list. Drug trafficking. Racketeering. Money laundering. Kidnapping. Assault. Those guys are going down for decades. And the police in Sacramento and Reno are shutting down the nursing homes, the laundromats, and the casino where they laundered the drug money."

"Another thing I don't understand," Amelia said, "is how all that can happen and the police never asked me many questions."

"Same with me," Ellison said. "I was still wearing my chest candy when the first cops arrived. They took note of my name and such, but I've never received a followup call about my involvement in our operation."

Cor said, "Two Bureau of Investigation agents came to talk to me at the hospital at UC Davis. It was like they were tip-toeing in stocking feet. Like they were consulting me for my opinion about the gunshots and the murder of the snake guy and our takedown of the drug runners."

"That was the governor's doing," Josie said. "He and I had a long video call, very likely recorded. I gave him a complete statement and full documentation of everything we'd done. I mentioned everyone's name and contribution and left out nothing except Cumberland and the details of how he does his work. At the end, I made a somewhat stern statement that I expected the authorities to lay off Cor, Ellison, Diane, Amelia and, of course, Sam and me." Josie sipped some of Amelia's coffee. "I think, but don't know, that the governor understands that I can give as well as I get."

"Meaning," Ellison said, "that if he treats you gently, you won't spread the sordid story of Sonja Gonsalves and her connection to the governor all over the media."

"Yes, that's a good way to put it."

Everyone was silent.

Ellison nodded thoughtfully. He turned again to Josie.

"Have you heard from the woman who was imprisoned as their chef?"

"Yes. Elena Soto, who Diane tracked to a cave-like shelter near a steep slope after the sun came up. Her mother Zoe called me. She is very happy to have her daughter back, and she's trying hard to cope with the loss of her husband, Juan. Elena is temporarily living in Zoe's apartment. Zoe said her daughter was psychologically abused but never sexually assaulted. She's getting therapy."

"Glad to hear it."

A small cheer went up at the volleyball court. Some people clapped. It was more subdued than the last match Josie had witnessed.

Ellison turned to a nearby spectator for an update on the match. Then he turned to Josie and the others.

"Sam's 'We'll Bust Your Balls' team lost their final match. But everyone agreed that it was well-played, and both teams deserve kudos."

Samantha emerged from the crowd near the volleyball net.

"Good job," Ellison said.

"Thanks. That was one of the toughest matches we've ever

been in."

Ellison nodded. "I could tell."

Ellison stood up as Samantha approached, and he handed her an envelope. "I brought you something."

"What's this, Ellison? A consolation prize?"

"No. Just a good-news notice. Remember when you said your dream volleyball experience would be the Origins Volleyball Training Camp? I received this yesterday and wanted to pass it on."

Samantha opened the envelope, pulled out a sheet of paper, and opened it.

She stared at the paper, a serious frown on her forehead.

"It's an email to you, Ellison," she said. "And it's from Origins Beach Volleyball Training Camp." She looked at Ellison. "I don't get it. Should I read this?"

Ellison nodded. "Sure."

Samantha read out loud.

"'Dear Mr. Ellison, As I explained during our phone conversation, the Origins Beach Summer Volleyball Training Camp is officially open only to high school students. As you may know, only a small percentage of applicants are admitted. The main qualification is that attending students have extraordinary volleyball skills. However, we also look at the student's character as evidenced by reports from their school staff and community members. Further, we consider reports of the student's grades and other school achievements.

"'Our goal is to invite the kind of exceptional volleyball players whose skills and demeanor will spread good associations to their current and future schools and communities.

"'However, as you intimated on the phone, it might be in Origin's interest to occasionally consider younger players who are in middle school if their attributes are exceptional.

"'As a past beach volleyball player yourself, your praise of Samantha Strong's volleyball technique and her overall character caused us to take a closer look at her. One of our staff knows of the school that she attends. That staff member watched two of Ms. Strong's games at a recent tournament and, further, called on two of her teachers and her headmaster for character comment.

"'As a result, we would like to offer Samantha Strong a position in our upcoming summer training clinic. We will be sending out our invitation to attend near the end of the school year, and Samantha Strong will be on that list. I'm sending you a courtesy note in advance should you like to notify her yourself.'"

Samantha shrieked and started jumping up and down. "Oh, my Gosh, Ellison!" She gave him a big hug. Then she pushed back and looked at him. Samantha's eyes went back and forth, searching Ellison's.

"You recommended me to Origin?"

"Sure did, Cap'n."

"All this time, the Origin people knew you and you never said?"

Ellison made his own frown and shook his head. "They have no idea who I am. I've never met any of them."

"Then how did they take your recommendation seriously?"

"I just threw some volleyball slang at them. They realized I knew something about the game. So they looked you up." Ellison put his hands on Samantha's shoulders. "Remember, being able to attend the clinic isn't Origin doing a favor for you. It's you doing a favor for them. You've got major chops on the sand, girl, and they want to attach their name to great players now and in the future."

Samantha was shaking her head. She took one of Ellison's hands, rotated so her back was against his chest, lifted up his other hand, and pulled his arms so he was hugging her. Then she leaned back against him.

Samantha looked at Josie and smiled broadly as she said, "Best grandpa ever!"

About the Author

Todd Borg and his wife live in Tahoe, where they write and paint. To contact Todd or learn more about the Josie Strong thrillers or the Owen McKenna mysteries, please visit toddborg.com.

A message from the author:

Dear Reader,

If you enjoyed this novel, please consider posting a short review on any book website you like to use, such as Goodreads and Amazon. Reviews help authors a great deal, and that in turn allows us to write more stories for you.

Thank you very much for your interest and support!

Todd

Made in the USA
Middletown, DE
19 September 2024

60722500R00194